Acknowledgments

A trip to the Grand Canyon and rumors of
the idea of this story. My gratitude goes ou
leading fabulous trips, and to my fellow b
there and teaching me outdoor skills.

Much appreciation and thanks go to members of Southland Scribes, especially Helen Osterman for her leadership, Lydia Ponczak for proofreading and her unfailing encouragement, and Ryan O'Reilly for his legal and marketing advice.

Appreciation and thanks also goes to:

Tim Bowden, Wildlife Biologist, Science and Resource Management, Grand Canyon National Park, for sharing his knowledge of canyon flora and fauna.

Dr. David Ciambrone, medical examiner, for answering my questions about snake venom and forensics.

Brittiany Koren, editor at Written Dreams.

From my father, I inherited the love of vocabulary and the gene that urges me to search for the perfect words and polish them until they shine. Thanks, Dad.

Thanks also to readers of my first draft—my sisters, my mother, my friends—for their kind words and support, without which I might have given up.

Of course, a big thanks goes to my husband of forty-four years, who gives me the time and means to pursue my writing career in comfort.

I believe in evolution. But I also believe,

when I hike the Grand Canyon

and see it at sunset,

that the hand of God is there also.

— John McCain

Everybody needs beauty as well as bread,

places to play in and pray in,

where nature may heal and give strength

to the body and soul.

— John Muir

Prologue

Nervous about my flight that day to Phoenix, I awoke at dawn and padded down the carpeted staircase in my bare feet. The cold marble floor in the foyer shocked me out of my groggy state. I tiptoed through the great room into the kitchen. The strong aroma of fresh-brewed coffee would reach John on the couch and wake him gradually. We could get to O'Hare on time and—if I made it easy for him—without an argument.

I nuked oatmeal for myself and sat with my hot tea in the bay window waiting, watching frosted leaves fall from the giant oaks behind the house. A familiar ache reminded me that he no longer held me, no longer said he was proud of me, but—when had he ever? I couldn't remember. I had tried to keep up: stayed trim, wore make up, covered bits of gray with a brunette tint. He liked my long hair at least, though it had become a bother.

I set out his favorite coffee mug and thought about how I had pulled him through college and was his cheerleader as he struggled with his business.

Shouldn't he encourage me now?

Going into the wilderness had been a lifelong dream, a postponed dream, a silly dream for a wife and mother. Still, I yearned to experience wildness, self-reliance, and to be strong enough. A thrill caught in my throat as I thought of the planned hike across the Grand Canyon—a huge step outside my comfort zone. Fear urged me to cancel.

I know I'm too old, but this is all I've got, this body, this time.

Frost on the windows began to melt, running away in tiny gray rivers. My reflection and my courage washed away with them.

I'd better wake him.

Only then, I noticed that the television wasn't flickering in the great room. His blankets weren't on the couch. *Maybe he never came home.* I checked the nearest bathroom.

"John?" I said aloud.

The furnace hummed and the grandfather clock dinged at the quarter hour. *Did he sneak into bed, and I somehow missed him?*

I stopped at the foot of the stairs when an envelope on the table in the foyer caught my eye. *That wasn't there last night.* I turned the fine linen stationery over and ran my finger over the raised embossed lettering in the upper left corner, *John H. Warren, Architectural Designs.*

AMY.

My name stood out in bold letters on the envelope's face. I slipped the note out and took it into the kitchen's light, squinting at the single sheet. I fetched my glasses and read what my husband of twenty-nine years had to say in twelve-point, Times New Roman font.

I'm moving on with my life.

I adjusted my bifocals to make sure I'd read that right.

My attorney will have papers drawn up by the time you return from this foolish trip of yours. You'll fail at that, too, of course. Get yourself a lawyer.

My head began to throb. I skipped over the list of attorneys he recommended, skipped over additional ridicule of my backpacking, how it embarrassed us both. No signature. I turned over the paper searching for a sign that he loved me. *Who am I kidding? This one is final.* I pictured John sneaking back into the house and pecking away at his keyboard to deliver the blow while I slept.

Damn him.

I sunk into a kitchen chair and let my tea grow cold.

1

PHOENIX SKY HARBOR INTERNATIONAL AIRPORT

My smart phone chirped as soon as I turned it on. I stood off to the side, out of the stream of passengers deplaning, and jabbed at the icons. The numbers disappeared. *Shoot.* Without my reading glasses, I couldn't have seen the message anyway. *Maybe John had a change of heart.* I pushed that fantasy out of my head.

Probably Karen looking for me.

I swiped and poked at the screen. The salesman said I'd hate the new phone for a week until I got used to it. He was half right. I bought the thing a month ago and still hated the electronic nightmare. Half my messages got lost. The clock was the phone's saving grace—at least I could see the huge numerals. 10:09. Karen's plane should have landed twenty minutes ago. The monitors said her Indianapolis flight had arrived on schedule, so I followed the signs to baggage claim. Maybe I'd find her there.

The weather back in Chicago had been wet and blustery, a typical October day. Yet, here in Phoenix the sun beat through the high windows, causing my fellow passengers to strip off their jackets and sweaters. *A good analogy for the start of my new life*, I thought. I stuffed that idea, along with my fleece, into my carry-on bag before scanning the crowd around carousel two for my hiking partner. I then glanced down the row of other, mostly empty carousels. No Karen.

I moved a short distance away from the crush of passengers to find a bit of quiet and dug my glasses out of my bag. My not-so-smart phone's call-log listed three messages from Karen. None from John. I groaned aloud. *She missed her plane. Or she's lost.*

I tapped the green phone icon and waited for her to answer.

"Amy," Karen cried. "I'm so sorry."

"What? Where are you?"

"I'm still in Indianapolis. We were on I-65, driving to the airport. A pick-up truck swerved into our lane and forced us off the road."

"Oh my god. Are you all right?"

"Yes, yes," Karen said. "Just banged up. We hit the guardrail."

"Your daughter was driving? Is she okay?"

"A little bruised. She's fine. But, Amy, I banged my knee on the dashboard. I can't even think about backpacking."

"No, of course not." Panic crept in. "You have to take it easy."

"I'm sick about missing our trip after we planned everything and trained so hard. Now I've left you in a lurch. I'm so sorry. Are you in Phoenix?"

"Yeah, I just arrived." I tried to sound calm and casual, but anxiety churned in my stomach. "The most important thing is that you and Tammy weren't seriously hurt."

Karen apologized over and over as we talked a little longer. All the while, my resolve withered. *How could I hike across the Grand Canyon without Karen?* Fear threatened to take over. I had to get off the phone before Karen caught on.

This can't be happening. I sank onto the metal mesh bench and wondered about the next return flight to Chicago. *But why go back? John abandoned me and now . . . How can I possibly spend five days in the canyon alone? I can use my achy knees as my excuse. Maybe I should skip the hike and get a room on the South Rim for the week.*

My misery must have shown as I argued with myself. People glanced at me with hooded interest while they waited for their luggage to appear from the baggage handlers' underworld.

I sniffled and turned away to find a tissue. *You'll never make it. You're too old.* John's pronouncements echoed and beat me up all over again. *Maybe he was right.*

4

Dang it. Fight back. I reminded myself that I trained all summer to prove John wrong. Karen had trained with me, plodding for hours up and down the Palos toboggan slide staircase, working out, building muscle. I choked back my fear. *One step at a time, Amy.*

The harsh buzzer sounded and the baggage carousel clattered to life. People jostled for position as suitcases, boxes, and golf bags tumbled down the chute. I spotted my green, wheeled duffle bag and moved to intercept it further along the conveyor belt.

Elbows and suitcases buffeted me as I fought my way to where I'd last seen my bag. I scanned the conveyor belt. My green bag with the yellow ribbon had moved to the opposite side. I glued my eyes to it and wove through the mob of passengers.

A young man in his late teens, wearing a gray tee shirt and black jeans, had his eye on my bag, too. He lifted it with ease from the logjam. It was the sort of kindness my son had done in his teenage years after he discovered his muscles. *Good things happen after all. This trip will be fine.* I wanted to thank the young man for extracting my luggage, but he turned away and dragged my duffle bag with him.

"Wait!" I darted around old people pushing carts and children sitting on piles of luggage. I tried not to pass judgment on the eyebrow rings and dime-sized gages poking through the kid's earlobes, but he strode away with my camping gear. I ran to keep up.

"Excuse me. Excuse me." I reached out to touch the spiderweb tattoo on his arm. "You have my bag," I said.

His goatee twitched in my direction. "It's mine." He didn't make eye contact and kept moving.

I ran ahead to put myself in front of him. "Check the luggage tag."

"It's my stuff," he growled.

I reached for the ID tag, but he jerked to the side and quickened his pace.

The claim stub that matched the airline's sticker lost itself in my carry-on bag. It would prove me right, if only I could find it. I spent five seconds searching. *To heck with that.*

I kept the kid's slicked-back hair in sight and sprinted after the gear I had so carefully collected. My tent, my backpack, my boots. I closed my fist around the canvas strap on the back end of the duffle and dug in my heels. I yanked the young man to a halt.

He glanced over his shoulder.

Ignoring his scowl and black gages, I mustered my courage, put on my stern employer face, and tightened my grip. "*This* is my bag."

With one jerk, he won the tug of war.

An abrasion burned the palm of my hand. I clutched the injury to my chest for a second, then lunged after the disappearing bag, clawing to get a hold of the handle. The crowd parted and flowed around my struggle.

"Stop!" A female voice of authority brought me to a standstill.

A woman, about my age, in a white shirt with a red bandana tied loosely at her throat blocked the young man's path. His momentum took him nose to nose with her. She stood an inch shorter, but made up for the lack of height with an attitude and a solid build. A dark green backpack, big enough for a week on the trail, hung from her shoulder adding bulk to her figure.

The man sidestepped. Her chest obstructed his path again.

He glowered at her. "Outta my way."

"The lady says you have her bag." Tight dark curls bounced around her fierce face, adding emphasis to her words. "Shall we call the guard to settle this?" She jerked her thumb toward a uniform leaning against a post fifty feet away.

The woman kept her eyes on the punk's face. Their scowls battled until his lip curled into a sneer.

"My bad." He dropped his end of the bag and stalked off.

I snatched up the canvas strap and stared after him, my mouth agape.

"What a load of crap," the woman said.

We watched the kid retreating through a throng of travelers, each dragging luggage of all shapes and sizes. Groups of twos and threes exited through automatic doors letting sunlight flash into the terminal. Silhouetted against one snapshot of brightness, a taller man shoved the tattooed kid in the shoulder in rough greeting. The doors blinked shut behind them.

"You okay?" the woman asked, her face softened. A grin accentuated her red-apple cheeks.

"No harm done." Still shaken by the experience, I offered my hand and received a firm, businesslike grip in return. The abrasion on my palm stung, but I ignored the pain. "Thanks for intervening. Nobody else seemed to care."

She was maybe fifty-two, tan and strong, the outdoors woman I aspired to be.

"He really wanted your bag. Do you want to report this to security?"

No more issues, please. I gave my head a quick shake. "We've seen the last of him."

"Hope so." She looked down at me and adjusted a leather thong around her neck. A joke played behind her brown eyes. "Have a nice trip." She shifted the backpack on her shoulder and turned toward the exit.

There goes a real backpacker. Her clothes were perfect: a breezy shirt, quick-dry pants, a brimmed hat hanging flat against her back. I had studied brands for months and bought the best, but she found the look I envied—an efficient pack, well-worn boots, and an abundance of confidence. My own inadequacy and jangled nerves added weight to the nylon duffle bag I dragged toward ground transportation. Reassured that such a woman existed, I put one foot in front of the other and moved on.

* * *

While waiting for the shuttle bus to the car rental agency, I found a quiet corner to calm myself, away from the flow of passengers exiting the airport. I sat on my duffle bag, propped my elbows on my knees, and tried to think of a reason not to turn around and go home. *This is your dream. Envision the Grand Canyon. Beautiful plateaus. The river.* I sighed and kneaded my fingertips into my forehead. *I can't do this.*

Weariness defeated me until I pictured John gloating over my failed hike. *I won't give him the satisfaction.* I yanked open the green duffle bag and pulled out my two-toned brown backpack, boots, and straw cowboy hat. *Look the part, feel the part.* I transitioned from traveler to backpacker.

The bus chugged to a stop at the curb, so I gave my bootlaces a final tug and threw my traveling shoes and carry-on bag into the duffle. I hoisted my pack onto my shoulder and rushed to join the line.

The driver greeted passengers and took their luggage. Unwilling to relinquish my gear to anyone, I said hello and climbed aboard to stow my own backpack and duffle bag on the rack. I settled into the nearest seat, leaned my head against the window, and rested my eyes. *Another step forward. I can do this.*

That odd feeling of being watched made me open my eyes and look around. Behind the tourists with their golf shirts and Bermuda shorts, I spotted the woman with the red bandana. She returned my nod with that little grin she had had earlier.

Now or never, Amy. The bus is filling up. A big man plopped down next to me, making the decision easy. I stood to switch seats and the woman put on a real smile. She nodded toward the long back seat next to her.

I held out my hand. "My name is Amy. Thanks again for coming to my rescue back there. My trip would've been over if he'd taken my bag by mistake."

"Sarah Rochon. Sit. Glad I could help, but that was no mistake."

She was right, of course, but I was working very hard to keep positive thoughts. "But why would he steal *my* bag?"

Sarah widened her eyes. "Because you look like a brand new backpacker and would have all new equipment?"

I groaned. "Do I really look like such a novice?"

"New Mountain Hardware shirt, new convertible pants." She laughed. "I wondered if you were a backpacker. Now I see that pack—as big as you are." She pointed to the rack. "You're a serious backpacker."

Though delighted with the description, my confidence faltered under her gentle teasing. I pushed the conversation to safer ground.

"Where are you headed, Sarah?"

"The canyon. South Rim."

"Same here." I loved talking about hiking itineraries, trailheads, gear —anything backpacking. "My plan is to shuttle from the South Rim to the North Rim and hike across the canyon from there."

"Really?" Sarah looked me up and down. "Have you trained?"

John's criticisms came to mind as I defended my plan to the woman —and myself. I told her about my mileage, repetitions on the stairs, and Karen's car accident. I hoped it was enough to prove I was capable.

"I've hiked the canyon twice," Sarah said with a light flick of her hand. "You'll be fine."

Her approval sent an unwarranted flood of relief through me. I grinned like a fool and quickly calculated what it might be to travel with the woman. *How bad could she be? No twitching, no furtive looks. She looked sane and responsible.*

I had hired hundreds of employees during my years in business. My character assessments were usually right, so I trusted my instincts. "Shall we carpool to the South Rim together—share expenses?"

"Absolutely. Anything to cut costs." Sarah jumped on the idea so fast, I began to second guess myself. *It's been a heck of a day. Maybe my judgment is off.*

I hoped my impetuous invitation wouldn't come back to haunt me.

* * *

The shuttle bus trundled through an industrial part of Phoenix and squeaked to a stop in front of the car rental agency, a simple building gleaming in the desert sun. A blast of arctic AC greeted each customer at the door. I took a number and got a good place in line while Sarah stood guard over our backpacks. Within ten minutes the paper work was done and I had keys in my hand.

"Ladies and gentlemen." An intercom announcement got everyone's attention. "Please bear with us. We are out of vehicles, but will have cars cleaned and ready for you as they are returned."

The gathering of polo shirts and Bermuda shorts buzzed in displeasure. Some grabbed mobile phones to make other arrangements, some rushed for the door. Resisting the urge to crow over our good luck, Sarah and I hoisted our packs onto our backs and joined the exodus.

Outside, backlit by painful brightness, an attendant pointed to a mid-sized car baking in the sun halfway down the second aisle. Sarah and I crossed in front of a blue car idling at the stop sign. Through the windshield glare, the impatient driver scowled. I scurried out of his way, but glanced back and got a moment's glimpse at his passenger.

"Sarah?" I wanted her to get a look at him, but she was several paces ahead whistling Willie Nelson's *On The Road Again*. "Sarah." I caught up to her. "That kid has black plugs in his ears—like the guy who tried to take my bag."

Sarah frowned and followed my point. "I don't see him."

"Back by the stop sign. Blue car."

We scanned the row of vehicles being returned, but the car and the kid were gone.

"You don't really think the punk from the airport followed us here?" Sarah asked.

"I couldn't really see through the glare off the window." My memory already blurred. "Never mind. I'm just on edge today."

I let the idea go with a shrug and identified our Taurus by popping the trunk with the electronic key. Sarah and I shared our first laugh. Our mid-sized car came with a shoebox-sized trunk and our two backpacks would have to ride in the back seat. I threw my half-empty green duffle bag into the trunk.

An uneasy feeling crawled up my back as I slammed the lid. I spun around to survey the parking lot, but saw only impatient people waiting for rental cars. I wrote it off as pre-trip jitters and slid into the driver's seat, eager to leave Phoenix behind us.

As I-17 ran north and the desert spread to the horizon, the tires on the road hummed in tune with my new sense of freedom.

2

THE SOUTH RIM—Elevation: 6,860 ft.

Hours of driving through the desert brought Sarah and I to our destination, or so we thought. A lone sign announced, *Grand Canyon National Park.* Ramshackle stalls lined the dusty road, deserted by souvenir vendors. Ragged pennants and banners blew loose in the wind as if welcoming us to a ghost town.

The road continued to curve and snake along, hemmed in by trees. Darkness descended into the pine branches and closed in around us. Through the gloom, the Grand Canyon was nothing more than a black hole in the ground looming off to my right. The void drew me to its rim. I swallowed hard and gripped the wheel to keep the Taurus on the road.

Sarah had chattered nonstop during the long drive from Phoenix, but now she watched the narrow road in silence. The asphalt shadowed the canyon edge and demanded my attention. I needed white noise to calm my nerves.

"Talk to me, Sarah."

She talked, but I didn't listen. We drove through the moonless night with no hint of civilization. The last unlit directional sign lay miles behind us.

"So, this year I'll write a charter school grant . . . Hey! That was a sign." Sarah sat forward and slapped her hand on the dashboard. "Too dark to read." My navigator twisted in her seat, grumbling in frustration.

"Let me back up and try again." I put the Taurus in reverse and maneuvered off the road in front of the sign.

"I still can't make it out." Sarah unfolded her long legs and stepped from the vehicle, shining her flashlight on the sign.

I exited the car, as much to stretch my aching knees after the three-hour trip, as to read the sign. "Grand Canyon Village 10 miles," I read. "Finally."

The sound of a car engine came from somewhere down the road behind us.

What a relief. Civilization.

The sound grew into a roar, coming at us, echoing from all directions. Still, I saw no lights; nothing—until I heard tires pulling at the tarmac. Blinding headlights switched on. Like guided missiles, bright beams aimed straight at me. Instinct propelled me onto my car where I sprawled across the hood clawing for a handhold at the base of the wiper-blades. The jolt of metal on metal vibrated my bones. I pictured my feet being torn from my limbs and pulled my knees in as a great whoosh of air ruffled my pant legs. The screech of steel scraped my eardrums. The car careened off. *No brake lights.* The vehicle hurtled and swerved down the road.

"Freaking drunk." Sarah jumped from the bushes behind the car and pumped her fist in the air. "He tried to kill us."

"He's *going* to kill himself." I listened for the sound of a crash, but the night kept its secrets.

Sarah leaned over with her hands on her knees. "I may be having a heart attack." She blew air from her cheeks and straightened up. "Are you hurt, Amy?"

She took me by the shoulders, like I would have done to my daughter, and led me in front of the headlights to look me up and down.

In spite of our similar ages, I let her mother me, but brushed aside her concern.

"I'm okay," I insisted. A nervous twitter escaped me. "I had no idea I could move that fast. Training for this hike must have done me some good." My hands trembled as I smoothed my blouse and patted perspiration from my forehead.

Sarah turned the flashlight toward the scratches on her arms and a ragged hole in her nylon pants. "Crap. These were new."

The shiny, white rental car still idled on the edge of the road. "Can I borrow your light?" Wishing I had signed up for extra insurance, I examined the damaged vehicle. Jagged scrapes creased the length of the car. I peeled off a paint chip and held it out to Sarah. "Blue car."

She nodded, put on her glasses and bent to peer at the ragged metal and broken tail light.

"Not bad," I said. "We can still drive it."

"Not bad," she yelled. "That's all you can say? We should chase that frigging guy down and pound some sense into him."

I wanted no part of a fight and backed away, looking at Sarah from a new perspective. *What am I doing with this woman?* I wondered if I'd saddled myself with an angry vigilante. "I just want to find the lodge and get to bed," I said.

The Taurus' fender supported me while I watched Sarah rage on. *John was right.* I groaned. *This trip is doomed. Karen canceled out. A kid tried to steal my gear and a drunk just tried to kill me. Now I find out my passenger is a raving lunatic.*

Sarah soon stopped her tirade and put both hands on top of her head. "It'll be all right." She sighed and bent to retrieve her hat. "Let's go. We'll call the police from the lodge." She brushed herself off and climbed into the passenger seat.

I shook my head at the change in attitude and my hands trembled as I tugged on the driver's side door. The handle snapped back into place. The door wouldn't budge. "Great."

Sarah tried to force open the buckled door frame from the inside to no effect. I climbed in from the passenger's side and wiggled into the driver's seat. We crept along the road on the canyon rim, hoping that our car hadn't suffered internal damage and that the Yavapai Lodge waited beyond the next curve.

Out of the blackness, my headlights reflected back at me, glinting off a piece of chrome. I slammed on the brakes. "There's the blue car."

With its nose in the bushes and up against a boulder, the old Chevy Caprice had come to an abrupt stop.

"I don't see anyone." I whispered, as if the drunk driver might hear me.

"He's probably passed out." Sarah sniffed.

"We should check on him in any case. He might be injured."

13

"Drunks are immune to injury. They kill everyone else." In the dark I heard the cluck of her tongue. "I'll go," she said.

Flashlight in hand, Sarah stepped from the car. "Shine your headlights on him and keep the motor running." She left her door open and approached the disabled vehicle from behind the driver's door. She tapped the butt of the flashlight against the window. "Anybody in there?"

Sarah waited. She shined the light in, put her nose against the window, and opened the door. Rap music blared from the Chevy's radio.

My curiosity got the better of me. I turned off the engine and climbed out the passenger side door.

"He's gone," Sarah said with a shrug.

The beam of my headlamp probed inside the Chevy. The windshield had shattered and scattered crumbled glass lay across the bench seat. Keys dangled from the ignition. Fast food boxes, gum wrappers, and drink cups littered the floorboards. A red gym bag sat on the back seat. Sunglasses hung from the visor. I leaned in and turned the key to stop the hip-hop noise. My hand brushed against a damp rag balled up on the seat. I picked the cloth up by its corner, sniffed, and dropped it.

"There's a bloody rag in here," I called. "Maybe he staggered away."

Half afraid that we'd find him bleeding to death in the shrubbery, I searched along the side of the road to the extent of the Taurus' headlights, but found nothing. Sarah's flashlight bobbed in the bushes.

"Sarah," I yelled. "Don't go in there. We're near the rim of the canyon."

"I know," she called. "I can feel the wind. It's as black as hell over here."

"Come back to the road." A shiver went down my spine. The air was too quiet. Even the night birds held their song, waiting.

Wanting to get this business over, I bent into the beam of the headlights to write down the Nevada license plate number. Twigs cracked behind me.

"Sarah, I . . ." I turned to look at her, but saw only darkness.

"Sarah!"

14

3

GRAND CANYON VILLAGE

"I'm right here, Amy." Sarah's voice came out of the night, and my heart started to beat again. Feeling exposed in the beam of the car's headlights, I stepped to the side and turned my flashlight toward Sarah.

"Where were you?" I demanded. "I thought you were right behind me."

"Sorry. I searched in the bushes down that way. You okay?"

"A bit spooked," I admitted. "Let's get out of here. We're not saving anyone tonight. Either the driver's healthy enough to walk toward the lodge or someone picked him up."

"We haven't seen another car for almost an hour," she pointed out.

"Whatever. We've done what we can, and this place feels unsafe."

"You've got the willies bad," she teased.

My tone turned sharp. "When my skin starts to prickle, I pay attention." The surrounding darkness seemed thick with tension. I edged toward our vehicle.

"You're serious," Sarah said, no longer amused.

My voice lowered to a whisper. "Get in the car. We're exposed here, and something or someone is watching us. I can feel it."

I kept my eye on the rear view mirror watching the wrecked vehicle, but nothing moved to validate my sixth sense. Maybe I was wrong. Maybe the eerie canyon had unnerved me. Maybe I was just tired.

Whatever it was, I wanted to get away from it and to the safety of the lodge.

The road curved and took us away from the scene. The further I drove, the more my adrenaline quieted.

Sarah sat forward in her seat and peered into the darkness. "If he walked along this road, we'd have seen him by now."

"Perhaps he doesn't want to be seen," I countered.

Eight miles down the road, our lights found a *Yavapai Lodge* sign, and we caught sight of the soft glow of low-wattage bulbs coming from the windows of a group of buildings. The National Park Service took light pollution seriously. We inched our way into what I thought might be a parking lot.

"I don't see an office sign. Maybe that's the door. I'll run up and see." Sarah jumped out of the car and disappeared into the night, reappearing a few seconds later, silhouetted against a window's light. She waved me inside.

A bright young woman tended the reservation desk in the small lobby. She wore a neat 'Grand Canyon Village' blouse complete with name tag: 'Kate – Australia'. Another employee's tag read, 'Camille - France'. I assumed college students from all over the globe applied for work at the canyon, and I envied their adventurous spirit.

'Kate - Australia' quietly told a young family that reservations were needed and no rooms were available. The poor man looked stricken and glanced at his exhausted wife and little boy.

Sarah and I made a quick, unspoken decision and sidestepped the line to inform the desk clerk that I would give up my reservation and share a room with Sarah. 'Kate – Australia' smiled. Our gesture saved her from turning the family away. The father immediately pulled out his credit card.

I remembered being young and naïve with my two little ones, and I sympathized with the mother. She thanked us over the head of the irritable child, and the dad shook our hands before gathering their belongings.

After the little family disappeared into the night, I joined Sarah at the desk where she was explaining the hit and run. 'Kate – Australia' dialed for help, handed the phone to Sarah, and turned to assist the next guest.

Sarah reported the drunken driver and the crash to the local rangers and glanced at me as she spoke. I nodded to confirm the facts.

She surprised me by hanging up too soon. "You didn't tell them about the keys or the bloody rag."

"The rangers will check out the car tonight," Sarah said. "You can tell them all the little details when we fill out a report tomorrow."

"An hour ago you wanted to track him down and beat the driver up. Now you're not interested?"

"No, not really." She held up her hands. "Let the rangers do their job, and we'll get on with our vacations. We shouldn't get involved."

She was probably right, but uncomfortable thoughts niggled in the back of my mind. *We're already involved.*

While waiting for her credit card to process, Sarah leaned comfortably against the counter. She engaged Kate in another conversation, as if they were old friends, and I envied her easy way with people. Sarah signed the paperwork and asked, "Where is the nearest scenic overlook, Kate? We have time for a little exercise before the shuttle tomorrow."

Kate had a map at hand and pointed with a pencil. "The canyon is awesome from anywhere you look, Sarah, but hike a mile or two to Yaki Point. You'll be amazed by the fabulous views there."

My excitement grew in spite of my apprehensions and exhaustion. We thanked Kate for her help and the map, and walked out into the night. Our sense of sight was useless in the inky blackness. I forced myself to trust the gravel path to stay beneath my feet. I smelled pine and sensed the wall of trees that blocked out the stars. Muted voices floated on the cool breeze. In spite of my willingness to open myself to nature, I appreciated the safety of the car. We used the headlights to find Building Five and lugged our packs up industrial grade cement steps to the second floor. Once inside, we gave the clean, practical room a cursory look and, armed with headlamps, went in search of dinner.

We opted to walk to the cafeteria in the main building, so I switched on my LED, giving us enough light to stay on the path connecting the parking lots. Oddly quiet, as if all the guests and staff had already gone to bed, only the crush of stones beneath our boots and the rustling of dry leaves in the bushes disturbed the silence.

"There sure isn't much night life around here," Sarah said.

I stopped dead in my tracks. "Darn. My money is in the car, and I forgot to lock the door."

We spun around and made our way back through the shrubbery lining the path. Our car was a hulking shadow in the parking lot. I had the sinister feeling that eyes still watched us from the trees or from behind the buildings. In the dark anyone could have been within ten feet, and we'd never know. I paused.

"What?" Sarah stopped behind me.

"Nothing. I thought I heard someone."

We listened.

"I guess not," I said, but my skin still prickled.

I retrieved my wallet and locked the car. We started off again, but this time my ears were on alert. Sarah listened rather than talked. My beam of thin light skimmed the path in front of us.

I stopped short and grabbed Sarah's arm. "What's that?"

"Don't know," she whispered and tugged me along the path.

I trained the light on our feet, and we quickened our steps. Suddenly, my light caught movement. My heart faltered and Sarah gasped.

"Holy cripes."

Not five feet in front of us, a huge animal stood on the path. We involuntarily jumped back.

"Elk," Sarah whispered. "Let's back off."

"There's a whole herd here." Unnerved, but thrilled, I froze in place.

The animals' earthy smell surrounded us. They pulled up grass and smacked their lips, while Sarah and I stood like trees until the herd passed on either side. Sarah whistled softly at the immense set of antlers worn by the last of the eleven elk, a majestic male. He seemed as benign as the others, but I prayed we didn't draw his attention. *He could impale us . . .* I put that thought away.

Within minutes the animals moved beyond the reach of my light.

Sarah nudged my arm. "Did you see that? Those antlers had to be four feet long."

"Impressive. Probably no big deal to the locals, but still . . . ."

* * *

We reached the lodge and found the cafeteria too late for a hot meal. The long row of kitchen equipment stood silent in dim light behind stainless steel barriers. The servers had gone for the evening, so we settled for sandwiches from behind glass-doored refrigerators and paid the tired cashier who perched on stool at the check-out counter. She was in no mood for conversation. A few of the banquet-style tables were occupied by people lounging or playing cards in the glare of fluorescent light. Sarah nudged me to the relative privacy of the atrium.

I surreptitiously considered Sarah while she ate her sandwich like a kid with a Happy Meal. *Should I ask her to join me on the trail?* Her dark curls bobbed above her smooth, tan face. *Was she the helpful person I met at the airport or the hot-tempered woman at the crash site? Would we be able to spend an entire week together?* I shredded my napkin, thinking about my options.

The thought of going solo put fear in my bones, but the specter of going home without completing the hike was worse. I recalled John's condescending smirk and his accusation that I never finished anything.

"Sarah?" I asked.

She stopped in mid-chew, and I barged ahead, afraid of rejection. "I'm not comfortable hiking solo. Will you join me on the rim-to-rim trail?"

"Well, sure. I thought you'd never ask." She took the shredded napkin from my hand, tossed it aside, and smiled. "I can squeeze an extra day in before my meeting at the Phoenix charter school. You know, I originally planned a rim-to-rim route myself, but didn't want to tackle it alone." She pointed a potato chip at me. "We could even share gear and cut a little weight, if you want."

Relieved, I got caught up in her enthusiasm. We chatted through our meals and headed for the door into the night. With my flashlight in my pocket, my eyes adjusted to the now familiar darkness. Forgetting my earlier apprehension, we strolled the short distance to our lodge engrossed in our new plans. I ignored the crunch of footsteps on stones and the slight movement in the bushes. More elk, I assumed.

4

Day 2: YAVAPAI LODGE

Excitement woke me early, but Sarah was already up and dressed. "I'm going out to look around. Be back shortly," she said.

How can people pop out of bed like that? I managed to get my hand from under the covers and waved, not trusting my voice. I appreciated having the room to myself and a few extra minutes to roll up in the layered blankets to visualize the coming day.

Five minutes later I stretched and put my feet on the chilly floor. By the time I washed and dressed, Sarah had returned, fumbling with the door key. I opened the door, and she filled the room with her cheerfulness.

"Coffee or tea?" she offered.

"Thanks. Tea would be perfect." I opened the curtains, and we sipped the hot liquids in the sunlight.

"They've got the weather posted at the cafeteria," she said. "Sixty degrees this morning, eighty this afternoon. Perfect." She frowned at my cosmetic bag. "Why don't you get rid of that stuff?"

"Habit, I guess. My husband insists I'm too pale and should cover my freckles."

She grunted in disapproval. "Your skin is perfect. You've got killer blue eyes and a great smile."

I laughed, embarrassed. My father had reprimanded me in seventh grade for deflecting a flattering remark. He said I'm to simply accept compliments and say *Thank you.*

"Umm. Thanks," I said.

"No, seriously," Sarah insisted. "Besides, the only cosmetics a self-respecting backpacker carries are sunscreen, deodorant, lip balm, and bug repellant."

Suits me just fine. I threw the cosmetics in my carry-on bag and switched to the task of coordinating gear with Sarah. Last night we talked for a long time while she studied my map and brochures detailing the campsites and popular scenic stops along the North Kaibab Trail. She now knew the elevations, mileages, and water stops even better than me.

During the night we had agreed that my tent would stay in the car, and we'd each carry parts of her tent, cutting about two pounds for both of us. Sarah's tarp and poles fit in my pack, but her pack still looked huge. "Do you have every piece of gear known to man in there?" I asked.

"Hey, I don't want to ever be without something I need." She laughed. "Let's haul this stuff down to the car."

The freshness of the canyon air welcomed me. Pine fragrance wafted down from trees towering over the buildings. I breathed deeply as if the scent were a tonic to enliven my mind and body. The pure air helped to settle my queasy stomach.

Daylight at Yavapai offered an entirely different experience than the night before had. Flanking bright parking lots, rows of two-story buildings lined up like soldiers—neat and clean. Squatted along any highway, they would be called motels, but here at the Grand Canyon they were called Yavapai Lodge. People with muffled footfalls strolled or jogged along paths of hard-packed earth strewn with pine needles. Faint chittering came from the bushes and trees, maybe birds, maybe squirrels. The sun peeked over the pines and warmed the breezes, promising a perfect day.

"Hey, now there are dents on the passenger side," Sarah said as we approached the rental car.

Her statement roused me from my commune with nature, and I joined her the car to examine the door frame. I looked around for what might have caused the new damage.

"Someone tried to pry open the door during the night," I guessed.

"There's nothing in there," she pointed out. "Why would anyone break into a damaged car?"

"Who knows? My insurance company is not going to believe this."

"The situation could be worse," Sarah said. "If our equipment got stolen, our trip would be over."

"That's my kind of luck," I groaned, glancing down at the gear I had almost lost at the airport. "What do I have that anyone would want so badly?"

"I can't imagine, but then I don't think like a criminal." She made a sinister face.

What could I do but laugh? We tossed our carry-on bags and my tent into the trunk and our packs in the back seat.

According to our map the backcountry permit office was less than a half mile from the cafeteria, but I inadvertently drove the long way around, weaving through parking lots and the narrow, looping streets of Grand Canyon Village. Like tourists everywhere, people strolled about without much concern for being run over in the street. Apparently, they thought their cameras, flip flops, and flowered shirts made them immune to death by automobile. I managed to miss the pedestrians, but nearly hit a parked car when I caught a glimpse of the canyon. It's grandeur took my breath away.

"Let's pull over and take a look." Sarah craned her neck like a child at a circus.

We found a parking space, locked the doors, and didn't give another thought to the possible theft of our gear. Following a crowd of tourists, we found our way onto an open plaza behind one of the pricey rustic hotels. I made a beeline for the low-stone wall on the far side of the plaza.

The canyon's awesome vista stretched as far as I could see. Layers of rock lined the canyon walls in striations of red, orange, purple and every shade in between. Mesas and ravines filled the horizon.

"Wow," I said.

Sarah's eyes were as wide as mine, trying to take in the vastness.

"This is so awesome—like a picture postcard." As a good tourist should, I exclaimed in delight, but couldn't admit my first view of the canyon had disappointed me. The postcard scene appeared lifeless, maybe even fake. I don't know what magic I expected. *Grand* and other superlatives used to describe the canyon were accurate, but the panorama before me lacked something.

Where's the wildness, nature unleashed? I didn't feel any of that power in the neatly packaged plaza. Too many people milling about, too much civilization. I itched to be down in the canyon, part of its natural world.

Sarah had seen enough, too. "Ready?" she asked. "Let's get our permit."

The Backcountry Office, hidden away from the scenic areas, sat near the railroad tracks and overflow-parking. A young ranger greeted us with a boyish "Hello," listened to our request, and canceled Sarah's permit.

"Okay, Ms. Warren, I've added Ms. Rochon to your permit for North Kaibab to Cottonwood tomorrow, two nights at Bright Angel Campground, then Indian Gardens and back here on the tenth. Correct?"

"That's the plan," I said. Hearing our itinerary excited me more than seeing the canyon.

"Here's your receipt. There are rules and instructions on the back." He folded the paper and slid it into a plastic sleeve. "Keep these with you at all times. The rangers will check permits."

As he flipped through a sheaf of papers, Sarah and I waited like well-behaved school girls. "Let's see. Snow flurries are expected on the North Rim tomorrow morning—and be careful on the trail near Supai Tunnel. Several feet of the trail collapsed, and the crew may be working to shore it up. Any questions?"

I motioned to the parking lot. "Will you give me a report for my insurance company? Last night our rental car got sideswiped by a hit-and-run driver. This morning we discovered additional damage, as if someone tried to pry open the passenger door."

The ranger arched his eyebrows. "Huh. Heard about the hit-and-run." He snapped a report sheet to a clipboard and headed toward the parking lot. In his neatly pressed, short-pants summer uniform, the ranger looked more like a young scout than an adult ranger. Pen in hand, he examined the car, taking down the license plate and VIN numbers.

"Do you have much theft here?" Sarah asked, pointing out damage to the door frame.

"Not at all, but those do look like pry marks," said the ranger. "We might get pick-pocketing, missing cameras, but seldom vehicle break-ins." He bent to inspect the long line of blue etched into the white paint, running his fingers along the grooves. "Was anyone hurt?"

"We weren't, but the other driver might be," I said. "Do you know anything more about the guy who hit us?"

The ranger continued writing and shook his head. "No. The report mentioned an abandoned vehicle, but no injuries. We don't have the plate ID yet."

He dutifully wrote down the details I forced on him: the bloody rag, the rap music and the eerie feeling at the crash site, then snapped his pencil into place under a rubber-band. "Thank you. I'll do the paperwork, and you can pick up the insurance report after your hike."

The ranger wished us a safe journey and returned to his office.

We dragged our packs from the backseat to get what we'd need for a short trek. Before catching the 1:30 shuttle bus to the North Rim, we'd do a warm-up. A five-hour bus trip with no exercise for the day did not suit either one of us.

I added a few necessities to my fanny pack—water bottle, car keys—but stopped with a groan. "We forgot to sign you up for the shuttle."

Sarah laughed at my worry. "I'm all set. I took the bus over to Bright Angel this morning while you slept. The bus to the North Rim had two seats left."

Sarah turned out to be a responsible, thoughtful friend. A thoughtful friend with a very heavy fanny pack. "What are you putting in there?" I asked. "We'll be gone for less than three hours."

She raised her chin in mock defiance. "I'm prepared for anything. I have water, snack, jacket, hat, sunglasses, a field guide to flora and fauna, binoculars, first aid kit and a few other basics."

"Sleeping bag?"

She laughed. "No."

"Flashlight?"

"Good idea, but no, I'll leave that here."

I loved the bantering. "Are you ready now?"

"I am."

After locking the car, we were off. I tamped down my excitement and restrained the urge to link arms and skip.

Mather Point proved to be an excellent vantage point to get another look at the canyon. The sun rose higher in the sky, and the colors of the distant plateaus and rock formations changed; more yellow and beige, less purple. Spectacular views presented themselves in every direction.

Two busloads of people thought so, too. Groups of twos and fours milled around the scenic overlook. A young couple struggled to push an umbrella stroller over the rocky soil toward the rim. An elderly man and woman sat on a bench, more interested in the baby in the stroller than the view. Two middle-aged couples took turns photographing each other.

Sarah approached them with her hand out. "Here, let me take a picture of the four of you." The woman entrusted the expensive Fuji to her, and Sarah positioned them with the canyon in the background. She handled the strangers well, chatting amiably, controlling the situation.

"Okay, everybody smile. One more. Got it." Sarah handed the camera back to the lady who thanked her profusely.

"That was kind of you," I said, after the couples moved on.

"I love meeting people like that," Sarah replied. "All you have to do is step in to say hello. They'll tell you all sorts of interesting stories. Almost no one says no." Sarah shrugged.

"That's how I met you yesterday," she said.

Only yesterday? "Well, I'm glad you stepped in to rescue my gear."

"Me, too." She grinned.

Three teen-aged boys caught my attention as they roughhoused on boulders at the very edge of the rim. "That's so dangerous." I raised my voice. "People fall over the edge playing around like that." Nobody paid attention.

"Those kids have no common sense," Sarah said. "There are warning posters everywhere."

"I can't watch. Let's find the trailhead and get away from here."

At the far side of the parking lot a wooden sign marked the beginning of the Rim Trail. Our brisk pace soon left the crowd behind, along with my worries for their safety.

Almost immediately the trees shaded the trail and obscured the view of the canyon. The trail roughly paralleled the canyon's south rim. The jagged edge jutted in here, poked out there. At times the canyon loomed breathtakingly near, giving us a majestic view at every step. A mound of rock or a thick stand of trees would then force the trail back from the rim and obscure the view. We trekked along without speaking, each enjoying the experience in our own way.

I broke the silence when a dark thought occurred to me. "There's an average of twelve deaths each year in the canyon."

Sarah waited for my point.

"I mean, you'd think so many deaths would scare us off, but most of them were suicides or stupidity. That made me less afraid. I don't intend to do anything stupid."

Sarah sighed and nodded. "Like the athlete who tried to run rim to rim in the heat with no water."

"Exactly." I looked out over the five-mile expanse and shook my head at the tragedy. "Hard to imagine the killer heat on the canyon floor right now."

I tried to shake off negative thoughts as we hiked along, but spotted a discarded pop can at the side of the path. "Why are people so careless?" I picked up the can, emptying the cola onto a rock.

"I don't get it either." Sarah shrugged. "I usually come back from my hikes with a full trash bag."

"Me, too. But I embarrassed my husband by picking up litter. He quit walking with me years ago."

Litter collection became a game as we hiked along the wooded trail. Soon, the junipers and pinion trees gave way, allowing a breeze to cool our skin. The canyon came into full view again, and we found a small outcropping that gave us a private, scenic overlook. A gorgeous landscape spread before us; the same canyon, but better.

"Let's sit here awhile to take all this in," I suggested. Small pebbles rolled from beneath my boots and skittered over the edge.

"Careful," Sarah said, grasping my upper arm. "It's a long way down."

Sarah sat further back from the edge and pulled a pair of binoculars from her fanny pack. "Check out the trail down there," she said. "The path winds all along that wall and out into the main canyon."

She handed them over, and I put the binoculars to my eyes. "These are really high-powered. I can see the trail clearly *and* a stand of trees in the distance."

"That's Indian Gardens," she said.

The close up views entertained me. "I can even see birds flitting around in the bushes clinging to the side of the canyon wall."

Sarah snapped a few pictures while I hogged her binoculars.

"Geez. That ticks me off," I said. "Can you believe somebody threw garbage into the ravine?"

She glanced over to where I pointed to our right and about two hundred feet down.

"What do you see?" she asked.

"Bright red." I analyzed the distant object. "More than litter, larger. Maybe a piece of cloth."

"Hmmm. Let me see." Sarah took the binoculars and scanned the ravine. "Maybe a scarf. That's really stupid." She clucked her tongue and handed the lenses back.

Something about that *scarf* nagged at me. What was it? How had it found its way into the canyon to spoil the view? To find out, I scrambled back from the edge and followed Sarah east on the Rim Trail.

5

YAKI POINT OVERLOOK

Tracking down the red cloth became a goal, a reason to walk several miles. When neither rocks nor trees prevented access to the rim, we sidled as close as we dared to the edge and scanned the rocks, boulders and ledges beneath and to the east of us. The trail veered away from the rim taking us into pine woods with thick underbrush.

I followed our progress on the map, though the simple lines of the map did not detail the meanderings of the trail nor of the canyon's craggy rim. "Pipe Creek Vista should be a short distance ahead," I said.

"You'd hardly know the canyon's behind these trees, but this is beautiful, too. Not so different from the Northwoods with the smell of pine I love." The sound of a bus's air brakes interrupted Sarah.

Fifty yards ahead, the trail and road converged at a point where the canyon rim opened up to a spectacular view. I found a trash container for the crushed pop can I had been carrying and joined a dozen tourists who noisily exited a bus, cameras and sodas in hand. The new set of visitors oohed and aahed at their first glimpse of the canyon. Pipe Creek gave such a gorgeous, wide open view that I oohed and aahed along with them. I almost forgot we were on a mission.

While the tourists looked straight out across the width of the canyon, Sarah trained her binoculars to the east. She motioned me over. "There. See the cloth?"

I took the binoculars and followed her point. "I see something."

We needed to get closer and turned to leave, sidestepping people who jostled each other to get to the rim to pose for pictures. Ignoring the danger, a few stepped over the obvious rock barrier. A man with a beer-belly the size of Texas stood in flip-flops on the very edge of a rounded rock. Worry for the man spiked my stress level. *Time for me to go.*

To take my mind off the careless tourists, I searched for litter along the trail. A silver granola bar wrapper tumbled across the ground pushed by the wind toward the rim. I stomped the foil beneath my boot.

Sarah got into my game again. A little further on, she picked up a long shoelace. "Now how can someone lose a shoelace? Nothing wrong with it." She rolled up the lace and stuck it in her pocket.

The canyon gave us another opening and a clear view of the ravine. The rock beneath our feet, beaten smooth by centuries of wind and rain, dipped away from us in layers, disappearing over the edge. We sat on our rear ends to scoot closer to the rim.

"See if you can see the cloth from here." I handed the binoculars to Sarah.

She scrutinized the ravine from side to side and then up and down. "There it is. Looks like a jacket or a . . . ." She dropped the glasses into her lap.

"What? Let me see." I focused the lenses on the red cloth. "Good God, a foot is sticking out from under the jacket." Sickened, I lowered the binoculars, but a morbid curiosity compelled me to look again.

Jagged rocks half hid the body. An arm splayed out to its side. A man's leg and foot were visible, but protruded oddly as if the body folded over on itself. He lay there like a broken rag doll.

"Could that be the hit-and-run driver from last night?"

Sarah refused the binoculars. "I can't look at blood," she said, cupping her hand over her mouth. "What should we do?"

I willed myself to think. "Call the rangers. Try 911."

Sarah fished out her cell phone and punched the buttons. "No signal. Now what?"

"Let's find the road and flag down a car." I started down the path to the east.

"I'm not getting any closer." Sarah held back, ashen-faced. "I'll run back to Pipe Creek and see if the bus driver has a radio."

She jogged off, as if demons chased her. I ran in the opposite direction, hoping to find the spot directly above the body, but I'm a better hiker than I am a runner. I stopped frequently to catch my breath and to check on the body—as if the limbs would reassemble themselves and walk off.

The roar of a tour bus came through the thicket of shrubbery. I waved my arms and shouted, but the bus zoomed by.

Dang. Sarah missed the bus at Pipe Creek.

Eighty yards further, the trail came within sight of the road. *This is the place.* I peered over the rim. The red jacket and mangled body lay directly below, about a hundred feet down.

I froze in place. *What if I'm trampling evidence?* I scanned the area. *Evidence of what?* I didn't know, but I looked for clues as to what had occurred on the rim overnight. *Footprints? Scraps of clothing? Was this one of those suicides?*

I closed my eyes and envisioned the poor man's last moments on earth. *A terrifying descent, a painful fall, what else? Maybe he left a note.* I searched around. *Nothing.*

The low bushes caught my attention. Broken twigs bent toward the canyon. Weeds lay matted. Bushes on the opposite side of the trail, adjacent to the road, were also broken. I wondered if the man had been dragged through the bushes. *Not a suicide?*

I stepped around the broken bushes and onto the pavement which stretched from Yavapai Lodge out to the entrance to the park. *This is the road we followed last night—about where the hit-and-run driver almost killed us.* I pulled the map from my pocket and traced the road to where it abutted the canyon edge. The abandoned car would be a short distance further east of where I stood.

Did the victim in the canyon have a connection to the abandoned car? I retraced my steps and checked again for footprints, but on the hard packed trail I found only partial prints. Not hiking boots, I thought. A tourist then, or at least, not a serious hiker. On my hands and knees, I examined a print. Engrossed, I almost didn't hear my name being called.

I stood and yelled. "Over here, Sarah."

She hung out of the window of a police car cruising slowly down the road. The vehicle pulled to the side of the pavement, and Sarah jumped out followed by a blond woman in a fitted National Park Service uniform.

"Don't come this way," I said. "There are footprints here." I directed them through the shrubbery several feet from my evidence.

The ranger extended her hand. "Hello, I'm Ranger Janet Beal. Sarah tells me that you may have found a victim."

Amazed that the ranger and Sarah were already on a first-name basis and excited to share the clues I'd found, I forgot to introduce myself. "Look over here. These bushes are broken. Don't step on those footprints."

Ranger Beal indulged me a few moments before saying, "Let me take a look over the edge." She sidestepped my clue area and cleared her own path to the rim.

I followed her in, but Sarah hung back.

"See him down there?" I pointed.

"I see," she sighed. "I'll call in a recovery crew." She spoke into the radio at her shoulder, and I joined Sarah back on the trail to give the ranger privacy. I couldn't make out Ranger Beal's exact words, but heard her firm, professional tone giving the facts. The response came in staccato bursts of static.

"You don't look so good," I said to Sarah. "Are you okay?"

Sarah sat slumped on a rock. She shook her head slowly. "Do you think he's the driver from last night?"

"I don't know. We're near the crash site though. I suppose he could have wandered this far and fell over the edge."

"We should have tracked him down when we had the chance," Sarah said and rubbed her forehead with her fingertips.

"Don't go there, Sarah. The victim in the ravine might not even be the driver. Maybe it's a suicide." I winced at my attempt to cheer her up.

She frowned. "What makes you think that?"

"I read that some suicidal people want to make a big statement. What could be bigger than the Grand Canyon? They drive out here and then to go over the edge."

31

Sarah accepted the information and sighed.

I regretted that our find caused her sorrow, but didn't know what to say to help her.

Ranger Beal approached us. Her robust figure and toned muscles countered the age showing around her eyes. Her blond hair was gathered in a neat bun beneath the stiff full brim of her hat. "Thank you, ladies, for reporting this incident." Ranger Beal put her hand on Sarah's shoulder. "I'm sorry you're upset. We'll take care of this." The ranger's aura of authority and competence seemed to ease Sarah's worry.

"I'm okay," Sarah said. "I just hate dead things and blood." She propped her elbows on her knees and stared out over the canyon.

Ranger Beal turned to me. "What were you saying about clues?"

I kept a solemn demeanor, but itched to show her my evidence finds: the branches, the footprints, the path from the road. "I think the man wore gym shoes. I found a few partial prints here, but there's too much rock to see a pattern."

The ranger jotted notes while she surveyed the area.

"Last night there was an abandoned vehicle a short distance east," I said. "There may be a connection."

Ranger Beal looked at me quizzically.

"A blue Chevy sideswiped our car on the road last night," I explained. "We found the car a few minutes later, but the driver was gone. We phoned in a report."

"Huh. You ladies get around," the ranger said, slipping her pen into her shirt pocket. "Good job. I'll mention your ideas to the investigation team."

Another squad pulled up, and Ranger Beal waved.

"We should go," called Sarah. "We need to catch that shuttle."

I looked at my watch. "We're going to be late. Do you need anything else from us?"

"Your name and contact information," Ranger Beal said. "Now that the other squad is here, I can drive you to the Village to save you time. Hang out at the car while I talk to the response team."

Ranger Beal spent a few minutes updating the other rangers before settling herself behind the wheel of her vehicle. "Call me Jan," she said.

Jan's cheerfulness and the increased distance from the Yaki Point tragedy calmed my surging adrenaline and seemed to ease Sarah's mind.

"So, where are you girls from?" Jan asked over her shoulder.

Sarah brightened, or made a good show of it. "I'm from the northwoods of Wisconsin. Amy is from Chicago. I met her less than twenty-four hours ago and it's been trouble ever since." She was only half kidding. "Must be that Chicago thing."

"I'm from a small town *south* of Chicago, but agree we've had an interesting twenty-four hours."

Ranger Jan played along, deftly deflecting our thoughts away from the ugly scene behind us. In spite of the dead body, we laughed—perhaps shamefully, maybe in self-defense. We soon arrived at the Backcountry Office with our damaged vehicle in the parking lot.

Exiting the squad car, I searched in my zippered pocket for the keys.

"You did get sideswiped," Ranger Jan said, surveying the Taurus as if we had overstated the damage. She extended her hand. "Well, thank you for going to so much trouble to report the accident—both of them." She shook Sarah's hand, then mine.

"Is there anything else we can do for you?" Ranger Jan asked.

I glanced at my watch. 12:14. "We could use a ride to Bright Angel with our backpacks. That'll give us time to grab lunch."

"Done," Jan said, but looked doubtful. "There's always a long wait at Bright Angel's restaurant. Let me make a call for you."

After the ranger disappeared into the building, Sarah and I busied ourselves with preparations. Sarah refilled our water bottles from the outside fountain, while I made a last check of the car. Sarah's stuff had gotten strewn all over the trunk. I gathered up her extra clothes and a plastic wrapped package and shoved them to the right. Shaking my head at her sloppiness, I slammed the trunk and locked the doors.

Ten minutes later Jan's squad car delivered us to the wide stone steps leading to the front door of the Bright Angel Lodge.

Several dozen people enjoying the sunshine milled around and watched our arrival with mild interest. A young man in a black tee shirt turned his back and melted into the crowd.

Jan unlocked the trunk and handed each of us our packs. She shook our hands warmly. "Look me up at the end of your hike. I'd like to hear all about your adventure."

Sarah pulled out her camera. "Amy, stand with Jan."

I followed directions and stood with the ranger in front of the squad car, while Sarah, the photo journalist, snapped a quick picture.

Jan wished us a safe trip and pulled away from the curb.

Large dark logs formed the walls and ceiling timbers of the vast lobby of Bright Angel Lodge. The room resembled a ski chalet with the huge stone fireplace and rough floor. Rather than skis propped against the walls and skiers clomping around in ski boots, backpacks lined the walls and hikers stomped around in hiking boots. People crisscrossed the mayhem in all directions, bumping shoulders, laughing.

"What do we do?" I yelled, hyped up by the anticipation of adventure which hung in the air, but unnerved by the noise.

Sarah shrugged. "Let's find out." With me in her wake, she plunged into the chaos.

We found a line to stand in, checked in with the shuttle bus reservation clerk and asked for directions to the restaurant. He highlighted our names in yellow on the boarding list and pointed across the lobby. "The line starts there near the gift shop."

We fought our way back through the sea of tourists and hikers. Would-be-diners, milling around in the hallway and slouched on benches, hampered shoppers trying to get into the store.

"I can't butt in front of all of these people," I whispered.

Sarah had no problem with that. "Excuse me. Sorry. Excuse me, please." She sailed up to the hostess desk.

I apologized my way through the crowd without looking at the hungry people leaning against the walls.

"Do you have a table for Sarah Rochon and Amy Warren?" Sarah asked the hostess.

The woman smiled from beneath a bouffant hairdo and winked. "I sure do, darlin'. Follow me." She looked as though she was last employed at a diner along Route 66, where the waitresses knew everybody in town and served the best pie. She even had the chewing gum going.

"Here we are, girls." She seated us in the busy restaurant next to a wall of railroad memorabilia and handed out menus. "May I recommend the cheeseburgers? They're our specialty."

Sarah slapped the menu shut. "Make mine medium rare," she said. "With onion rings. I hear they're to die for."

I sighed and gave up. "To heck with the diet. I'll have the same. Medium."

The waitress jotted down our order and hurried to the kitchen.

"Relax and enjoy," Sarah said, sitting back comfortably. "I can get used to this personal service." Her countenance showed no trace of the morning's misadventures.

"This *is* a great place. Did you see that lobby?"

"Like something Paul Bunyan built," she said, launching into her own version of the mythical northwoods lumberjack and his big blue ox digging the Grand Canyon. Her comical story made my stress level plummet.

"In spite of everything, I've laughed more in the last twenty-four hours than I have in the entire last month," I said, "maybe six months."

Sarah shook a playful finger at me. "A good chuckle releases endorphins to get rid of stress and anxiety."

"I'm used to daily bouts of stress."

Sarah's good humor faded. "Being run down by a drunk driver, having your car broken into, and finding a dead body causes more than average anxiety."

"Yes, but you're here to help me handle those issues." I decided not to add news of my husband's threat of divorce to Sarah's worries. We were friends, but I didn't know her well enough to share my personal problems.

"I don't cope well with dead bodies," she admitted. "Blood makes me faint, and the thought of that poor man down there freaks me out."

The change in her demeanor saddened me. "The rescue crew is probably already there, getting him out."

"But why did he jump?" she asked. "Do you think he's the hit-and-run driver?"

"Maybe not. Could be a guest at one of the lodges. He got blind drunk and stumbled over the edge. Or maybe his lover in Iowa jilted him. He drove out here to prove his love for her by jumping, or something like that. If we weren't leaving for the North Rim, I'd stay and find out more."

"I'm glad we're leaving. I want nothing else to do with your mystery," she said. "I've had enough death in my life."

Her announcement caught me off guard. "I'm sorry." I mentally kicked myself for ignoring how our discovery of the body had shaken my friend. I patted her hand and wondered what sadness her past held. "Do you want to talk about it?"

"Not really. It was . . ."

"Here you are, girls. Two cheeseburgers hot off the grill." Our waitress delivered our meals, and Sarah took a huge bite to avoid talking, I suspected.

"This is delicious." She garbled the words and pointed to the burger.

The food was great, I agreed and pretended that Sarah's soft side hadn't peeked through her armor. "Don't worry. I'm out of the mystery business." I chewed with my hand in front of my mouth. "Ranger Jan will probably have the case solved by tomorrow anyway."

We dropped the conversation and concentrated on the old fashioned, cholesterol busting cheeseburgers and onion rings. Leaving half the sandwich on my plate, I checked my watch. 1:15. "We should go." I signaled for our server.

"Let me get this," Sarah said. The bill barely left the waitress's hand before Sarah swooped it up and handed over her credit card.

We hurried to the exit where a line of people still stood, waiting for tables. I avoided their eyes, in case we had passed some of them on our way in. The lobby, however, had emptied. Only a few backpacks leaned against the walls. I frowned at a jacket sleeve hanging from an open compartment of my pack. With no time to mull over my sloppiness, I tucked in the jacket and dashed to the shuttle stop.

6

ON THE ROAD AGAIN - 236 Miles

We need not have rushed. No buses were at the entrance when we arrived. Hikers sat on the stone steps or on their packs, basking in the sun. Within minutes two shuttle buses pulled into the circular driveway. The clerk from the reservation desk stood next to the minibus calling out names from his list. Sixteen of us were directed to the first vehicle.

The driver climbed on top of the bus, ready to receive backpacks hoisted to him by the clerk. They tossed my pack easily. Sarah's made them grunt with effort. The two men then covered the pile of backpacks with a blue tarp and secured the load with bungee cords. Sarah got on the bus several minutes before me and claimed two seats in the front. Once I saw our gear safely stowed, I stepped aboard.

"Thanks for grabbing these seats," I said, as I plopped next to her. "Riding in the back of any vehicle makes me nauseous."

"No problem. I like the front seats," Sarah said, "so I can watch the road and talk to the driver."

The upcoming adventure caused an instant camaraderie among the sixteen passengers, all new friends. The general mood turned jovial. Hikers and backpackers jostled into their seats and found places for their fanny packs and miscellaneous stuff.

A broad-shouldered young man with sun-bleached hair tapped a skinny student wearing a tie-dyed T-shirt on the shoulder. He ushered the student out of his seat and took his place.

"Is this seat taken?" the bully asked the pretty blond girl sitting next to him.

"Now it is." The girl giggled. "Hi, I'm Kylie."

"Eric Prescott," he said. "You're the hottest looking girl on this bus."

I cringed at the clumsy flirting and noticed the tie-dyed student slumped into the back seat with his long, scraggly goatee pressed against his chest under his crossed arms. He glared at Kylie and her new friend.

The driver, in cowboy boots and long-legged jeans, climbed behind the wheel right on time, and the passengers settled in for the long journey.

Sarah snapped pictures of our traveling companions, as I listened to the conversations around us. Two male voices off to the side bantered back and forth about the merits of Deet. Behind me, the bully's smooth voice contradicted his arrogant exterior as he impressed the girl with tales of his adventures on the Appalachian Trail.

"I hiked the entire A.T. last year, two thousand one hundred seventy miles," he boasted.

An experienced woman would be wary. I casually twisted in my seat to see Kylie's reaction.

The awestruck girl twirled her long blond hair between her fingers. "That's so incredible, Eric. How many days did you hike?"

"I went all the way to Maine in four months, six days," he said. "Most people drop out before they get out of Georgia."

"That's, like, awesome," she purred, batting her long lashes.

If Eric was truthful, I wanted to hear his stories, too. If he wasn't, Kylie's future included heartbreak.

I eavesdropped on various conversations for a long time to make the trip go faster and to gain vicarious hiking experience. Eventually, the noise level dropped. People slept, some stared out the windows. The girl and the hiker whispered together, and I lost interest.

Sarah sat forward in the seat to engage the driver in talk about himself. "Hey, Chet. What's the best story you have about tourists in the canyon?"

He took time to pick over his words. "Well, ma'am," he said in a western drawl. "Some ain't got a lick of sense. Last year a dern fool drove over from Vegas in one of them SUVs, him and his family. He ran around the gates somehow. The North Rim's at nine-thousand feet and snow piles up in November, ten feet easy. Bunch of us brought 'em out on snowmobiles. They was lucky."

"You saved them," Sarah said.

"Aw, I got the snowmobile anyway to tend my cattle. We get called out now and again to help."

While Sarah interviewed Chet and a couple in their fifties in the opposite front seat listened, I scanned the passengers behind me to put faces with voices. As I expected, they were of both genders and spanned a wide range of age and apparent physical abilities.

My fellow passengers were in their element, having a great time talking about their adventures or the latest gear craze, but backpackers can be a quirky lot. Most I'd met were the friendly, helpful sort, although many were socially uncomfortable.

There were also a few serious loners among the ranks of backpackers, social misfits. They might hike alone for months, avoid human contact, and go into towns only to replenish supplies.

I thought one such loner sat in the seat, one back and on the other side of the bus. The lean man, maybe in his mid-twenties, stared out the window from under heavy dark brows, ignoring the people around him.

During a lull in her conversation, I nudged Sarah to take a peek. "That fellow doesn't look happy."

She agreed. "His body language says *leave me alone*."

His seat mate had figured that out, too, and turned with his legs in the aisle to talk to his new buddies behind him.

The loner intrigued me, so I pretended to need a stretch and stood to get a better look at him. "I'll bet he's an ultra-lighter," I whispered, as I slid back down in my seat. "His pack can't weigh more than fifteen pounds."

Of all the passengers, only he did not stow his backpack on the top of the bus. Instead, he laid the old, worn pack across his lap; his arms resting on top. He looked disheveled, as if he had already spent several nights on the trail.

"Ultra-lighters are nuts," whispered Sarah. "How can he hike the canyon with so little gear?"

"Maybe he's sleeping under the stars and has no extra clothes," I said. His pants looked like cotton, not the typical nylon. "Maybe he does everything on the cheap."

Sarah snickered. "And maybe he drilled holes in his toothbrush to shave an ounce."

"I admire some of the ultra-light tricks. I got my pack down to thirty pounds. That's about all I want to carry."

"I take the opposite view," said Sarah. "I carry as much as I can." She swaggered proudly in her seat. "My pack weighs forty-five pounds, including food and water, but I also weigh a lot more than you."

Sarah obviously took pride in her strength and height, comfortable with her body. I envied that. My scale probably showed fifty pounds less than hers, yet I constantly dieted.

I took another covert look at the motionless ultra-lighter. A five-o'clock shadow darkened his jaw. "I'm surprised he didn't hack the extra straps off his pack," I said. "That would save an ounce or two."

Sarah shrugged. "He probably didn't even bring a toothbrush."

We turned our attention to fish stories being exchanged between the driver and the couple in the other front seat. The balding husband with a little paunch protruding from his belt chuckled at Chet's tale and launched into his own. As his voice grew louder, his wife's attention drifted to the scenery outside. No doubt, she had heard all his stories before, but I *hadn't* and listened with interest.

Still chuckling over the ending, the storyteller sat back in his seat. His wife looked at him with obvious love. My heart ached. I wanted to be that couple; still in love, having fun, traveling, growing old together. John had shattered that dream for me.

The route to the North Rim covered 236 miles. The map showed only one road that made its way east, north and then west to get around the many arms of the canyon. Much of the landscape appeared arid and barren, but spectacular in its own way. Even so, the view became monotonous, and my eyes grew heavy. Sarah borrowed the map, and let me rest my head on her shoulder.

"Folks," Chet announced. "We're going to stop here for gas."

Jerked awake by the driver's loud voice, I opened my eyes to see a few buildings in a dusty parking lot.

"There's a restroom out back," he said. "We'll be here for fifteen minutes."

Sarah and I were out of the bus in seconds and stood off to the side to stretch. The rustic rest-stop boasted few amenities: two gas pumps, a windmill, a water cistern, a small house in the back, and a souvenir shop disguised as a convenience store with restrooms on the outside. The flat, dry land offered nothing more for as far as the eye could see.

"These buses are probably the only business they get all day." I shook my head at the desolation before wandering inside to spend a few dollars on snacks and bottled water.

People herded into the cluttered store as I looked over a limited array of Indian crafts mixed in with the usual tourist trinkets. A display of knives with hand-carved handles caught Sarah's eye. While she exclaimed over the artistry, I picked up a Buck knife and tested its heft. *Too much for a minimalist like me.*

Ultra-lighter stood at the counter, his backpack slung over his shoulder. He dumped a collection of candy and snack cakes on the counter and paid the clerk. The loner took his junk food and, without a word, exited the store.

Sarah leaned down to me. "He's going to need that toothbrush."

After buying water and two bags of mixed nuts, we wandered outside to see if the line to the restroom had dwindled. It hadn't. While we waited our turn, Sarah asked the gray-haired, retired lawyer from the back of the bus to take our picture. The working water cistern provided the perfect backdrop to help us remember this forlorn place. Sarah and I linked arms.

"Okay, girls, smile pretty." While our photographer lined us up for another shot, Ultra-lighter ducked behind one of the outbuildings. The skinny student in the tie-dye shirt, his shoulders tight, looked left and right before following.

"You were frowning," the ex-lawyer said. "Let's try another one. Okay, one, two, three. Smile."

After the picture, I tugged Sarah along to check behind the outbuildings.

"It's none of our business," Sarah said.

"I know, but I'm nosey."

Ultra-light and Tie-dye had disappeared, and we were on private property, so we roamed back to the parking lot. Another vehicle, identical to ours, had arrived. The last of its passengers entered the store, letting the screen door slam behind them.

The storyteller, Ron, and his wife, Kathy, who had introduced themselves on the bus, soon joined Sarah and me in the dusty parking lot.

"Where are you from?" Sarah asked.

They said they hailed from San Antonio, though their accents sounded more like southern Illinois.

"Indianapolis," Ron corrected me. "I was a corporate banker there, but transferred to Texas years ago. Retired now."

Kathy added, "So we travel the country and life is grand."

Sarah was right. All you have to do is say '*Hello.*'

I wore no watch, but knew our fifteen minute rest stop had stretched into twenty or twenty-five. Our driver waited in his seat reading a magazine. Some of our group still posed for pictures, and a dark-haired girl, Tie-dye's new seat partner, scurried back into the store.

"Chet isn't even trying to collect everybody," I complained.

Sarah nodded. "As useless as herding cats."

Eventually, most of our passengers gathered near the vehicles.

"I count twelve." Impatient to be on the move, I glanced around to find the missing souls. I nudged Sarah. "Ultra-lighter is on the wrong bus."

"Should we tell him or let them have him?" she asked.

"I'll be kind."

My footsteps on the stair echoed in the hollow vehicle. He jerked up in his seat, as if ready to pounce. Perhaps I had startled him out of sleep. His animosity surprised me, pushed me back, but I blurted the message. "Our bus is over there."

He sniffed in disgust, and I could read his mind: *Busybody old lady!*

Backing out, I rolled my eyes and headed to our vehicle.

That seemed to be the cue for our fellow travelers to board. Chet put down the magazine and greeted each passenger. As people are wont to do, everyone took the same seats they had occupied earlier, including Ultra-lighter.

Chet sank into his seat and put the key into the ignition, but stopped when he saw a leathery tan woman run out of the store waving her arms. Chet opened the doors to admit her. "What's up, Janie?"

"I'll tell you what's up," she said angrily. "I'm sick of these people swiping my merchandise."

My ears perked up, and I sat forward to hear the gossip. Janie caught everyone's attention.

"You. You took a knife from the display." Janie pointed and glared at my side of the vehicle, so I turned to see who she had skewered.

"You!" she insisted.

"Me?" I gaped at the angry woman. Both my hands went up with open palms. "Not me. I don't have a knife." Heat crept into my face. "You can look through my things." I held out my fanny pack.

Disgusted, Janie threw her hand at me and glowered at the entire busload of suspects. More hands went up in surrender.

Chet stood behind the red-faced woman and patted her shoulder. "I'm sorry, Janie. Questioning my passengers ain't gonna work." She turned on her heels and stormed out of the bus.

"Janie has a hard life in this here desert," Chet announced. "If anyone forgot to pay for that knife, jus' leave it on your seat when you get off, and I'll see that her merchandise gets returned."

I surreptitiously scanned the bus for the guilty party and found several pairs of eyes staring at me. I slipped further into my seat.

"Don't worry about it," said Sarah and patted my knee.

Declarations of innocence buzzed through the bus as passengers relived their visit to the store. I kept my head down. Little by little the noise level subsided. People grew bored with the incident and were lulled by warmth, road noise, and the now-familiar desert views.

Sarah's quiet conversation with the San Antonio couple, Kathy and Ron, took my mind away from my embarrassment.

"What we really want to try is kayak camping," Kathy said.

"I love kayaking," Sarah said. She perked up to tell her own story. "I used to live on the East coast and kayaked the rivers for weeks at a time, camping along the way."

43

Kathy interrupted. "By yourself?"

"Mostly." Sarah nodded. "A friend joined me when she could. We never had a problem, but I carried a gun just in case.

"A gun?" I said, surprised.

"Just a starter pistol, but anyone messing with me wouldn't know that."

I had a quick image of her as one of Charlie's Angels. "Do you have the gun with you now?"

"They would've arrested me at the airport if I brought a gun. Now I pack my trusty knife in my checked baggage." She pulled up her shirt to reveal a leather sheath. I looked closely, a frown gathering between my brows.

She yanked her shirt down. "This is not the knife from the store," she said in a low voice. The hurt in her eyes wounded me.

Before I could cover my gaffe, a scream filled the bus, and male voices erupted in anger. Men wrestled and yelled. Tie-dye stood over the dark-haired girl with his hands around her throat. Her legs thrashed in the air until a meaty fist smashed into Tie-dye's cheek, upending him on the back of the seat.

Chet slammed on the brakes. The girl scrambled on her hands and knees from beneath the melee up the center aisle of the bus. Sarah put out a hand and helped her to her feet. Kathy reached for the girl and pulled her into the front seat. The girl hid her puckered face against Kathy's shoulder.

Trapped in our seats, Sarah and I watched the bedlam in the back of the bus. Tie-dye cursed and screamed. Men jumped over seats to catch his ankles and wrists. Four passengers struggled to subdue Tie-dye's skinny arms and legs until the retired lawyer put his knee into the crazed man's chest, and the others got control of Tie-dye's thrashing limbs.

I fished in my fanny pack. "Duct tape," I yelled and passed the roll to the back of the bus. Chet jerked open the bus's back door and helped bind Tie-dye to his seat. Calm returned, except for Tie-dye's gasping anger. Finally that ended, too, and the busload of passengers collectively exhaled.

"Anybody hurt?" Chet took control, surveying the combatants. "What the hell happened?"

The men sank back into their seats, but kept their eyes on Tie-dye. One of the men spoke. "He suddenly went crazy and grabbed the girl. She was reading a book."

Chet shook his head. "Let's take a breather," he said. "Y'all, out of the bus." Chet motioned to the front door. Everyone obeyed and filed out.

Except me. I dawdled behind, intrigued by the student's sudden transformation from mild to violent.

Chet stroked his leather-brown jaw and stood over the bound student. Tie-dye fought against the duct tape and glared up at the bus driver.

"Off the bus, Miss," Chet ordered with a jerk of his head toward the front door.

"Sorry." I blushed and joined the other passengers gathered on the side of the road.

The dark-haired girl clung to Kathy's arm, but appeared uninjured. Her collar, no doubt, hid the imprints of the man's fingers on her slim neck. Kathy led her a short distance from the bus, while everyone else gabbled and speculated about what set off Tie-dye.

Unable to quell my curiosity, I sidled up to the back door of the bus to eavesdrop on the conversation between Tie-dye and Chet.

"Okay, kid. What's going on here?" Chet sat in the opposite seat with his fingers spread on his knees and with a scowl on his face. Tie-dye appeared to have fallen asleep.

"Kid?" Chet reached out to touch Tie-dye's shoulder. The young man's head lolled onto Chet's weathered hand. Chet yanked back his hand and sat up straight. His panicked eyes locked onto mine.

"He ain't breathing."

"Get him out of there," I yelled.

Chet ripped the duct tape from Tie-dye's wrists and dragged him by the shoulders from the bus. I caught the dead weight of the young man's legs and helped Chet lay him on the road. I put my fingers to the boy's carotid artery. Nothing.

"Are you trained in CPR?" I asked, praying he'd say yes. Chet's head jerked a quick negative. Sarah appeared behind him. "Sarah, do you know CPR?"

Her eyes went wide. "No."

"Ask the others," I ordered. Chet scrambled up from his knees and rounded the corner of the bus.

Sarah knelt beside me on the gritty stone next to the young man. My brain went numb as I fixated on Tie-dye's clean, clipped fingernails and the acne scars on his neck.

Suddenly, a Bee Gee's song popped into my mind along with my scout leader CPR training. *Staying Alive, Staying Alive, Ah, Ah, Ah, Ah.* I straightened my elbows and thrust the heels of my hands firmly into his chest to the beat of *Staying Alive, Staying Alive, Push, Push, Push, Push.*

"Sarah, breathe for him." My own breath became labored.

"I don't know how. What should I do?"

"Tilt his head back, pinch his nose, and breathe into his mouth." *Staying Alive, Staying Alive.* Sarah and I fell into a rhythm. After several minutes sweat broke out on my forehead and my arms ached. An audience gathered, but no replacements came.

"I need to stop. Can you do this, Sarah?"

"I'll try," she said between breaths. Sarah put her hand onto Tie-dye's chest. I crawled to his head and pressed my lips to his.

The passengers sweated in the empty desert and jabbered on about the student's crazy outburst. Sarah thrust downward to the beat of *Staying Alive*, and I blew into Tie-dye's mouth. When the second shuttle bus pulled up, Sarah continued to thrust downward on the young man's chest in regularly timed motions, and I breathed for him. A tourist shoved his way off the second bus, claimed to be a doctor, and ran to take over Sarah's efforts. She fell back exhausted. Ten minutes later the doctor pronounced Tie-dye dead.

7

NORTH RIM - Elevation: 9,000 ft.

Ron threw a blanket over Tie-dye's body, while Chet took roll call to determine the young man's name . . . Darren Kreminski. The doctor noted the name on a handwritten death pronouncement, added his signature, and handed the paper to Chet.

The remaining passengers tentatively boarded the bus. A few patted my shoulder or Sarah's as if to say, "Nice try." Chastened by the presence of death, they glanced at the blanket in the rear seat and took their seats in silence. The dark-haired girl squeezed in with Kathy and Ron again.

All eyes went to Chet as he boarded and held up a cell phone. "There's no reception out here, so we're going to ride on into the North Rim the way we are." He slid into his seat, started the engine, but stood up again to address the passengers in a weary voice.

"Doc says his heart gave out." Chet cleared his throat. "We owe thanks to the gals for that CPR. They done what they could." He nodded at Sarah and me and touched the brim of his cowboy hat.

As Chet pulled onto the road and cranked through the bus's gears, Sarah whispered in my ear. "His heart? Is that what the doctor said?"

I closed my eyes, looking for the sense in the situation. "Cardiac arrest he said, maybe a drug overdose."

"Who brings drugs on a backpacking trip?" Sarah moaned. "What a shame. So young." Her voice cracked, and she turned to stare out the window.

I touched my fingers to my lips, swollen from the pressure against the dead man's mouth. Fighting off nausea, I fumbled for my water bottle and wiped my lips clean with my bandana around my neck. I closed my eyes, but sleep wouldn't come. The road noise took on the rhythm of *Staying Alive*.

* * *

By late afternoon, the scenery changed from desert to pine grove valleys on both sides of the two-lane road. We gained elevation, and cooler fresh air poured in the few open windows. The dust was gone.

Fellow passengers no longer murmured about Darren Kreminski's death. They seemed to be inured to the blanket in the back seat, but held conversations in low funeral tones.

Since the bus had become a hearse, Chet decreased his speed and drove with care around each curve. "Sometimes there's elk here," he muttered. "Don't want to hit 'em."

Sarah and I took turns questioning our CPR techniques, blaming ourselves for the failure. I urged her to take pride in our attempt, but faulted myself for missing something that might have saved Tie-dye— Darren's— life.

The pristine forest flashed past the windows while I pondered the student's death. Why use drugs on the bus? Did he bring them or did someone sell them to him? Is anyone else using the same deadly drug?

Sarah refused to look at the body in the back of the bus and kept her eyes on the road ahead, but I glanced back every now and then to make sure the dead man hadn't slipped off the seat. Eric stared at me each time, a smirk on his face and Kylie now asleep on his shoulder.

After many miles, I gave up my vigil, rested my chin on my chest and closed my eyes.

When the bus slowed and made a sharp turn, Sarah gave me a little nudge. "Looks like we're here."

Rows of miniature log cabins were scattered along paths meandering through tall, straight ponderosa pines. The place resembled an upscale summer camp. The other shuttle bus stood empty at the curb, and an ambulance and squad car waited nearby.

Chet pulled the vehicle into a circular drive surrounded by log structures, the largest of which boasted a hand-carved sign—*Grand Canyon Lodge*.

"Here we are, folks," Chet announced. He turned off the engine and stepped out to stretch his long legs. Without a word he unlocked the back door and motioned for the EMTs to bring a gurney. They whisked Darren Kreminski away.

Passengers disembarked through the front door while Chet unhooked the bungee cords and folded back the tarp that had protected our gear. He scampered onto the roof of the vehicle and handed down backpacks one by one. Passengers gathered at the rear of the bus craning their necks, watching for their packs, and calling out "Mine" or "Here." Much like buckets in a fire brigade, backpacks were passed along until each reached its rightful owner.

Ultra-lighter, or Michael Rap according to Chet's roll-call, made no effort to help. The loner stood off to the side, clutching his small pack and staring at the gear being unloaded.

Our backpacks were last to come down, and Sarah stood at the back of the bus to receive them from Chet. By then most of our fellow travelers had busied themselves with their belongings or wandered off. Ultra-lighter must have seen my dirty looks and hurried away between the buildings. A few others gathered near the squad car to hear the dark-haired girl's story.

Sarah and I lugged our packs to the side while Chet jumped down to fold the tarp and throw the bungee cords into a box. He stowed the remaining backpack, the one belonging to Darren Kreminski, in the bus.

The driver of the other shuttle bus sauntered over to Chet and thumped his back. "Tough day, buddy."

Chet rubbed his forehead and exchanged stories with the other man. Though I stood too far away to hear the conversation, I caught the words 'Yaki Point' and 'went over the edge.'

Sarah buckled her pack, ready to leave, but I detained her. "I think they're talking about Darren *and* the guy who fell from the rim. Do you want to ask if they heard any news?"

"Not really," she said. "I've had enough of dead bodies, but you go ahead. I'll wait over there by the gift shop."

After his buddy left, Chet ducked into the bus and walked to the back, checking each seat, cleaning up.

The thought of the stolen knife heated my face, but I held fast to my innocence and greeted the driver as he exited.

"Hi, Chet. Thanks for getting us here safely." I handed him a tip which disappeared into his hip pocket.

"Thanks." His weather-beaten face reddened.

"Did the doctor say anything more about Darren?" I asked.

"Says they'll do an autopsy to say for sure what killed him."

"So sad." We shuffled around in silence for a few seconds. "Did you find the knife?" I asked quietly and hoped that the blunt approach removed suspicion from me.

"No, ma'am." He regarded me with a sideways look.

I rushed on. "I heard the other driver say something about someone falling over the edge."

"That's so."

"I wondered if there is any news. We saw him this morning."

Caught off guard, Chet squinted at me. "A bus driver reported two women were with the rangers near Yaki Point. Saw the guy fall."

"Sarah and I didn't see him fall. We spotted him lying in the ravine."

"The canyon grapevine don't always get it right." Chet stroked his stubbled jaw. "Not a pretty sight, I reckon."

"We had binoculars—about a hundred feet down." I pointed toward Sarah. "She's still upset and wants to forget the sight—and now Darren . . . "

Apparently, Chet trusted me enough to fill me in with what he had heard. "They say the guy at Yaki Point was on drugs, too."

"Accident or suicide?"

"Don't know. Another driver said Coconino County PD got involved after the Park Service hauled him up." Chet seemed tired. "If you don't mind, I gotta give a report to the rangers and get some dinner. I got another full load to go back."

I thanked him and joined Sarah near the gift shop. I watched Chet amble toward a side building. In spite of the tragic day, I appreciated the way the man walked in cowboy boots and jeans.

Sarah tugged at my arm. "Come on, hot pants, let's check in."

Embarrassed by my thoughts and for getting caught, I reddened. "What's wrong with looking?"

"Nothing at all." She shook her head. "Beats talking about the dead."

* * *

We yanked open the heavy wooden doors to the Grand Canyon Lodge and stood inside waiting for our vision to adjust to the dimness. A massive deer-antler chandelier gave off weak yellow light. Eventually, the interior's construction became visible. Whole logs, darkened with age, supported the building's walls and rafters. The Park Service probably went through a lot of trouble making the building's décor look like it hadn't been touched since it was built in 1907.

"This is wonderful," Sarah whispered.

Backpacks were stashed in a row on the side wall, so we added ours to the group. Ron and Kathy nodded from the middle of a long disorganized line. The check-in clerks stood behind wooden window frames like those you might see in an old Western bank robbery. We had stepped back in time. I enjoyed every bit of the experience, even the slow registration process.

With room keys in our hand, we opted to explore the lodge before finding our cabin. Stepping around the first corner, I gasped and staggered. Nothing but sky and canyon lay before us. I fought off vertigo, forcing my brain to process my surroundings. Large panes of glass spanned the entire back wall of a viewing room hanging over the canyon.

"Whoa. I didn't expect that."

"You can let go of my arm now, Amy," Sarah said.

I laughed and freed her arm.

Once I got my bearings, we ventured up to the glass. The panoramic view was the break we needed from our long travel and thoughts of death, and I didn't mind looking like a rube to the dozen or so people lounging on overstuffed furniture. After we exclaimed over the view from every direction, we settled into comfortable chairs and blended in with the more blasé visitors.

Sarah jumped up, energized. "Hey, why don't we hike out to that point to watch the sunset?"

"Excellent idea." A dazzling orange sun sliding behind the canyon walls would take our minds far away from the melancholy day. I looked at my watch. "We'll have to hurry. Sunset's in an hour."

We rushed to stow our packs in the clean, homey mini-cabin and were out the door in five minutes, headed for the promontory. Shadows already crawled up the side of the canyon.

A dozen people wandered either before or behind us as we navigated the narrow path around stone outcroppings with a steep drop off to our left. We hopped over a ten-inch crevice. *Would all the trails in the canyon be as dangerous?*

I swallowed a mouthful of fear and focused on planting my feet on solid rock. I didn't raise my eyes from ground level until the path ended at a metal railing on the point. The best of the sunset hid below the horizon, but a dusky rouge light left its impression on the far canyon wall. The scene made a gorgeous backdrop, so Sarah asked a bearded man to take our photograph.

"Glad to." He snapped two pictures. "Oza Butte and Manu Temple will be behind you in the photo."

I turned to the west to look. "The peaks have *names*? What's that flat area with the red and white slopes?"

"That's Walhalla Plateau," he said, sweeping his arm to the east. He then identified a dozen mesas and peaks.

I appreciated his knowledge and leaned on the railing to wonder about the stories behind the strange names.

In long deep silence, Sarah and I watched the last of the sun's rays disappear behind the distant rim. The quiet was so intense, it was as if no one else was there. I turned around in the cold blackness to discover that no one else *was* there. They had all left us, and they had reason to. We could not see our hands before our faces, nor the path, nor the edge of the abyss. A moment of panic gripped my heart.

"Sarah, how will we get back? I can't see a thing."

She turned around and sucked in her breath. "I have a flashlight," she murmured and produced the mini-light from her keychain. Sarah led the way by taking a few steps and then shining the weak LED backwards, so I could watch my feet.

I prayed to my God to keep me safe, and to the canyon gods, promising I would forevermore respect the dangers of the canyon.

We inched along for an eternal fifteen minutes.

Lights from the lodge finally became visible, and the path more solid, wider, and brighter. We saw people inside the lodge milling around, talking and laughing. Theirs was another world. They had no idea what we had been through. I touched a fence post to reassure myself that we'd reached civilization. It didn't make me feel any better about breaking the first rule of backpacking—plan ahead.

"That was dumb," I muttered.

"And exhilarating," Sarah countered. "Let's find something to eat."

The aroma of food reminded me that the dinner hour had long since passed. "My money is back at the cabin," I confessed. "Sorry. I didn't plan well for this. No flashlight, no money."

"Don't apologize. I don't have cash on me either." Sarah laughed and nudged me. "Hey, we're on vacation."

Sarah proved to be an unflappable travel companion. My husband would have been aghast at the incidents on the bus and very angry about being caught in the dark, about forgetting to take money, and about his late meal. Sarah rolled with the flow.

We strolled back to the cabin with Sarah's mini-light illuminating curbs, roots and rocks. The North Rim didn't waste any more electricity on outdoor lighting than the South Rim had. Out of range of the lights from the lodge again, our route became a guessing game.

Suddenly, a woman's scream shattered the silence of the blackened forest. Sarah and I stopped mid-stride. Another scream sent fear racing down my spine.

"This way." I turned off our path and yelled into the darkness. "We're coming!"

"We're coming!" Sarah echoed with double my volume. We ran as well as we could within the bouncing circle of light thrown by her LED. The maze of pathways tripped us up, and we paused to listen.

"I don't hear anything. Sarah, call out."

"Where are you?" Her booming voice reached into the distance.

"Here." The thin word strained to reach us.

"Keep talking," I shouted. "We're coming."

Small strangled sobs came from our left, and we followed them. Sarah's light scanned across several darkened cabins and fell upon a blond girl huddled with her back against a cabin door. She sobbed and held her knees to her chest.

I knelt down beside her. The girl turned her terrified face into the light. I recognized Kylie, the girl who had been talking to the A.T. hiker on the shuttle bus.

"Are you hurt, honey?" I asked.

"He ran when he heard you," Kylie whimpered.

Sarah's knife slipped from its sheath. "I'll be right back."

"No, Sarah," I gasped. "Don't go out there."

But she was gone, taking the light with her.

I muffled my fear for Sarah's safety and turned my attention to the girl. "Kylie, do you hurt anywhere?" Afraid to move her in case she had injuries, I held her still.

"My hair hurts. He yanked my head back hard when I bit him." She cried anew, and I gathered her into my arms.

"Good girl. What a good girl you are. Shhh. You're okay now." We rocked back and forth until her sobs quieted, and she breathed more normally.

Sarah returned in minutes. "He's gone. I didn't see anyone." She turned up the volume. "No one except that guy hiding behind those curtains who could have helped. Freaking coward!"

My angry friend knelt beside me. "How's she doing?"

"I think she's just scared, but we should get her inside. Where's your cabin, Kylie?"

"Right here," the girl said. "He grabbed me when I came out and tried to shove me back inside. The door slammed shut, and I threw the key that way."

"Smart girl." Her presence of mind impressed me.

Kylie pressed the heels of her hands to her forehead. Her words spilled out in a rush. "He had me, like, in a head lock and had my mouth covered, so I bit as hard as I could. He cussed at me and yanked my hair until my teeth let go." She touched the back of her head gingerly and moaned. "I screamed, and he put his hand over my face, and I tried to, like, kick him, but he had me."

Tears welled up in my eyes. *No one should have to go through that.*

Sarah bristled in anger and barely controlled her voice. "Then what happened?"

"Then he stopped." Kylie sniffled and looked up through the darkness at Sarah. "I think he heard you yelling. He threw me here and ran away." She pointed behind the cabins and sagged against my chest, exhausted.

"Sarah, let's get Kylie inside. Can you find that key?"

Sarah jiggled the handle of the door. Locked. Her light scanned the area under the window, and she got on all fours to search. Kylie clung to me while we waited.

"Found it."

"That was quick," I said, trying to lighten the mood.

Sarah unlocked the door and switched on the lights. We helped Kylie to her feet and into the small room.

"Why don't you lie down, hon. We can talk while you rest." I took off Kylie's jacket while Sarah pulled back the bedspread. Kylie didn't object and slumped into bed.

Sarah averted her eyes from Kylie's bloody mouth and stood by the door with her hands on her hips. "I'm going to the lodge to report this attack to someone. He's still nearby."

"Try your cell phone first," I suggested.

"I did. Nothing." Sarah put the useless gadget into her pocket.

"I'd feel better if the three of us stayed together," I said. "Can you wait a few minutes? Maybe we can all go to the lodge."

Sarah agreed, but remained on edge, keeping watch at the window.

I brushed Kylie's long blond hair back from her face and dabbed her cheek with a wet washcloth. The bruises and abrasions didn't look too bad yet. The blood on her mouth looked awful, but I couldn't find its source. Her only other visible injuries were scrapes on her hands and elbow.

"Sarah, do you have your camera?" I asked. "Maybe we should take a picture before she gets cleaned up."

"Do I look that bad?" A faint pink had crept onto Kylie's cheeks.

"Not bad," I assured her. "Like you've been in a fight."

After I took the picture, Kylie stumbled into the bathroom.

"Oh, shit," she said.

"Sounds like she just saw herself in the mirror," Sarah said, smiling.

Kylie looked better after washing her face, but where the blood had been, she now had Angelina Jolie lips.

She let me examine her mouth. "I suspect that wasn't your blood on your face."

"Do you think I bit him that hard?" Kylie asked, her eyes wide, impressed with herself.

"He deserved more than that," Sarah said.

I tried the gentler approach. "Do you feel up to reporting this at the lodge, or would you prefer a ranger come here? I'd stay with you."

Kylie tested her arms, her legs, and her willingness to go out in the dark. "We can go. I'm okay, just hungry." She set her bruised lips in a straight line. "I was going to dinner when he . . ."

She looked away and dumped a few things out of her fanny pack, then gathered her LED light and jacket. "I'm ready."

Sarah and I flanked Kylie and walked toward our cabin in a tight line to take advantage of the two small light beams. The closeness gave me a sense of security, and their body heat warmed me. We passed the cabin with its lights on, and Sarah rapped sharply on the window.

"Coward!" Sarah shouted.

"Sarah." I sounded like my mother. "Don't give our witness a heart attack."

"I get so angry when people don't help," Sarah said. "What if we hadn't been nearby?"

"Shhh." I glanced at Kylie.

"It's okay," Kylie whispered. "I know how lucky I am."

We got our money and jackets from the cabin and trooped down to the lodge.

The place buzzed with activity, people coming and going. The tangy aroma of barbecue ribs permeated the air. My hunger reached the danger zone.

"Ask about getting a table, Sarah," I said. "I'll find someone to take a report about the attack."

Kylie and Sarah went in the direction of clinking silverware, while I headed for the reception area. The sign read, *Office Closed*, and those old Western movie windows were shut tight, but I heard the sound of movement from behind the door. I knocked and poked my head in.

"Excuse me," I said. "I need to call the police."

In spite of her age, the park employee jumped to her feet. "What's wrong?"

"A man brutally attacked a girl down at the cabins."

"Good Lord! Will she need an ambulance?"

I assured her Kylie didn't need emergency help, but the news shook the poor woman. She had the number to the ranger station memorized and jabbed at her phone's buttons with the eraser end of her pencil. She spoke a few hurried words into the phone.

"They'll be here soon, maybe five or ten minutes. Is there anything I can do?"

"Thank you, no . . . maybe tell us where to get food."

The woman's tension dissipated a bit. "You need a reservation in the dining room, but the deli outside the lodge has sandwiches. You can buy them there and eat them in the lobby or take them to the pub next to the gift shop."

"Perfect," I said. "Please tell the rangers that we're in the pub."

"Sure will. Sorry about your friend," the woman said, and hurried to whisper an account of the attack to her co-worker before I was even out the door. The grapevine's tendrils began to spread the news of a predator on the loose.

Sarah and Kylie approached me, and the two office women peeked out to eye Kylie's bruises, wagging their heads in sympathy.

"No tables for at least a half hour," Sarah reported.

We opted for the deli as Plan B and carried our sandwiches to the pub on the other side of the courtyard.

The creaking door welcomed us into a warm, friendly place with rough, wooden floors and heavy furniture and bar, probably dating from the last century. The goodwill and camaraderie of the pub engulfed us.

"I'm buying the beer," Sarah announced.

Her cheerful mood brightened my own. I shouted over the din. "What are we celebrating?"

"We're here and we have food." Sarah slapped her hand on the table, getting into the party mode.

"And Kylie is safe," I said. "Are you old enough to have a beer?"

Kylie took umbrage. "I'm twenty-three."

Gad, she's five years younger than my daughter. "Sorry. I forgot what twenty-three looks like." I made light of my faux pas, but wondered how time had flown.

We were still chewing the last of our sandwiches, when a ranger, dressed in creased pants and a winter jacket with an official logo on the chest, stepped inside the bar room door. The scene reminded me of the good-guy sheriff called into the bar to check out the bad guy who just rode into town.

Our good guy stood tall like Jimmy Stewart, but had broader shoulders and more muscle. High cheek bones, firm jaw, and quick eyes gave him the look of a hunter, but his clean, fresh skin made him approachable. He removed his stiff-brimmed hat, revealing closely cropped, dark, thinning hair.

I added several years to the estimate of his age . . . closer to my own, maybe late forties. He scanned the patrons in the bar with a practiced eye, but didn't see us in the corner.

I slid out of my wooden chair and went to speak to him. "Are you looking for a girl?" I had not intended the double entendre and laughed inwardly at the situation.

"Are you looking for a ranger?" His face refused to smile or betray emotion, but I saw a wicked little sparkle in his hazel brown eyes.

"Why, yes, I am." I smiled up at him, but resisted the urge to tease in such a serious circumstance. "My friends and I need to make a report."

"So, are you the woman who left a message at the lodge?" he asked in a kind voice.

"Yep. A man attacked Kylie outside her cabin." I pointed to the girl.

The ranger and I made our way through a sea of curious patrons to the corner table where Kylie and Sarah waited. I introduced each of us and invited him to pull up a chair.

The noise in the pub required conversation at close range, so the four of us leaned toward the center of the table.

"Pleasure to meet you, ladies. My name is Ranger Glen Hawk." He studied Kylie, whose bruises had swelled and darkened since we were in her cabin. "Do you require medical attention, Kylie?"

"No. I'm hiking tomorrow."

The ranger hid a smile. "Tell me what happened."

She closed her eyes and nodded, ashamed. Her face drained of color, but in a clear steady voice, Kylie told the same story to Ranger Hawk as she had told it to us.

The ranger's eyes never left her face as she spoke. "Do you know the man?" he asked.

She shook her head.

"Can you describe him?"

"No, I'm sorry. He jumped out of the dark, and he grabbed me from behind." Ranger Hawk's gentle concern urged Kylie to continue. "I think his arm is bleeding where I bit him."

Sarah took that as a cue to show the ranger the digital picture of Kylie's mouth before she washed her face.

"That's a lot of blood," he said. "You got him good." He pulled a camera from his pocket. "If you don't mind, I'll take a picture for the report."

Kylie smiled timidly at the ranger's praise and raised her face to the camera.

"You reacted in exactly the right way, Kylie," Ranger Hawk said. "You fought and screamed and refused to be a victim. Good for you."

The ranger had said what the girl needed to hear. I liked him for that.

Kylie sat up more confidently. "Thank you."

Ranger Hawk turned to Sarah and me. "Can you add anything to Kylie's report?"

"At about seven-thirty P.M. we heard a woman's scream and then a second scream," I said, "so we ran toward her and yelled that we were coming to help."

"Did you see the man?"

"No." Sarah sniffed. "I checked the area, but didn't hear or see a thing—except a guy, a witness, peeking out from behind a curtain. Cabin two-twenty-one. The coward."

The ranger hid a smile. "I'll interview him tonight when I search the grounds. You and Amy did a fine thing by coming to Kylie's aid."

We both shrugged and Ranger Hawk went back to writing, as he had been doing all during the interview. We sat in silence while he added a couple of sentences and finally looked up.

"Are you hiking tomorrow?" he asked.

"Sarah and I are taking the North Kaibab Trail to Cottonwood in the morning. Kylie?"

"Me, too," the girl said.

"Okay," Ranger Hawk said. "I'll find you if we need more information. If you think of additional details, contact any ranger and ask for me." He handed his business card to Kylie and then stood up, scraping his chair back. "If you'll excuse me, I want to get this information out over the radio in case he's still around."

I watched him stroll to the door and half expected to hear his spurs a-jingling. We went back to our beers. Kylie poked my arm. "He likes you."

"Why would you say that?" I asked, taken aback.

"Because he asked me the questions, but looked at you when you weren't looking."

"Do I have lettuce in my teeth or something?"

Kylie and Sarah laughed and assured me that I did not. We finished our beers and cleaned the table before heading outside. Kylie ducked into the gift shop while Sarah and I discussed plans for the morning.

"Should we ask Kylie to join us on the trail?" Sarah asked.

"Go ahead. I like her," I said, "though I don't know why she'd spend time with old folks like us."

"Hey." Sarah shoved my shoulder. "Age is just a number. We're not old yet."

A few minutes later, Kylie skipped out of the store to show off her new cap. "This says, *I Survived the Grand Canyon.*"

Her spunk took me off guard, but I admired that she poked fun at her near-miss. "Good thought, Kylie, but first I want to make sure I *do* survive the Grand Canyon."

"Sure you will." Kylie had more confidence in me than I had myself.

Sarah took the new cap and patted it into place on Kylie's head. "Amy and I were wondering if maybe you'd want to hike out with us in the morning—if a couple of fifty-year-olds wouldn't slow you down too much. Sounds like we have the same itinerary."

"Sounds awesome," Kylie said, adjusting the cap. "Like, what time do you want to get started?"

We planned the next day's hike and then trooped into the darkness, away from the public area, along the meandering walkways. My eyes darted from shadow to shadow along the string of mini-cabins, alert for movement, for unusual sounds, for danger. Sarah kept her hand on the hilt of her knife.

A welcoming light shown from Kylie's cabin window and a comfortable silence greeted us. Still, Sarah made a circuit around the small building while Kylie fumbled to get the key into the lock.

"Are you sure you won't stay with us tonight?" I asked.

"I'll be okay, but—could you check in the closet and under the bed?"

A thorough search was the least we could do.

8

Day 3: NORTH KAIBAB TRAILHEAD

Elevation: 8,250 ft.

Sarah's blankets lay neat and tight across her bed. From under my blankets I forced my unfocused eyes to check the time. 6:42 A.M. In the next moment the door swung open, and Sarah struggled in, juggling two steamy cups and accompanied by a draft of cold air. I pulled the covers over my face.

"Wake up, sleepy head. Come look at this."

"What?" I croaked.

"Come see." She motioned outside with enthusiasm. With the blanket wrapped around me, I became vertical and ventured outside.

"This better be good."

Overnight the world had been transformed. An inch of snow decorated the pine trees and trimmed the eaves of the log cabins. A Currier and Ives Christmas card had come to life, but with the added scent of clean snow. Even my breathless gasp sounded inappropriate in the muffled silence. My bare feet burned in the snow, so we retreated indoors.

Behind the closed door, I whispered as if in church. "That's so gorgeous. Thanks for dragging me out of bed." I jumped back on the bed to sit cross-legged, warming my frozen feet under the blankets.

Sarah handed me a cup of hot tea and sat nearby with her steaming coffee. "I thought the snow might melt by the time we got moving."

"Thanks for thinking of me. Brrrr. Right now I'm looking forward to my last hot shower for five days. Do you want to go first?"

"Either way," she said. "I don't take long."

"Me, neither. Not anymore. Not since I chopped off my hair."

"You had long hair?" Sarah asked. "This style suits you. When did you cut it?"

"A few days ago."

"Really? For this trip?"

"Well, yes. Partly for the trip, but partly for spite."

Sarah gave me a sideways glance. "Spite? Whom were you spiting by cutting your hair?"

I wished I hadn't brought up the subject.

"My husband," I admitted. "He always loved my long hair, but forever nagged me about taming the frizz. I got angry with him the other day, so I cut off ten inches."

"You are a real hoot. So, are you sorry you cut it, or do you like the style?"

"I love it . . . so much lighter and easier to wash and dry."

She chuckled. "Well, you showed him. What did he say?"

"Oh, he hasn't seen it yet."

She laughed all the way to the bathroom and turned on the shower. I put my empty cup aside and looked in the mirror. The stranger there ran her fingers through her short waves of brunette hair. My long hair had been my signature. "Amy Marie, for such a smart person, you do dumb things." The woman in the mirror looked as if she wanted to cry and turned away to wait for her turn in the shower.

A half hour later we were squeaky clean and on our way to breakfast at the lodge. The temperature headed toward the forecasted forty degrees and the snow began to melt. I pulled the hood of my fleece sweater over my damp hair and shoved my hands into the pockets of my jacket.

"Do you suppose Kylie will join us for breakfast?"

"Let's at least knock on her door to see if she's up," Sarah suggested.

"Here's 219. Looks different in daylight."

The layer of pure snow obscured the scene of last night's attack. I wondered what evidence might be hidden under that guise of innocence.

Sarah stopped and gazed at the open area between the cabins. "Too bad the snow wasn't here last night," she said. "We could have tracked his footprints."

"That would've helped. Still, I prefer this way, clean and fresh."

Sarah tapped on Kylie's door.

No response, so she knocked louder. The window curtains parted, and then dropped back into place. The door lock clicked open.

"Hi. Come on in. I just got up." Kylie's eyes were puffy; her hair, a rat's nest.

"Rough night?" Sarah sympathized.

"Yeah. I kept, like, hearing noises. I should've stayed with you guys."

She looked so young and vulnerable.

"I'm sorry," I said. "We should have insisted."

Kylie shrugged off our concern.

"We're on our way to breakfast," Sarah said. "Do you want to get some pancakes?"

"No. I'd better, like, get my stuff together here. Bring me a bagel or something?"

"You got it. Coffee?"

She nodded, and we stepped back into the cold.

"Lock this door," Sarah ordered.

"Okay. See you at eight-thirty." The lock clicked into place.

* * *

A 1,000 foot drop-off outside the window gave an odd sensation to eating pancakes with huckleberry syrup. All of my senses were heightened, making the orange juice tangier, the syrup fruitier, and the pancakes fluffier.

During breakfast, Sarah pointed out several of our fellow bus passengers among the throng of diners. "Almost everyone is here," she said.

"Any one of these men could be Kylie's attacker." I scrutinized each man in the room for bite marks on his arms, but everyone wore a sweater or long-sleeved shirt.

"You can cross Ron off your list. He and Kathy were at dinner," Sarah said.

"We don't know that for a fact, but they did have reservations."

"The retired lawyer and the two thirty-something guys from the bus are behind you along the wall." She pointed with her chin. "Maybe one of them attacked her."

"Possible, but they're good guys. They jumped in to help the dark-haired girl while Darren Kreminski strangled her."

"I don't see Ultra-lighter." Sarah twisted around in her seat, scanning the room. "What'd Chet call him?"

"His name is Michael Rap. He headed for the canyon the minute we got here."

None of the fifty possible suspects in the room revealed criminal tendencies while eating breakfast. "Kylie's attacker could be anybody," I said. "Maybe he rode the other bus, or maybe he works here."

A busboy hurried by with a tray of dishes. I stole a glance at his bare forearm and crossed him off the list.

"Eric Prescott." His insolent face popped into my mind. "He's missing—and I don't see the dark-hair girl either."

"Prescott?"

"The smart aleck who kept Kylie entranced with A.T. stories. She said he camped at the campgrounds last night."

"I got the impression she liked him," Sarah said.

"She does, but *I* think he's a jerk. He didn't lift a finger to help on the bus."

"All swagger and no character, but why would he attack Kylie when she seems to be all over him?"

"Maybe he's got a sick thing about violence against women." I cringed at the thought.

"Hmmm. Maybe you're right. Let's keep an eye out for him."

* * *

At 8:20 we arrived at Kylie's cabin and knocked to deliver her breakfast. She opened the door fully dressed with her pack loaded and ready to go. Sarah handed Kylie the bagel and coffee.

"Everyone missed you at the lodge," I said. "Almost all the passengers from the bus ate breakfast."

"Eric?"

I smiled at her eagerness to hear about him. "No, not Eric."

She didn't hide her disappointment, and I regretted saying anything.

"Take your time eating," Sarah said. "We need a few minutes to get our packs together."

"Okay, I'll be right there," Kylie said. "Thanks a bunch."

* * *

Sarah paced with her gear outside our cabin door melting the snow underfoot. She looked at her watch. "Eight-thirty. Packs on."

"Yes, ma'am." I saluted. "Here she comes."

Kylie trudged toward us with a backpack which rivaled Sarah's in size. Plumes of vapor formed in the cold air with her every breath. She groaned. "I'm having a hard time breathing." Yet she didn't pause and continued tromping east. We fell in line behind her.

Within a quarter mile, the thin air affected even Sarah. "Ugh. I feel so out of shape. I shouldn't have eaten that last pancake."

"The brochure warned that higher elevations take some getting used to. We're at nine thousand feet right here." I threw out that factoid, but saved the rest of my breath for hiking. I wondered if I had trained adequately by dragging myself up and down the hundred-twenty steps of the toboggan slides all summer. I worried about my abilities and plodded along in silence through bright sunlight and slush.

After twenty minutes we found the North Kaibab trailhead at Roaring Springs Canyon and took our first rest stop. We pretended that the stop was to read the map and remove a layer of clothing, but our lungs were desperate for a break.

"We need a trailhead photo," Sarah announced. She balanced her camera on a boulder and fiddled with the adjustments. "Amy, Kylie.

Stand in front of the sign. Little more to your right. I'll set the auto-timer and then get in the picture." She pushed the button and hustled to stand between Kylie and me, throwing her arms across our shoulders. I grinned at the rock and waited ten seconds for the flash.

Sarah previewed the image and gave us a thumbs up. With no more excuses, it was time to start our big adventure, to go below the rim. My apprehensions were alleviated by the sight of ordinary pine trees and shrubbery—beautiful, but familiar. Maybe this hike would be no more difficult or dangerous than my hiking trips in Indiana.

The trail, cushioned by layers of humus and pine needles, immediately fell away in a downward slope. Walking became easier. Gravity helped take us lower and lower into the canyon. The trail meandered through the woods and descended to a more breathable elevation.

A man and two women hikers staggered up the trail toward us. Though they carried no backpacks, they struggled and gasped for air. I suppressed the urge to gloat about being more physically fit than that group. I knew *my* reckoning would come in four days when I tackled the ascent to the South Rim.

Before long, the curtain of pines gave way. This time I wasn't viewing the canyon from above; I was inside, on its wall. I could easily see individual shrubs and rocks on the opposite wall of Roaring Springs Canyon. We were in a narrow arm of the big canyon, more close and intimate than the grand expanse.

"What's wrong?" Sarah's loud voice startled me.

"Nothing. Why?"

"You're limping."

"Oh, a twinge in my knee started about a half hour ago."

"That's not good," Kylie said. "My physical trainer told me that downhill is, like, so hard on the knees, especially with weight on your back. Every step jars your knees. Bang. Bang, Bang." With each 'bang' she slammed her fist into the palm of her other hand.

"I'll be fine," I said, but in truth, I worried. Two years earlier I had slipped on an acorn-covered hill and twisted my knee. The meniscus took eighteen months to heal, or at least I thought it had healed. Mostly I worried I'd be a drag on my hiking partners. I concentrated on not limping.

The trail brought us into constant sunshine and became a staircase rather than a path. Timber-framed stairs, each unique in width, height and condition, made our steps uneven and awkward.

Mules and their iron shoes had created ruts and imprinted the dried mud, leaving the surface rough and unstable. The animals also left piles of green, grassy-looking dung. I held my breath to avoid the odor until I realized the droppings smelled like dried parsley flakes. Mule dung seemed to be a valid subject to occupy my mind and helped me avoid thinking of my aching knee.

"Move to your left, please."

The request came as a shock in the silence. A woman riding one mule and leading two others with loaded packs came up the trail from around a bend. She was dressed like an extra on a Western movie set, except for the NPS logo on her shirt. We dutifully found a place to squeeze ourselves in amongst the boulders on the inside of the trail to give mules and rider plenty of room to pass.

"Good morning." Sarah's hearty greeting elicited a friendly nod from the rider as the first mule came abreast of us.

More than happy to take a moment's rest, I leaned the weight of my pack against the stone wall. I wondered if the mules transported mail as the Pony Express did in the Old West, but slower. "What sorts of things do the mules carry in and out?"

The mule rider pulled her steed to a halt, ready to talk. "Everything. Yesterday I brought supplies and food down to Phantom Ranch. Today I'm bringing up waste."

"Waste?" I asked.

"Human waste. We use composting toilets at the Ranch and haul the compost out."

"Oh." So much for my romantic notions and comparisons to the old West.

Sarah enjoyed my discomfort. "That is *Pack it in, Pack it out* on a grand scale," she said.

Kylie giggled behind her. The rider laughed along with them.

"Day-to-day living in the canyon is not easy," the mule rider offered. "The smallest things can become big problems. We don't have sewers and can't pump waste into the Colorado River. It's a job."

I regretted asking.

"By the way," the rider said, "a slide covers the trail down past Supai Tunnel. The work crew is there, so stay close to the wall and wait for them to wave you through."

The four of us chatted awhile longer, and then the human waste express went on its way. I held my breath until the last two mules passed, in case the air didn't smell like dried parsley.

"Ready?" Kylie asked.

I breathed in. *Fresh as a meadow*. "Let's go."

I pushed off from my comfortable niche amongst the boulders and followed my friends down the trail. Every twist and turn of the trail led to eye-popping scenery; a pine-covered valley below, a red rock outcropping, a purple mesa outlined against a clear blue sky. It was amazing how one gorgeous view after another became common place. Not boring exactly, but my brain pushed the dazzling scenery into the background to avoid sensory overload. So, we trekked in, under, around, and through one of God's greatest creations as if it were routine.

We talked of other things, though mostly I listened. Sarah entertained us with stories about her student's antics, trips to Europe, crazy backpackers. Her jokes and stories passed the time.

We came upon a point of rock hanging over the edge which gave a fantastic long view of the narrow arm opening into the main canyon. The breathtaking vista provided a good place to stop for a short rest. Kylie asked for my map and hopped onto a boulder. Sarah and I stood together on the bare rock overlook. The heat of the sun radiated from the stone and gave off a certain summertime smell. I closed my eyes for a moment to breathe in the feel of the place.

"Can't you see the hand of God in all of this?" I asked.

Sarah shook her head. "Water and wind erosion created the canyon. I believe in science, not God."

Uh-oh. "Well, I *might* concede that God doesn't involve himself with humans anymore, but some higher power got the ball rolling for this to be created."

"Do you mean that a super being put us here and then turned away?" she asked.

"That is a possibility, yes," I said.

Sarah sniffed.

I glanced at her expression, fearing we might launch into a heated discussion of religious beliefs, but her thoughts seemed far away.

"Years ago I had a friend," Sarah said. "Melanie wrote a poem from the perspective of humans on earth looking upward at the very moment that a massive claw-like tool ripped through the fabric of the sky. The claw grasped the earth and pulled it from the experiment. The lab technician put the sphere on the pile of other failed projects."

"That's depressing," I said.

"You're right. I'm sorry." After a moment of sadness, her smile came back. "If it turns out there is a God, this canyon is His gift to us."

"That's better." I preferred the happy Sarah. "Can you reach my water bottle for me?" I turned so she could extract my bottle from its mesh pocket on the side of my pack.

"Sure." She handed me the bottle.

"Guten morgen, Damen." The male voice startled me, and I spun around as fast as my heavy pack would allow. Two men, one gray and balding, and the other with a full head of blond hair, hailed us from the trail. They shared a strong resemblance, probably father and son. Both were dressed in quality hiking apparel and carried a good brand of internal-frame packs.

"Guten morgen." Sarah repeated. I smiled politely and moved away from the overlook to give them their view.

"Passen Sie auf einen Dieb auf der weiter ist den Pfad hinunter," the older man said.

"Do you know German, Sarah?" I asked.

"Just hello and good bye."

"Same here. *No sprechen Sie deutsch.*" My clumsy German got the message across.

The father heaved a sigh and shook his head. The younger man took over and pantomimed, as if playing charades. He pointed down the trail and then to the map in his hand.

"Supai Tunnel." I caught that, though the words were heavily accented.

"*Ja.*" He put his pack on the ground and made motions as if frantically pulling out items and then ran a short way down the trail. Both father and son looked at us hopefully. Our confusion must have shown. He tried again. He pantomimed removing an item from his pack, made his hand into a circle on his forehead and looked around with his eyes squinted.

"A head lamp," cried Kylie from her seat on the boulder.

"*Ja. Licht.*" He put the imaginary light under his shirt and ran down the trail.

"Somebody took his headlamp," suggested Sarah.

We all nodded up and down.

"A thief is near Supai Tunnel?" I slowed each word and spoke distinctly.

"*Ja.* Thief, *ein Dieb.* Supai Tunnel."

A disturbing thought quickly replaced the thrill of solving the riddle. *A thief in the Grand Canyon?* Up at the lodges, yes, but the idea of being mugged on the trail seemed absurd.

Kylie jumped to her feet. "There's a thief down here?" Agitated, she clearly hadn't gotten over her assault yet.

"I think that's what they're saying." I had shamefully forgotten her frightening incident. Last night seemed a long time ago and in another world, but then I wasn't the one attacked.

Sarah rushed to reassure Kylie. "I'm sure there is no connection to the guy last night. The rangers probably already tracked him down and hauled him off to jail."

Kylie didn't look convinced.

The German men moved away and took out their cameras, so Sarah offered in pantomime to take their photo. In a stage whisper she asked me, "How do you say *cheese* in German?"

I hid a smile. "Fromage?"

"That's French."

"Close enough."

The father and son duo grinned into the camera while Sarah took several pictures from different angles before returning their camera.

"Danke. Auf Wiedersehen."

"Any time." Sarah's smile was universal.

9

SUPAI TUNNEL - Elevation: 6,800 ft.

For most of the morning Kylie had hiked much faster than Sarah and me. She now hung back with us. I guess the prospect of running into a thief on her own unnerved her. We had an interesting chat. In spite of her youthful appearance, she held a responsible job as a medical illustrator for a publishing company in New York. The odd combination intrigued me.

Kylie and Sarah talked art for a while longer before the subject turned to Sarah's job situation. "There's a woman in our school district that drives me crazy." Sarah launched into her story, so I increased my hiking pace to stay within earshot.

"Her name is Nadine the Nazi," Sarah began. "She was in charge of the school district budget and stuck sticky notes on every appliance in every school declaring its cost of electricity. You know, three cents for a clock, five cents for a clock radio."

Uncertain of the story's veracity, I waited for a punch line. Sarah spotted my incredulity.

"No, seriously. Each teacher gets an electrical budget and is charged personally for using more electricity than allowed. Heaven forbid, if you have an aquarium in your classroom." Sarah's indignation and growing anger told me she wasn't joking, but how could I keep from laughing?

"It's not funny."

"I'm sorry to laugh." I hid behind my hands.

Sarah tore into her nemesis. "Nadine cheats the charter school kids. She budgets hamburgers for the regular schools and says the charter school kids can eat ketchup sandwiches."

"You're kidding." I looked askance at her.

"That's the truth. I came unglued a few months ago and let Nadine have it." Shaking her head, Sarah sniffed. "She's the reason my teaching contract is not being renewed next year."

"They fired you?"

"Basically."

"Did you punch her out?" Kylie asked.

"No, of course not. I lost my temper and yelled. Maybe she *imagined* a danger to her life," Sarah said.

"You intimidated her." I nodded in approval.

"I wouldn't want to get in your way," Kylie said.

"I love the kids and the teachers, but I hate the politics."

"Give a petty person a little power," I said, "and they abuse it."

Sarah's shoulders rounded under the weight of her pack. "Nadine won the battle and left me worthless. I expected my accomplishments would save me, that friends would intervene, but I'm out." She kicked a rock off the trail. "The good news is—one school after another asked about my project-based learning ideas, and now I have consulting work all over the country."

Sarah's triumph didn't surprise me. Still, I wanted to punch Nadine myself.

Real conversation became difficult while hiking single file, but Sarah's voice carried forward to Kylie and back to me. She entertained us with further tales of Nadine the Nazi. Time and distance passed, while Sarah held our attention and the rhythm of our steps kept us moving.

Before long, the trail led to a large sheltered area with no view of the canyon, but with trees offering shaded areas to rest.

"This must be Supai Tunnel." Somehow I expected a tunnel, but found nothing resembling one. I checked my map. "There's water and a latrine here somewhere," I said.

"Good. Then let's take a snack break." Kylie deposited her pack on a nearby boulder.

Sarah settled herself on the ground and asked for the map. "If this is Supai . . ." She did the math. "We've descended twelve hundred feet."

Our accomplishment impressed me, but Sarah and Kylie took the feat in stride.

While they went in search of the latrine, I removed my boots and sweaty socks and laid them on a sun-baked boulder, propping my aching feet on a rock. I rested my eyes. A slight breeze blew over my damp feet and the sun dried them.

"Hey!"

"What?" Startled, I jerked up.

Sarah chased off two chipmunks. "Dang micro-bears. They were into your pack."

"Micro-bears? Cute. I didn't even hear them."

"Cute?" Sarah exclaimed. "They gnawed a hole into your pack. In another minute they would have done real damage—like eating your dinner."

Sure enough, the chipmunks had tried to tunnel into my food sack compartment. "Dang micro-bears." I waved my hiking pole at the varmints while we rested. Still, they foraged brazenly.

"They know exactly where to find food," Sarah said. "They're habituated." Her exasperation entertained me as much as the chipmunks' antics.

"Kylie, will you stand guard over my pack while I look for the water?" I asked.

She nodded and took my pole.

Slipping into my lightweight camp shoes, I took our water bottles and shuffled down the nearest path which led to a small grotto and a spigot. Clean, cold water burst from the tap. No filtering needed. When I returned, Sarah stood up, her impatience showing.

"We'd better get out of here before these guys make nests in our packs."

"As soon as I get my boots on." I rushed to find dry socks and hung the damp pair from my pack's bungee cord.

"Yeew." Kylie grimaced as if tasting goat cheese. "Your toenail's all purple."

"Lovely shade, don't you think?" I wiggled my painful toes at her. "They scrape inside my boots every time I step downward."

"Lace your boots around the ankle," Sarah commanded, stomping her foot at a micro-bear. "That'll get worse. Don't let your foot slide forward."

I tugged on the laces. "Do you know everything there is to know about backpacking?"

"I try," she said with a grin. "Well, look who's here." Sarah jerked her head in the direction of a young man, tanned and blond, coming up the trail.

Kylie jumped to her feet and trotted toward him. "Hi, Eric!"

"Hey. How ya doin'?" He stopped short of Kylie, uncertain. "What . . ." He pointed to her bruised face.

"It's, like, nothing." Kylie waved away her injury.

Eric's face didn't register emotion. "I need to fill my water bottle."

"I'll show you where." She led the way to the hidden spigot. Poor Kylie fluttered about him, her voice in a twitter. He took the attention for granted.

"She's got it bad." Sarah shook her head sympathetically as we watched the romantic-comedy play out. "I'm so glad not to be twenty."

"I don't trust him."

"Really? Why not?" Sarah frowned, but didn't sound surprised.

"How do we know he isn't the thief," I asked, "or even the guy who attacked Kylie last night?" I watched the path for the two of them and kept my ears on alert.

"She said she didn't know the attacker."

"She said she didn't *see* the attacker, Sarah."

Kylie and Eric returned with his full water bottle. She grinned ear to ear. Apparently, Eric decided that there were benefits to cozying up to Kylie. He slipped his arm around her waist. They made an attractive couple.

"Where did you come from, Eric?" I asked. "We didn't see you on the way down." He had come up the trail as if headed back to the lodge. His eyes bore into mine.

"There's a side trail down further," he said, looking down his nose at me, daring me to find fault with his plausible explanation. "I explored a slot canyon, but I needed to backtrack here for water before I start down again."

Kylie gazed up at her Superman, twirling her hair around her fingers, but then remembered we existed. "I was, like, thinking that maybe I'll go ahead with Eric. You don't mind, do you? I mean, okay, if you really want me to, I'll hike, you know, with you." Her eyes pleaded with us.

Eric pulled away from Kylie's grasp. "Gotta take a piss."

When the latrine door slammed, I pleaded with the girl. "Please stay with us, Kylie. You don't know Eric well."

"He's a great guy," she said.

"Is it possible that he attacked you last night?"

She jumped back. "No way. He wouldn't hurt me. Besides I would know—I bit that guy."

"Eric's wearing long sleeves," I pointed out gently.

"It wasn't him," she insisted.

"Kylie, please, at least get a look at his arm."

Sarah joined us. "You hardly know him, Kylie. You gotta be smart."

"I'll be okay, seriously." Kylie tilted her head and whispered, "I really like him."

Kylie was a grown woman and a stranger to us. We had to let her go. "If you need us, we'll be at Cottonwood this evening," I said.

Kylie hugged each of us around the neck. "You guys are super. Thanks for last night and all. It's been great." She swung her backpack onto her shoulder, leaving the straps dangling and trotted after Eric like a faithful beagle. He glanced back in smug triumph.

"See you in camp tonight, Kylie," I called.

She didn't hear me.

Sarah shook her head. "Even if he's not a bad guy, her infatuation is painful to watch."

"I hate to admit that I've acted that way a number of times in my life."

"That's what makes it so painful." Sarah's laugh released the tension that had built up in the last few minutes.

We picked up our hiking pace to keep the young people in sight, but they sped up and disappeared.

Below the sheltered area of Supai Tunnel fewer timber steps confronted me, but after ten minutes, I could not keep up the speed. Breathing hurt. I pointed to our right, about two hundred feet below. "There's Kylie and Eric," I gasped.

"Where?" Sarah's eyes followed the gritty, stone-covered trail which narrowed to a single track, switching back and forth along the face of the canyon wall.

"Three or four tiers down. Are they trying to get away from us?"

"Young legs move fast. Let 'em go," Sarah said. "How's your toe doing?"

"It's best I don't think about it."

"Well, take your time," she said. "There's no point to rushing through all of this scenery."

"Thanks. You're being good to me."

"Oh, pshaw!"

We took water breaks, scenery breaks, and picture-taking breaks at the start of each new switchback. As if everyone had left us behind, the canyon loomed large and empty. I focused on the placement of my boots on the narrow path and did not immediately see the bearded young man wearing an orange helmet sitting on a boulder at the side of the trail.

"Wait here, please," he said.

Startled, I looked around for a reason. He was part of the crew repairing the rock slide that the mule driver had mentioned. The young man's eyes never met ours. Even Sarah's direct questioning got little out of him—only that more of the crew waited below for a signal.

"You can go now," he said.

Afraid he'd pass judgment on my hiking style, I did my best to walk normally. Halfway down the next switchback, we arrived at the work site. Four strapping men with pick axes and shovels at their sides sat on the upside of the path and waited for us to pass. They nodded a polite greeting. I expected a warning or suggestion for how to cross the rock slide, but they gave none. About fifteen feet of trail had crumbled and slid into the ravine.

I looked back at Sarah. "What do you think?"

"Hug the wall, I guess. Kylie and Eric must have crossed."

With one hiking pole looped over my wrist to leave a hand free to feel my way along the wall, I thrust the other pole into the loose scree for support. Each foot placement sent bits of gravel onto the trail below.

Sarah waited on solid ground. "Be careful."

I ignored the yawning ravine to my right and advanced across the sliding gravel, testing with my hiking pole for firm ground. When the edge of unbroken trail was finally within a few steps, I confidently planted my foot on a protruding rock.

To my horror, the rock pulled loose from the earth and broke into shards under my weight. As if ball bearings were beneath my feet, my boot skated out to the side.

I launched my body forward. My chest hit solid ground first, and I rolled onto my side. My heart hammered. With perfect clarity, I watched my water bottle bounce several times against the canyon wall below and come to rest forty feet down at the base of a spiny cactus.

Sarah yelled and was at my side in seconds. She grasped my shoulder straps and dragged me away from the edge. "Are you okay?" she asked loud enough to wake the dead.

"Just resting." I lay there a few moments appreciating the cool, solid, unmoving ground before rolling onto my knees. Sarah grabbed my arm to drag me up.

I dusted off my legs and arms and glanced back at the rock slide and the four young men watching in shock. I signaled that I was okay and let them off the hook.

"You got across quick," I said to Sarah.

"No problem." She surveyed me from head to toe. "You banged your knee."

"Yeah." My knee hurt, but not as much as the embarrassment. "Let's get away from these guys before I clean up the blood."

Sarah understood.

I limped along, but paused several times to shake out my leg, hoping to put the knee cap back where it belonged.

Two tiers below we came upon another helmeted young man. "Ma'am," he said, holding up my water bottle. I thanked him for it. Once we moved out of range of falling rocks, he signaled to the men above to begin work.

Beyond their sight we found a shady spot and sat to doctor my wounds. "We should have ice for that," said Sarah while I poured cool water over the scrapes.

"I'll take an ibuprofen now and soak my knee when we get to a stream."

Sarah nodded. "Thought I almost lost you there."

"Close call," I agreed. "I think I scared the work crew." I finished bandaging my knee, and we took to the trail again.

Conversation while trekking along had become our routine and kept my mind off my aches and pains. My near tumble into the canyon, made me talkative. I babbled about my grown children, selling my father's bicycle factory, and my brother contesting Dad's will. Sarah listened politely. Perhaps I divulged too much, but the cathartic effects kept me talking.

"If you hadn't worked with your father," she asked, "what would you do?"

"I really don't know." My dream of becoming a lawyer had faded decades earlier. "I had a year of college. We got married and couldn't afford two tuitions, so I ran Dad's office. There was no point in thinking about a different career."

"What about now?" she asked. "You can do anything you want to."

"Don't know." The sun beat down on me like an interrogation lamp. "Maybe I'll hang back for a while and see what grabs my interest."

"Is your husband old enough to retire, too?" Sarah asked.

I muffled a groan and adjusted my shoulder straps. *Husband?* The divorce hanging over my head humiliated me. "John's whole identity is wrapped up in that job."

"He's an architect, right?"

"A VP for a Chicago firm." *Stay positive.* "He loves the corporate life, the wining and dining, the country club."

"You don't?" She looked over her shoulder at me, waiting for a reply.

I had avoided that question for years. "I guess not. The women are nice, but I don't fit in." I shrugged. "Isn't this a gorgeous view?"

"Yep. So why do you hang out with them?" The cross-examiner glanced over her shoulder and raised her eyebrows.

I couldn't think of an answer right away. Sarah stopped and faced me.

"I don't know," I said. To my own ears, I sounded defensive. "My wifely duty, I guess. John thinks a successful man's wife should help further his career."

My shoulders slumped before I could stop them. "He says I embarrass him because I won't wear furs and jewelry. His golf buddies will think he can't afford luxuries."

"May I be blunt, Amy?" she asked.

"What would you do if I said no?"

"I'd be blunt."

Disarmed by Sarah's impish grin, I motioned for her to speak.

"I don't like your husband."

"How could you not? You've never laid eyes on John. Besides, he's a nice guy."

"Maybe so, but everything you've told me about him is negative. He doesn't like your hair. He thinks picking up litter is beneath him. He insists you wear make-up. He's obviously into image and tries to control everything about you."

"I guess I made him sound worse than he is," I muttered, ashamed of complaining about the husband I had chosen.

"That's not it," she said. "The point is—you feel bad because of him. He hasn't made you feel beautiful or confident."

I didn't want to look at her. *Too awkward to admit the divorce now.* "It's not like that."

"Isn't it? Does he cherish you?" She spoke softly.

"I don't want to talk about it."

She touched my shoulder. "I'm sorry. I have a big mouth. In any case, I'm proud of you for standing up for yourself by taking this trip."

"I almost chickened out at the airport."

"That shows there's hope for you. You really do have gumption."

"Gumption?" I shifted the load on my back and stood a little straighter. *I like gumption.*

The surface mood lightened. We trooped down the trail again, but a burr of trouble nettled my mind. My personal life had followed me into the beautiful wilderness.

Engrossed in my thoughts and oblivious to the changing scenery, I followed Sarah's lead, descending another hundred feet of twisted switchbacks. Then abruptly, the trail turned and thrust us into deep shade. My eyes needed time to adjust to the change in light, so I slowed my steps, not wanting to stumble blindly on the narrow path. There was no margin for error.

"Hold up a minute, Sarah. I need my jacket." Coolness seeped from the smooth stone all around us as if we had stepped into the mummy wing of the museum.

"I don't think the sun ever reaches this area," she said. "Are you getting hungry?"

Since she mentioned it, yes. "I'll be ready to stop when we find a good place."

Canyon-bliss calmed my thoughts as we descended further into the basement of the "museum". The trail had been chiseled into the face of the canyon wall, an awesome feat. I had no clue whether natural forces, dynamite, or men with pick axes had accomplished the impossible. I wondered at my lack of fear.

We plodded along on the five-foot narrow strip of rock with towering stone walls on my right, but to my left—nothing. Somehow the immoveable rock gave me a sense of security and anchored me to the earth.

"How about right here?" Sarah called back to me. Thirty yards ahead, she didn't wait for my answer. She dropped her pack, rummaged around for her lunch, and took her first bite by the time I reached her.

The ledge measured about eight feet wide at that point. We sat with our backs against the rock and stretched our legs out without fear of impeding hikers who might pass. For the next thirty minutes the little oasis would be our home.

Looking across the chasm at the opposite canyon wall, I could see the depth to which that wall went, but I didn't want to equate that to my own location. I didn't want to know that we perched on a tiny ledge clinging to an escarpment with hundreds of feet of rock above us and hundreds of feet below. Awestruck, I moved slowly and chewed quietly.

There were no birds, nor bushes for them to land in. No sound of leaves rustling, nor of wind whispering. No trickling stream. Not even flies or mosquitoes to swat away. *Silence.* We were too deep to hear life above us and too high to hear life below. The place held a deep and thorough peace, and I loved it.

Drawing in the pure sweet air, I tried to grasp the miracle of such a place and the miracle of me there as a witness. Maybe I overdramatized.

I glanced at Sarah, and she caught my eye. "Wow," she said. I had to agree.

As if seated before a stage, I anticipated a grand drama. The sun that had been on us all morning shone on the opposite wall, highlighting terra cotta layers in brushstrokes of color. I gazed at the artwork on the opposite expanse and discerned a barely visible zigzag line scratched across the flat wall.

"Look, another trail." I pointed.

Sarah squinted to see. "Mmhumm. And a hiker."

"Really, where?" I followed her gaze to see a lone hiker picking his way along the trail on the distant wall. The tiny human made the enormous wall look that much more enormous.

"That sure gives me a new perspective," I said. "His position looks so precarious."

"And we look like that to him, spots on a wall."

I absentmindedly watched the other spot move along the opposite wall, wondering if someone from the bus had wandered off-trail. He moved out of our field of vision and was forgotten.

I pondered the solemnity of the scene, overwhelmed by the hushed beauty of the spires and depths. A profound sense of my own insignificance enveloped me. Silence hummed in my ears like muffled cotton. *Am I worthy to be here, tuned into the earth's secret sounds?*

The rustling of plastic broke into my thoughts. I glanced at Sarah. She robotically popped jelly beans into her mouth while balancing her artist's pad on her knees. She, too, seemed mesmerized by the drama before us.

"I love this," I whispered.

"Gorgeous." She made swift strokes of color and chewed on her jelly beans.

Eventually, my imagination wandered to an unwelcome vision. I imagined the poor man at the bottom of the ravine at Yaki Point and involuntarily reenacted the scene in my mind, as if he were falling from the rim above us. *Did he flail his arms? Could he see the ground coming up to meet him? Were his screams lost in the darkness, or did they echo through the canyon?* I hated those thoughts for despoiling this sacred place, but could not banish them from my brain.

Giving up, I stood to stretch my aching back and knees.

"I could stay here all day, but we'd better get a move on," I said. "I don't want to get caught up here after dark."

"No way," she said, "but we'll be down in plenty of time."

Sarah stashed her artist supplies, and then stretched her back and rubbed her fanny. The rocks were awe inspiring, but they were also cold, hard, and unforgiving. I stowed my garbage in a zip-lock baggie and tucked it away. Hoisting my pack to my knee, I deftly swung the weight onto my back. The maneuver had become second nature to me.

The long rest stop did my knee good, and I walked with less limp, though with tentative progress. A persistent picture imprinted itself in my mind of me and Sarah on a precarious, wall-hanging trail. I identified too easily with the crumpled body in the Yaki Point ravine and hugged the inside wall, touching the stone now and then to assure myself of its solidity.

Eventually, I beat back the images, and the routine of hiking quickened my step.

After an hour of steady trekking, the smooth wall portion of the canyon gave way to a craggier section with fewer switch-backs, but a steeper slope.

That slowed me down again.

I regretted that my pace held Sarah back. I suspected that, like a race horse or a greyhound, she itched for speed. I appreciated her consideration and didn't mind when the gap between us grew to fifty or a hundred feet. She stopped at intervals and waited for me to catch up.

The Park Service brochures warned us to stay hydrated, and we took the advice seriously, each carrying two water bottles and stopping frequently for water breaks. To prevent muscle cramps, I mixed a lemon-flavored electrolyte replacement powder into my water—*a little sweet, but not too bad*. Sarah stopped at the bend in the trail ahead, and I assumed this would be our next water break. Instead, she turned abruptly and jogged back toward me, waving her arms.

"Something's coming," she yelled.

"What?"

"Move to the inside!"

Over Sarah's shoulder I spotted a full-grown bighorn sheep round the bend at a fast clip. It closed in on Sarah.

Awkward, under forty-five pounds of backpack, she ran toward me, looking for a way to get off the narrow trail. She could not see behind her.

"Get out of its way," I screamed and gestured wildly.

The four-foot wide trail offered no hiding places, but she immediately flattened herself to the inside wall. The three-hundred-pound beast trotted past her without giving her a second look.

I stepped quickly into a safe niche amongst the boulders to give the ram the entire width of the trail, but instead of passing me, the ram came to a halt six feet from where I stood. I had trespassed in his domain, and he stood stark still, considering me. His eyes stared, as expressionless as a shark's.

I studied him. He could have been the model for the 'ram tough' pickup truck logo. Massive horns of thick bone curled around his head, and his sleek hide rippled with muscle. He was no lethargic zoo animal.

I did not want to provoke him, but to relieve my tension, I said to him, "The trail is all yours." I made a slight sweep of my arm, indicating the length of the trail.

That small movement broke his trance and spooked him.

He ran at me so fast, I had no time to react or shield myself, though how do you protect yourself from a ram-tough truck? Images flashed. I feared he'd gore me with his horns and toss me into the abyss, or smear my body against the rocks behind me.

Instead, he sprang over my shoulder. I heard the clatter of his sharp hooves next to my ear. I looked above me. He had disappeared. My legs went weak, and I sat down.

Sarah ran the short distance between us. "Holy crap. Are you all right? Where did he hit you?"

I managed a giggle and a weak flutter of my hand. She checked me all over frantically searching for blood. Finding none, she gave me a huge bear hug. "Holy crap."

Sarah didn't release me for several moments and, in truth, I could have used the strength of her arms around me for a while longer. We scanned the steep escarpment above us, but saw no sign of the brawny beast.

"How can he disappear like that?" Sarah exclaimed.

I hadn't yet found my voice and shook my head in wonder.

Sarah did enough talking for both of us. "That was amazing. He scared me to death when he ran up behind me. I couldn't find a place to get off the trail and I thought he'd ram me off the cliff. He jumped right over you. I was terrified he had kicked you in the head." Hyped-up, Sarah nattered for several minutes, but eventually she ran out of steam and sat beside me.

"I need a drink," I sputtered.

Sarah laughed. "Scotch would work well." She handed me a water bottle and lowered her voice. "I'm so glad you're all right."

My pulse still pounded in my ears, but I calmed down enough to replay the incident in slow motion in my mind. "What are the odds that I was standing in his favorite spot to climb the mountain?"

"A million to one," Sarah guessed. "I wish I had my camera out. *National Geographic* would have loved the face-off between you and him."

"Ha. You probably would have pointed the camera the wrong way and taken your own picture, panic stricken." I made a face of mock terror, and she poked me with her elbow.

I hefted myself from my seat and glanced up the side of the canyon. The ram nimbly perched on an outcropping hundreds of feet above us, king of his realm.

Sorry that we had trespassed in his territory, I took a few tentative steps on my rubbery legs and went on my way.

10

COTTONWOOD CAMPGROUND

Elevation: 4,080 ft.

Chattering about our close encounter, we ambled along for another half hour until the canyon began to bottom out. Hiking became easier, and the scenery changed again. The trail followed the route of an angry stream continuing the work of erosion, digging the canyon deeper and deeper, one grain of sand at a time. The water collided with itself, frothed and bubbled, barging between boulders, shoving its way to the bottom of the canyon to eventually surge into the Colorado River. In some places, the stream shared its water with the land. Reeds crowded the wetted soil. Tamarisk and cottonwood trees grew tall and lush.

During our mid-afternoon snack break, I dipped my bandana in the icy water and soothed my swollen knee. I found a slice of shade and pulled out my dog-eared map to find a stretch of trail that paralleled a stream.

"I think we're here." Pointing, I noticed my fingernails were dirty. "Or here."

Sarah popped a cherry jellybean in her mouth and took the map. "You could be right. We probably have an hour to go." She glanced at her watch. "That puts us in camp about four-thirty."

"As long as we get there before dark."

"Well, let's drink up and get going," said Sarah. "How's your knee?"

"A little swollen, but not really painful." I had taken an ibuprofen and hoped that my assertion would soon be true.

We were on a wide flat plain or mesa, and for that I was grateful. The canyon gave us a break for the next hour; no pounding descent, no stair stepping. Having been on the trail for seven hours, my entire body complained. Beads of sweat ran along my spine from between my shoulder blades into my waistband, and my hair clung to my head in wet ringlets beneath my limp cowboy hat.

Our descent for the day totaled almost 4,200 feet, and I wanted our trek to be over. Fatigue prevented me from rejoicing when we finally hobbled past the small sign pointing the way to Cottonwood Campground.

The sign toyed with us. The trail went on and on. The next mile took an eternity, and the quarter of a mile through the campsites strung out along the creek took another eternity. My body yearned to plop down at the first unoccupied campsite. Sarah, energetic and diplomatic, suggested I sit at a picnic table in an acceptable site while she scouted for a better location.

I rid myself of my backpack and lay on the seat of the picnic bench with a water bottle held to my head. Shrubbery struggled to shade me from the merciless sun, but we had entered a natural kiln. The canyon walls and scree-covered floor radiated the sun's intense heat from every direction, baking all occupants to a wilting one hundred plus degrees. Still, the ten-minute siesta in the shade revived me enough to be ready when Sarah came back to announce that she found the two best tent sites in the campground.

"Come on, I want you to choose," she insisted.

I didn't have the heart to tell her that I didn't care. Every site we passed featured the same raised flat area bordered by timbers, a large T-shaped bar with hooks, presumably to hang our packs and negligible shade provided by the stunted trees and shrubs. Instead, I surveyed the second site and said, "This is perfect."

Sarah flashed a toothpaste-commercial smile. "Great. I'll sign us in."

She's way too peppy, I moaned to myself.

When she was gone, the residue of her energy goaded me to do my chores. First, I needed shelter from the sun, so I located Sarah's tarp and ropes and tied one end to the T-shaped bar. I looked around for branches to secure the other ropes.

Before the job was done, Sarah returned and offered her help. She looped the end of a rope over a thin branch of a nearby shrub, knotting an expert taut-line hitch. "We're not supposed to do this," she said.

"What? Put up a tarp?"

"We are not supposed to tie anything to trees and bushes. A flyer on the bulletin board says it's a ticket-able offense."

I stopped my attempt to tie a proper knot. "So . . . should we take the tarp down?"

"I'm betting that a ranger won't come around until later. Besides we need the shade. We'll plead ignorance, and you can charm him into forgiving us."

"Oh, great," I said. "He'll give us two tickets."

She laughed a full-throated laugh. "Let's get set up and go for a dip in the creek before supper time."

Under the shade of the thin nylon tarp, we worked together and set up her single-wall tent in five minutes. We unrolled our mattress pads out on the picnic table to allow them to self-inflate, then fluffed out our down sleeping bags and threw them into the tent.

I arranged the sleeping bags and looked around our neat little campsite, satisfied we had chosen the best one in the entire campground. "What are these things? They look like ammunition boxes."

"Those must be the metal boxes the flyer mentioned," Sarah said. "We're supposed to lock our food inside so animals can't steal it."

"Huh. Great idea. I guess our government actually recycled something."

Sarah rolled her eyes and handed me her food sack.

One ammunition box provided ample room for our food. I forced the stiff hasp over the metal loop and tested its strength. For good measure, I put the heavy box on top of the picnic table. We suspended our nearly empty backpacks from hooks on the T-bar four feet from the ground. Our camp thus protected from marauding animals, I grabbed my bandana and a fresh shirt and followed Sarah to the creek.

The creek's sun-sparkled water ran through reeds and polished a bed of stones. The paradise lured us in. I intended to sit in the cool stream to soak my swollen knee, wash my shirt, and decrease my body temperature by several degrees. One foot in the icy water, changed all that. "Oh, dang! It's freezing."

The cold burned my ankles. I couldn't bear having them submerged for more than thirty seconds. Sarah toughed it out a few seconds longer. Both of us hopped to the shore to perch on rocks and splash ourselves clean. Sarah dipped her head into the stream and howled at the cold shock. She scrubbed her scalp and then shook her curls like a big, friendly sheepdog.

"I'm going back for a jacket," she said, shivering. Sarah dried herself with a small towel and hurried toward camp. She called over her shoulder, but the high decibel white noise created by the creek drowned out her words.

Alone in our oasis, I dawdled on my rock blotting moisture from my skin with my bandana. I indulged in an image of myself as a river nymph basking in the sun—until camp chores nagged at the nymph. With only two shirts, one to wear and one to carry, I'd have to do laundry—a small price to pay to keep pack weight down and to prevent stinkage. A few purists out there insist that human odors are a part of wilderness camping. I disagree.

Not wanting to be a stinking purist, I disregarded modesty, stripped off my sweaty shirt and doused my armpits with cold water. I slipped into a fresh shirt and knelt on a slab of stone to swizzle my thin nylon shirt in the current and scrub the fabric. I then twisted and knotted the shirt to coax water out. I whirled it over my head, hoping centrifugal force would speed the drying.

While twirling my shirt, a movement twenty yards downstream caught my eye. I focused on the spot and recognized Ultra-lighter from the shuttle bus. He turned away and bent to the water to drink and wash his face. Not wanting to invade his privacy, I turned to whirl my shirt in the opposite direction. With a shock, I realized that Mr. Rap might have witnessed my bathing. How long had he been staring? My face heated up, but it comforted me to know that a young man would certainly turn away from an older woman's momentary nude display. *Wouldn't he?*

I put Ultra-lighter out of my mind and concentrated on wringing moisture from my shirt. The sun lost its heat, so I hurried through a confusion of paths back to our campsite. By the time I got there, my blue skin prickled with goose bumps. Shadows crept toward us.

Sarah met me dressed in her jacket and long pants. "You'd better hustle up," she said. "The sun's going fast."

"This is amazing. First, we fried, now we freeze." I pulled my clothes sack from my backpack and dashed into the tent to change into long pants, dry socks and two layers of fleece.

In the meantime, Sarah took down the tarp and removed the illegal ropes from the trees. With impeccable timing, she handed me the tarp to tuck into my backpack just as a uniformed ranger stepped through the bushes.

"Good afternoon. I'm making the rounds to check permits and to make you aware of a few rules for camping in the park."

I noted his name tag. "Hello, Ranger Paul."

Sarah pointed to the plastic sleeve hanging from her backpack. He glanced at the permit and checked us off on a report on his clipboard. His abrupt manner left no doubt that the tarp would've gotten us a ticket.

"Are you familiar with the rules for food storage?" he asked.

"I guess we use the boxes," I said. "Are these World War II ammo boxes?"

"They're from the Gulf War. Put all of your food, toothpaste and scented creams in the boxes and lock them. Also, jam the boxes under the bench." He took the locked box from the picnic table and slid it under the seat. "Animals have learned that the lids pop open if they knock the boxes over."

"Raccoons?" asked Sarah.

"No raccoons," he said flatly. "We have squirrels, ringtail cats, mice and chipmunks. I've seen three squirrels team up to push over one of these boxes. They want your food. Don't leave anything unattended even for a minute. That is a ticket-able offense."

He wasn't kidding, but seemed to soften. "Your site looks good." He glanced around in approval. "You wouldn't believe what some people will do. Yesterday, a camper strung a clothes line from tree to tree."

Sarah attempted to get on his good side. "Are there other ticket-able offenses we should know about?" She controlled a smirk.

I swear his chest puffed out. "No fires. No collecting wood or breaking branches. No soap in the creek. No littering. Don't hang anything in the trees. No loud noises after ten P.M."

When he finished his litany, I asked, "Does your permit list show names of campers? We're looking for our friend, Kylie Wells."

He shook his head. "Sorry. No names, just numbers. If she's not on this end, maybe she's at the west end." Ranger Paul said his good-byes and wished us a good night.

We waited for him to begin his spiel to the campers in the next site before we laughed.

"That was a close call." Sarah's voice tended to carry.

"Shhh. He'll hear you."

"And that would be a ticket-able offense."

I suppressed a grin and shushed her, but then got serious. "It's none of my business, but I'd feel better if I knew Kylie was in for the night."

"Me, too," Sarah said. "I already scouted the west end. Maybe they set up and are out exploring."

"I hope so."

I strung a lightweight rope between the T-bar and a tent pole to hang my wet shirt. My stomach growled. "We'd better start dinner, or we'll have to cook in the dark."

While Sarah filled our water bottles at the spigot, I dragged out the ammunition box and removed our food bags. Mindful of scavenging animals, I kept an eye on our food while I dug through my now disorganized pack to find my miniature stove.

My chicken-and-rice recipe was simple; open packet, boil water, and wait, but Sarah produced a titanium pot and an eight-inch skillet from her pack.

"You carried a skillet? No wonder your pack is huge." I didn't intend to sound critical, and she didn't take it that way.

"This is my favorite pan." She held the skillet lovingly and demonstrated how to remove the handle to save space. "I have a cool foldable spatula, too." The toy-sized spatula fit in her pocket.

I fought back gear-envy, knowing that my priority should always be minimum weight. I screwed my little stove to the top of its orange fuel canister with a simple twist and noticed Sarah's tiny soda-can stove nested in her titanium pot.

"May I see that?" I loved the idea of recycling an aluminum can into something useful, and examined the design.

Sarah beamed. "I found the instructions on a website."

"Very interesting. Where does the fuel go?"

"Watch." She poured alcohol into the reservoir and struck a match. The flame came through the series of holes punched around the top edge of the aluminum can. Her stove threatened to tip under the weight of the skillet, but did the trick.

While she cooked, Sarah told stories of menu successes and failures, but occasionally paused mid-sentence to flip her crab-cake patties in the hot oil. We waited in quiet domesticity while my meal rehydrated, dusk gathered, and our conversation lulled. I recalled then what I had seen down at the creek.

"Do you remember Ultra-lighter from the bus?"

"Yeah. Michael Rap," Sarah said. "What about him?"

"He was down at the creek earlier, just standing there, staring at me."

"What happened?"

"Nothing much—gave me a creepy feeling—and he drank straight from the creek."

"No purifying?" She shook her head. "That's like playing Russian roulette with your intestines."

"I can't imagine being on the trail with exploding innards."

"The guy's nuts." She shuddered. "Can we change the subject? I'm cooking here."

I gave my chicken and rice a stir and waited, mesmerized by the flame of the stove.

While we were busy with our meals, darkness snuck in. Suddenly, nothing emitted light: no moon, no stars, not even animal eyes in the night. I tried to force my pupils to dilate to their maximum, but there was no stray light to be gathered.

"I can't see a thing." An unreasonable fear pinched my shoulder blades. I fished my headlamp from my pocket and hung the strap around my neck.

Sarah patted her shirt and pants with one hand, searching for her light, and balanced the skillet with the other. "I forgot my headlamp," she said. "Would you look in the tent, maybe in the blue gear bag?"

With three LED bulbs reinforcing my bravery, I found our tent, sitting squat in the night, a short distance away. Its yellow nylon warmly reflected my light. I unzipped the door—a sound much too loud for the darkness—and bent into the tent to find Sarah's headlamp. I zipped the tent and stood to return to the picnic table, but stopped.

A stealthy rustling came from the low bushes between us and the creek. My light picked up nothing, so I took another few steps and then paused to listen.

Sarah noticed my hesitation. "What do you hear?"

"Something's in the bushes."

Like a search light in a prison yard, my LEDs swept over the immediate area, but could not penetrate more than fifteen feet into the night. Finally, the light met a sound, and two sets of eyes stared back at me.

"An animal," I hissed, "no, two animals." My pulse rate soared as I tried to remember if dangerous carnivores lived in the canyon.

Sarah put her skillet aside and jumped up. As fast as a gunfighter, her camera appeared in her hand, aimed at the far end of my light stream. She moved toward the bushes, stalking the two sets of eyes.

I turned on her headlamp and put it into her hand. Her more powerful beam immediately showed the outline of two animals ducking behind thick bushes. They moved like big weasels and sported long bushy tails with black stripes.

"Those are ringtail cats," I whispered. The Park Service brochure featured a picture of the scavengers. My heart thumped against my rib cage. You'd think I'd spotted a movie star.

Sarah moved in on the animals like a hunter, one step at a time, camera held high in one hand and flashlight in the other. "There they are." She bounded forward. Her camera flashed and snapped pictures in quick succession. The ringtail cats scampered away among the rocks.

Sarah laughed in triumph, and waded back through the brush. She urged me to view her photos as proof of her hunting prowess. The first picture showed only bushes, the second caught the tip of a striped tail, but the third captured one of the animals looking over its shoulder with disdain, its proud tail the center piece of the photo.

Very satisfied with her photographic safari, Sarah returned to the picnic table to finish her meal. She sliced a crab-cake bagel in half. "Here try this."

The sandwich tasted delicious, hot and crispy around the edges, and I nodded my approval with my mouth full.

"I love outdoor cooking." She patted her stomach. I heard her humming and smiling in the dark.

Clean up was quick. We stowed our food sacks and garbage bags into the ammunition box under the bench. The ringtail cats would find no leftovers.

We switched off our lights and sat for a while in the dark to accustom ourselves to its texture and sound. The rustling of the bushes continued, but was no longer an unknown. Eventually, sleepiness overcame me, and I looked at my watch.

"Eight-ten," I said. "I don't know how much longer I can stay awake."

"Let's visit the latrine before turning in," she suggested.

The paths that had been familiar in daylight became a maze of wrong turns and missteps. We twice blundered into other campsites, our lights shining on their tents before we could tiptoe away. No sign of Kylie and Eric. Everyone in camp had retired to their sleeping bags early and surely heard us whispering and shushing each other. A campfire ban changed the dynamics of a campground after dark. No beer drinking, no ghost stories, no camaraderie.

We located the fresh-smelling latrines in a clearing. While I waited outside for Sarah, I turned off my light to enjoy the night sky and the millions of brilliant stars in the Milky Way. For the first time in my life, I saw the flow of its river from one side of the sky to the other.

"Looking at constellations?" Sarah asked as she joined me.

"I hoped to see a shooting star."

"Okay." She stood with me to search the sky.

What a pleasure to have someone beside me to whom it made perfect sense to stand in the cold, waiting for a shooting star.

Suddenly, I missed my husband. Not the John who really was, but the John I had dreamed he would be, my kindred spirit.

"There's one." Sarah nudged me and pointed to the right.

How exciting. "There's another with a long red tail."

Satisfied, we started back, and the notion of John being a kindred spirit deleted itself from my mind. We stopped at the water spigot to brush our teeth, spitting into the drain at our feet. That minty-fresh feeling is another of life's pleasures that I appreciate on the trail so much more than at home.

"Ahhh." Apparently Sarah appreciated minty freshness, too.

"All done." I pocketed my toothbrush. "Which way?" I had lost my sense of direction.

"This way."

Sarah always knew the way. Or so I thought. We should have attached a glow-stick to our tent.

The maze of paths led us to several dead ends, and we had to backtrack. Finally, we recognized the oddly shaped rock which marked our turn. Too tired and achy to traipse around, I was relieved to find our site. I swept my light over the area to ensure the camp truly was ours and found two pairs of eyes watching for our return.

"Shoo. Shoo." We yelled in a whisper and ran at the ringtail cats sitting on our picnic table sniffing around, probably finding a crumb or two after all. At their leisure, they took us seriously and bounded off the table into the bush.

"They'll be back," Sarah sighed.

"No doubt about that."

To be on the safe side, I added my toothpaste and brush to my toiletry bag in the ammunition box. The last thing I wanted was for one of those scoundrels to slice into our tent with a sharp claw and snatch a minty-fresh snack. I loaded everything else into my backpack, zipped and snapped every opening, and suspended the pack from the T-bar hooks. Sarah was on the same page and secured her gear.

"Go ahead and get situated in the tent," she said. "I'll finish up here and will climb in when you're settled."

Sarah's tent was roomy, as far as backpacking tents go, but only one person at a time could change clothes, move around, or rearrange the sleeping bags. I climbed into the tent and immediately zipped the door behind me. Though I had not seen crawling critters, I wanted to prevent them from sneaking inside.

I hung my headlamp from a loop in the tent's peak a few inches above my head and groped around for my long underwear. The soft merino wool long johns were a luxury treat to myself and perfect for sleepwear in colder temperatures. After stuffing my jacket and clothes into a flannel pillow case, I slipped into my sleeping bag.

"Your turn," I called and scooted to the side of the tent to give Sarah as much room as possible.

Sarah unzipped the door, ducked inside, knocking the dirt from her camp shoes. While she got ready for bed, I turned my face to the nylon wall to give her privacy.

My prone position eased my groaning back. My aching body welcomed the half-inch thick sleeping pad as if it were a feather bed. I settled my head onto the luxurious, makeshift pillow and closed my eyes.

Two sighs later, a cramp seized my calf muscle. I gasped as if stabbed and clutched my lower leg. "Ow. Ow. Ow." My back arched, my leg went rigid, and I was afraid to move lest the pain increase.

"What's wrong?"

"Ugh. My leg," I moaned.

Sarah pulled back my sleeping bag and knelt at its foot. She picked up my leg by the ankle and ran her fingers lightly over my calf.

"Relax. Let the pain go." Her voice coaxed and coddled. "Release the muscle. Let it go. Let it go."

I followed her smooth, creamy words, letting the pain dissipate and flow out through her fingers. Her touch worked like magic to relax my entire body. Able to breathe again, I sagged back into my bedding.

"Better?" she asked.

Exhausted, my words came breathlessly. "Yes. Thanks."

I expected that she'd remove her hand from beneath my calf and put my leg down. Instead, she took my foot into her hands and began to knead her thumbs into its sole, moving methodically up and down the length of my foot, and then massaging the ball of my foot and the joints of each toe.

I hadn't realized how badly my foot ached, until the ache was gone. Wanting more, I neglected to say that I was fine and she could stop. I was disappointed when she did stop and tucked my foot beneath the folds of my sleeping bag. When she picked up my other foot, I did not say no. I took advantage of her good nature and the free professional massage.

I finally roused myself from a stupor enough to say, "That was great. Where did you learn massage?"

"Years ago I took a class with a friend of mine, and we practiced on each other. Do you want me to do your back?"

Her offer surprised and delighted me. It had been ages since anyone had touched me with such wonderful, magic hands, professional or otherwise. "I never turn down a back rub."

"Well, then," she said, "flip over."

I did as I was told and got myself comfortable. "After this, I'll repay the favor."

"Don't worry about that," she said. "I enjoy giving a massage even more than getting one. You've had a hard day. Tonight, you relax."

Her thumbs kneaded the muscles on either side of my spine all the way up to the base of my skull, while her long fingers extended around my rib cage soothing the soreness. I melted like butter left in a dish on a summer day. Gentle pressure on my lower back drew out my aches and pains and more than a few groans.

Perhaps I dozed off or maybe she had finished her massage routine, but she stopped and settled herself beside me. My sleepy haze prevented me from expressing my gratitude for the massage. I rolled onto my side and curled up for the night.

Sarah reached over and brushed my hair back from my face and ran her fingers over my cheek bones. I wondered if there was a facial massage in her repertoire. Her finger tips grazed my lips, and my face relaxed even further. After a few moments, I realized that tiny kisses were being placed on my cheek and lips.

"What are you doing?" Alarms went off in my head. "Stop, Sarah."

We were dangerously close to the line that can't be crossed. Her hand left my face and stroked the curve of my neck. *Surely, she knows we're over the line.*

"Stop, Sarah. Stop. I can't do this."

"No?" She tilted her head in a question, but her fingers continued to caress—so unlike John's clumsy grabbing. I closed my eyes and savored the friendly touch. *It's been so, so long. Years. Decades.* Her hand slipped beneath my shirt. *She'll stop soon,* I assured myself.

John's frown popped into my mind. My mother clucked in the background.

I clamped my hand over hers. "No! Stop now." I shoved her hand away and turned toward the wall.

"Okay. I'm sorry," she whispered, putting her hand on my shoulder.

I jerked away. "Leave me alone." Confused and unable to think, I hugged my sleeping bag and curled up like a defensive hedgehog.

"Amy?"

I had no idea what to say.

"Hey. I'm sorry," she said. I could hear regret in her breathing. She eventually moved away and turned out the light. A large, empty space grew between us.

I listened to her every small movement and eventually to her sounds of sleep. I wanted to cry. I regretted that I had been so harsh, certain I'd hurt her feelings. My face flushed hot red at the thought of her touch. Sarah had become the friend I always dreamed of and now that was gone.

My sadness kept me awake. I heard the night noises and the scratching of the ringtail cats at our backpacks, but didn't rouse myself to chase them off.

11

Day 4 - RIBBON FALLS TRAIL - Elevation: 3,720 ft.

In the morning Sarah was gone. I lay in my bed angry at her for complicating our friendship, but wanting to hear the sound of her tinkering with her stove or humming Willie Nelson songs. I feared that she had hiked down the trail without me. No. Her sleeping bag lay in a heap next to mine. The door zipper gapped open a few inches, so I knelt and peeked with one eye, hoping to see Sarah sitting in silence at the picnic table.

Not a soul in sight.

The air in the tent suddenly seemed old and stifling. I unzipped the door and let a fresh breeze blow through the mesh screening. *Was last night really so horrible?* Sarah had been kind and caring, and I felt—special.

And I returned the favor by shoving her away.

I threw myself into my bedding and curled up. Never in my life had I considered a woman as a lover, yet I'd almost let it happen. I touched my cheek where Sarah's kisses had been. Guilt and embarrassment swirled like reproachful shadows. The incident seemed like a rejection of my husband, of all men, and against every image I'd had of myself. *Who was this woman that missed her so much?*

My head throbbed, so I wrapped myself in our entangled sleeping bags and allowed myself that brief comfort. *What's done is done.* I roused myself, dressed, and climbed from the tent. We had planned to be on the trail at 9:00. I vowed to uphold my end of that agreement—even if Sarah no longer wanted to hike with me.

My breakfast called me, so I headed for my backpack hanging on the T-bar to get my stove and titanium pot. Oddly, a plastic baggie lay on the ground beneath my pack in the otherwise pristine campsite. Tooth marks stippled the plastic around a ragged hole. *So much for the efficiency of the T-bar and protection from scavenging animals.* I examined my pack, expecting shredded nylon, but found no damage. The zipper to an empty compartment had been neatly opened. I marveled at the ringtail cat's dexterity. *Ha. It got only a few licks of salt for all its efforts.*

Sarah's undamaged pack hung limply on the T-bar, her fanny pack missing. *Where'd she go? No doubt, she's avoiding me.*

While I waited for her return, I boiled a pot of water and dawdled over my oatmeal and a cup of hot tea. The babbling creek and dry cottonwood leaves kept me company. Every now and then a hiker trekked past just beyond the leafy border of our site. I'd sit up straighter, expecting Sarah, and was disappointed each time.

After breakfast, I washed my pot and spork, took my dry shirt down from the clothesline, and bundled the ropes. While I cleaned up, I mulled over my situation and concluded that Sarah was angry, too, or maybe embarrassed. Either way, we needed to get on the trail soon. I stuffed my sleeping bag into its compression sack and deflated my sleeping pad. I tidied up the tent removing my belongings, leaving hers.

A slight movement caught my attention, and I turned to the campsite entrance.

"Amy, may I come in?"

She didn't sound angry. Only my startled expression welcomed her. "Yes, of course." I couldn't risk a smile and shyness garbled my words. I motioned her to the picnic table.

"Did you get your breakfast?" I asked, unable to look at her.

"Yeah. I took my coffee and granola down at the creek so you could sleep."

I didn't know what to say.

She tried again. "How's the knee?"

"Seems fine."

"Did you take a painkiller?"

"I'll take an ibuprofen." My answers sounded curt, but I couldn't help myself. I stared at initials carved in the picnic table, and hoped she didn't give up on me.

Sarah zipped and unzipped her fanny pack. "Did the scavengers get any of your stuff?"

"They chewed up a plastic bag."

"My stuff was all over the ground this morning," she said. "They dragged off my soda-can stove. I searched the area, but didn't find anything."

"Mmm. Maybe we should take inventory to see what else is missing."

The task gave us something to do rather than try to make conversation. We removed every item from our packs and lay them on the table. I brought the rest of our gear out of the tent.

She broke the silence. "Where'd you get a bag like this?"

We both reached out to pick up my mesh food sack, our hands brushing against each other. She jerked back as if burned.

I hated the strain between us, so I held out the bag to her like a peace offering and forced myself to speak as if everything was normal. "Last Easter's spiral ham came in this netting. I trimmed one end off and threaded macramé cord through the holes."

"Good idea." She fingered the plastic sack. "Tough and washable material."

"Yep," I said. "It stretches to fit all my food."

"Huh. Clever."

I basked in her approval, wanting to please her. *But why?*

In the awkward pause, I turned back to the task at hand. "All of my things are here."

"Mine, too. Except my soda-can stove." Sarah frowned and tapped her finger on her lips. "And the fuel it uses."

Our minds clicked onto the same conclusion. We synchronized our nods.

"That's one smart ringtail cat."

"Too smart," she agreed.

"Who would stoop so low as to steal a fellow hiker's stove?" I fumed. "That's like taking food out of your mouth." I could not fathom a fellow camper rifling through backpacks. A thought struck me.

"I heard noises last night while I lay awake, but I assumed the ringtails foraged around and didn't bother to look outside. I'm sorry."

"You aren't to blame." A shadow of guilt clouded her face. "Besides, there's no harm done. I have an emergency stove and will make another pop-can stove when I get home." Her lips set a firm line. "That thief's nerve riles me."

"Sure it does." Our clumsy conversation stalled, and I stood still in prickly silence.

"Amy?" she asked.

"Yes?"

"Are you mad at me? I mean about last night." She stumbled over her words and flopped her arms at her sides. "I apologize. I overstepped my bounds."

"I'm not angry, Sarah." It was my turn to stumble over my words. "I'm just not . . . I didn't know . . . I guess I sent the wrong signals, but I'm not mad." I looked right into her eyes so she could see I spoke the truth. "I consider your attentions a compliment, and I'm sorry if I hurt your feelings. Are you angry with *me*?"

"Heck, no. I was the one out of line." Sarah's shoulders relaxed. "Thank you." She looked down at her boots. "This morning I thought . . . well, I thought you'd want to get away from me."

How could I explain without giving her the wrong impression? "No, Sarah, that's not it." I paused to find the right words. "I needed a friend, and you were, are . . . wonderful, but I didn't know you were, you know . . . interested in women. And, well . . . I like men. I was confused last night."

I could almost smell incense from a darkened confessional. "The massage relaxed me. I loved it. Apparently, I really needed a human touch. I wasn't thinking about where a massage might take us." I took a breath. "I'm sorry I misled you." My voice trailed off to nothingness.

"My fault entirely." Sarah sighed. When she raised her head, her cheery demeanor surfaced. Forced or not, it changed everything. "I thought anyone could tell that I prefer women, and obviously you're into men."

"What do you mean *obviously*?" I challenged.

"I can see it whenever a man is around."

"Oh, you cannot!"

"Yes, I can," she said. "I see your reaction. You get all perky."

"Perky? No way." We needed the friendly banter.

"Your body language screams perky," she insisted. "Last night with that young ranger? And the ranger on the North Rim . . . big time."

The old Sarah was back, joshing with me, making me laugh—but *perky?* Well, she probably pegged me right, so I didn't argue further. Her contagious grin showed her even white teeth, and the sun shone brighter.

Sarah had more to say and continued in a quieter voice. "You remind me of someone, and I got carried away. I thought maybe . . . I was hoping . . ." She stopped.

"So, tell me who I remind you of," I said.

She looked up into the cottonwoods, but probably didn't see the leaves quaking in the breeze. An aura of sadness and old pain seemed to grow around her.

"Her name was Melanie."

"The friend with the poem."

"Mm-mm." Sarah sighed. "Mel was an activist, an idealist. She was determined to make the world run according to her Utopian plan and wouldn't take no for an answer. She loved to be outrageous and was always happy—except when railing against homelessness or abusive husbands or nuclear proliferation. I loved when she got fighting mad about injustices. Always something."

Sarah seemed lost in her memories, so I waited.

"She was so feisty. I loved her immediately, but she didn't notice me for months. We were together for fourteen years." Her words trailed off, replaced by a hint of a smile.

"What happened?" I asked.

"She died."

"I'm so sorry."

"That's okay. She's been gone fifteen years. I'm getting to the point where the pain is bearable, and I can remember the good times."

"Tell me about her."

"If you get me started, I may not stop." Her smile didn't quite reach her eyes.

"We have all day."

"True," she said, "but we can't sit here all day."

We began to pack our backpacks with automatic motions, and I prompted Sarah to talk. "So how did Melanie die?"

"Mel died because she wanted a baby. She decided that in-vitro was the way to go, and when Mel wanted something she went after it. Clinics in Chicago and New York turned her down because she had a spot on her liver that made her a poor candidate to receive growth hormones."

We sat down again so I could listen. Sarah's broken heart was reflected in her eyes. She went on to tell about the unethical "doctor" in Philadelphia who gave Melanie growth hormones each time in-vitro failed to produce a baby. The hormones grew cancer in her liver.

"Mel never complained, but I wanted to kill that quack." Sarah shook, red in the face. "He ended up going to jail for using his own sperm on his patients."

I brushed tears from her cheeks.

"My heart was torn from my chest when she left me," Sarah said in a ragged whisper. "Anger boiled inside me for months; sometimes at that filthy *doctor*, sometimes at Mel for being so bull-headed."

I hugged Sarah, and she held on to me until she calmed.

"Hate and anger ate me alive," she said. "After a while, I had to let it go."

I marveled at how well Sarah had hidden her pain.

"Eventually, I found peace." Sarah wrapped her arms around her knees and rocked herself back and forth on the bench. She laughed. "Now I can remember her grin, her outrageously wild hair, and her really impressive diatribes."

Sarah stopped rocking, and I waited for more.

"Sometimes I feel her with me, especially when I'm solo in the wilderness." An intimate smile warmed Sarah's face. Her eyes softened and she gazed into the distance.

I let her have a silent moment with her dear friend.

"I miss her," Sarah said. "Thank you for letting me talk. I've never said all that out loud to anyone."

I found my packet of tissues and offered them to Sarah. "She sounds like a wonderful person."

"She was." Sarah sniffled and sighed.

"So did Melanie hike with you?"

"*God no.* She hated backpacking." Sarah laughed. "She tried. She loved campfires, but hated bugs, dirt, sweat and sleeping on the ground."

"Sounds like my husband."

"Either you love camping, or you hate it."

I enjoyed her memories of Melanie, but when Sarah fell silent, my own thoughts crowded in. Nothing in my background told me how I should feel about her loving another woman. Maybe I should feel sorry for Sarah and Melanie for not having a *normal* life, but that seemed arrogant. Obviously, their relationship had been happier than my marriage.

Envy crept in. Real love can be so fleeting. One must grab a hold and let love grow where it will. I thought about Sarah's kiss last night. She had honored me. I heaved a long sigh, making her glance at me with a sad, half-smile.

"We'd better get moving," she said. "It's almost nine."

Full sun had reached our campsite and began steaming the air. We worked together, playfully racing to meet our self-imposed deadline. In a matter of minutes we had the tent down, the rest of our gear stowed in our packs, and boots laced up. I checked my watch. Nine o'clock on the dot.

"Packs on," Sarah said.

I followed my good friend down the trail.

* * *

We emerged from the oasis that had been Cottonwood campground and fell into the routine of hiking; sometimes talking, but more often alone in our thoughts. The narrow trail zigzagged through craggy gorges lined with rock walls less smooth and less polished than those at higher elevations. I supposed that the river scraped more recently through these rocks, exposing their youth to give humans a hint of what the area looked like millions of years ago when the canyon was merely a valley on a high plain.

The creek that lulled me to sleep last night searched elsewhere for its route to the Colorado River, leaving the land and the air parched and dusty. I missed the white noise provided by the gurgling creek, but instead tuned into the dryer sounds: crunching stones, tumbleweeds, and buzzing insects.

Vistas became more confined, though no less spectacular. Odd, I thought, how we take less notice of the grand scenery and focus on our own lives as if we could be the center of the universe. Time after time, the canyon underscored that we are not. Is that a human failing? Nature simply went about its business.

"You're deep in thought," Sarah said.

"Just thinking that this type of scenery is beautiful, too."

"You seem wistful. Is something wrong?" She looked unsure of herself, perhaps worried that, after our earlier heart-to-heart, my judgment of her had changed.

"Don't worry," I assured her. "I'm thinking that I should have spent more time with my kids, traveled maybe. Now all they do is work. I was a bad example."

"I seriously doubt that," Sarah said. "Get them hooked on your Grand Canyon stories. There's plenty of time."

"Maybe." I fought back melancholy. "I'm ready for lunch. Do you mind if we have a packs-off break?"

"Sure. There's shade ahead."

The rock overhang resembled a stone lean-to and provided ample room in the front for us to sit sheltered from the sun. The roof tapered to the ground in the back, creating a dark recess and a possible home for snakes and scorpions. I ran my hiking pole along the ground, poking it into narrow crevices to flush out inhabitants. None scurried forth, so we dropped our packs, and I lowered myself to the ground with a groan.

Sarah propped herself on her pack next to me and dug into her lunch. She ate with gusto, but chewed each mouthful completely. Between bites she prodded me to talk about my kids.

"Are you sure you want to get *me* started?"

"I want to hear it all," she said. "I enjoy kids vicariously whenever I can."

"Okay, then." I took a sip of lukewarm water. "Meagan is twenty-eight now and married to Ed. He's a sweetheart. You should see her face light up when he enters the room."

"Any children yet?"

"Not yet. They're hoping to get pregnant soon."

"So you're going to be a Grandma." Sarah leaned forward, intent on hearing the details, and I swelled with happiness at the thought of my future status. I chattered on about my accountant daughter and her career in Atlanta.

"Is she close to her Dad?"

"John doted on Meagan as a baby, but by the time she turned eleven, he hardly recognized her. She lashed out at him during her teenage years. I didn't fare much better, but I think we're okay now."

Sarah listened so well, I talked more about my daughter than I ever had. I missed Meagan acutely—and James. I missed their childhoods when they needed me and anything was possible. *Where had that time gone?*

"What's your son up to?" Sarah asked.

I shook my head and thought a moment. "I worry about him."

When I didn't continue, Sarah prodded me.

"He's not happy," I said. "He needs to think better of himself and meet a good, strong woman."

"Has he tried counseling?"

"*Ha.* The men in my family don't do counseling." I rested my forehead on the heel of my hand and shook my head. "That would say to the world *I am a wacko.*"

"You're kidding. I thought everyone's seen a therapist. Have you?" she asked.

"Several times," I admitted, "but the outdoors is my real therapy. My outlook improves, and I like myself better. How about you?"

Sarah's voice went soft. "My therapist probably saved my life—or at least made life worth living." Her gaze fixed on a saguaro cactus, its arms raised in surrender. Her thoughts obviously traveled back to memories of Melanie. A little tic quivered her eyebrow above her otherwise placid countenance.

I opened my mouth to ask more about her friend, Mel, but Sarah pulled herself back to discuss my son. The conversation deflected her sadness, so I spoke freely about my kids.

She looked at me while I talked, as if she were deeply interested; no glazed-over eyes; no glancing over my shoulder; no fidgeting to prompt me to cut my story short. The experience exhilarated me. She cared enough to hear my entire spiel. She encouraged me to complete my unfinished sentences and capture dangling thoughts. *So unlike John.*

Our thirty-minute water break had turned into forty, but I was as loath to end our conversation as I was to again expose myself to the heat of the day. The rock overhang's shade cooled the air by at least ten degrees, but the sun had advanced on us from a new angle, cutting our oasis in half.

I sighed in resignation. "I guess we should get moving."

Sarah stretched her arms above her head. "A siesta would be more sensible in this heat."

I cocked my ear toward a sound. "Shhh. Listen." I strained to hear more.

Sarah peered outside our rock lean-to and stood to survey our surroundings, her hand on the hilt of her knife.

"What do you see?" I whispered.

"Don't know. Something moved over that way."

I shook my socks to dislodge possible scorpions and shoved my feet into my boots before I joined her. Bright sun glared off rocks. Sharp shadows dotted the rough terrain. I shaded my eyes and scanned the trail in both directions and the desert on either side. No hikers. Nothing disturbed the red dust.

"Maybe just a big lizard," I said.

From under her wide-brimmed hat, Sarah stared out over the cactuses littering the canyon floor and shook her head. "Bigger," she said.

"Mountain lion?" NPS brochures had mentioned the rare cats. My eyes darted from boulder to boulder and to the branches of the few trees in the area. *Look big*, the pamphlets advised. *Don't run.*

"Probably nothing," Sarah said, but frowned as she swung her pack onto her shoulder. "Let's get going."

I knotted my bootlaces and shoved stuff into my pack. In sixty seconds we were flushed from our resting spot and on the move. Silent and on alert, we kept an eye on the austere landscape.

What ever lurked back at the lean-to was left behind, I hoped, but the conversation had opened new worries about my kids. Had John told James and Meagan about the divorce—and put his spin on it? Would they blame me? I'd rather face that cougar back there than disappoint my children.

12

PIT VIPER

I had taken the lead, but soon started to hobble. Sarah pretended not to notice and stayed behind. *I'm such a wimp.* Knee pain and throbbing toes began to consume my thoughts. I tried leaning on my poles and kicking my heel into the dirt to give my toes more room.

Complaining was pointless. I distracted myself by wondering what might have crept up on us back at the rest stop. The mountain lion no longer seemed likely. Ringtail cat? Gila monster? With no answers, I reflected on the cactus varieties, planned my dinner, and thought about Sarah's friend, Melanie. Odd, how your body goes into auto-mode. My legs kept putting one foot in front of the other.

Time passed unnoticed. The trail leveled out for longer stretches and our vigilance relaxed. My toes and knee took less of a beating and allowed me to focus on details. More sunlight, a wider trail. The canyon walls stood further apart, fewer cliffs. An insect buzzed nearby.

Sarah lagged behind, taking pictures.

"Oh, a bee!" Her cry sounded strange in the silence.

I turned to look back up the trail. She bent over to brush at her leg, and then jumped back.

"Snake!" Sarah screamed. "Snake!"

She and her forty-five pound pack came careening toward me with her arms flailing and her eyes wild. Her pack grazed and bumped along the canyon wall. Her feet tripped over rocks and sent them clattering over the edge. She was a runaway truck, and I stood in her way.

"Stop, Sarah, stop!" I held out my hands like a traffic cop, but in her panic, she could not see me. Afraid that she'd knock me into the abyss, I backed into the wall to let her charge past.

Suddenly aware of me, she jolted to a stop and put my body between her and the snake. I grabbed a hold of her shoulder straps and shook her.

"Sarah?" I said.

Her eyes riveted on a point back up the trail.

"Sarah, look at me."

She groaned, still gripped by terror.

"Shhh, shhhh." I crooned, as I had to my children.

She finally saw me and breathed a little easier.

"It's way back there, and you're here." I brushed stray curls off her forehead. "You're safe now."

Sarah nodded uncertainly. "Okay, okay. I'm okay."

"Yes, you are. Now, let's sit for a minute." I helped her unbuckle her straps, and she let her pack slide to the ground.

"Sit."

She sat on her pack, and I dropped mine next to her. "Tell me what happened."

Sarah held up her hands in a helpless gesture. "I heard a bee buzzing near my knee and swished it away." She reenacted the part. "I looked down and there was a snake right there next to my boot—and I ran. I freaked out. Sorry. I hate snakes."

"Did the snake bite you? There's blood on your arm."

Startled, she stared at the blood oozing bright red from a small hole on her forearm. Her face went from pale to ashen.

My panic threatened to show. "What kind of snake was it?"

"I don't know. Big, coiled up. *A snake.*" Her voice rose to soprano levels.

"Just relax. Let me get my first aid kit." I fumbled through Band-Aids, Immodium and Q-Tips while searching my brain for information on snake bites. Terror seized me when I remembered a scrap of advice. Step one: *Get to an emergency room immediately.* Oh, God!

"What should we do?" she asked. "Am I supposed to suck out the poison?" She looked at the flowing blood as if the snake might bite her again. She broke out in a sweat and lost all color.

"Sarah, lie down." I yanked my sleeping bag from my pack and threw it on the trail. She swayed and crumpled. I caught her head like a softball before it cracked on the ground.

"Sarah!" I straightened her legs, propped up her feet, and covered her with half of the sleeping bag. *God, help me!* I spilled water onto my bandana and dabbed her clammy face. *Did the poison hit her instantly?* I knelt next to her and patted her cheek while hunting through my memory for first-aid training. I checked her breathing and called her name.

A few harrowing minutes later her eyes fluttered.

"Sarah. Hi."

"I hate snakes."

"Me, too." I grinned at my friend. "Do you feel numbness, pain?"

Pink returned to Sarah's cheeks. "I think I fainted."

I prayed it was that simple. She struggled to sit up, but I held her down. Fear weakened her enough for me to win the battle.

"Sarah, please lie still and let me figure out what to do about the snake bite. Give me your arm." I quelled my shakes and swabbed the wound with an antiseptic wipe. "The main thing is to remain calm so the venom disperses very slowly." I made up facts as I went along, and she believed me.

"Does it hurt?" I asked.

"Yeah." She gave me a playful smirk and grimaced with each dab of antiseptic.

The area around the wound radiated heat. I put on a confident face, but my hands trembled while I poured water over her forearm and ripped open a bandage. I pressed the gauze on the wound and had visions of the poison blackening her skin. *How do I get help? Can the venom kill her?* I had to believe that an adult would be okay, but what did *I* know?

"Do we have to suck it out?" she asked again.

With her phobia, she should have studied snake bites.

"Experts don't recommend that anymore," I said. "The first aid books tell you to be gravity-neutral."

"What?" She squinted her eyes.

"The bite should be no higher and no lower than your heart, so stay down and put your arm to your side." I patted her shoulder. "It's a precaution in case the snake released a little venom. Here, take a clean gauze pad."

Sarah nodded and did as she was told. Her total trust intimidated me.

I don't want this responsibility. "Now, you relax," I said, "and I'll go search for the snake."

"What do you mean?" She started up. Fear drained color from her face again.

"To see what kind of snake it is." I stroked her arm and settled her down. "Don't worry and stay here."

With a trekking pole and Sarah's camera in hand, I sidled up the trail to where she'd started running. I inspected every rock and crevice, every shadow, until finding the snake coiled up in the shade of a boulder. He raised his tail and shook furiously. In spite of the serpent's bravado, he produced a soft buzz, not a threatening rattle.

Sarah's description had been less than accurate. This creature measured only about twenty inches. With a diamond-patterned back, it resembled the pink rattlesnake pictured in the canyon brochure. The reddish skin gave the snake perfect camouflage in the surrounding red dust.

I took a quick picture and backed away from the little guy. *What had the books said about rattlesnake bites?* I fought down panic and tried to recall snake-facts as I hurried back to Sarah. She seemed to be napping, but opened her eyes when I approached. She still looked wan, but strength had returned to her voice.

"Did you see it?"

"Yes, it's just a little snake, and the buzzing came from it, not a bee."

I sat on the ground next to her. "Here's our options. Either we rest here and wait for the next person to come along and send him to get help —or we walk slowly down ourselves, but you'd have to hold your arm still and up like this. Gravity neutral." I held my arm up with my elbow level with my chest. "If you got any venom, you need to see a doctor to get the anti-venom shot. We can't waste time."

Taken aback, weighing the options, she stared for a moment. She then nodded her understanding. "It could be hours before anyone hikes through here."

"True."

"I'd rather do something."

"It's your choice," I said. "Phantom Ranch is an hour or two away at a normal pace, but we'd have to go slow."

"I say we walk."

"Okay. You shouldn't overexert yourself, so we'll leave your backpack here. I'll leave a note and maybe some kind soul will bring your gear down." I ripped off the bottom of our permit and found a pen. "I'll carry your food and water and tie your sleeping bag to my pack. Anything else you absolutely need?"

"I guess not." She looked better, though not quite right. Was it the stress, the fear, or the poison? The faster I got her to civilization, the better.

Sarah stood, but wobbled. "I'm fine," she insisted and brushed off my helping hand.

"Put your arm up as high as your chest."

She put her right hand on her left shoulder to support her arm, and we began our journey. Sarah looked back at her pack with longing.

"If nothing else, we'll come back tomorrow to get your gear." My assertion didn't fool her.

What a pair we must have looked—if there were human eyes anywhere within miles to see us; her with her arm held up in an awkward position, and me limping behind. The few extra pounds on my back made a difference—or maybe the extra burden of worry weighed me down. I worried myself sick that walking might be the exact opposite of what we should do, but we trudged along in silence, not willing to share our burdens.

Sarah wanted to speed up, but I begged her to move slowly. We inched along for an hour or more, leaving the shade of the canyon walls

116

behind. The sun burned hotter, switchbacks were fewer, and our rate of descent decreased.

Sarah stopped. "Listen." The sound of a creek rushing over rocks was somewhere below us. "We're almost down."

Our morale improved and our steps came easier.

"Hello!" The voice came from behind us. We turned to see a young man trotting toward us. He was in his twenties, an athlete. The pack on his back bounced around but seemed not to hinder his speed. He at least had the good grace to breathe heavily. "My buddies and me read your note. They're bringing your gear."

Sarah brightened. "Thank you."

"I thought I should catch up to you to see how you're doing," he said.

"We're doing okay," I said. "Do you know anything about snake bites?"

"No, ma'am, sorry. Jim, my buddy, thinks walking out is probably a good move."

That relieved me some. Just having a healthy human nearby took pressure off me.

He took a swig from his water tube. "How about I run ahead to Phantom Ranch and find a ranger for you?"

"That'd be great," I said. "We'll rest here until the ranger comes." I hoped that the venom hadn't already spread too far.

Sarah nodded agreement, but with some consternation.

"Anything else I can do for you, ma'am?" His youth and cheerfulness lightened the whole situation. I wished he would stay.

"No, we're good. Sarah?"

"I'm okay."

"So what's your name?" I asked to stall him.

"Jeff."

He looked barely old enough to shave.

"This is Sarah. I'm Amy. If you can't find a ranger, will you come back and tell us?"

"Yes, ma'am. I'll drop my gear and run back. Might take an hour or two." He bopped up and down, anxious to leave. "See ya later." He waved and trotted away, so we settled ourselves in at the shade of an overhanging rock and watched him until he rounded a corner.

"He's cute," she said.

I rolled my eyes and wondered at her recuperative powers. "Way too young to even think about."

"You like him," she teased.

"Of course I do. He's the Boy Scout who is going to rescue us."

Sarah's mental state had improved. Still, I hoped her pallor was from worry, not snake venom. I made conversation to pass the time. "Did you notice his little pack?"

"See, I knew you liked him."

"What? Oh, stop it. I mean his backpack. It's a simple design, probably carrying eighteen pounds or less, another ultra-light hiker."

"That's not for me." She grinned like an imp. "I like to bring as much as I can carry."

"Well, those guys back there will thank you for that."

Her musical laughter lightened my mood. Without thinking, I took a gulp from my water bottle.

"Will you hand me my water?" she asked.

"Uh, no. If I remember correctly, you're not to have anything to drink or eat."

"You're kidding?" Her voice turned shrill. "Which is worse, to die of thirst or from snake poison?"

I shrank from her harsh tone. "How am I supposed to know? I'm repeating what the books say." I tugged her water bottle from my pack and thumped it in the dust between us.

She let the bottle sit there. "I'm sorry." Her voice went back to normal. "I couldn't have done this without you, but I'm parched."

"Take a sip." I put my head in my hands and closed my eyes.

She snatched up the Nalgene bottle and flipped open the top, but sipped slowly and put the container down before drinking an ounce. "I promise I'll be fine," she said.

"You're supposed to be gravity-neutral." I sighed, tired and exasperated.

"Okay, you're right." With her left hand she pulled her sleeping bag from my pack and tossed it on the ground where she settled herself with her wounded arm at her side. Within minutes, she slept. Her soft, even breathing seemed to say that all was right in her world. I envied her. Sleep was beyond me, but I closed my eyes and willed my body to relax and the worry to drain away. Numbness would have to do.

With my eyes closed, I listened to the canyon's quiet melody until a distinct distant sound interrupted. My ears homed in. Footsteps. I leaned forward peering into the bright sunlight and waited until the owners of the feet came into view. Two young men hustled down the trail with Sarah's pack suspended between them. I gave Sarah a nudge and stood to greet them.

"Hello!" I waved and waited for them to approach. "Are you Jeff's friends?"

"Yes, ma'am, most of the time." The clean-cut young men beamed and introduced themselves as Jim and Conor.

From the shadows, Sarah yelled hello and waved from her prone position. "I'm supposed to stay gravity-neutral."

"Yes, ma'am." Conor lugged the pack into Sarah's shade and stepped back, running his fingers over his stubborn cowlick.

She thanked him, but frowned at the open backpack and disorganized mess inside. "What the . . ."

"Sorry, ma'am," the young man said. "I repacked your stuff as well as I could."

"What happened," I asked, examining the broken zipper. "Did an animal get at her pack?"

Conor exchanged a look with his buddy who took a position at his side. "We saw a man climbing down the slope near the pack," Jim said. "We figured the gear was his until we read the note."

Sarah reached for her pack, but I motioned for her to lay still. "I'll inventory your things." I pulled her tent, cooking supplies, food bag, and clothing from the pack and lay them across the rocks.

"Everything is there," she said, eyeing each item, "except my second water bottle. I guess he just needed water."

"What'd the guy look like?" I asked the men.

"Tall, thin," Jim said. "Like he'd been deployed in Iraq too long. We called to him, but he kept going."

I looked out over the desert land and wondered what caused a man to roam the unfriendly terrain without adequate provisions. *These men would have helped him. We would've shared our water.*

Jim, who was as broad-shouldered as a made-for-TV lifeguard, asked about Sarah's condition. Conor, shorter, as muscled as that ram had been, and with all the exuberance of a ten-year-old boy, wanted to hear about the snake.

Sarah invited them into the shade. We all settled in around her as if she was a turkey on a Thanksgiving table, and she took the attention in stride. Jim and Conor seemed content to wait with us until the ranger arrived.

The young men had hiked from the North Rim that morning and planned to stay the night at Indian Gardens and pick up the Tonto Trail the following day. They assured us that they were in no hurry and suggested they carry Sarah's pack to Phantom Ranch on their way down. I believe they would have carried Sarah, too, if we asked them. They were strong enough—in their mid-twenties and in excellent shape.

"Are you firemen by any chance?" I asked.

They both sat up straighter and squared their shoulders. "No ma'am, we're Marines."

I got up from my rock to shake their hands, intending to thank them for their service, but tears formed. Their self-sacrifice and patriotism put a lump in my throat. I could only manage, "Thanks."

They smiled, but averted their eyes. "Thank you, ma'am." Jim busied himself with the tube of his hydration unit, while Conor took interest in a map.

"Too bad Kylie isn't to meet these young men or Jeff," I thought. Any one of them would have been a better match for her than the lump she had chased after.

When my voice returned I asked them about their deployments. They responded by asking each other: "Do you remember . . ." or "What about the time . . ." They told their stories more easily to each other rather than to speak to Sarah and me directly. That was okay. We got to hear about their experiences without intruding or pretending that we could understand what they had gone through.

After a while our questions ended, and we each leaned back in thought. The boys refused the snacks I offered. Sarah napped, and we waited.

In time, I heard the thump of footsteps. Our new friend, Jeff, jogged up the trail with a ranger right behind him. They ran with the ease of marathon runners. My heart quickened when I realized that Ranger Hawk had come to our rescue.

"Sarah, more heroes are here." A thousand pounds of worry lifted from my shoulders.

"Yahoo."

"Hey!" I called. My smile of welcome must have spread from ear to ear.

"Good afternoon, Amy, Sarah," said Ranger Hawk. He shook hands and introduced himself to Jim and Conor before the Marines moved a discreet distance away.

I was pleased that the ranger remembered us from our meeting on the North Rim, but he was all business. "Jeff tells me one of you was bitten by a snake," he said.

Sarah raised her hand. "I'm gravity-neutral."

"I'm impressed," the ranger said. "Did you get a look at the snake?"

Sarah's face reddened. "Well, yes and no. Amy took a picture."

Ranger Hawk turned to me, and I showed him the camera. He nodded. "That's our pink rattlesnake. How long ago?"

I checked my watch. "What do you think, Sarah, maybe two hours?"

She shrugged. "I guess. Feels longer."

"That's good. Symptoms of envenomization generally show up within two hours." He looked into Sarah's face. "Do you feel tingling in your tongue or your lips?"

Sarah ran her tongue over her lips and shook her head.

"Let me take your pulse and temperature to make sure." He stuck a thermometer under Sarah's tongue and put his fingers on her wrist.

With little else to do, I appraised our rescuer. His football-player sized hands tended to Sarah gently. He had a clean, open, and intelligent face, but was not what you'd call good looking. Maybe forty-eight. A bald spot highlighted the top of his head, but not an ounce of fat on him. Well-defined calf muscles.

"Normal." His pronouncement shook me from my reverie. I looked up to see Sarah eying me with a knowing grin.

"Let's take a look at the bite," he said.

Sarah indicated her right arm, and the ranger knelt beside her with a first aid kit at his side. He easily removed the sweaty bandage and peered at the wound. He unwrapped an antiseptic wipe and gently cleaned the area. "Not bad, a little swelling. The skin still looks healthy, good color." His brow furrowed. "Huh, are you sure you were bitten?"

"Well, yeah. I think. All I know is I saw a snake at my foot. I ran away and there was blood on my arm."

"This doesn't look like a typical snake bite."

"You're kidding," she said.

"Mm-mm." He peered again at Sarah's arm and reached into his kit for a tweezer. Sarah winced as he prodded her wound.

"Ah. There it is." He held up the extraction.

"Is that a fang?" Sarah's eyes were wide.

"No," he said, "but almost as painful. You impaled your arm on an agave cactus spine."

I replayed the incident in my mind, Sarah barreling toward me. Yep, greenery had sprouted along the trail. I knew he was right. Relief flooded through me while Sarah hid her face.

"I'm such an idiot," she exclaimed.

"This is my fault," I said. "A snake bite made sense at the time. I'm sorry we created all this fuss." I steeled myself for the ranger's annoyance or anger, but instead he smiled at our discomfort.

"I'm so embarrassed." Sarah groaned and sat up from her gravity-neutral position.

"Don't be," Ranger Hawk insisted. "Now we don't have to rush you to an emergency room for anti-venom shots." He swabbed Sarah's arm with antiseptic and covered the wound with a bandage.

"If you ladies will excuse me, I'll cancel the helicopter." He brushed the grit from his knees, walked several yards away, and spoke into his radio.

"Helicopter?" I raised my eyebrows at Sarah.

"I am so embarrassed." Sarah knelt on the ground stuffing her gear into her pack. "Let's get moving."

While she packed, I approached our three good Samaritans. "Sarah will be fine, so I want to thank you and let you get on your way."

Jeff and the others stood. "Is she okay? We'll carry your stuff down to the ranch if you want."

I loved their eagerness to help. Ranger Hawk joined us and answered for me.

"We're going to wait awhile longer and, when the ladies are ready, I'll escort them down. Thanks for your help, guys." The ranger and the younger men did the manly handshake, shoulder thumping thing before the Marines set out at a fast pace.

What a thing of beauty, watching those three young bodies jog off in formation. They were built to pit themselves against the rigors of the canyon. I envied their self-assurance and strength, but hoped that testosterone and overconfidence never led them to take foolish chances. The canyon had beaten many athletes in the prime of their lives.

The ranger, too, watched the boys trot into the distance. "Good men," he said with husky satisfaction.

"Yes, indeed," I said, noting their youth, but appreciating the maturity of the man next to me. "Well, Ranger Hawk, thank you for coming to our rescue." I offered my hand in formal greeting, but let my eyes twinkle at him.

He engulfed my hand with his calloused paw. "My pleasure, but call me Glen. When Jeff reported that two good-looking women were in trouble, I raced up here."

I liked the tune of his laugh. "I am so sorry to drag you out here needlessly."

A grin dimpled his cheeks. "No problem. My day needed excitement."

"So if the snake bite had been real, did we do the right thing by hiking this far?"

"Probably," he said. "Out here there is not much else you can do. If help was nearby, Sarah should have rested."

I was extremely relieved that Sarah was okay and that I didn't do anything to screw up. "She fainted, or seemed to go into shock up there, and I was frantic."

"Really? Well, thinking you've been bitten is traumatic." He looked over at Sarah, who had calmed down and sat on a rock in the shade. He ducked into Sarah's shade. "Amy says you fainted. How do you feel now?"

"I'm fine," she said. "Just have a stress headache, I think."

"Do you have enough water?" he asked. "Dehydration can cause a headache."

"My nurse wouldn't let me drink." Sarah winked at me, popped an ibuprofen and drained the last of her water bottle.

Glen poured half of his bottle into hers. "Drink up," he said. "Rest as long as you want. We'll leave when you're ready."

The sun had moved and our patch of shade shifted, so I put my sit-pad nearer to Sarah leaving enough room for Ranger Glen to sit.

"I have more nuts and raisins, if you'd like some." I wanted to get a pair of dry socks anyway, so I got up to retrieve the snacks from my pack. I offered the baggie to the ranger and to Sarah.

"Thanks," he said. He munched and seemed to consider the food, but said, "You know, I can drill your toe for you."

"What?"

"You're limping," he said. "I'll bet you have a blackened toe nail. It throbs, right?"

I nodded. "But the limp is caused mostly by my twisted knee."

"Without ice there's not much I can do for your knee, but let me take a look at your toe."

I'd let him look and hoped he had a suggestion for pain relief, but there was no way I'd allow anyone to drill. I peeled off my sweaty sock, and he took my foot into his hand, cupping the heel gently.

"Yep, this happens all the time. People aren't used to descending anything as steep as the canyon. You have blood pooling under your nail." He examined the nail more closely. "You should let me drill."

Uncomfortable with the focus on my toe, I teased, "I'll bet you say that to all the girls."

"No, only the one I want to get to know better."

My mouth dropped open and my mind went blank. I had no snappy comeback. I became aware that he still cradled my foot in his hand. My skin buzzed and my entire body came to attention. I looked at Sarah for help, but she rolled her eyes. I took my foot back. "Thanks, but I think my toe will be fine."

"Tonight when the pain is bad, you'll think of me."

Egad. Was he kidding? His straight face told me nothing.

Sarah finally came to my aid. "Maybe it's time to get going."

I inserted my bruised toes back into my socks and laced my boots. I extracted my battered hat from my pack and jammed it on my head, suddenly conscious of its ridiculous look. If I didn't need sun protection, I would have stuffed the ratty thing back in my pack.

"Interesting hat." Ranger Glen's eyes hinted at mischief.

"I like it." I smoothed out the brim with aplomb before toiling inelegantly to my feet and collecting my gear.

"I'll carry your backpack to take weight off your knee," Glen said.

"Absolutely not." No self-respecting backpacker lets someone else carry their gear, and I wanted very much to be a self-respecting backpacker. He shrugged, and I hoisted the cumbersome pack and twisted into the straps, hoping I looked graceful. He took the lead, then Sarah, then me. There was no way I was going to fall behind, blackened toes or not.

* * *

The stream we heard earlier came into view. Rocks dotted the creek bed causing water to find its way over and around the obstacles any way it could. Crashing water droplets dispersed a fine mist which drifted over our hot skin.

Sarah opened her arms wide to the spray. "Ah, that feels wonderful." She seemed to have forgotten the 'snake bite'.

"What's the name of this creek, Glen?" I knew its name from the map, but wanted to start a conversation to keep my mind off my aches and pains.

He took on a tour guide demeanor. "This is Phantom Creek which runs through the Phantom Ranch and into the Colorado River. When we get reports of snakes, they're typically in reedy areas like this."

He kept talking and I listened. The ranger's bank of information impressed me, and I enjoyed hearing his stories of rescues and odd tourists. "The Park Service seems to depend upon you a lot," I said. "You were on the North Rim to take our report, and now you're at Bright Angel campground. That seems like a big territory for you to cover. Is that normal?"

"Normal? No, but the morning after the attack on your friend, we had a report of a suspicious person along North Kaibab. My supervisor asked for a volunteer, so I hiked down to keep an eye on the trail and double up at Cottonwood and then Indian Garden." He glanced at his watch. "I should be going on duty right now."

"You mean you're not on duty now?"

"No. I'm on my own time." He casually motioned to a cactus. "Be careful. That's an agave."

While I contemplated the prehistoric plant, Sarah pressed the issue of Ranger Glen being with us when he should be on-duty. "You know, if you need to report for duty, we'll get to the campground on our own. The trail is easy to follow, and we're doing fine."

"Sarah's right," I said, "and I'm worried about getting in late and not getting a tent site. Maybe you could hike ahead and reserve a site for us—and report for duty?"

He cocked his head like an attentive German Shepherd and looked at Sarah and then at me. "Okay," he decided. "I'll let you get rid of me. Are you sure you won't need help?"

"No, seriously, we'll be fine," I said. "Just slow."

"I'll run ahead then. When you get in, stop at the cantina, and I'll buy the lemonade."

My mouth suddenly tasted like lint, so I reached for my water bottle laced with lemon-flavored electrolytes. "Give us an hour and a half before sending out a posse, and then we'll take you up on that lemonade."

Ranger Glen hiked off, leaving us in his dust. I was sorry to see him go, but also relieved. "I can limp now. How about a five minute rest, and then we'll head for the lemonade?"

Sarah laughed, and we both let ourselves sag.

"Snakes," she said.

"Where?"

"I mean, let's check out the area before we sit."

"Ah, once bitten, twice shy. Isn't that what they say?" I couldn't resist, and she groaned.

I ran my pole under and behind rocks and into the crack at the back of the rock base, and then made myself comfortable far away from the threatening cacti. We sipped from our water bottles and relaxed. The presence of men had infused the air with tension, not necessarily unpleasant tension, but still, their absence liberated us.

"You know he likes you." Sarah regarded me seriously. "He hiked down from the North Rim in hopes he'd see you again; and when Jeff told him one of us had a snake bite, he ran right out here."

I suspected she was right, and the idea warmed me, but I didn't want to admit my feelings. "That's his job."

"He *volunteered* to hike down, and he came out here *off-duty*," she insisted.

"He's being a gentleman."

"Maybe so, but he likes you."

"It doesn't matter," I said. "I have a husband."

"And you're flirting with Glen, why?"

"Nobody takes that seriously," I said. "Besides there is nothing wrong with sending men home feeling a little more attractive, maybe amused that some nice woman stroked his ego. I'm sure he flirts with every woman that hikes through here, and I'll bet he gets a good response. Women love a man in uniform."

"You mean the khaki shorts and Smokey the Bear hat?" Her laughter echoed through the canyon.

I shot Sarah my most baleful glare, but she thought that was funny, too, and hooted even louder. I couldn't resist. In spite of myself, I got the giggles.

Whoever said 'Laughter is the best medicine' was right. We were soon perked up and ready to hike.

13

BRIGHT ANGEL CAMPGROUND

Elevation: 2,480 ft.

Fifty minutes later Sarah and I hobbled like refugees into Phantom Ranch. I almost resented the few people we passed, all of whom looked healthy and rested.

My energy level rose when I spotted a cluster of cabins. Constructed of dark wood and river stone, they fit into the landscape with an aura of the Old West, as though they had invited a century's worth of hikers up their stone steps. Further along, the path brought us to a larger stone structure under a canopy of shade trees.

"Welcome to the Phantom Ranch." Ranger Glen's voice boomed from the dusty yard of the cantina.

"We made it." Though my aching body said otherwise, I infused my words with cheerfulness to give the impression that we had been up to the challenge of the trail.

"Why don't you take a seat at the picnic table, and I'll get each of us a lemonade, or would you prefer a beer?"

"Lemonade sounds great," I said.

Sarah wiped the sweat from her forehead with her bandana. "Cold beer for me." She offered Glen money, but he waved the cash away.

"My treat," he said.

He bounded up the stone steps into the cantina, catching the screen door behind him with his foot before it slammed shut. That was a practiced move. I wondered how often his job brought him to the Ranch and if he treated all the guests as well as he was treating us. I took stock of the many visitors and our surroundings. My body may have been bone-weary and sore, but my mind was thrilled to be there.

"I love this architecture," I said. The cantina's rock walls and chimney looked solid and timeless. "I can picture this building riding out a flood surging through the canyon, washing the newer cabins downstream."

Sarah had undone the bandage and examined the wound on her arm. She glanced at the cantina as if for the first time, impressed. "Yeah, looks like it's been here forever."

"Since 1920 anyway."

"I'm sure glad to be here," Sarah said and got up to rummage through her backpack. She came back with her jellybeans, offering me the baggie.

"I wonder if we'll see the Marines again," I said. "They were so sweet."

Sarah chewed her jellybean before speaking. "They're long gone, I bet, doing a forced march to Indian Garden and the South Rim."

I never understood the lure of a testosterone-fueled forced march. At any rate, my hopes for Kylie meeting the Marines were dashed.

Party noises drifted from the screened windows. Hikers, runners, and tourists came and went. Two robust young women exited the cantina dressed in skimpy shorts and moisture-wicking singlets. They stretched in various yoga positions. The taller of the lithe female specimens stood on one leg and reached up and pulled her foot to the back of her head.

I wondered how many men ogled the athletic ritual from behind the screened windows. I remembered then that Sarah might have the same response to the display as the male spectators, but her expression was like my own—painful disbelief. The young women jogged off.

"Gawd!" The word burst from Sarah's mouth. "I feel like a fat, old cow."

"You and me both."

Our images of ourselves suffered in comparison to the girls made of rubber and spandex, but we enjoyed a bonding moment and soothed our bruised egos.

Ranger Glen swung the screen door open while juggling three large, plastic cups. He handed me a drink. "Lemonade for the lady." His bright brown eyes held mine and rebuilt a bit of my ego.

"Cheers!" We clinked plastic cups. The cold lemonade went down smoothly and tasted especially delicious; maybe I was relieved to be off the trail, maybe I was glad to find two good friends. The lemonade revived my body and made me eager to find our home for the night.

"Were you able to reserve a campsite for us?" I asked.

"I pulled some strings," Glen boasted playfully, but then paused. "Honestly," he said, "I didn't have to. Your permit holds your site until late this evening, but I did scout around and saved a good one with shade and a little stream."

"Sounds perfect." Sarah swung her heavy pack onto her back. "Show us the way."

We followed Ranger Glen past a wooden rail corral with several mules in residence. The earth in and around the corral had a green tint; dry manure had been pulverized by the trampling hooves of daily mule trains. I didn't flinch and tromped right through the parsley dust.

The path led over a well-constructed iron bridge spanning Phantom Creek and then narrowed before entering Bright Angel Campground, cutting through lush shrubbery and past neat square campsites occupied by a variety of aerodynamic tents. The area resembled a well-organized botanical garden, with the creek bordering one side and a cliff wall on the other. I was home.

"Here we are." Ranger Glen stepped onto a tiny path through low growing shrubs and over a thin burbling stream. "Can I help you set up?"

"Thanks, but we've got the routine down to a science." I deposited my pack on the picnic table and pulled out the tent.

"Okay, then." He seemed reluctant to leave and looked up and down the path before asking, "Will you have dinner at the cantina tonight?"

"We have reservations for the six-thirty seating," I said.

"Good. Do you mind if I join you?"

I glanced at Sarah. She shrugged, so I accepted.

One of his dimples appeared. "I'll see you in an hour or so. Sarah, keep that puncture wound clean."

I returned his wave. Sarah stopped unpacking and watched him leave. "We're going to see him a lot, aren't we?"

"Not if we don't want to. This is our trip and we are partners. Okay?"

"Sure, okay." She seemed not herself.

Our tent was up and our food stored in the ammo box in less than ten minutes. I slid my inflated sleeping pad into the tent and tossed in my sleeping bag. I leaned in to stow my clothes and decided to collapse into my bedding. Every muscle thanked me.

"Are you all right?" Sarah asked.

"I'm resting."

"Can I get my stuff in there?"

"Sure." I unzipped the tent for her and she threw in her sleeping pad and bag.

"I'd love to get a thirty-minute nap in," I said and a yawn nearly escaped me.

"Mind if I join you?"

I scooted over and she flopped herself down on her side of the tent. "Oh, that feels good." She fell asleep instantly. Her rhythmic breathing lulled me to sleep a few minutes later.

* * *

"Hello in the tent." A male voice pulled me out of sleep.

As if drugged and disoriented, I called, "Hello?"

"Park Service. I am here to check your permit."

"Okay, hold on."

Sarah roused herself and pulled up her legs to give me room to crawl from the tent. Still groggy, I struggled to my feet. Before me stood a short, sinewy Hispanic man, stern and authoritative.

"Good afternoon, ma'am." He frowned. "Your permit is not displayed as required. That is a ticket-able offense."

From the tent I heard a low, "Oh, for gripe's sake."

I covered Sarah's outburst with a friendly smile while looking at his name tag. "Oh, Ranger Geraldo, hello. I was hoping I'd meet you. Glen

Hawk said you'd be the man to go to if I needed help here at Bright Angel." I fished the torn permit out of the side pocket of my pack and handed it to him.

Geraldo loosened his shoulders slightly. "Ranger Hawk. I saw him earlier."

"He mentioned that you take care of everything here," I said, "the reservations, the injuries, even the plants."

The ranger's pride and ego visibly grew. He checked our number off of his list and handed our permit back to me. His voice softened as if to take me into his confidences. "Yes, there is much to do. Visitors do not understand how important these plantings are to resist erosion. I planted many of them myself. People must not trample them."

"They're beautiful," I said, and they were. I had taken them for granted and was relieved Geraldo hadn't seen me take a short-cut into our campsite. The ranger outlined the usual ticket-able offenses and instructed us to use the ammo boxes to store our food. Sarah had joined me, and we listened politely.

Suddenly, Geraldo ran from our campsite. "Stop. Stop!" He waved his arms and chased after an older backpacker who had trudged through the plantings into the campsite opposite ours. Geraldo berated the man until a more diplomatic camper calmed the situation and begged forgiveness on behalf of the older man. Geraldo relented and let them off without a fine. He continued his rounds shaking his head in frustration.

Sarah and I watched the comedy sketch play out and chuckled, glad that he had forgotten us. Sarah glanced at her watch. "He woke us up just in time. Dinner is in twenty minutes."

We zipped up the tent, grabbed our fanny packs and hung our headlamps around our necks, ready for nightfall. In familiar territory now, we strolled through the lush shrubbery, across the iron bridge, and past the crowded pen of mules.

Even from a distance, I immediately recognized Ranger Glen. His strong jaw, his solid chest. Dressed in civilian clothes, he sat on a tree stump in the cantina's yard flanked by two female visitors who murmured their good-bye as we approached. Glen stood up like the lord of the manor and welcomed us with a bright grin. "Hello, Amy, Sarah."

"Hi, Glen." A hug seemed inappropriate, a handshake too formal, so I stopped a few feet short and smiled. "We met your friend, Geraldo. He wanted very badly to give us a ticket."

Glen chuckled. "How did you get away?"

"That's a whole different story." Sarah and I laughed together.

"Hey, you guys." Kylie bounded over and gave Sarah and me a hug. Eric shuffled behind her with his hands deep in his pockets. His *hello* was a barely discernible grunt. Kylie took Eric's arm and intertwined her fingers in his. She pointedly caught my eye and ran her other hand down Eric's smooth, unbitten forearm. *Okay, so he wasn't the man who attacked her.* I still didn't like him.

I introduced Eric to Ranger Glen who pumped the younger man's hand and greeted him heartily. While Glen drew Eric out with questions about his Appalachian Trail adventures, Sarah and I pulled Kylie aside.

"Is Eric treating you okay?" Sarah wanted to know.

"He's great. I'm like having the best time." Kylie acted unnecessarily eager.

"We missed you last night at Cottonwood," I said.

Kylie shrugged. "Yeah, we got in early, set up, and hiked to some waterfall and didn't get back 'til late."

Something didn't ring true. Kylie was too vague, so I prodded for information. "I'd love to see the waterfall. What did it look like?"

"Really sweet. You should go there." She smiled as if she had answered my question.

"Where is it?"

"I don't know. Ribbon Falls; somewhere between here and Cottonwood."

"We can hike back tomorrow," Sarah said. "I'd like to paint a waterfall."

"I wish I could," I said. "My knee needs to rest, but you should go."

While Sarah questioned Kylie about the waterfall, I listened for clues as to what troubled me about the girl's story. I detected nothing. Maybe my suspicious mind heard problems that didn't exist.

"Come and get it!" A red-faced woman with a blond braid hanging down her back unlocked the screen door and waved us in. Each of us handed her our dinner ticket and filed up the steps. Kylie slipped a ticket into Eric's hand. He followed her through the door and to the far side of the room where there were seats for all five of us. Ranger Glen pulled out a chair for me and then for Sarah and sat between us.

With diners shoulder-to-shoulder, the room seemed chaotic, but the din was charged with energy and camaraderie. Hikers, rafters, and mule riders, each in their own groups, were united by a common hunger. Everyone, eager but polite, reached for big bowls of salad which made their way down each row of tables. The famous Hiker's Stew and vegetarian chili came next. We ladled the steaming concoctions into man-sized soup bowls.

"This looks delicious." I breathed in the savory steam.

"Hmm-hmm." Sarah had just bitten into a crusty roll.

"This stew's my favorite," Glen announced. He didn't say another word until he consumed a second bowl. Plentiful food and the sound of clinking dishes minimized conversation. People became sated, sat back and patted their stomachs.

The various groups switched to party mode and the noise level rose considerably. Even Eric loosened up and talked about the Appalachian Trail. Sarah and I peppered him with questions, listening for untruths.

"What was the hardest part of the hike?" Sarah asked.

"Loneliness," Eric said. "I went days without seeing anybody, so I'd sidetrack into town just to hear people talk."

Glen leaned forward, urging Eric on. He seemed to believe what he heard. The conversation at our table attracted others, giving our experienced hikers an audience. Glen, with a beer in his hand, kept us entertained with ranger jokes, animal adventures, and tales of stupid tourist tricks. I glanced at the dozen or so rapt listeners and liked the effect that Glen had on them.

People began to wander out and the room cleared enough to move around. My knee had stiffened, so I got up to explore the place.

The shelves lining the walls were filled with books, maps, games, animal bones, and other treasures. A sign above a coin jar read, *Feed the mules. Donate your heavy change.* If I had had any change, I would have rid myself of the weight. I picked up a post card with an image of Phantom Ranch's cantina which was stamped *Mailed by mule from the bottom of the Grand Canyon.* I wondered if I would beat a postcard home and then remembered there was no one home to receive it in any case. I dropped the card into the display and moved along.

Haphazard notes and flyers tacked to a bulletin board fluttered in the breeze and caught my attention. I read several cryptic notes. *Crash – Here early. Tonto camp tonight – Stomper.* Another less helpful message read, *Rooster – We were here. Where are you? – Cow Patty.*

The notes were like scraps torn from a travel journal. The fun bits and pieces were enough to pique my interest in the characters with odd names, but too scant to tell a story. I was engrossed in the snippets and announcements when a shadow eclipsed the messages.

"Will you attend?" His voice warmed me like creamy hot chocolate.

"What?"

Glen's finger tapped a Park Service flyer. "I'm presenting an interpretive program about canyon bats tomorrow night at seven-thirty."

I smiled, but didn't turn in his direction. "Bats?"

"They're very interesting and necessary creatures."

"I thought you said you were headed back to Cottonwood in the morning."

"The ranger scheduled to do the program is sick in bed, so I volunteered."

"They're lucky you're so versatile."

"I do what I can." He placed his hand over his heart and bowed in mock humility.

"Are you two coming?" Sarah, with a knowing look on her face, held the door open.

"Right behind you." I hadn't realized everyone had left. The waitresses were clearing the mess of dishes and cleaning the room. Glen stood aside for me to exit and then followed, catching the screen door behind him before it slammed.

Not quite ready to venture into complete darkness, we stopped in the pools of light coming from the cantina's windows. Sarah and Kylie chatted as Eric tugged at Kylie's hand.

"You'll love the waterfall," Kylie assured Sarah. "Okay, okay. Bye everybody. See you at breakfast." Kylie giggled and let Eric drag her toward her tent.

With a feeling of unease, I watched them go. "I still don't like him."

"All we can do is keep an eye on him," Sarah said.

"Are you talking about Eric?" Glen asked.

"Yeah, we don't think he's good for Kylie. What impression did you get, Glen?"

He squinted his eyes to block the beam of my head lamp. "Don't know. I think he exaggerates. He obviously hiked parts of the Appalachian, but I doubt he completed the entire trail. He doesn't know enough about menu planning and supply drops."

"Something isn't right," I said. "He should be watched."

"I'll keep my eyes open," Glen said, "but he's probably just a braggart."

Sarah and I said goodnight to Glen and watched him step from the pool of light and disappear into the dark before switching on our headlamps to make our way to our campsite. Our tent seemed like home, welcoming and cozy.

We wasted no time before preparing for bed and climbing in. I thought I'd drop off to sleep immediately, but my nerves buzzed. "Are you awake?"

"Yep," she said. "I've been laying here thinking it's been quite a day."

"Me, too. How's your arm?"

"Sore to the touch, but not otherwise," she said. "How's your knee and toe?"

"I'll live. Glen was right about one thing, maybe I should've let him drill. My toe throbs."

"Here." She sat up and tucked a pile of clothing under my foot. "Keep it elevated." She lay back down. "Is that all you're thinking about him?"

"It'd be a lie, if I said no. I like him, but I don't want even a platonic relationship with him. I've got a marriage to figure out."

"What's up with your husband?" she asked.

I blew out a slow breath, deciding how much of my personal problem to divulge. "We've grown apart, as if we're orbiting two different planets."

"What does that mean?"

"We do so little together. He won't do anything I like to do. At least, I'll attend his corporate dinners. I clean up pretty well, you know."

"I believe I pointed that out," she said.

"You did. Thank you. I can stand up against those trophy wives at his country club." I paused, suddenly depressed. "Maybe not. I've gotten too old. Several times he suggested I get breast implants."

Sarah stifled a guffaw. "That's crazy. I can't imagine you with these glued on your little chest."

I heard her thumping her ample bosom in the dark. She was outrageous and lightened my mood.

"That doesn't bother me." I took a deep breath and let it out. "I managed Dad's business. Met ordinary people. John couldn't imagine why I wanted them as friends. I covered for him, but they eventually stopped inviting us."

Sarah sniffed. "Sounds like you devoted your life to him."

"I tried. My mother preached that a wife should dedicate her life to her husband. By the time I turned fifty, that attitude seemed ridiculous. This year I found my own interests—and I trained for this trip."

"He wasn't happy?"

"Not in the least."

"Well, nobody likes change."

"Exactly. He refused to try anything new, but griped at my full schedule. I've had to go alone to most events. He probably went alone to some cocktail party tonight."

"I'm sure he'll go home alone, too." She reached out and patted my arm.

"Probably." I didn't have much confidence in that and couldn't work up any distress over the possibilities either.

"You sound depressed," she said.

"I guess I am."

"Maybe when you get home, he will have missed you so much he'll treat you like a queen."

"Maybe so," I said, knowing nothing was further from the truth. "Good night, Sarah."

I couldn't stand to tell her the rest of the story. She had been a good listener and deserved my silence.

14

Day 5 - PHANTOM RANCH - Elevation: 2,546 ft.

I awoke before dawn with the delicious feeling that I had nothing to do but relax for the day. Already I heard the soft thuds of boots on the dirt path ten feet away. Hikers marched past our tent, getting an early start to beat the heat. I did not envy them. My plan for our layover day really wasn't a plan at all . . . Go with the flow and no hiking.

The soft morning light gradually warmed the yellow nylon of our tent, suffusing the interior with a buttery glow. Surprised to see Sarah still snoozing in her sleeping bag, I barely moved so as not to wake her.

Like everything else she did, she slept in a carefree, uninhibited way. No tight fetal position for her. She sprawled half out of her mummy bag with her arms flung over her head.

Sarah would have made a fine sister. What would it have been like to have a close sister; someone who knew your mistakes, faults and foibles and loved you anyway? A champion for your dreams and secret wishes? A pang of disloyalty to my sister hit me, and I regretted that our age difference kept distance between us.

Sarah opened one eye. "Good morning." At least that's what I think she said.

She put her watch in front of her eye and groaned. "Six o'clock. How long have you been awake?"

"I've been dozing off and on since before dawn."

"You should've woke me up," she grunted. "Did you fix coffee?"

I cringed. *How could I be so selfish?*

On other mornings she'd brought me hot tea, and I never thought to return the favor. "I am so sorry. I didn't think of it."

140

I pushed my sleeping bag off and grabbed my camp shoes. "I'll heat the water now."

"I'm kidding." She laughed and blocked my exit. "Relax, this is our day to lounge around."

I flopped back onto my bedding, relieved that I didn't have to start the day yet. "So what's your plan for the day?"

"We could hike to the waterfall Kylie mentioned," she suggested. "I want to spend time painting."

I held up my hand. "No hiking for me. My knee may heal up if I baby it today."

"I hoped it would be better this morning." Her disappointment showed. "What will you do?"

"Not much. Roam around here, find something to read. I'm looking forward to it."

"I hate to leave you on your own."

"I'll be fine," I insisted. "You should go—find a quiet place to paint."

Sarah seemed relieved to have my blessing and suddenly became energized. She dumped out her pillow sack to find a semi-clean T-shirt and pair of shorts, dressed, and exited the tent in two minutes. She smiled back at me.

"I'm firing up the stove for my coffee. Do you want tea?"

"I'll do it." I threw off the covers. "Really. After I find my clothes."

I dressed and rolled out of the tent, feeling rumpled and refreshed, and then sat to enjoy the new day. So many hikers had pulled up stakes early that we had our end of the camp to ourselves. We lounged in the sun, sipped our hot drinks and commented on the stragglers heading out. A troop of mule-riding tourists waited to depart next. The dozen or so mules milled about on the opposite side of the creek, jostling for position. There must have been cliques or a seniority system at work, but eventually the mules sorted themselves out and lined up nose to tail to plod down the trail.

Our indolence couldn't last in the face of hunger, so we roused ourselves and headed for Phantom Ranch fifteen minutes early. We had been lucky to get a last minute reservation and did not want to miss breakfast. Outside the cantina, a dozen people waiting to be fed, milled around much like the mules. The door remained locked while the staff cleaned up from the earlier seating.

In the shade of a huge tree Kylie sat on top of a picnic table with her feet on the seat, her elbows propped on her knees, and her head bowed low. We climbed onto the table beside her before she noticed us.

"Hey girlfriend, what's going on?" Sarah nudged Kylie with an elbow.

"Nothing."

Sarah and I shared a knowing look over the top of Kylie's head.

"Isn't Eric joining us for breakfast?" I asked.

Kylie looked up, her eyes dull and her face pulled tight. "He didn't have a reservation and, like, wanted to leave early. I asked him to wait for me to eat, but he's gone."

Tears weren't far below the surface, so I put my arm over the girl's shoulders.

"We'd love to have you hike with us tomorrow," Sarah said.

"Thanks, but I'm gonna, like, catch up to him after my breakfast. I'm all packed."

"He sets a fast pace," I said. "You'd have to run to catch him. Hike with us." I knew she'd refuse my invitation, but I hoped she'd abandon her chase and let Eric hike out of her life.

"I think I can do it," she insisted. "He said he might, like, stop somewhere for a nap during the heat of the day."

"What about you?" Sarah asked. "They predict ninety-seven degrees today. You'll need to rest and get out of the heat, too." Sarah had a good point, but logic didn't sway Kylie.

I worried she'd ignore the warning signs of dehydration or heat stroke. "Be sure to carry two or three liters of water and stay hydrated," I lectured.

"I know. I know," she said.

Compelled to make Kylie see that Eric wasn't worth pursuing, I poked at her image of him. "So what did Eric do for breakfast this morning?"

Kylie sighed. "I didn't, like, have money to lend him for the reservation, so I gave him tomorrow's breakfast."

"He took your last breakfast?" The pitch of Sarah's voice rose and color came into her cheeks.

"He didn't know it was my last one." Kylie spat out her words, ready to defend him. I signaled Sarah that I'd take up the battle.

"That's okay, honey. I have extra oatmeal you can have for tomorrow. Did you lend him anything else?"

"No," she said. "Well, yes, a dehydrated dinner, but that was an extra one."

I hid my disdain for the man. Real backpackers pride themselves on being self-sufficient. Eric didn't fall into that category no matter what his claims were for completing the Appalachian Trail. Veteran A.T. hikers have some name for hikers who pack little and plan to beg and borrow food along the way. *Trail rat? Even if that's not the right phrase, rat suits Eric well.*

The screen door to the cantina swung open, and thirty-some people shuffled into a line to present reservation tickets to the cantina employee. A few people pushed ahead, hungry and perhaps afraid that the food would run out. Not wanting to get trampled, I hung back, but a gentleman held the door open for us. I rewarded him with my best smile.

Sarah leaned down to whisper in my ear. "You're being perky again."

I shot her a look. Her laugh was lost in the din of people jostling for seats and scraping chairs on the wooden floor boards. To each table, young servers brought platters heaped with pancakes, sausage and scrambled eggs; enough to satisfy the hungriest of hikers.

We sat with an elderly woman with a fluff of white hair and soft, paper thin skin tinted blue by her veins. I could not imagine how she got to Phantom Ranch, so I diplomatically pressed her for information. "Have you been to the Ranch before?"

"I've been coming here since I was a girl," she said, "but I'm afraid this is my last trip."

"Why is that?"

"My husband won't let me hike alone anymore."

"You hiked down? Alone?" I was astounded. Sarah stopped chewing to listen, and Kylie cocked an ear to hear what the lady had to say. Her name was Violet.

"I've been visiting the canyon since I was ten years old," she said. "I fell in love with the canyon then and still love it."

"May I ask how old you are?" I said.

"Eighty this year."

Shocked, I compared myself to the intrepid woman who seemed so healthy and sharp. My ridiculous aching muscles and knees embarrassed me. I vowed to never whine on the trail again.

Violet entertained us with recollections of the canyon's old hotels and colorful characters, but Kylie had no time for an old lady's memories. After wolfing down a pancake and a scoop of scrambled eggs, she excused herself.

We let her go, and she dashed across the dusty campground in a big hurry to hunt down her heartbreak.

While a couple from Iowa relayed their mule train experience the day before, the creak of the screen door caught my attention. A vaguely familiar man stood to the side of the door scanning the room. I stared at him for several minutes before I recognized the ultra-lighter, Michael Rap. In comparison to the hearty bunch that chowed down on the mounds of food on the tables, he looked unkempt, almost unhealthy. He furtively slipped into a seat at a table recently vacated by four women.

Rap snatched a pancake from the stack, folded it around a couple sausages, and shoved it in his mouth. He hunched over the table like a pit-bull protecting its food dish.

Sarah caught sight of my stare and turned to watch over her shoulder as he shoveled leftover scrambled eggs onto a piece of toast. "I guess we have a party crasher."

None of the staff noticed the unscheduled diner.

"Let him eat," I said. "They'd have to throw out the leftovers anyway."

We left Michael Rap to his scavenging and turned to our table where the woman from Iowa engaged Violet in another story. The noise level rose several decibels as people, jovial and full, finished their meals and leaned back to talk. I caught a partial sentence. ". . . fell off the rim."

I leaned forward and strained to hear.

"Excuse me," I said. "What are you talking about?"

The woman's husband took over her story in a booming voice. "The *Canyon News* printed the story yesterday morning. Some guy got murdered. The police found his body down at the bottom near Yaki Point."

Sarah and I pulled our chairs in closer to get the update. "Why did they report it as a murder?" Sarah asked.

"Paper didn't say."

The term 'murder' unsettled me. A Grand Canyon murder seemed like an oxymoron. I preferred an accident, or a stupid tourist trick. A suicide or a heart attack death ended there—at least as far as the public was concerned. A murder continued as a worry. Who did it? Is he still out there? Will he strike again? Sarah and I put our heads together.

"That's got to be our red jacket guy," she said.

I agreed. "I can't imagine there'd be more than one in such a short time."

"More than one?" Violet exclaimed.

"No, no. Only one. The newspaper probably reported the man we saw who fell from the rim on Saturday." Sarah tried to reassure Violet that a rash of killings hadn't blighted her beloved canyon.

The voice of the man from Iowa rose above the rest. "You saw the murderer?"

Not wanting to disturb the entire room with the news, we drew our chairs in and told our story to our table-mates. As much as I'd tried to forget the incident over the past few days, its sordidness had followed us. The image of him plummeting over the edge in terror haunted me. That image merged with other thoughts like bits of glass in a kaleidoscope: the attack on Kylie, the heart attack on the bus, the string of thefts, the sense that someone watched us. *Could all those disturbing events be connected?*

No, I decided. *Too many miles in between. Just coincidences.* I shook off the depressing notion, but it crept into the shadows of my mind.

I sat back and tried to sort out my thoughts, while the group exhausted the news of the murder. When the subject finally turned to more pleasant topics, we realized the wait staff had cleaned most of the tables and few guests remained in the cantina.

"I guess we've been here long enough." Sarah checked her watch. "I want to get in a hike this morning."

We stood to follow the Iowa couple from the building, but Sarah remembered that we had pre-ordered box lunches. She rang the bell for the cashier while I asked Violet about her plans for the day.

"I hope to find and photograph Precambrian rocks today. There are two billion years old remnants nearby," said Violet with a sparkle in her eye. "That's even older than me."

"Are you going alone?" I pictured her scrambling over cliffs and boulders. "Does anyone know where you'll be?"

"Don't worry, dear." Violet patted my arm with her cool fingers. "I have befriended one of the rangers. She'll walk with me."

Relieved that I didn't have to volunteer to hike with her, nor keep up with her pace, I held the door open for the amazing woman.

"Bye-bye," she said.

As I watched Violet's straight back and sturdy legs stride down the path, Sarah returned with two bags of food.

"Good stuff." She smiled and held up the bags as if they weighed several pounds each.

"What'd we get?"

Sarah stopped at a picnic table to examine the contents. "Let's see. We have a big sandwich, ham and cheese on whole grain bread, mayo and mustard packets, pickle and tomato in a zip-lock bag. A small pack of Oreo cookies, a Red Delicious apple. And a sleeve of salted peanuts. Not bad. And a napkin."

"Such a deal."

Sarah and I sauntered toward the primitive campgrounds, crossing the footbridge over the cascading creek. In true canyon fashion, nature graced us with a show. A small herd of mule deer bounded from the foliage in front of us and trotted briskly along the narrow dirt path which followed the curves of the creek. With their white tails up and their rabbit-sized ears twitching, they tolerated our presence and led us to our campsite.

I transferred my lunch into my mesh food bag and dragged the ammo box from under the picnic table. I hoped that the sun didn't turn the box into an oven before lunch. In the meantime, Sarah rinsed a shirt and a pair of socks in the tiny rill that ran at the edge of our site. She hung her clothes on a line and dried her hands on her shorts.

"I'm going to hike out to try to find that waterfall and do some painting," Sarah said. "Are you sure you don't want to come with me?"

"I think I'll stay in camp. I woke up too early this morning and will take a little nap before the sun heats the tent."

"In a few minutes I'll leave you in peace," Sarah said. "I have to organize my watercolors and stuff."

I retrieved my tattered map. "Show me where you plan to be, in case I have to come rescue you."

"Ha," she said, but squinted at the map and traced a line about a mile to the East to a short unnamed trail. "Kylie said the waterfall was here. In any case, I won't go further. I'll be back before two, so don't call out the search dogs."

"Okay, but don't take chances."

"Don't worry, " she said. "I won't."

I unzipped the tent. "Need anything from in here?"

"Nope. Don't think so. Have a good nap."

I kicked off my shoes, crawled in the tent, and zipped up the mesh screening. My sleeping bag welcomed me, and I punched my clothing sack into some semblance of a pillow. I heard Sarah rummage through her pack for her painting supplies and her emergency items. The ammo box clanked open as she, no doubt, packed her lunch.

"I'm running down to the cantina to fill our water bottles. Be right back," she called.

"Okay. Thanks."

Silence. Except for the rustling leaves, the chipping of birds, and the trickling of water in the rill. My heavy head sank into the pillow. I closed my eyes and let nature's music lull me into a doze.

The sound of rattling paper brought me back from the edge of slumber. I listened as Sarah moved about trying to be quiet and letting me sleep. "I'm awake."

No answer, but the sound continued. I finally got to my knees and peeked from the tent's screened window. A squirrel as fat as a football sat on our picnic table filling his cheeks with Oreo cookies as fast as his little teeth could nibble.

"Hey!" I jumped from the tent and waved my arms at the football. Reluctant to leave, the marauder grabbed a last bite, leapt from the table, and trundled into the underbrush. The professional thief ignored the crazy woman making such a fuss.

Disgusted, I spread the remains of my food across the table and moaned over the hole in my homemade mesh bag. The thief had gnawed right through the mesh, taken several bites from my Red Delicious apple, and shredded the Oreo's tinfoil wrapper. My packets of oatmeal and hot chocolate were untouched.

One by one I examined my meals and snacks for contamination.

Sarah strolled into the campsite. "What's going on?"

"Some stupid squirrel ate my lunch." I fumed. "Look at him sitting there waiting for the next stupid human to leave him a feast."

Sarah's eyes flashed fire. "Are you calling me stupid?"

I snapped my mouth shut.

"I didn't leave your food out on purpose." She raged on. "How dare you call me stupid!" She slammed my water bottled onto the table. "You're the stupid one, flouncing around after that ranger."

Sarah grabbed her fanny pack and made a show of shoving supplies into it while I stared at her. She growled and groused under her breath, but did not storm off.

I sat down, afraid to speak.

Finally, she sighed deeply. "Look, I'm sorry I left your lunch out. You can have mine."

I wanted only to smooth things over. "Don't worry about it. I have plenty of food. I was frustrated and didn't mean you're stupid. I'm sorry."

Sarah looked miserable. She sat down across the table from me, but looked over my shoulder rather than at me.

"Sarah? This isn't about the squirrel is it?"

With her elbows on the table, she leaned her forehead onto her hands, half hiding her face. "I'm sorry I snapped at you. I saw Ranger Hawk at the cantina, and he asked about you and your plans for today. He'll probably be here in the next few minutes."

"Okay. And?"

"I think I resent the time you've spent with him. I'm afraid you'll want me to get lost, or you'll ask him to join us for the rest of the trail." She hung her head low as if confessing to mass murder.

Touchy-feely conversations weren't my thing, but she was obviously worried, so I tried. "Listen, Sarah. You and I are friends, and I truly value that." I took my turn in the confessional. "I have too few woman friends, mostly sports buddies or work associates. You and I have a good relationship. I wouldn't push you aside for a man, and I'm in no position to start something with him anyway."

Embarrassment still colored her cheeks, but she nodded.

"Besides . . . I do not flounce." I challenged her with a smile.

"You flounced." She grinned.

"I've been known to sashay and sway, but never flounce." I demonstrated the moves.

Friends again, I put the incident behind me and the contaminated food in a garbage bag. Sarah zipped up her fanny pack.

"I guess I'll go find some scenery to paint," she said. "Here comes Prince Charming."

She headed east toward the waterfall and gave a friendly wave to Glen.

"Morning, ladies." He stopped at the entrance to our campsite. Not in uniform, he looked good anyway, clean-shaven and fresh in his *Grand Canyon* ball cap, tee-shirt and zip-off nylon shorts. His sturdy leather boots must have weighed two pounds each; they'd certainly hold up against canyon rocks for years to come. I welcomed him in.

"Good morning, Glen. Have you had breakfast? Would you like hot tea?"

"Thanks, Amy, but no. I had breakfast at the first seating."

He joined me at the picnic table. "I wondered if I could be your guide today and maybe show you Ribbon Falls, or we could climb a small slot canyon no one visits." He rushed on. "Or I know of a secret gorge with stromatolite fossils in a bed of shale about a mile west of Bright Angel Trail."

Stromatolite? His nervous chatter surprised me. His enthusiasm almost tempted me. I stopped him before I took the bait. "Whoa. All that sounds great, but I'm not hiking today." I pointed to my knee. "It needs a rest."

The energy drained from his face.

I backpedaled a bit. "The river isn't too far. We could watch the rafts float by."

"Good plan." He brightened immediately. "Now, or wait awhile?"

"Now," I said. "I have a sack lunch. Maybe we can picnic on the shore."

He flashed his contagious smile and patted his small day-pack. "I happen to have my lunch packed and ready to go."

"Do the rangers have a *Be Prepared* motto like the scouts?"

"That's my personal policy," he said. "You never know when you'll be called upon to have an emergency picnic."

I shook my head at the silliness and looked forward to a good day. I gathered a few necessities and retrieved my lunch from the ammo box. "Lead the way, Glen."

The flat, sandy ground did not bother my knee. I almost regretted not taking advantage of Glen's offer to share secret sites. I followed behind his well-defined calf muscles and neat little seat and wondered if I should be more adventurous.

The route from our campsite took us past the empty group-camp area and the ranger station. The rustic building fit in well with the canyon.

"Not exactly deluxe," I said.

"It's home—when I'm here." He shrugged.

"So where's home when you're not here?"

"I keep a small place in Duluth near my son and ex-wife. I stay there in the off-season and do substitute teaching to pay the bills."

"Sounds like a simple life."

"That's the way I like it." He turned a happy, little-boy grin my way.

What does he want with me?

15

THE COLORADO RIVER - *Elevation: 2,400 ft.*

The quarter-mile walk turned hot and oppressive when we left the shade of Bright Angel campground and veered away from the creek. Deep roasted sand radiated heat. I wiped my fogged up sunglasses and stopped at an information board as much to get into shade as to see what the placards had to say.

Glen chatted amiably about the area, its history and the wildlife. He had more than a working knowledge about every topic I broached and interspersed facts and statistics with anecdotal tidbits. I'd picked the perfect tour-guide, a walking encyclopedia of wilderness lore.

Our stroll took us to a beach on the shore of the Colorado River. The river's mocha-latte water appeared denser than average water, perhaps thickened by the silt carried in its flow as it rolled westward. The waterway appeared calm, but I knew the current had treacherous possibilities.

We headed for the thickest shrub on the sandy shore. I parked my sit-upon in the meager shade and Glen sat next to me, but at a comfortable distance. I downed a couple ounces of water and removed my boots to wiggle my toes in the sand. He followed my example and set his boots and socks off to the side. His long legs stretched to the water's edge.

"We'll have a good view from here of the rafts coming down river," he said. "Most guides stop for lunch at the Ranch." He pointed upriver with his chin. "Here comes a couple now."

Two colorful vessels rounded the curve in the distance. The closer they came, the larger they got. The lemon yellow raft led the way. Seven or eight people perched on the vessel's thwarts, but one man did all the work. His long oars flew up and down in strong, frantic motions as he maneuvered the rubber balloon-like craft out of the main current and into the protected arc of the beach. The bright blue raft held back. Its captain fought the current to stay out of the way until the first craft beached. Given the *all-clear*, the second captain expertly guided his oversized raft onto the sand next to its partner.

Each raft looked like a floating party. The passengers held drink cans high and saluted their captains. Their arms waved toward the other raft and their sunburned faces laughed. They presented a stark contrast to the quiet, austere nature of my own travel choice.

Glen and I watched the entertainment. The girls wore bathing suits, some covered by gauzy tops or oversized tee-shirts. The men preferred baggy swim trunks or cut-off jeans. Passengers disembarked by rolling themselves over the rubber gunnels of the rafts and into the shallow water. More than a few flip flops had to be caught before being lost to the current. I enjoyed the show.

The most important piece of gear on the rafts appeared to be the white plastic coolers. While the captains stowed ropes and oars, hefty guys took opposite ends of the coolers and headed toward the Ranch, no doubt to replenish the ice and beer.

"Groups coming in at this time generally stay for lunch," Glen offered. "Others may stay a night or two and then hike up to the South Rim."

"Rafting the Colorado is on my bucket list," I said. "Where do the trips begin?"

"I guess most start at Lee's Ferry up near Lake Powell. Some end here, but others do a float through the entire canyon, ending in Lake Mead; takes two weeks."

"Fun." My adventurous juices got revved up. "I'll sign up for rafting when I can't hike anymore."

"Many years from now." He was being kind. I had serious doubts about even getting myself out of the canyon in the next few days.

"I don't know," I said.

"Keep on going. You'll build muscle." He had more faith in me than I had.

The passengers disappeared in the direction of lunch, but the two boat captains remained, struggling to anchor one of the rafts to the shore.

"Excuse me." Glen jumped up and trotted over to give the men a hand. The three of them hauled the heavy craft further ashore and buried an anchor in the sand. The men shook hands and stood in the sun, ankle deep in water, casually talking.

I admired Glen's strong back and muscular arms and the ease with which he engaged the strangers. They responded heartily to his friendship. *He's comfortable in his own skin*, I thought. His bearing conveyed confidence without a hint of arrogance. I liked that.

After a few minutes Glen handed each of the captains his business card, took theirs, and returned to my shade.

"Great guys," he said.

"You're a great guy, too."

"Thanks." He brushed aside the compliment. "They put in at Lee's Ferry. It's a three-day trip, and they'll push off again in two hours." He held up the business card. "This is for my son. He wants to be a river guide for the summer."

"Good experience," I said. "What's his name?"

"Todd." Pride filled his voice. "He's in his first year at the University of Arizona, Tempe."

"Great campus. What's his major?"

"He hasn't chosen a career yet. Right now he vacillates among river guide, teacher, and botanist." Glen shook his head as every parent does. "He'll be content as long as he gets outdoors. He is especially interested in cacti." He winked.

I responded to his gentle reminder with only a smile. "He must love to visit you here."

"I hope so. I see him two weekends a month. He uses visits here as part of his course work."

"I'll bet he gets his love of the outdoors from his Dad."

"I guess. I started Todd camping with me when he was four. By the time he was ten, he wanted to hike out alone."

"You let him camp alone?"

"Not exactly." Glen chuckled. "He didn't know, but old Dad was never too far away."

"What about your wife?"

"Ex-wife. Marie thought she had married a teacher. She couldn't understand that classrooms made me feel closed in. This is the perfect job for me; being outdoors, sleeping on the ground, watching the sunrise. Life is simple here."

He grinned. "The work is interesting, the people are generally pleasant, and occasionally I get to rescue a fair maiden."

I acknowledged the compliment with a slight blush. "To be fair, I'm not exactly a maiden." I played the straight man and he laughed.

"I love backpacking for the same reason you love your job," I said. "I eat, sleep, and hike. The simplicity calms me from the inside out. Marie didn't want you to be a ranger?"

"Not at all. We tried for eleven years, but we had two different definitions of success. She found someone more stable."

"Are you okay with that now?" I asked, wondering if I'd ever be okay with my new marital status.

"Yeah, I want her to be happy. He's good to her and Todd."

My questions were intrusive, but I wanted to hear his history. "What did you teach?"

"High school biology for eighteen years. Then I applied with the Park Service. That was thirteen years ago."

"You've been in the Canyon ever since?"

"No, no. This is a plum assignment. Can you believe they took five years to recognize my brilliance?" His mock boasting made me laugh.

"Are you always so happy and content?" I asked.

His laughter relaxed into sincerity. "You have that effect on me, I guess. You're here and I'm happy. Very simple."

I smiled at Glen and accepted his compliment with grace. What a difference from the man I married, I thought. John had to work at being happy and seldom succeeded. Certainly, I hadn't been able to make him happy. *What a waste.*

My stomach told me lunch time had arrived, so we propped our picnic goodies on our daypacks and continued to chat about his love for the canyon and his son. While we ate, another group of rubber rafts bumped into the sandy beach and spilled out their passengers. The camaraderie and vacation atmosphere entertained us until they headed for the Ranch, leaving the beach empty again.

"Glen, may I ask a question?"

He nodded with some apprehension.

"Why me? Why are you," I hesitated, "spending time with me? You must meet many women looking for a friendly guy in uniform."

His booming laugh rolled across the river and echoed back. "Surprisingly, not all women are impressed with the uniform." He chuckled to himself before becoming quiet. "Dating typical visitors is useless, so it's not worth flirting with them."

"You've been flirting with me, and I…" I wiggled my ring finger at him.

"I know and I'm sorry if I've offended you, but sometimes things aren't what they seem. Maybe you wear the ring to fend off guys."

"People do that?"

He shrugged.

"My ring is real," I said, almost certain I did the right thing.

"Oh." He cast his eyes downward. "Then I apologize. When I saw you on the North Rim, I thought here's a woman worth some effort, and took a chance."

"Sarah tells me that my friendly flirting can be taken as a come-on. I guess I've been married so long that I'm naïve, but I can't follow up the flirting with—with anything. I'm sorry if it…if you…"

"I understand, but I'm not sorry I took the chance."

"You're a good guy."

"One of the best." His silly grin came back, but not quite as big.

"I need to stretch my legs," I said, breaking away from the awkward conversation. I packed up my lunch debris and waded into the water to rinse my hands.

The intense sunlight broke into golden spangles thrown across the water's surface. His glittering reflection joined mine creating a beautiful vignette, but the image splintered as I splashed cool water over my heated skin.

"Ready to go back?" he asked.

I looked up at him to see if he was okay, but his facial expression hid in the glare. I spoke to his dark sunglasses. "Sure. Let's head to the Ranch for lemonade. You've got me hooked."

"Whatever makes you happy."

I think he meant it. I responded with a genuine grin of my own.

* * *

A number of the boat people made themselves at home in the cantina; eating, playing cards, and stacking up beer cans. Their's was a portable party. The raft captains hailed Glen, and he waved amiably rather than join them.

We brought our cold lemonades to a quiet table, away from the ruckus, and sat in the breeze near a window. I was pleased he still wanted to be friends, wanted to spend time with me. Glen pulled his chair close to the table and leaned forward.

"People have all sorts of reasons for hiking the canyon. Why are you here?" He probed in a genial manner and made me want to answer; made me want for him to know me. That's what friends do.

"I've wanted to hike the canyon for a long time, since fourth grade actually, but I feel guilty for taking this trip. The timing is bad."

"Guilty?" he asked.

"Yeah, there are things I should be doing at home."

He tilted his head like that attentive German shepherd again. "You have to live your life in ways that make you happy."

"Being in the natural world makes me happy."

"Here we are then," he said.

He stared at me, watching my face, beaming his bright smile. I tried to take the scrutiny in stride, but had to look away.

"Please don't stare," I said.

"I like what I see."

"I'm one of those useless visitors who'd waste your time."

"No, you're good company, and I'm enjoying the little time I have with you. I don't often meet intelligent women my age who feel comfortable in the wilderness."

"What age group is that? How old do you think I am?" I challenged him to tread on *that* thin ice.

"Maybe forty-nine or fifty," he guessed.

That deflated my ego. People generally judge me to be ten years younger. "What makes you say fifty?"

He paused, obviously knowing a thing or two about thin ice, but decided not to heed the danger signs. "Because you have crow's feet at the corner of your eyes." He put that little tidbit out there as cautiously as offering a dead chicken to a snapping alligator.

My mouth fell open and I laughed out loud. His unexpected candor tickled me. "Most guys know not to say such things."

"You asked a direct question—and I'll never lie to you."

What a concept. I sat back in my chair to think about that and watched him from a new perspective. He waited tentatively until I nodded my head in approval. His relief was visible.

"They have games here," he said. Apparently the serious talk had ended. "If you want to stay inside during the worst of the heat, we could play something."

"Scrabble is my favorite."

He got up to search the game shelf and returned in triumph with a battered Scrabble game. "My college buddies and I used to play this all the time." He sounded quite confident, and I took the challenge.

"I plan to trounce you." I topped the trash-talk with a smile.

"I don't doubt that for a minute."

"In a friendly way, of course."

"Of course."

We played with such cheerful intensity that we were unaware the rafting gang had gone and we had the place to ourselves. Without a dictionary, we both had to accept a few possible misspellings, and in the end I won handily. Though I couldn't swear he gave his best effort. We dumped the tiles back into the box just as Sarah marched through the cantina's yard.

"In here, Sarah," I called through the window screen.

Dusty and tired, she dragged in and dumped her stuff on the table and herself in a chair. "Hi, guys."

"Beer or lemonade?" Glen asked.

"I need a beer."

Glen went to the counter to get her drink.

"You're back early," I said. "Did you finish painting?"

"No. I got interrupted."

Glen put the sweating beer can in front of Sarah.

"Thanks," she said, taking a sip. "I had Ribbon Falls all to myself—I thought. The place is gorgeous. The water falls into a narrow ravine, and I climbed to the top to take pictures from each side and from behind the falls. What a great place." She guzzled an ounce or two of beer. "I climbed back down and sat on a rock to sketch the scene. But I had a weird feeling that someone was there."

Sarah sat straighter in her chair as her story built up steam. "I looked around occasionally, but saw nothing. The waterfall drowned out almost all sound, but I heard a little noise from up on the cliff, and caught sight of a man before he ducked out of sight. A few stones slid down. I got nervous and put my supplies away. All of a sudden, a rock the size of a basketball bounced down the side of the cliff and landed ten feet from me!"

"You think he started an avalanche?" I asked.

"No, I think he heaved the rock at me," Sarah said. "On *purpose*."

Glen instantly became Ranger Hawk. "Could you identify him?"

"Not really, no, but something seemed familiar," Sarah said. "I got an image in my head of that guy."

"What guy?" I asked.

"The one we called Ultra-lighter. He snuck into breakfast this morning."

I gasped in disbelief. "Michael Rap? Why would he try to hit you with a rock?"

Ranger Glen stood up. "Can you give me a description of this guy, of Michael Rap?" He reached for the pad of paper that we had used for our Scrabble scores.

"Probably wasn't him. Could have been any thin, youngish backpacker." The incident clearly troubled Sarah. "Maybe it *was* an accident."

"I'll find him in any case," Glen said. "Interviewing him won't hurt. How tall is he?"

Sarah and I gave a short description before she remembered taking Rap's picture on the bus. She scanned through her camera's memory card. "Here. This is him." She held out the camera to Glen, and I peered over his shoulder.

"He's scruffier now. More hair or something," I said.

"Thanks." Glen studied the picture and made another note. "I'll take care of this." He hurried away.

Half way across the room, he said, "I'll see you at dinner, Amy."

I waved to him and turned back to Sarah, trying to imagine her harrowing incident. "What'd you do?" I asked.

"I went after him. But by the time I climbed to the ledge, he was gone." She threw her hands up in frustration. "I tried to finish painting, but he had me spooked. I didn't want to get ambushed again."

"I should have hiked with you," I said, troubled by yet another disturbing event.

"Nothing would have changed except the rock might have hit you."

"I'm glad you weren't hurt."

Sarah drank her beer in silence while I worried. *Was the rock an accident? What could anyone gain by hitting Sarah?*

"You should see it," she said.

"What?"

"The waterfall pours down and has carved a basin into the top of a tall domed rock." She held out her camera, tapping her finger on the screen. "You gotta see this. I climbed up behind this curtain of water. It forms a tiny pond and then spills another forty feet." The pictures showed a glistening pool with strands of emerald moss trailing twenty feet over a cliff.

"Gorgeous." I scanned picture after picture. "Did you paint this scene?"

"Not yet, but I finished a few others." She hesitated, but then opened her case and handed the tablet to me.

I flipped open the cover. "That's from the North Rim," I said. She had perfectly captured the winter scene with the mini-cabins in a blanket of new snow. "This is wonderful."

The next one stunned me. "That's where we had lunch."

"The title is *Cathedral,*" she said.

"Exactly." I looked up to catch her watching my reactions and smiled directly into her eyes. "These are perfect, Sarah. So professional."

She ducked the compliment and tapped her finger on the next sheet. Subtle colors captured a pink dawn as the sun rose above the canyon wall and sparkled on a creek. "That's the creek we passed on our way into Cottonwood."

"That's where you went for breakfast yesterday morning?"

"Yep."

"I love every one of them." I went back to the beginning of the booklet and took time to study each painting again. "Beautiful. You got the layers of color perfect." I gushed while Sarah drank in my praise. Finally, I closed the cover and placed my hand over the precious collection. "These are fabulous."

"Thanks."

I put the booklet in her hands. "You're an artist. You could sell these and cross that off your life-list."

She didn't believe me.

"Art lovers would buy these," I insisted. "I would buy these."

She carelessly tossed the booklet into its case.

"I'm serious, Sarah, and I'm jealous."

Sarah shrugged, slapped her knees, and stood up. "I could use a nap. Are you ready to head back to camp?"

"Sure, let me find a book to read." I thought I'd bone up on bats before Glen's presentation that evening. While Sarah bought each of us lemonade, I searched the shelf of tattered books and found the one I wanted.

"Hey, the mules are coming in." She forgot about her nap, and we wandered down to the corrals with our plastic cups to watch the tourists. A rough bench in the shade provided a good view of the newly arrived horde. In their haste to get to fresh feed and water, the mules kicked up dust and dried green droppings with their iron shoes. They knew the routine and exactly where to go.

The dust-coated riders appeared relieved to reach the ranch and its promise of rest and refreshments. The riders, with slow and creaking bones, dragged their legs over the backs of the mules. Most slid on their stomachs down the mule's side, their feet searching for the ground. Audible "ughs" accompanied the thud of their shoes.

As the achy riders hobbled around to test their land-legs, Sarah called out and waved. "Welcome to Phantom Ranch!"

I waved, too, but could not bring myself to be so boisterous.

The saddle-sore, imitation cowboys smiled or groaned, rubbed the seat of their jeans and headed for the cantina. With each step, it appeared their muscles loosened up, as did their spirits. Within minutes the noise level and the party-atmosphere surged. We headed in the opposite direction, to the peace and quiet of our campsite.

"I've been thinking, Sarah," I said. "I'm really worried about your *accident* with the rock at the waterfall."

"That was no accident."

"I know," I said, "and that's what I mean. So many nasty things have happened all around us—First the body in the ravine, then Kylie was attacked, then the boy on the bus died. There are too many tragedies in a short time. It can't be a coincidence."

"Weird and scary," Sara said, "but each of those events happened a hundred miles apart. There's nothing to tie them together."

"There must be," I said, "but right now I see only one common denominator."

"Like what?"

"Us."

"Us?" she said, "as in you and me?" I was kidding when I told Ranger Jan that trouble follows you everywhere because you were from Chicago."

I sniffed a little laugh. "I haven't figured it out yet . . ." I hesitated, uncertain whether I should broach the subject. "Sarah, is it possible that somebody is after you? I mean, there was the hit-and-run accident and now the rock."

Sarah turned and gaped at me, shaking her head. "I can't imagine a soul who'd bother to follow me to the canyon. Besides I deal mostly with fourth graders." Her face clouded over. "If one of us is the target of some sick plan, it must be you. Think about it. That kid in the airport gave you trouble. You mentioned your brother is angry about your father's will and . . ." She took a deep breath. ". . . and you have a husband who seems to be a jerk."

John? The thought that he might have followed me to the canyon struck me like a thunder bolt. It's not possible to live with someone for thirty years and not know what they're capable of. Or is it? I gripped the iron railing for support.

"Hey," Sarah said. "I didn't mean it. Take that look off your face." She nudged me with her elbow. "Amy."

I blinked and shook thoughts of my husband's treachery out of my head. "That's so far off. It's impossible. There's something else going on."

"Yes. And it has nothing to do with us."

"I hope you're right." But I feared she was wrong. All the terrible happenings did have something to do with me, I knew it.

"Come on," Sarah said, giving me a gentle shove toward our campsite. "I have a nap waiting for me."

16

TRAIL RATS

Groggy from her nap, Sarah crawled from the tent. She merely nodded in response to my greeting. She yawned without covering her mouth and stretched her arms wide, reaching to embrace the entire day and her place in it.

"What did I miss?"

"Not much." I held up my half-read book. "Says here that miners took in ringtail cats as house pets to eat mice and rats, so they're also called miner's cats. And they have purple eyes." In truth, I'd only scanned the book and spent most of the hour thinking of the terrible events of the last few days.

"You're full of trivia." Sarah smiled.

"Yep, useless trivia is my specialty." I put my book down, and Sarah joined me on the picnic table.

"Have you recovered from your traumatic day?" I asked.

"Guess so, but you got me thinking. Why would Michael Rap, or anybody else for that matter, want to crack my head open with a rock? If someone dislodged a rock by accident, they would have yelled, 'Watch out.' Don't ya think?"

I agreed. "Rap struck me as odd from the moment we saw him, but I never guessed he was dangerous. No more solo hikes, okay?"

"None planned. Whoever was up on that cliff is a coward. Let me take him on face to face. I'll twist his nuts off." Her fists were already balled as she built up steam.

"Whoa, girl. Save your energy until we know who threw the rock. Maybe Glen will have information for us at dinner."

She relaxed and laughed. "Sorry. Speaking of Prince Charming, how'd your day go?"

"Pleasant."

"Aw, you're blushing," she teased. "What happened?"

I shook my head to drain the extra blood from my cheeks. "Nothing happened. We had a picnic down at the river, watched the rafts come in, and I beat him at Scrabble."

"What else?"

"Nothing."

She raised her eyebrows in a question.

"Seriously. Nothing," I insisted.

"But you like him."

"He's a great guy. What's not to like? I told him I'm married and that's that."

"Was that before or after he let you win at Scrabble?"

"Before," I said, "and I beat him. To be more precise, I trounced him."

"Good. I'm sure his ego is healthy enough that you don't have to pretend to be stupid."

"No way." I pulled my cap down to shade my eyes.

"Just checking."

How did she know that the old me might have used that little ruse? Sarah certainly never played the subordinate to anyone.

She looked at her watch. "Getting close to dinner time. Do you want to mosey on down?"

"Yes, ma'am," I said. "I'm famished." Glad the personal talk was over, I hopped off the picnic table, zipped up the tent to deter ringtail cats, and checked my fanny pack for my headlamp.

Dinner repeated itself, same routine, same food as last night, though I had the vegetarian chili. We should have cooked for ourselves. The charm had worn off the chow, though that didn't stop us from eating our shares. The best part of the meal was watching others enjoy rustic grub for the first time.

While we ate, I scanned the room repeatedly looking for Glen. My disappointment in not finding him surprised me.

During dessert, I spotted two uniformed men enter the crowded cantina. Glen towered over Geraldo and raised an arm in greeting when he caught sight of us. Geraldo disappeared into the kitchen, and Glen made his way through the maze of tables and chairs toward us.

"Hello, Sarah, Amy." He nodded to the other guests and dragged a chair from the corner to squeeze in at the end of our table.

Sarah got right to the point. "Did you find him?"

"Not yet. We hiked to Ribbon Falls and searched the ravine and the surrounding cliffs, but didn't spot him. He apparently came back here. We talked to others who may have seen him." Glen kept his voice low even though our dinner companions were engrossed in their own conversations.

"Someone matching Rap's description rifled through the coolers left on the rafts. One of the river guides chased him away after he took several cans of beer. The guide said he didn't look well, kind of wild and uncoordinated. Does that sound like him?"

"I don't know about uncoordinated," I said, "but otherwise, yes."

Sarah agreed and pulled her camera from her shirt pocket to check his picture again. "He looks like any other scruffy backpacker to me," she said.

The entire situation sounded illogical, and I said so.

The other guests finished their meals and most drifted outside. Another chair was available at our table by the time Geraldo arrived carrying two large bowls of hiker's stew. He set one in front of Glen.

"Thanks, buddy."

"You are welcome, my friend," Geraldo said. "Good evening, Miss Amy, Miss Sarah.

The two famished men dug into the stew. Between bites, they discussed their search for the suspect as if Sarah and I weren't there.

"He's hanging around the Ranch, not really running away. Hiding," Glen said.

"He is hiding from me because he is not registered to camp." Geraldo took his job seriously. "I will find him."

Glen nodded. "Unless he hikes out. Eventually someone will spot him."

"If he goes off-trail, he will get lost, and we will be required to rescue him."

"Maybe he's an expert outdoorsman," said Glen.

"That is not my impression," Geraldo said.

Ranger Geraldo spread a trail map on the table and studied the lay of the land. Glen finally looked up at me.

"Amy, do you recall what type or color of backpack Mr. Rap carried?"

"Not much of one. Navy blue, I think. I'd call it a school book-bag rather than a real backpack. It's not big enough to carry much gear."

"That may explain why he snatches food and drinks," Glen said.

"But that doesn't explain why he threw a boulder at my head." Sarah wanted the search to remain focused on the attacker rather than on the beer thief. "Maybe they're not the same guys."

"Maybe," Glen agreed. "All we can do is keep an eye out for him— or them."

"We will do our best, Miss Sarah, to locate him and question him. We will find out what is going on."

"Thanks, Geraldo." Sarah replaced her frown with an indulgent smile for the earnest ranger. "Most likely he's a petty thief, and the falling rock was an accident."

Sarah made light of her worries. "He's probably no worse than a ringtail cat looking for food."

I shook my head at the comparison. "Shall we call him ringtail Rap?"

"I'll bet Sarah would like to wring Rap's tail," Glen chimed in.

I rolled my eyes, but Sarah threw him a big grin. "You betcha," she said.

Glen laughed aloud and slapped his knee. "Don't take him on yourself, Sarah. We want him to be able to answer some questions."

We all enjoyed the lighter mood, though Geraldo looked puzzled over our word-play. Glen glanced at his watch and scraped back his chair.

"I have to do the presentation at seven-thirty. Best show in town. Will you girls be there?"

"Sure." I answered too quickly, but Sarah covered me with a playful barb of sarcasm. "We were going to go bar hopping, but bats sound more fun."

"They are." Glen winked. He made a slight bow, collected his dirty dishes and headed for the kitchen. "No heckling from the audience," he called over his shoulder.

"No promises," I called back.

* * *

Ranger interpretive programs tend to be very casual affairs. This one was no exception. When we arrived at the semicircle of wooden benches, a number of people had already congregated; some chatted, some waited quietly in the dark. Sarah and I took seats in the back row and struck up a conversation with a mule-riding couple from Vermont.

Campers continued to meander in to fill all the bench space. I switched off my headlamp to let my eyes adjust gradually to the dark. Several people forgot that bright beams would blind the person sitting opposite them. I pulled the bill of my cap down to protect my eyes from errant beams.

Promptly at 7:30 Glen strode into the semicircle and greeted his audience. He had an easy rapport with the crowd. He spoke in a relaxed, conversational manner and soon had every visitor eager to learn about the twenty species of bats in the canyon. He deftly embedded bat factoids in amusing anecdotes to spice up the otherwise dry material.

I learned that bats are not blind, are seriously endangered and live in the caves high on the canyon walls.

"He's good, isn't he?" I whispered to Sarah.

"Yeah," she agreed. "Very entertaining."

Her objective opinion meant a lot to me; a reality check in case I didn't see him clearly. Pride grew inside my rib cage. *I'm proud of him.*

168

He's my friend. I mulled that realization over in my mind and missed some of the presentation.

My attention came back to bats when he asked everyone to turn off their lights. He explained that, as a whole, bats eat hundreds of thousands of tons of insects each year, including the common and dangerous scorpions found in the canyon. He switched on a black light and held the lamp to the ground while roaming the aisles. White scorpions, about one and a half inches long, skittered about, glowing fluorescent under the black light. I put my feet up on the bench in front of me.

"Holy crap." Sarah grimaced. "I'll never sleep without a tent again."

"Or go barefoot," I whispered.

"These little creatures are nocturnal and hide in dark places," Ranger Glen said. "They sting only in self-defense. The sting is nasty, but won't kill a healthy adult." He completed his rounds through the audience and switched off the black light. "Always shake out your boots and clothing while in camp and never put your hands into crevices or under rocks."

I watched the audience, wanting them to think he was smart and entertaining. They listened to him in rapt attention, and I smiled widely. Half expecting Sarah to tease me for the foolish grin, I snuck a peek in her direction. Her seat was empty.

I straightened up to look through the crowd. Where had she gone? I stood to peer into the darkness behind the benches. Something moved in the glow of the cantina's light, so I switched on my headlamp and abandoned the bat presentation.

"Sarah, where are you?" I hissed.

Only droning insects answered me.

To my right, dry weeds crackled. I whirled toward the noise. Adrenalin warned me to become invisible. I switched off my headlamp and veered away from the sound, not slowing until I reached the light of the cantina.

"Sarah?" I whispered into the shadows.

"Over here." She stepped out from the side of the building.

"Where have you been?" I demanded. "I thought you went to the bathroom."

"No, I saw him lurking around and I tried to sneak up on him."

"Him who?" I couldn't believe my ears. "Rap?"

"Well, yeah—probably," Sarah said.

"What if he tried to *kill* you? What if he has a gun?"

"If he had a gun, he would shoot me, not throw rocks at my head. He's probably foraging for food."

"In any case, you shouldn't chase after him alone." I heard my own exasperation and sighed. "I think someone's over that way."

Sarah tugged my elbow. "Okay. Let's go."

Together we left the comfort of the light and circled the cantina. For good measure, we shined our lights into corners and tested the locked back door to the place. A ringtail cat leapt away from us in the direction of the cabins. We followed.

Outside a dark cabin, we turned off our lights and stood still to listen. Sarah put her hand on my arm in warning. The sound of a heavy footstep came from the far side of the cabin. One footstep. Three seconds later, another footstep. A twig snapped.

Sarah nudged me to go to the side of the cabin. She tapped my headlamp, so I held my finger at the ready on the button. She disappeared to the front of the building, while I crept to the side. At the corner, I strained my eyes to see a dark silhouette.

Sarah made her move, jumping behind the man. "Ah ha!"

I switched on my light and shined the high beam into the man's face.

"Eric!" I said.

He protected his eyes with a hand. "What are you two up to?" he deadpanned. "You scared the heck out of me."

"Where's Kylie?" I demanded.

"Haven't seen her all day," he said. "She planned to have breakfast with you."

Sarah maintained her half-crouched stance. "She followed you out of camp."

"Then you know more than I do." His singsong voice infuriated me.

"Why are you here skulking around, Eric?" I asked.

"Okay, you got me," he sneered. "I'm too lazy to walk down to the latrine, so I peed on the side of the cabin here." He pushed past me. "If that's a crime, report me."

Adrenalin pounded in my veins as we watched him stomp away. "What a jerk," I said. "I'm afraid for Kylie."

"Maybe they missed each other on the trail," Sarah said, "and she's camped at Indian Gardens tonight."

"I hope so. Maybe he meant to ditch her and didn't have the guts to tell her in person."

"That fits," Sarah said. "What was he doing here?"

"I don't know, but I don't see wet spots on the side of this cabin." To confirm our suspicions, we shined our lights at the bases of several cabins. All were dry.

We returned to the benches in time to hear Glen conclude his lecture. He talked informally with several people who had questions for him. Sarah and I waited outside his circle of fans until they drifted off, and he noticed us.

"So how was the presentation?" he asked.

I avoided shining my light in his face and could not see him, but his deep voice warmed the space between us. I smiled in the privacy of the darkness. He wanted to hear compliments, and I didn't disappoint him. "You were great. Everyone was fascinated."

"Very interesting." Sarah was succinct, but sincere.

"Thanks. I get a kick out of giving talks," he said. "The audience responded well, especially with questions at the end."

"We missed that part," I confessed.

"Oh?"

"Sarah thought she saw Rap sneaking around the cantina and went to investigate. I followed her."

Glen's jocularity disappeared. "You're kidding. Did you find him?"

"Turned out to be Eric Prescott prowling around the cabins," Sarah said. "He didn't hike out this morning after all."

"Kylie's not with him, and I'm worried," I said.

The ranger's headlamp shined toward the cabins. Several lights bobbed in the distance as guests returned to their rooms.

"I'll see if I can find Eric and ask him a few questions," Glen said. "Are you okay? Do you want me to escort you to your campsite?"

"We'll be fine." I assured him. "Eric is a jerk, but he doesn't scare me—not as long as Sarah is nearby. Good night, Glen."

"Yell if you need me. See you at breakfast?"

Sarah answered for us. "Yep, the first seating. We want to hike out early."

We headed into the black night with our headlamps leading the way. Eyes watched us, I knew. Malicious or benign? Ringtail cat or human? Rap or Eric? I couldn't tell.

At the bridge I turned to watch the powerful beam of Glen's lantern penetrating dark corners and hiding places, flushing out vermin. I kept my gnawing suspicions to myself.

17

Day 6 - BRIGHT ANGEL TRAIL - 9.6 Miles

Rows of lounge chairs covered with plush white towels lined the pool behind the hotel. Soft breezes blew through the palms and furled the full skirt of my sun dress. I lay like the Queen of Sheba with my arms thrown over my head in complete abandon and relaxation.

A mountain of a man appeared at the foot of my chaise lounge. His black curls shone in the sun framing his broad tan face. Nonchalantly, he fingered the hem of my dress with his football-player hands. His smoldering, dark eyes watched me, wanted me. He raised one eyebrow. I raised two.

Suddenly, I was awake and became aware that I was in the tent, and —I was not alone. My eyes flew open. Sarah lay on her side of the tent propped up on one elbow with a sly grin on her face.

"That looked like fun."

My arms were still over my head, and I brought them down to cover my face.

"Oh dang! I'm sorry. Did I say something?"

"You were smiling," Sarah said with a laugh. "I enjoyed watching you."

I pulled my sleeping bag over my head, and she hooted loud enough to wake the neighbors.

"So tell me about your dream, Amy." She reached over and uncovered my face.

"What? No." I shook my head and blushed. Some dreams I don't want to forget. "There was this beautiful man at the hotel pool. His job

173

was to make the women happy. He looked like a romance novel hero with silky long hair."

"Must have been quite a dream. You grinned from ear to ear," Sarah laughed. "You're still grinning."

"Mmmm."

"Looks like your hero didn't finish the job," she said. "That can be unhealthy."

She looked intently into my eyes. "Do you want me to put an emergency call out to Ranger Glen?"

It was my turn to hoot. "Would you?"

She laughed with me. What a great way to start the day. I dug my crumpled slacks from my pillow-sack. Putting them over my feet, I rolled on my back and hiked my pants up to my waist in one smooth motion.

"I'll get the hot water started." I zipped up my fleece and crawled out of the tent.

I intended to deliver Sarah's mug to her in the tent, but she climbed out and rolled up her sleeping bag before the coffee finished brewing. We sat at the picnic table with our hands cupped around the hot mugs.

"Don't you love the part of the morning when it's too early to do anything but sit and watch the dew dry," I asked, "when the day is pure and everything is possible?"

Sarah tilted her face up to the fresh and fragrant air. "Absolutely. I could stay here forever."

After ten minutes of indolence, we roused ourselves and packed the bulk of our gear, laying the slightly damp tent over the T-bar to dry. Still early, we meandered down the path, taking note of Geraldo's plantings, birds skimming the surface of the creek, and the mules with their noses stuck in the feed trough. We leaned on the corral's railing.

"Look at this place," I said. "You get the sense that life doesn't change here, like the canyon is forever."

Sarah bobbed her head. "These rocks were here millions of years before us and will be here millions of years after us." She flicked a straw of hay toward the trough.

"That's what I mean," I said. "We are nothing. The canyon is oblivious to us and goes about its business." Sarah waited for an explanation. "I mean, no matter what I do, nature doesn't care. That takes away the stress, and I don't have to try so hard."

"Try so hard to do what?"

I shrugged. "To be someone special, I guess, better than I am."

"You don't have to do that," she said. "You're fine the way you are."

"I'm beginning to understand that. I feel free here, like it's okay to be me. My hair is chopped short. My crow's feet show. I don't have a job— and that's okay."

"You should feel that way everywhere, Amy. All the time."

I stared blankly in the direction of the animals and nodded my head. Positive vibes warmed my thoughts and produced a sense of well-being. A hundred yards away the cantina's door slammed, and people lined up for breakfast.

"Right on time. I'm famished." Sarah strode off toward the dining room while I lagged behind, in no hurry to face the commotion.

The cantina rocked with the noise of hungry campers, hikers, and mule riders waiting to eat. The din inside the building jarred my hearing after the comforting sounds of nature. If not for the prospect of lively conversation with table mates and the probability of meeting Glen, I would have returned to our campsite for a quiet meal of oatmeal and dried fruit.

Sarah, with the advantage of height, spied open seats at the far end of the room. We were headed in that direction when I spotted the familiar color of the Park Service uniform. I was disappointed that it was only Geraldo who approached us. He'd been waiting.

"Good morning, Miss Amy."

"Good morning, Geraldo." I scanned the room over his shoulder for another Park Service uniform.

"Ranger Hawk requested that I deliver this message to you." He withdrew a note from his shirt pocket and handed the folded paper to me.

"Thanks, Geraldo." I tried to stop emotions from playing across my face and smiled at him, putting the note into my pocket.

"Have a very good day, Miss Amy." He made a serious little bow and hurried out the door.

"What was that all about?" Sarah had waded back to me through the crush of people, tables, and chairs.

"Geraldo delivered a note from Glen."

"He stood you up?" I could see that her remark was meant to be a friendly tease, but she saw me flinch from the sting of her comment and asked more gently, "So what's he say?"

"I don't know." I took the note from my pocket and read it. "He's following a lead and left for Indian Gardens early this morning. Hopes to see us there this evening."

"That's not bad," she said. "Why don't we eat and get an early start?"

I wondered how she knew that the camaraderie in the cantina would not be the same for me without Glen. With a tiny smile, I silently thanked her for understanding and for not making the situation into a big deal.

An hour later, Sarah and I stood on the heavy-duty bridge spanning the turbid water of the Colorado River. Looking back, Phantom Ranch appeared to be an oasis in the desert and underscored the stark difference between the dry, rocky soil for miles around and the leafy land bordered by the creek and river. The contrast was intriguing and beautiful in its own way, like a green gash of hope in the midst of desolation.

"The desert looks forbidding," said Sarah. "More people than I care to think about get caught out there with no water."

"That's what the book says," I said, and patted my two water bottles for reassurance.

Sarah turned toward the far shore. I figured I'd never again see Phantom Ranch, so I took a moment to imprint the scene in my brain; one of life's joys filed away.

We reached the opposite side of the bridge, and I took a last glance upriver. Three rafts in primary colors bobbed along like toys in the swift current, incongruously bright and playful in a very serious landscape.

The trail on the other side of the Colorado quickly took us away from the river and snaked through the dust in the general direction of up. The temperature rose faster than we did, and shade became scarce. Even so, movement invigorated my body. As on our previous hiking days, we fell into the rhythm of a steady slow pace, but with a difference. The pounding descent of our first two days in the canyon bruised my toes and injured my knees, now the ascent burned my quad muscles. Of the two, I preferred the climb up.

"This would be easier if Illinois wasn't so vertically challenged." I paused on a flat area, stalling—gasping for breath. "I should have trained on steeper stairs."

"You're doing fine," Sarah assured me. Her labored breathing made me less self-conscious about my insufficient strength.

We took several mini-breaks throughout the morning to make the trek manageable. The trail took us through arid dun-colored landscape, once dipping into a ravine split by a narrow coursing stream. Water careened against tight, tumbled rocks and sprayed our heated skin.

When the sun stationed itself directly overhead, I noticed a cave gouged into the wall of stone forty feet up. A gnarly tree made the place look inviting, so I suggested we stop for lunch. After several ounces of water and a homemade energy bar, we took to the trail again.

The afternoon progressed as the morning had, slow and hot. Conversation stalled, but my thoughts did not. It was tempting to forget the world outside the canyon, to forget that tragedies had occurred. I reminded myself that whoever attacked Kylie and the man who heaved the rock at Sarah were still out there. I tried to stay alert, but we had not seen a living soul for hours.

"This is supposed to be a busy corridor," I said. "Where is everybody?"

Sarah shrugged. "If we had a medical emergency on this trail, we'd never get help."

I suspected she was right. My imagination conjured up images of real snake bites, broken bones, heatstroke, and heart attacks. I pushed those negative thoughts away and concentrated on planting my feet deliberately to avoid a twisted ankle or nasty fall. My knee pain became part of the routine, background noise.

The dry afternoon dragged on. The monotony was finally alleviated by a shallow creek undercutting a cliff. The trail edged along the slit of water hemmed in by reeds on one side and the canyon wall on the other.

A lone pink flower, perhaps a mallow, clung to a niche in the rock wall and enticed me to stop. A perfect reason to remove my boots, I thought.

I swear my swollen feet sizzled as I plunged them into the icy water. My lungs sucked in air and exhaled a scream chopped into little puffs of breath.

"Cold?" Sarah laughed and waded right into the stream to splash herself.

"Cold is an understatement." My feet turned blue.

Sarah bent over and dunked her head into the current, four inches deep and barely enough to wet her scalp. I chose a less radical course. I dunked my bandana into the stream and tied it loosely around my neck. The frigid shock nearly popped my eyes from their sockets. I also submerged my straw hat and put it dripping wet on my head. Sarah hooted.

I didn't know what I looked like and didn't care. Style and fashion are ridiculous ideas in the wild where the lack of common sense can kill.

When we neared Indian Garden Campgrounds and civilization later in the day, I removed my rumpled hat and smoothed down my hair. I wasn't sure I succeeded, but I tried not to look like a mangled dog toy.

18

INDIAN GARDENS - Elevation: 3,800 ft.

Like desert rats, we limped into a grove of cottonwood trees. A cool breeze wafted across my sweaty skin. I yearned to dump my pack and take the weight off my aching knee, but Sarah continued trucking along. I followed her.

"This must be Indian Garden," I said, "but where are the tents?"

Sarah only shrugged. She seemed energized knowing we had reached the end of our trek. Still, the path went on and on, finally leading us to a length of split-rail fencing and a mule corral.

Several cowboys sat at ease astride docile mules and turned to watch our progress.

"I can drill that toe for you," one of them called.

"Oh for gripe sakes." I groaned under my breath and held out my hand to stop any further talk. "No thank you!" I waved, smiled and maintained my course. "What's with these guys and drilling toes?"

Sarah shook her head. "That's the worst pickup line I've ever heard, but they must get a good response."

"They weren't trying to pick us up. He saw me limping and thought he could help."

"Yeah, right."

"I'm sure his offer was sincere," I insisted.

She squinted at me from beneath her wide-brimmed hat. "You don't get out much do you?"

"Not really, but I have good instincts."

"Uh huh. You better stick with me."

I appreciated her concern, however unnecessary.

Five minutes later we came upon a row of colorful, two-person tents in neatly partitioned campsites. No one was in sight.

"Maybe everyone is napping," I whispered.

"Or out exploring," Sarah said.

We dragged ourselves along the hoof-imprinted path to the far side of the campground before finding an open site.

After five hours on the trail and ascending 1,254 feet in elevation, my body begged to get horizontal. Instead, we worked to make the campsite our home for the night. Within ten minutes we had the tent up, our gear unpacked, and the empty packs hung from the T-bar.

Ranger Glen found us as I stowed our food sacks in the ammunition box.

"You made it." He greeted us both.

"Barely." I welcomed him with a smile.

"Some of your cowboy buddies offered to drill her toe." Sarah motioned toward the other end of the campground.

He grinned at her playful challenge. "They were just being helpful."

"Uh-huh," she said. "I'm going to find a water spigot."

"Up the hill there." He pointed toward a grove of trees.

Glen stood at the entrance of our site, his feet squarely planted and his thumbs hooked into his belt loops. He must have taken the time to wash up; his face was fresh, pink cheeks shone through his tan. Canyon life agreed with him.

"Sit down," I said. "I'll make lemon drinks for us."

He joined me at the picnic table where I opened two zip-lock packets and poured powdered flavoring into each water bottle.

"Seriously," he said, "you should think about drilling your toenail if the throbbing has gotten worse."

I detected no teasing, only concern. "My toe is not my biggest problem, though a lovely shade of violet has developed. After several hours of hiking, my knee is what's killing me."

"Well, sure. The thirty pounds you hauled down here is hard on the knees. Do you want me to carry some of your gear tomorrow?"

I frowned, miffed he thought I didn't measure up as a true backpacker. "No. I want to do this hike myself." That's the answer a real backpacker would give.

"Okay." He nodded in approval.

I had misjudged his intent, so I backed off. "Thanks for asking," I said before changing the subject. "I'm worried about Kylie. Have you seen her—or Eric? Have you been here all day?"

"I haven't seen either one today. I just got in from patrolling the side trails looking for our thief. We got two more reports of stolen food and gear, so my boss asked me to take a stroll up here." Glen swirled his bottle of lemon drink, frowning. "Last night when I questioned Eric, he swore he hadn't seen Kylie since yesterday morning."

"If Kylie never caught up to Eric," I said, "she should be on the Rim by now, on the way to Tucson."

"That's probably where she is. Don't worry," Glen said. "We haven't had any injury reports."

Sarah ambled back into our campsite guzzling water. "Ah. Fresh and cold." She deposited herself on the seat opposite mine. "What's up?"

"No sign of Kylie or Eric," I told her. "There's been a couple of more thefts and Glen's been tracking down the thief."

"A trail rat like that could be anywhere." Sarah gestured down the row of tents. "He'll blend in with all the other backpackers."

"Probably so," Glen agreed.

"Is this much crime normal?" Sarah asked. "Murder, theft, ambush."

"It's been a bad week." Glen nodded with a dour frown. "The canyon is a big place, and we have to deal with undesirables here and there, but this is rare."

We sat in silence, stewing in our own thoughts, until Glen's face brightened. "How about we forget the problems for a while, do some exploring? We rangers know of a fabulous place to watch the sunset."

Pointing to my knee, I shook my head, but Glen looked so disappointed, I relented. "Maybe after I nap for thirty minutes. How far is this secret ranger place?"

"About a mile." He gestured to the east. "It's called Plateau Point and juts out into the deep canyon so you have views on every side. The colors are gorgeous."

I warmed to the idea. "Why don't we have a picnic there, so we don't have to rush dinner, and I can rest for a while?"

"Good idea. Sarah?"

"I'm in."

"You'll love the plateau," Glen declared. "Meet me down at the corral when you're ready." He clapped his hands on his knees and stood up. "Get a nap. We have at least two hours before sunset."

When he was gone I unzipped the tent and crawled in. Sarah already had her painting supplies arranged on the picnic table.

"Have a good nap," she said.

"Wake me in thirty minutes."

She nodded, already engrossed with her watercolors. I pulled the mesh door zipper closed and settled my head on my makeshift pillow.

19

PLATEAU POINT - Elevation: 3,740 ft.

A minute later Sarah shook the tent and her voice pulled me out of a stupor. "Wake up, sleepyhead."

I sat up slowly. "What's the matter?"

"Nothing. I let you sleep for forty-five minutes, and now we're late."

"Oh." My brain worked as fast as molded clay. "I'm coming." I stumbled from the tent and dashed cool water on my face to clear my head. We rushed to pack our cooking supplies and headed for the corral.

The fresh air and brisk pace revived me. By the time we met Glen, I was ready for the promised adventure. He had been watching for us, waiting with a foot propped up on the corral's lowest rung and his forearms resting on the top rail. He straightened up when we approached. A smile spread across his face. "How was the nap?"

"Good," I said. "Hope you weren't waiting long."

"Nah. I enjoyed watching the mules." He tossed a bit of straw into the corral. "Ready?"

"Lead the way," Sarah said.

A dirt path, spongy underfoot with layers of woodland debris, trailed through a stand of pine and cottonwood. Before long, the path branched at a Y intersection. An arrow and the word 'Plateau' burned into a wooden sign directed us to the right. Fifty yards further the path left the deepening shade and took us into an open, rocky area. From that vantage point, we saw the well-worn path leading downhill toward the canyon precipice in the distance. Thirty or more people traipsed along the crooked trail ahead of us.

"I thought you said this was a secret ranger spot," I said.

He grinned like a rascal. "I said gorgeous, not secret."

I hid my disappointment. "Well, a site this popular must be gorgeous."

"Looks like the in-place to be," Sarah said.

The line of people trooped along as if making a pilgrimage. We were among the privileged few who would view nature's astonishing beauty from a spectacular perspective. The footpath snaked along for another half mile and the land around us fell away. Like the state of Florida hangs off the continental U.S., this peninsula of land jutted into the thin air of the main canyon.

The temperature dropped as we neared the precipice. Cracks cleaved the foundation rocks beneath our feet. I hopped over them with some trepidation and prayed that an earthquake did not choose that particular moment to shake the bedrock and open additional chasms.

Glen stepped over a wide, deep cleft and turned back to me. "Need a hand?"

I took the offered help without hesitation, held my breath, and jumped. "Thank you, sir." I attempted nonchalance, but my words sounded thin.

Thirty or forty pilgrims stood or sat among the layered rock that formed the platform overlooking the canyon. A metal railing near the edge seemed out of place, but a barrier was necessary to warn the unwary that slipping off the crumbling rim would mean certain death. Still, a group of girls ventured beyond the railing and sat with their legs dangling over the edge. Their flirt with death gave me chills and I looked away, wishing their mothers had kept them safe at home.

"Here's a good spot." Sarah had chosen a group of smooth rocks that formed natural benches and low tables.

The picnic that had seemed like a great idea now seemed a nuisance. I wanted to ogle the scenery, not attend to the mundane chore of cooking. While the food re-hydrated, I wandered to the railing, gripped the metal with white knuckles and looked into the abyss.

"This is why we came here." Sarah viewed the horizon with a dreamy look of contentment.

"What a truly gorgeous scene." I relaxed, willing my senses to open to every sensation.

Glen stood behind us. "Look to your left."

Two big birds; their wings spread wide, were silhouetted against the golden sun. They neared the plateau and appeared larger and larger. The swoop and shape of the wings seemed familiar to me. "Vultures?" I asked.

"Condors," Glen said.

"I thought there were only a few condors left—in California," I exclaimed.

"We were down to twenty-two worldwide, but that's up to almost four hundred now. They've been reintroduced here in the canyon and are doing well."

I detected pride in Glen's voice as he spoke of the National Park Service's hand in protecting the birds.

"This plateau is one of their favorite areas," he said. "They have a cave nearby."

The birds effortlessly soared on the thermal updrafts up and away from us. Our own personal tour guide spoke with awe in his voice and filled us in on the efforts to save the birds.

"Here they come again." Sarah had her long-range lens trained on the condors. The magnificent birds soared no more than fifty feet in front of us and then dipped below the level of our feet. I could see them clearly. Their heads were a featherless pink making them as ugly as turkey vultures, though I didn't want to say that aloud and spoil the moment.

"They're twice the size of vultures," I marveled.

Glen corrected me. "Five times the size. Their wingspan is nine and a half feet wide, and they weigh about twenty-five pounds."

"Wow," Sarah said from behind her camera. Her shutter clicked continuously until the condors flew out of range. "I think I got some good ones." She held out her camera to give me a preview.

Nearly everyone on the plateau had been focused on the condors, but with their departure, the excitement died down. People went back to their own conversations, though a few near to us listened to Glen's explanations. They feigned disinterest, but I could tell their ears were tuned into Glen.

When the free ranger program ended, we settled onto the rock seats and ate our meals. Our vantage point was perfect for watching the sunset. The sun's rays came in at a lower angle and dusted the orange and yellow layers of the distant mesa in pink and purple. None of the masters: Monet, Van Gogh, or Bierstadt could have adequately captured the scene.

I knew that Sarah's photographs wouldn't either, but maybe they'd jog my memory. She had agreed to burn a CD for me.

"What causes the layers of colors?" I looked at Glen, expecting him to have answers, and he didn't disappoint me.

"The reds and orange are from iron, of course, but there are traces of many different minerals which create the subtle hues from dark red, to yellow and even green. I suspect the green is from copper."

"Mix in the sun coming through the clouds and you have a masterpiece," I added.

We shared the transformation of the landscape. Dusk arrived and the other visitors began to straggle back toward camp.

Sarah put her camera away and announced she'd return to camp with them. "Why don't you two stay to enjoy the stars?"

I considered leaving with her, but wasn't ready. "I'll be back at camp soon."

"Take your time."

Sarah hopped nimbly across the several crevices and down to flat ground. She struck up a conversation with the young girls who had dared to test gravity at the edge of the plateau. Eventually, the trail of dust kicked up by the departing groups settled down, and Glen and I were alone.

We sat with our backs supported by one of the layered rocks. I slipped into my jacket to ward off the evening chill and appreciated Glen's warmth nearby. At ease and happy that I had allowed him to pursue me this far, I ignored a hint of guilt.

Neither one of us needed to fill the silence with conversation. The scenery was enough. The last rays of dying sun threw glorious colors against distant plateaus and mesas. Shadows loomed up from the depths and engulfed entire mountain ranges. Nature controlled the choreography, and we humans could only witness the drama. It was a humbling experience. We were intruders who had stumbled into a sacred ritual.

"Isn't this spectacular?" Glen spoke softly with genuine awe.

"I know of nothing that compares."

The moon had yet to rise, and stars began to prick through the night's black curtain.

"There's the Milky Way," Glen said.

Hoping that he didn't read anything into my actions, I lay on my back to view the brilliant stars. "This view isn't possible in Illinois. The galaxy stretches across the entire sky."

I wanted to enjoy the panorama and gaze into the cosmos, but suddenly became aware that my little body was stuck out on a promontory above a yawning black hole. My imagination got the better of me. I sensed eyes peering at me from outer space. Perhaps a satellite snapped my picture, maybe aliens cruised in stealth formation through the blackened sky. My vulnerability overwhelmed me. I feared I would vanish without a trace and needed to get under the trees and away from the open.

"Do you mind if we head back?" I asked.

Surprised, Glen agreed immediately and stuffed our gear into his pack.

A fright built within me making me anxious to move. Glen apparently sensed no danger, so I shook off my fear, but hurried away from the plateau's edge. His powerful light pierced the wall of darkness, but still wasn't adequate for my peace of mind. The crevices which we had so blithely hopped across in daylight seemed treacherous in the night, as if some unseen force would grab at my ankles and pull me down. Glen stepped across the largest crevice and held his hand out to me.

Not soon enough for me, we got to flat ground. I breathed easier, until I realized that beyond the reach of our light beams, the winding trail and the edge of the drop off had become invisible.

"Talk to me, Glen. I need to keep my mind busy. Something is making me jittery."

"There's no need to be nervous."

"I know," I said, "but tell me a ranger story. Why do people take the job?"

"Not for the pay." He chuckled and kept up a steady stream of light conversation which freed my mind from the terrors of the night. His deep voice told legends about the canyon and tales of rangers who had come and gone.

Nothing, however, worked to ease the pain that had taken a hold of my left knee. I regretted leaving my trekking poles back in camp.

"Do you mind if I take your arm? My knee is killing me."

"My pleasure." He held out his arm, and we negotiated the rocky trail together.

My knee muscles rebelled in a continuous ache. Suddenly, my knee seized up in a spasm of pain. A gasp escaped me.

"Are you okay?" The concern in his voice encouraged me to tell the truth.

"No," I whispered. "The pain in my knee is terrible."

"Do you want to rest?"

We paused, but mostly I wanted to keep moving and get to my tent. I shouldn't have stayed late on the plateau and wished I was already tucked into my sleeping bag. I clung to Glen's arm and hobbled forward until another pain grabbed me. The intensity of the spasm took my breath away.

When my fingers grasped his bicep, Glen's large, calloused hand covered mine and gave a gentle squeeze. I caught my breath and willed my knee muscles to relax. "I can walk now."

One step further and pain seared through me again. He heard my gasp. I couldn't hide my agony anymore. Tears formed.

"Take it easy," he said. "We'll go one step at a time."

We struggled along with his beam of light scanning the trail in front of us until Glen made an abrupt stop. "Look."

Several pairs of yellow eyes loomed in the darkness as if they floated over the open ravine. "What is that?"

"Deer maybe," he whispered. "Maybe ringtails. Harmless, whatever they are."

"I hope you're right," I said. "I'm in no shape to run."

The eyes didn't move. I imagined something stalking us in the dark and wished he could train the light on them, but we needed the light for the trail lest we miss a curve and topple off the edge.

Suddenly, a howl tore the inky night and careened off the canyon walls followed by a series of ever more alien screeches. "What was that?" I gasped. "Wolves?"

"There are no wolves in the canyon." He tried to sound reassuring, but I could tell the howling disconcerted him, too.

My imagination was in hyper-drive. "Sounds like a banshee screaming for its dead."

The wailing spiraled through the canyon, and I gripped Glen's arm tighter. I tried to decipher the noise and filter the echoes from the original howls.

Glen came to an unbelievable conclusion. "That's human."

His deduction was difficult to fathom. "Creepy."

"Don't worry," he said. "Some idiot is just fooling around."

Knowing that a human capable of making those hellish sounds was out in the dark was no comfort. "Sounds like he's taunting us," I whispered.

Glen didn't answer.

The echoing howls subsided, and I lurched along in silence dragging my left leg and leaning heavily on Glen's arm. The pain again seized me. I dug my fingernails into his forearm. When the spasm ended, I realized that I must have hurt him. I relaxed my fingers. "Sorry, sorry." I patted his arm where the scratches must be.

"It's okay," he whispered. "Why don't you let me carry you? It would be less painful."

"I can handle pain."

"I meant less painful for me."

My laugh came out in a moan.

My ears listened for the howls, my eyes searched for lurking figures, but my mind could think only of the pain in my knee. It was getting worse. The trail seemed endless, and tears rolled down my face, hidden in the dark.

Each time Glen's headlamp swung in my direction, I ducked my head, but I could tell he wasn't fooled.

"Please let me carry you."

"That's not necessary," I insisted.

"Piggyback. It would be easy."

I sorely wanted to be swept up into his arms and have him take the pain away. "No, I have to do this myself." I didn't say that I feared I'd make him clumsy, and we'd both tumble off the edge of the cliff. Or, that if we were jumped by the howler, he'd need his hands free.

"You are such a trouper," he said.

"I am such a mess."

Our return from the plateau should have taken twenty minutes, but had dragged on more than an hour. Finally, my torture neared its end. The trail led into tall trees, and our headlamps reflected off man-made objects: the mule corral, a shed, tents nestled among the trees. We had found civilization, and relief flooded through me.

I hobbled past darkened campsites. Three hundred feet further I recognized Sarah's yellow tent. "Home sweet home."

Our campsite was silent and dark.

"Will you be all right?" he whispered. "If the howling idiot makes you nervous, I can pitch a tent nearby."

"I'll be okay," I said, but suspected otherwise. "Sarah's here. I'm going to take two ibuprofen and get to sleep."

"Do you want me to hike out with you tomorrow?"

His concern touched me. At that moment I would've loved to be pampered; but tomorrow, I'd want to complete the canyon myself, on my own two legs. "No, thanks. I'll be fine. Be careful going back."

He gave my arm one last pat. "Don't worry about me. I'll stop by in the morning to say good-bye."

"Come for coffee," I said. "Good night."

"Good night, Amy."

His whisper was already moving off into the dark. In quiet stealth, I fished the first aid kit from my pack and popped the pain relievers into my mouth.

There was no way to unzip a tent quietly, but I tried. Sarah's moist, rhythmic breathing assured me she was asleep. I climbed over her to my side of the tent and removed my boots and jacket in slow motion. I eased my aching head onto my pillow and closed my eyes.

A second later Sarah said, "So tell me everything." She sat up in expectation. "You were gone a long time."

My eyes were too heavy to open. "There's nothing to tell," I said, "except we heard the most ungodly howling somewhere in the canyon, and my knee is killing me." I moaned. "Can we talk tomorrow? I'm exhausted."

"Promise to tell all?"

"Yes, I will."

I barely had the strength to tug off my clothes and pull my sleeping bag over my shoulders. Sarah soon breathed deeply, but I could not quiet my mind enough to sleep. My body was beyond exhaustion, my toe ached, and pain gripped my knee. I indulged in a pity party for myself and wished I had been with a loving husband on the plateau. *A husband should protect his wife. Glen is wonderful, but at my age I should not be in this situation. John was right. I'm crazy for hiking the canyon. I always take on too much and fall on my face.*

Tears rolled from the corner of my eyes and into my ears, so I turned on my side and stared at the pitch blackness with the tent wall five inches from my nose. *There's a murderer out there, I just know it. I miss my kids.* I sighed miserably. It was supposed to be a silent sigh, but came out a ragged sob instead. I hoped Sarah was asleep and didn't hear.

"Are you okay?" she asked.

I tried not to sniffle. "I'm feeling sorry for myself, I guess. I don't think I can hike out tomorrow. I'm no good at this." I heard her turn toward me.

"Are you kidding me?"

I couldn't trust my voice to say anything without a sob.

"Hey." She gave me a little poke. "You're doing great. You kept *me* going. I could see you were in pain, so I had to suck it up myself. We've come so far. Do you realize how many people never get to see this canyon from the inside? How many women our age would never dare? We are one in a million. Well, two in two million. Right?" She jostled my shoulder. "Right?"

I rolled onto my back. "Okay, you're right."

"Seriously, I'm right. You were determined to hike this far and you succeeded. You are stoic, Amy. Good word, huh? Stoic."

How could I not laugh? "I'm fine, just tired."

"Of course. You get a good rest and tomorrow you'll be strong."

"Then, we go home," I said.

"Yep, back to civilization."

I heard her settle back onto her pillow and reposition herself in her sleeping bag. The rustling of nylon fabric masked another deep sigh. I tried to muffle a sob with my pillow, but the quiet magnified every sound.

"Amy, please tell me what's wrong."

"I'm thinking too much," I managed to say.

"About what?" she coaxed.

I forced the words out in a hoarse whisper. "He left me."

"What? Out on the plateau?" She started up angrily.

"No, no. Not Glen. My husband left me. John." The words broke from me, quiet and deadly. "He wants a divorce."

Her arms reached for me, and I turned to her. I hadn't cried like that in years. Her voice was soothing and sincere as she cradled me. "I'm so sorry, Amy."

"It's not fair." A sob stuck in my throat, hurting. "This is not the way it's meant to be. John should be here with me, and we should be having the time of our lives. Instead, he's through with me." I couldn't quite get my mind around the idea.

"Do you want to talk about it? What happened?"

"Nothing really." An invisible weight sat on my chest. "He said we've been together too long—and I can't disagree." I couldn't believe what I was saying and drew out each syllable of every word.

Sarah's whisper was barely audible. "Is there someone else?"

"I doubt it, maybe." The night hid my failure, and the words spilled out. "He loves when the bar-types hang all over him at the club. When he gets home, he tells me how some floozy pushed her boobs against him or ran her hand up his leg."

"Why does he tell you all that?"

"He said he was being open and honest with me. In his mind, he's the good guy, but gets to push the envelope."

"Kinda disgusting."

"That's what I said, but it never was worth getting upset about. He claimed I was smarter and classier than any of those women. Now I wonder." Sniffling, I sat up and rested my throbbing head on my knees.

"Are you angry yet?" Sarah demanded.

"I don't feel much of anything. I'm just numb. I hope he *is* having an affair. That would at least be an explanation."

"Do you love him?"

Her question sucked the air from my lungs. "I think I have to say yes." I suspected my answer disappointed her. "My duty is to love him. He's family."

"Not very romantic."

"We've been married for twenty-nine years."

"Hey, I'm not criticizing," she said. "I'm wondering if it's been enough for you—to keep you happy."

"I'm not sure what happiness is anymore."

"That's not right. You deserve to be happy."

I shook my head in the darkness.

"Will you try to change his mind? Try marriage counseling, or something?"

The unbelievable answer came to me. "I don't think I care enough about John to fight for him." The thought that a long marriage would end with so little fanfare saddened me. "He must have planned this for a long time. He already hired a lawyer and suggested I get one, too. We'll split everything down the middle . . ."

She let me trail off, then asked, "How do you feel about giving him a divorce?"

"Exhausted." My world looked black. "Mostly I'm tired of him controlling my every move. What to wear, what to say in public. How to cut my hair. *Gad.* He even tried to tell me when to take a shower." I took an exasperated breath.

"Let it out, Amy. Get angry."

"He treated me like I was a chore or a belonging, like a car in need of maintenance. He was once excited to have me, to take care of me, but now he's done. Ready to move on."

The flood gates had been opened, and Sarah let me run on. "I'm relieved, sort of. We've been spinning around in separate worlds. Still, I assumed we'd always be a family and grow old together. I thought I was doing a good job by putting up with him—apparently, he was putting up with me."

"Don't go there, Amy. He's the jerk, not you."

Like a confessional, talking into the blackness was easier than face-to-face in daylight, and telling a new friend was more simple; no preconceived opinions of me, or John. No history.

"I haven't even told my kids, no one. They'll be so disappointed. I wanted to be a good example for them."

"Don't you think they see how he treats you?" she asked. "You can teach them to find happiness by finding your own."

Everything she said was true, but the sadness would not leave me. "I feel so worthless."

"Oh, honey, that's so untrue. You have so much going for you. Without him messing with your mind, you can go out in the world and be yourself, like you are here in the canyon. Witty, warm, smart."

"Don't forget stoic."

She stroked my hair, tucking a strand behind my ear. "And stoic." I could almost see her kind eyes through the darkness. I had finally drained myself of words.

"I think I'm done. Thanks for listening, Sarah."

"That's what friends are for. This isn't something you should go through alone."

"Good night, Sarah."

As if a hot fever had broken, I relaxed and could think in clear, cool lines. Someone had finally said it: John is a jerk. I had to travel a thousand miles to see the truth, but there it was. Sarah had vindicated me.

I rolled over in my sleeping bag to rethink my world. Vignettes of happiness poked holes through the darkness. My kids would embrace me. I'd learn to kayak—and buy a starter pistol. Dye my hair red. I pictured myself atop the peak of a snowcapped mountain, my arms raised in triumph.

20

Day 7 - THREE-MILE REST HOUSE

Elevation: 3,048 ft.

An early dawn arrived. I'd dreamed too much and rolled over to give sleep another try. My hip hit the hard ground without the benefit of a layer of air. I groaned and reached up to test the air valve. Sure enough, I had failed to close the valve and my sleeping pad had gone flat. No wonder my hip and back ached. I opened my eyes and began to complain to Sarah, but I was alone. She had managed to slip out of the tent without a sound. I rolled over onto her comfortable sleeping pad and dozed off.

"Is she still asleep?" My eyes flew open at the sound of his voice.

"Yeah. Rough night."

"I'm worried about her," he said.

"Me, too. Coffee? What happened out there?" Cups clinked.

"Thanks. Her knee was so painful she couldn't walk. I offered to carry her, but . . . you know how stubborn she is."

"Hey, I can hear you." My voice croaked like a machine in need of oil. Glen's husky laugh made me eager to start my day.

"Good morning, Amy," he called. "How do you feel?"

I didn't know yet, so I took inventory: knee, toe, emotions. I cringed thinking Sarah might tell him about my breakdown last night. "I think I'm okay. I'll be right out."

Within sixty seconds I rolled myself out of the sleeping bag and into my clothes and then unzipped the tent. The two of them stood with titanium mugs in their fists expectantly watching me. I straightened up, put weight on my left leg and wobbled my knee back and forth. "Feels fine now. I don't understand. Maybe I was overtired last night."

"Maybe," said Glen, giving me the benefit of a doubt.

His bemused look made me wonder if my crying jag had wrecked my face. I self-consciously ran my hand through my hair and wished I had gotten up earlier to brush my teeth. I turned my back to him to swallow an ibuprofen followed by a gulp of water.

I gathered my courage and joined them at the picnic table. Sarah tapped the titanium pot with her finger tip. "Hot water for your tea. We don't have much else. Something got into our ammunition boxes during the night." She pointed to a pile of dirty packets and baggies.

Glen frowned. "They can't get at your food if you secure the boxes under the bench."

Sarah rolled her eyes and clucked her tongue. "They *were* jammed under the bench. Your ringtail cats figured that out."

The ranger raised his eyebrows, but was smart enough not to question Sarah further.

My raisins, granola bar, and other snacks were safe, still wrapped in the mesh bag. I examined my trampled tea bags and oatmeal packets. "We can salvage these," I said, looking for toothmarks and finding none. "Are you sure it was *animals* that broke into the boxes?"

"Stuff was scattered all over this morning," Sarah insisted. "Our packs were on the ground, empty."

"Sounds more like a thief looking for valuables," I said, getting up from the table to inventory my pack.

"I've got to catch this guy," Glen said in disgust, his poised pen over a small notebook ready to make yet another report.

"All my gear appears to be there." I shrugged. "What are you missing, Sarah?"

"I don't know, maybe nothing." She plopped herself down on the picnic bench, still making a case against the ringtail cats. "A thief would steal something, don't ya think?"

"Unless he searched for something specific and didn't find it." I contemplated the possibilities and dunked a tea bag up and down in my mug to color the water.

"Maybe he hit other campsites," said Glen. "I'll check around." He had been watching me from behind his coffee cup. "You're favoring your left leg."

Sarah slid her eyes over to me. "I don't have a problem with staying another night here so you can rest your knee."

I bent and stretched my leg under the picnic table, hoping that I'd get through the day without a recurrence of last night's pain. "I'll baby myself, but we should stick to the schedule."

"Don't push too hard, Amy," Glen said. "If that knee is bothering you, I'll get a permit for another night and scrounge up food for you."

"Amazingly, my knee doesn't hurt right now. Besides I have a hotel reservation in Phoenix and a plane to catch." My response snuffed out a bit of brightness in his eyes. I sensed he wanted more from me, but I couldn't trust my emotions. Not after this week's turmoil.

Keeping a friendly tone, I invited him to breakfast.

"No thanks," Glen said. "I just stopped by to check on you and say good bye. I've got some investigating to do." He glanced at what remained of our supplies and added two sticks of beef jerky to our food stash before moving toward the path, leaving.

A mild panic urged me to stop him, but I got myself under control and said, "Thanks for your help, Glen. You've been great."

"My pleasure, Amy. I'm glad to have met you. Sarah, you too. Be sure to keep that puncture wound clean."

"Sure, Glen," Sarah said. "Thanks."

She turned toward me when he was out of range. "I thought you liked him," she shot at me. "You kinda blew him off."

"I do like him, but there's nothing I can do. I can't get into a relationship. I'm still married."

"Technically."

I moaned and put my mind to cobbling together a sufficient breakfast. We talked in hushed voices as if someone would eavesdrop on our conversation.

"I don't know what I feel about him," I said after a while. "I have no experience with this. What if I'm confusing loneliness with attraction?

Maybe it's a vacation aura, and he only seems attractive because he is in this beautiful place."

"Vacation aura?"

"You know, when you buy a souvenir you love, but when you get the thing home you say, *What in the heck did I buy this for*? I don't want to do that to him."

"So you think of him as a souvenir?" Her belly laugh relieved my tension.

I smiled into my mug and paid more attention than necessary to the last bit of oatmeal in the bottom of my bowl. "You know what I mean."

"Yeah, I do, and I can't argue with your logic, but when you find a good one . . ." She shook her spoon at me for emphasis. ". . . you have to go for it."

"You're right." I sighed and stood up to gather my dishes. "But I can't see myself as single right now."

She clasped her fingers together and bit on the first knuckle. "Okay. I'll let the subject drop," she said as she gathered up the salvaged food. "So do you want to shoot for packs-on at nine-thirty?"

"That works for me."

We cleaned up in short order and had plenty of time to relax and to take in the sights of Indian Garden. Sarah took pictures and penciled sketches in her tablet, while I made myself comfortable on a bench with a view of the trail—a good vantage point to eye up possible thieves. Only a few innocent looking backpackers hiked out to take advantage of the cooler morning hours.

A cowboy whistled a warning and the hikers stepped into the bushes at the side of the wide path. Riderless mules thundered by like wild horses. The mules seemed to run for the joy of running. Perhaps the beasts have fooled us humans with their plodding, dowdy demeanor, while underneath they have the souls of sleek thoroughbreds. The thought made me want to run with them, my hair streaming in the wind.

Sarah collected her art supplies and stowed them in her pack. She took pride in being on time, so I roused myself and made final adjustments to my pack. At 9:30 on the dot, we cinched ourselves into our backpacks.

Feeling like I left something behind, I scanned the area near the picnic table and where the tent had been.

"I guess that's everything," I said.

* * *

The well-worn path angled steeply out of the campground, and I soon found myself huffing and puffing. The day's schedule required a five-mile hike to the South Rim, but that included an elevation gain of 3,060 feet, so our pace was slow, maybe less than one mile per hour. The trail rose like a flight of stairs, as if we trudged up a skyscraper's stairwell. I was comforted by the notion that my muscles would adapt and my breathing would be more normal once my body accustomed itself to this physical exertion. Miraculously, only a twinge bothered my knee. Even so, I soon signaled to Sarah that I needed a rest stop.

From our perch on a cliff, we could see the grove of trees that shaded Indian Gardens. I scanned the camp to see if maybe Glen waited there for us to turn around and wave. I chastised myself for being so silly and fought down the urge to borrow Sarah's binoculars. Instead, my sight followed the trail out of camp and up the side of several hills, checking our progress.

"That doesn't look like we've gone far at all," I said in exasperation.

"The zig zagging trail makes the way longer, but we can't climb these walls." Sarah shaded her eyes and looked up at the towering mesa as if she might consider doing just that.

"There's a mule train coming down," she said.

Shielding my eyes from the glare of the sun, I looked in the direction of her point until I spotted the string of animals and their riders rounding a corner of the mesa wall. Too proud to let the mule riders see me looking exhausted, I took a last gulp of water and hauled myself up from my comfortable rock.

Ten minutes later we heard the scrape of iron shoes against rock, announcing the approach of the mule train. Sarah and I automatically sped up our pace to reach a niche in the rocks to step into and give the animals room to pass.

The nine-hundred-pound mules picked their way along the trail with their heads hung low. The weary animals lifted their hooves lazily, stumbling over and unearthing softball-size rocks. Their huge bellies swayed side to side, threatening to throw the beasts off balance.

Blue-jeaned riders, a few of them nearing the two-hundred-pound weight limit, straddled the ungainly mules. To block out dust kicked up by the animals, several of the riders covered their mouths with bandanas. Every one of the tourists sat hunched in the saddles, their faces slack with boredom. They leaned awkwardly backwards to avoid being pitched over the necks of the animals on the downhill trail. Man and beast appeared miserable.

When the third of a dozen mules came abreast of us, the animal tripped over a stubborn rock and lurched forward. Its rider grabbed for the saddle horn, stared into the ravine, and turned another shade of pale. The mule caught itself on its other three feet and regained its balance. The wide-eyed young man gave us a weak smile, sweat glistening on his upper lip.

Near the end of the string rode a red-headed woman more alert than the riders in front of her. I envied her the cute cowboy hat, fresh chambray shirt, and the clean bandana tied neatly around her neck. She looked the part of a cowgirl and was probably the one to suggest the mule-riding adventure to her family. She appeared to enjoy the canyon, so I smiled and waved. "How's the mule ride?"

"I'd rather hike with you," she said. "I have saddle sores."

"Ouch."

She laughed and waved over her shoulder to us. Sarah watched her awhile longer. "Maybe I'll ride the mules down when I can't backpack anymore."

"Not me," I said. "I can't imagine entrusting my life to a dumb beast this high up. We just saw one of them almost go over the side."

"Nah. They're sure-footed. One of the cowboys said they've never lost a rider, and only one mule, as far back as he could remember."

"I couldn't stand looking down into the ravine like that." I imagined the scenario, and my stomach lurched.

"I know, but if I'm not physically capable of hiking, I'll ride."

She was right, of course, but at the moment my body was healthy and strong—relatively anyway, and wanted no part of saddle sores. My goal was to be like the little lady down at the Ranch, and hike until I'm eighty. As if to underscore that ambition, an adrenalin surge prompted me to take to the trail with a brisk step.

The adrenalin didn't last long. The heat and exertion soon took their toll on me. The ascent seemed increasingly arduous, but frequent stops helped me recover and continue.

"We've got all day," Sarah assured me. "We may as well enjoy the scenery while we can."

So I relaxed and congratulated myself for each step and switchback. After another hour, exhaustion set in. At the next hairpin I sagged onto a boulder to catch my breath and study the map.

"There is something called Three-Mile Resthouse coming up." I held out the map with my finger pointing to the spot.

The idea of a resthouse tantalized me. My eyes hurt, my body ached, and my mood had soured. I needed a long rest, but didn't want to admit to Sarah my lack of energy and strength.

"Good," she said. "I could use a rest—and lunch."

A couple of switch-backs later a structure came into view. A simple metal and stone pavilion had been built next to the path, a welcomed break in the trail tedium. Several day-hikers lounged in its shade.

Sarah and I nodded to the group and deposited our packs on the concrete floor before sitting on the low, stone wall. She dug right into her oversized energy bar. The heat had given me a headache which muddled my brain, so I moved slowly and deliberately, unfolding my bandana and opening Glen's beef jerky.

"That's all you're eating?" Sarah's loud voice made me wince.

"I have crackers and dried fruit, too." I spoke in a near-whisper.

"You'll have a calorie-deficit. We're burning five-hundred calories an hour."

"Whatever."

Suddenly, I resented her know-it-all attitude, her strength, and her cheerfulness. I bit back an abrasive retort, but my annoyance must have shown on my face.

Sarah gave me a hard look. "I'm just saying. You need more calories."

"I know what you're saying and thank you, but you can keep your advice to yourself."

"Hey, don't be like that. I'm offering to share." She held out a piece of her oatmeal and fruit energy bar.

"I don't need your food," I spat out. Irritated, I let my mouth run on. "You think you're always right, and I'm sick of it." I heard my nastiness and regretted my tone, but could not stop myself or retract my words. "I can't take it anymore, okay?" My frown hurt my forehead.

Sarah withdrew her outstretched hand and sniffed. "I'm out of here." She snatched up her lunch debris and grabbed her backpack.

I watched her stomp off and hated myself for what I'd said. *Why did I snap at her?* Maybe I was hungry or dehydrated, or just plain exhausted. There was no logic to my response, but I could not think of a way to undo the damage, so I focused on eating my lunch which tasted bitter in my mouth. I washed the jerky down with several ounces of water and then lay on the stone wall with my eyes closed.

After twenty minutes, the pain killers kicked in and my body began to repair itself. But my emotions were in turmoil. I castigated myself for being nasty and mulled over several scenarios which might make amends.

Feeling better with food in my stomach and a plan in my head, I headed outside to apologize to Sarah. Ready to eat crow, I walked behind the pavilion expecting to find her sitting in the shade or chatting with one of the day-hikers.

She was nowhere to be seen. I followed a small path leading away from the main trail in the direction I thought Sarah had headed.

Apparently, tourists routinely stopped at the pavilion and took the path a short distance to relieve themselves. Paper roses sprouted every ten feet or so where people had squatted behind the larger rocks for privacy. *Did they never hear of Leave no Trace? Disgusting.* My bladder reminded me of all the water I drank, so I took advantage of the quiet area myself— but I tucked my toilet paper into a zip-lock baggie.

I turned my back on the leftovers of civilization and followed the untrampled path that Sarah must have taken. Wilderness survival books tell you to take note of your surroundings in unfamiliar territory and memorize the shape of landmarks. I tried.

I checked my watch and promised myself fifteen minutes of searching before I gave up and returned to the main trail. My heart sank. If I didn't find Sarah by then, I'd continue up to the rim alone.

The path hugged the edge of a narrow side canyon. The track was flat and free of obstacles, yet ignored by hikers. A rock strewn escarpment bordered the path to my right and a steep hill dropped off on my left. I watched my footing and hoped I wasn't entering into the realm of bighorn sheep.

A noise came from behind. I whirled around and backed into the cliff wall in case a ram charged around the bend. Rock on rock, I thought. I listened, but heard nothing more and continued forward.

A few minutes later, I spotted a dark green backpack and wide brimmed hat. "Hey, Sarah!" I waved and sped up, hoping she'd welcome my appearance.

"Feeling better?" She smiled and seemed to forgive me.

"I'm sorry, Sarah. I needed food and water."

"Forget about it." She reassured me with a touch to my arm. "I know I'm bossy."

"No, my fault." I shrugged helplessly. "I get waspish when I'm hungry."

"If you'd warned me, I'd have tossed you a candy bar and gotten out of the way."

She had me laughing again. "I really am sorry."

Sarah waived vaguely behind her. "I explored most of this path. There's not much to see. We could check out the rest of the way or head back to the main trail."

"We should go back."

"Am I being too bossy?" she asked.

I smiled ruefully, shook my head, and gave her a friendly shove toward the main trail.

21

OVER THE EDGE

We stopped to look out over a steep, narrow branch of canyon leading into the larger canyon in the distance. I ran my fingers over the craggy rock wall and examined the interesting layering in various hues of orange, red, green, and purple. "I wish I knew something about geology. This must be the iron Glen mentioned."

"He'd be here to tell you, if you hadn't blown him off." Sarah leaned her shoulder against the stone wall and crossed her arms.

I gave her a withering look, but broke off my comeback when a movement behind her caught my eye.

She turned to follow my stare. "What?"

"I thought I saw something move further up the trail."

"Oh crap, not another ram."

"Don't think so," I said.

We sneaked forward expecting to spot a ringtail or a mountain goat. From a blind spot around the curve of the wall, we heard a growl. We froze, listening.

"Try to see what that is," I suggested.

Sarah sidled up the path with her back to the face of the cliff and peered around the curve. She jumped back, throwing her arm out to push me into the wall. Her intensity startled me.

"What's back there?"

"A man," she whispered. "He looks deranged."

I held my breath and spied around the rocks. About a hundred yards back, a thickly bearded man in ragged clothing stomped down the path toward us, gesticulating wildly. With ungainly gestures, he jabbed at the air in bizarre patterns punctuated with snarls and hisses. The hair on the back of my neck stood up on full alert.

"What should we do?" I asked.

"Let's get out of his way."

Our only choice was backwards, further into the canyon. We didn't need to discuss the situation and turned to hustle up the path, occasionally checking behind us to see if the agitated man was still there. He should have seen us, but perhaps he was in his own crazy world. His pace never altered.

On the move, Sarah briefly consulted her map then shoved it back into her pocket. We covered another sixty yards when the cliff on our right became merely a steep hill, and Sarah made a hairpin turn.

"Here," she said. "Let's climb up there and let him pass."

'Up there' was a small overhang about a thirty-foot fall to the path below, but the ledge was our only sanctuary. We scrambled across the escarpment upward, hoping that the man did not see our dart up the incline. We ascended until we reached the ledge and could go no further. A pile of scat left by the last resident somehow indicated that we were safe.

"I think we lost him." Sarah leaned against the wall, breathing heavily.

I nodded, but scanned the path below us, expecting to see the wild man.

"Where is he?" I wondered.

She peered over the edge and from side to side. "There. He's gone past."

His hissing and mumbling floated up to us, but steadily faded away as he stomped beyond a bend in the trail a hundred yards away. We relaxed.

"Let's sit for a while," Sarah suggested.

"He's probably a harmless canyon guy," I whispered.

"Or a psychotic. Looks like he's on something."

Sarah kept a lookout for movement below. Perched in the aerie with a good view and Sarah on guard, I relaxed. I held out my water bottle, but she shook her head.

"Crap." She held her finger to her lips and flattened herself to the ground.

More afraid of not knowing where he was, than of being seen, I peeked over the edge and watched the crazy guy coming toward us from the right. He prowled slowly, scanning the cliff and stopping occasionally to listen, his arms quiet.

I held my breath when he approached the rocks we had used to climb to the ledge. Thank God, he didn't see the difference between those rocks and any of the other millions of rocks. He passed beneath our position and then turned around and covered the same ground again.

I was certain of one thing; he was hunting us.

The hunter came to a halt. Had we dared, we could have heaved a rock over the side and hit him squarely on the head. Instead, we ducked far back from the edge. His muttering stopped, but we still heard his hissing breath.

I closed my eyes and prayed. I got through two or three Hail Marys.

"He's leaving." Sarah's whisper gave me the courage to open my eyes and peer over the ledge. She pointed left to the tattered man moving away from us, disappearing around a rugged crag. Somewhere along the way, Sarah and I had grabbed each other's hands. I unclenched my fingers and let her go.

"I'm not going down there," I said, "until I'm absolutely sure he is far, far away."

Sarah agreed with a slow shake of her head and continued to stare at the trail to our left. "We've got all afternoon."

We waited quietly, listening to canyon noises and watching vultures drift over a far-off mesa. Everything in nature seemed to be in order. The tension had drained from the air in the hour since our climb.

"He must be gone?" My statement came out a question.

"Yeah. I think we're okay." Sarah didn't sound any more certain.

The climb down was more hazardous than going up. With the gaping canyon in front of us, each step was precarious. I was tempted to scoot down on my butt, but didn't want my shorts full of stickers and stones. Lending one of my hiking poles to Sarah, we each skewered the ground ahead of us to arrest our slides. Crouching low and inching forward got us to the bottom.

Once on flatter ground, we scanned the path.

All was serene. A potentially nasty situation had been avoided.

I sighed in relief. "All clear. Let's get back to the pavilion," I said.

Heading toward the main trail, we quickly resumed our normal hiking pace. The encounter had been harrowing, but turned out to be a minor blip to our day. Peace had returned.

After a short distance, I noticed a few pebbles falling into the path ahead of me and glanced up to the rocks above. I stopped in shock. Sarah bumped into me from behind.

About ten feet above the path, the mangy man clung to a rock niche. When our eyes met, he snarled. Stunned, I stared at him.

With a screech he flung himself from the rock, pouncing like a cougar on the path in front of us. He had the look of a feral animal; unkempt and uncaring. The beast crouched there with saliva glistening in his beard which had obviously become a sieve for all matter of canyon debris. There was a stink about him, like hair balls dropped by vultures.

Through a matte of filthy hair, his red-rimmed eyes glowered, drilling me with his stare. I knew then that our encounter had not been an accidental meeting; he would never have passed us by. Murder was in those eyes, and terror rooted me to the ground.

"Run!" Sarah grabbed my arm and pulled me along behind her.

I jogged as fast as my leaden feet would go. My backpack grew fifty pounds heavier. In seconds my lungs burned, my calf muscles rebelled. I prayed for a place to hide, but we were hemmed in by the face of the cliff on one side and the ravine on the other.

We rounded a bend, and I dared to look over my shoulder, hoping that his aggression had been a bluff.

The maniac maintained a relentless advance. He didn't run or even hurry.

That gave me hope. If we didn't falter, if we could maintain our speed, maybe we could lose him.

"Stop!" Sarah's husky gasp brought me to a crashing halt.

"He'll catch us." I panted and couldn't believe she had given up.

"There's no more." Sweat poured from her red face. She motioned to a rock barrier beyond which there was no path, only thin air.

I fought down panic and searched Sarah's face for her plan. The hardness in her eyes told me that there would be a fight. I held her gaze for a moment, and my mind cleared. Fear built resolve. We turned to face our predator.

Sarah's hand went to her belt and came up with her four-inch blade. I berated myself for not having my knife handy, but held one of my trekking poles in front of me like a lance. A grim determination seized me. I refused to be a victim.

Our defiant stand did not deter our pursuer. He was fifty feet back and approaching steadily, still angry, still beating the air with his fists.

"Stay back!" Sarah barked the order at him and flashed her knife.

I grabbed a loose rock from the wall and heaved the weight in his direction only to have it bounce short and careen off the cliff. I lobbed a few smaller rocks while Sarah threw a barrage of obscenities. Neither had any effect. The gap between us closed quickly. I gripped my lance tighter, planted my feet, and stared into his face.

Something about him looked familiar, maybe the blue pack swinging from his shoulder. A memory flashed through my brain. I had seen that pack before. On the bus, in the lap of Michael Rap. I focused on the man. The lunatic descending upon us was Ultra-lighter.

"Sarah, that's Michael Rap."

She shot a glance at me as if I was the lunatic, but then shifted her stare to the oncoming man. "Whoever he is, I'm ready to beat the crap out of him."

I wanted that courage, but his unwavering intensity scared me—like a wildebeest about to be devoured by a lion. My adrenalin rushed through my body, preparing me for battle, building my resolve to fight tooth and nail. But then something in his hand glinted in the sun and took away my bravado.

"Sarah. He has a knife."

"I see it," she said in a low and dangerous voice, gripping her own cold, steel blade in front of her.

He was twenty feet away when I heard his growling and garbled threats. His words were slick with saliva. "You bitches. You bitches."

"Michael Rap, you stop right there!" I yelled. I don't know where I got the nerve or the volume, but the shrill tone familiar to my kids came from deep in my lungs. "You stop this right now. You have no right to chase us. Stop it!"

Miraculously, he did. He lurched to a halt ten feet away and pointed the knife at us. "I'm sick of you, bitches. Give me my stuff."

"We don't have your stuff," I said. "What do you want?"

"Go away and leave us alone," Sarah shouted.

We yelled over each other, but he wasn't listening in any case. He snarled like the animal he had become.

"Cut them guys. My wack." Rap swayed back and forth, like a drunken prize fighter looking for an opening to attack. Sarah and I stood our ground thrusting our weapons in his direction.

"Gonna slit your throats." His tongue ran along his crusty lips. He contorted his face and raised the knife above his head.

He ran at us.

In an instant Sarah closed the short distance, launching herself at him, coming in low to take out his knees. As his body hit the ground, his head flew back, and the air left his lungs. He lay still.

Gripping my trekking pole as a weapon, I moved closer to survey the damage. Sarah pushed herself away from him to get to her knees.

In a flash Rap sprung to his feet and away from Sarah's grasp with a hideous laugh. Her backpack made her clumsy and no match for his agility. His fist came from behind his back aimed at Sarah's head. She shielded her face, taking the force of the blow in her upper arm. She went down.

My anger made me brave. While Rap grappled with Sarah, I charged at him and thrust the pole into his spine several times. He swatted at me, but I skipped out of his reach to come back at him from his other side, taking a baseball swing at his head. The aluminum pole made a metallic twang and bent in half.

Rap turned his attention to me, grabbed my weapon from my hand and threw the pole against the wall. In that moment Sarah rolled away from him and jumped to her feet. In attack mode, he turned to me, hate contorting his face.

More than anything I feared his knife and expected to see steel flash out in an arc of death. I stood stupidly like a raccoon in headlights. Sweat rolled down my spine—but the knife was gone.

Emboldened by his empty hands, I swiped a rock from the cliff wall and hurled it at him, hitting the bull's eye in the center of his chest. He raged in anger and lunged at me. I jinked away, turning, but his fingers caught the back of my pack. With a grip on the straps, he thrashed me from side to side.

I brought my flailing arms under control long enough to grasp at my hip belt and find the buckle. His mad howling filled my ears, but I finally heard the click. The buckle snapped open and freed my hips. Still ensnared by the chest strap, I couldn't get my balance.

He laughed like a maniac and shook me from side to side. I caught sight of Sarah beating his back with her fists, but he focused on me, dashing my body against the stone wall. The chest strap rose up and dug into my neck. I got my fingers to the buckle and pinched. With a tiny click, I was freed from the restraint of my backpack and fell to the ground at the edge of the abyss. My hands clawed the dirt for a grip, my nails left grooves in the loose scree. I slid over the side.

Somewhere in my brain I heard Sarah screaming, but I needed all my concentration to cling to the edge of the cliff. My boots scraped into the loose gravel sending a shower of stones into the canyon below.

Near to panic, I forced myself to think about my situation. What could I feel with my toes, with my knees? There had to be somewhere to get a toe hold. I did a tactile search of the few inches around my feet. Finally, my foot found a bump in the escarpment. The lugs on the sole of my boot caught on the rock and held. I began to breathe again.

Daring to look beyond myself, I saw Sarah and Rap still crashing into each other. Her eyes caught mine, and I gave her a thumbs up. Her face relaxed a bit, and she threw herself at Rap with renewed vigor. She knocked him against the wall and made a dash for her knife on the ground.

"Sarah, behind you!"

She swung around on him with the knife flashing in her hand, but he seemed to have no fear and advanced on her, catching her arm in full swing. I sickened at the sight of Rap nose to nose with Sarah, breathing his foul breath into her face. She grimaced as he twisted the knife out of her hand, but then brought her knee up between his legs.

It must not have been a direct hit. He fell back and screamed, "I'll kill you, bitch!"

The knife swiped at Sarah in wide arcs, and she backed into the wall. He could have closed in on her at any time, but seemed to be having fun. Laughing, watching her angry determined face, he parried and lunged. At any moment his game could end.

Sarah stared at Rap and studied his movements. Her hands slowly rose to the straps of her backpack and unsnapped the buckles. In one smooth movement she swung the pack from her back and held it in front of her by the shoulder straps. The forty-five pound pack became her shield or more precisely, a battering ram. Sarah ran at Rap and knocked him to the ground, but he jumped up in an instant ready to slash her with her own knife. She swung the pack from side to side, advancing on him, pushing him to the edge.

As crazy as he acted, Rap knew where the cliff ended. He danced along its edge until he jigged off balance and tripped. Rap went down and caught the full-weight of Sarah's pack on the side of his head. The force of the blow sent him sprawling in the dirt; his pack flew from his shoulder, landing an arm's length away from me.

Sarah stood over Rap and could have easily shoved him into the abyss. She blinked. I saw her hesitation and the enormity of her decision. In that moment of uncertainty, Rap gathered himself up and shook his head as if to clear cobwebs from his mind.

The pummeling had merely made him angrier and stronger. He hurled himself at Sarah, tearing the battering ram from her hands and throwing her pack to the ground. She was left open and vulnerable to the slicing of the knife. She dodged the blade again and again, losing ground and pushed to the edge. He wasn't playing this time.

212

I watched the battle helplessly, desperately searching for a way to distract him so Sarah could run or get the upper hand. His backpack caught my eye. He valued what hid inside. Whatever his treasure was, he was willing to kill for it.

The pack lay inches beyond my grasping fingers. I stretched to the limits of my arms, sending loose stones bouncing into the canyon. Two more inches. I dug my toes in and sprung upward, lunging at the backpack. My left hand caught the strap of the pack, but the effort pulled me off balance, and I began to slip again. The weight of the pack did nothing to arrest my slide. I grabbed at small rocks, but they pulled from the ground in my hand. My feet scrambled and scraped until one of my boots found a foothold.

I teetered on the ball of my foot on a nub of rock. My elbows dug into the ground, and I used all my core energy to cling to the lip of the cliff. I found air in my lungs and screeched, "Hey, Rap. Hey!"

Sarah caught sight of me. Her look of horror caused Rap to turn toward me and spot his precious backpack perched on the brink. He screamed and lunged at the pack. Before he reached me, I gave his treasure the push it needed to plunge below.

The backpack careened and bounced several times. Without thought, the madman ran onto the steep escarpment to chase after his pack. His first step over the edge pitched him forward, somersaulting, and cartwheeling.

Watching his wild plummet from over my shoulder was a mistake. I lost my toe hold and began to slide again toward the yawning maw of the canyon. I grabbed at the pebbles and dirt in desperation.

Sarah dashed across the short distance between us and threw herself flat out to catch at my hands.

"Amy! Hold on, Amy." Her fingers grasped and scratched at my wrists, but I slid away from her. She hung over the edge grabbing at my sleeves, at my hair, at empty air.

I couldn't scream or think. I hugged the slope. Relentless gravity drew me toward the drop-off below. With a swimming motion, my legs continued to pump and crawl. Rocks lifted my shirt and scraped skin from my belly. The friction slowed me.

My descent became almost controlled, though my breathing and tumultuous thoughts did not. My boots finally dug in and found another toe hold, and I stopped.

Too terrified that I'd look down and see nothing but air, I looked up at Sarah's ashen face twenty feet above, her hands still reaching out to me. Seeing her gave me hope. Breathlessly, she spoke to me.

"You're okay, Amy. You're near a ledge. Don't look around. Step down about seven inches to your left."

I nodded and gulped dust down my dry throat. Hands firmly planted, I reached with my toe for the ledge and found a stable base for both feet. My courage returned, so I unglued myself from the wall and turned around. The canyon in all its grandeur intimately surrounded me, taking my breath away. My knees began to buckle, so I slid to the ground and sat.

Sarah called, "Are you okay?"

Unable to speak, I waved.

"Stay where you are. Let me figure some way to get to you."

"No," I screamed. "You stay up there." The thought of her sliding down here scared me more than my own predicament. "Tell me what you can see from there."

"He looks dead," she said.

"Who?" My mind must have gone blank when I concentrated on surviving my drop in elevation. Fear finally loosened its grip and allowed me to remember the man's insanity and evil intentions.

Seven feet away from me, Rap's body lay on the ledge against the boulder that had prevented him from plunging another fifty feet. Blood stains showed where he'd struck the rock and slid down its face. Seeing him maimed and torn made me gasp at my own close call. I sent a silent *Thank you* skyward and got a nudge of courage in return.

I surveyed my situation. The ledge was a thin lip of stone tacked to a sheer wall; maybe twenty-five feet long and no more than six feet at its widest, narrowing to a foot or less at both ends.

"Sarah, what else do you see? Is there a way up?" I was afraid to move, but could look up as long as my butt was planted on the ground.

Sarah, silhouetted against the blazing afternoon sun, appeared again over the edge off to my left side. "The ledge runs out over here," she called.

She disappeared again, and I glanced back at Rap. I didn't trust him to be dead. Watching blood run into his hair from the gash on his forehead gave me something to do while waiting for Sarah's report.

"The ledge is wider over on your right, but I don't see a way up." She stationed herself directly overhead again. "What should I do?"

"Do you have a rappelling rope in your pack?"

She took me seriously. "I have a rope, but it's thin and rated for seventy-five pounds."

Her earnestness made me smile inwardly, but my amusement was short lived.

My eye caught a small movement. The wind riffled Rap's shirt . . . or did it? I zeroed in and gasped. "He's breathing, Sarah. I think he's alive." I fought down my panic and inched further away from the body.

"Are you sure?" Sarah shouted. "How could he survive that fall? "

"No, I'm not sure. What should I do?"

"Poke him with something," she yelled. "If he moves, I'll throw a rock down on him."

"You can't do that!"

"Hey, if he wakes up, he'll kill you. Get serious."

No long sticks lay about. A gnarly shrub grew below the rim at my feet, but its branches were thin and useless and, in any case, out of reach.

"I don't have anything to poke him with." I knew I sounded petulant, but my courage faltered, and I wanted to be safe at home.

"Here. Use this." Sarah slid my bent hiking pole over the edge toward me. The pole hit a rock on its way down and flipped into the air, end over end, and continued downward into the canyon. Several seconds later a clinking sound traveled up to us.

"Tie the other one to your rope," I suggested.

After a long minute, she returned to the edge with her rope and tied it to the wrist-strap of my second hiking stick. She lowered the pole to me, and I picked at the knot with fumbling fingers.

"Don't poke him yet," she called.

I was in no hurry to disturb the madman and took my time to extend the pole to its maximum length. Sarah appeared above, this time with a large rock ready to hurl onto the man should he awaken violent and vicious.

"Okay," she said. "Go ahead."

I crawled along the base of the cliff toward the prone man and reached forward with the pole. My initial tentative poke got no response, so I jabbed roughly. Still no reaction. I didn't even feel guilty about wanting him dead. I studied him intently and could now see the rhythmic movement of his chest.

"He's definitely breathing."

The panicked voice above said, "Get away from him."

I scuttled past the body to the back wall of the ledge at its widest. Sarah disappeared and within thirty seconds returned to the edge with her sheathed knife tied to the end of the rope. The blade slid to my side, and I eagerly fitted its haft into my hand, though Rap looked helpless and hopeless.

"Sarah, we have to help him."

"What? No, we don't. He tried to kill us. I hope he dies." She moaned out loud. "Besides, there's nothing we can do. We have to get you up here."

My mind ricocheted from one repercussion to another. "That's too dangerous. You have to go for help."

"I'm not leaving you down there with him."

"You have to. They may not look for us for days." Cold fear flooded my body.

Sarah paused a long time. "Okay. If I run, I can get to the South Rim in two hours. I'll bring a rescue crew back."

"Sarah?" A realization hit me. "The sun will be gone in an hour. You can't hike in the dark, and they won't come until morning anyway." I looked up to her for a solution, some alternative to spending the night with a bleeding maniac, but knew there was none.

"I'll leave my pack and run as fast as I can." She hopped up to go.

"Wait, Sarah." I wasn't ready to be alone. "I need some stuff."

She stood on the ledge with her hands in her hair. "Amy, I'm so sorry this happened."

"I'll be okay. Let me think." With my addled brain, thinking wasn't easy. What might I need to survive a night clinging to a cliff?

Sarah called down, "Do you want me to lower your backpack?"

I was afraid I'd lose my gear all at once if the rope broke or the knot came undone. "Could you send things down one at a time? I'll need my sleeping bag, water and whatever snacks I have left over. See if you can find my first aid kit." In no time at all she lowered the basic necessities to me.

"Sarah, do you still have two headlamps?"

"Of course."

"I need the second one to keep an eye on him."

"Done. What else?" She added her headlamp to my fanny pack and lowered them down, giving me all that I'd need to wait out the night. Yet, I was afraid to let her leave.

"I guess that's all I need. Sarah?"

"Yeah?"

"Could you stay for a minute while I put a bandage on his gash?"

"Are ya kidding me?"

"No, I'm not. I can't stand looking at all that blood."

After an exasperated huff, she humored me. "Okay, that I understand. Let me get my rock."

Crawling toward the unconscious man with Sarah's knife and the bandages in my hand, I carefully placed gauze pads onto his oozing wounds. I was alert to his breathing and ready to jump away if he grabbed for me, but he lay there peacefully. Finished, I moved to the widest point of the ledge, as far as I could get from the body.

"Is he still alive?" Sarah stood above holding the rock between her hands.

"He's breathing." I shaded my eyes to look up at her. "Sarah—he has teeth marks and bruises on his right arm."

She whistled softly. "Amy. Listen to me. If he comes at you, you must use the knife. Stick the blade in below his ribs, pointed upward. It's self defense. Please don't hesitate."

I could not picture knifing a man's ribs, but I emblazoned the image in my mind, hoping my instinct to survive would kick in gear if I needed to stab him. I nodded up to Sarah.

"Please, Amy, promise me."

I promised fervently and watched her disappear from the edge.

The crunch of Sarah's footsteps faded to nothing. The silence was deafening. I could almost hear Rap's shallow breathing.

To keep my sanity, I needed to be busy, to make the narrow ledge my overnight home, so I gathered all of my belongings and retreated to the spot furthest from Rap's body. Suddenly, having my stuff seemed supremely important. Each of the items was a link to my known, safer world; a link to Sarah; tools to keep the terrors of the coming night at bay and to defend myself from the lunatic.

I unfurled my sleeping bag and positioned my hiking pole and fanny pack along the bottom edge of the wall, my water bottle next to me. I slid Sarah's sheathed knife into my thigh pocket and hung my headlamp around my neck. My back fitted into a shallow depression in the wall, giving me a sense of security. I settled in to wait.

In the quiet, I became uncomfortable. Burning pain radiated from my torso, so I lifted my shirt to examine my abdomen and rib cage. The slide down the escarpment left me with red welts and bloody scrapes encrusted with dirt and bits of stone. The oozing had begun to dry and stick to my shirt. I flushed out the scrapes with water and fanned my shirt in and out to dry them and to avoid melding the fabric with the scabby crud. Tending to my wounds was trivial—but concrete and within my control.

My doctoring complete, I watched faraway mesas in purples and oranges change hue with the angle of the sun. After my near-death experience, the beauty was more sublime than at Plateau Point. With no place to go and no one to interrupt my reverie, I contemplated raw nature.

My mind took the perspective of the condors soaring on thermal updrafts searching for carrion, patrolling their realm. My imagination flew with the majestic birds above chasms and gorges following the brown river snaking through the canyon toward the setting sun. My flight of fancy raised my spirits and brushed aside worries of impending danger. I imagined myself floating, free and open.

Like the proverbial elephant in the room, Rap lay on the ledge. I averted my eyes and occupied my mind with a review of the day, of Sarah's bravery, her valiant defense, her flushed and worried face, Rap's insanity.

Everything came back to him. As long as he breathed, he was a threat. I watched the fabric of his tattered shirt rise and fall. What if he awoke? There was nowhere for me to go but down. Confidence in my ability to defend myself hovered near empty. The warm steel blade in my pocket gave me a dab of courage, but what if I fell asleep, and he pounced on me?

I thought of my dad. I missed him. He had accepted death so gracefully a year ago. I didn't think I could. I didn't exactly fear death, only the dying part. Dead would be okay, though I mourned what my life could have been.

Sadness overtook my every emotion, even anger at my husband. *John had been right after all. This trip is a disaster.*

The Grand Canyon was supposed to be my step into a brave new world. Ever since I sold the factory Dad and I owned for thirty years, I dreamed of traveling the continents, meeting interesting people, doing something memorable. *Instead, I'm alone on a chip of rock watching a crazy guy die.*

My kids had no idea how close I had come to being thrown into the abyss. They probably were going about their daily lives, not even remembering that my grand adventure was scheduled for this week though I had e-mailed my itinerary to them both. *Did they even open the attachment?*

A weight settled around my heart when I pictured the world without me in it. I missed my kids terribly. Maybe I'd be so lucky to be a spirit, able to watch their moments in life; James' flourishing career; Meagan pregnant, her baby being born. I could almost see those luminous newborn eyes looking up at her, trusting that he'd be fed, sheltered and loved. I wanted that for them and vowed that if my soul had powers, I would make it so. I'd be there for eternity.

Melancholia sapped my energy. My head nodded; my eyelids drooped, so I sat up straighter and stretched my legs. Clearly, I'd have to fend off exhaustion, keep a better vigil, and focus on Rap. I steadied my chin on my arms and stared at the breathing corpse.

To pass the time, I matched the rhythm of my breathing to Rap's. I watched the rise and fall of his chest through the slits of my eyelids. I listened to air rasping in and out of his lungs until I could hear no more.

* * *

With a start and gagging fear, my eyes flew open and darted to the maniac. *Thank God, he's still half-dead.* I berated myself for dozing off, aghast at my stupidity. The sun had dropped near the horizon, and shadows deepened in the canyon and ravines. I thought I was prepared for nightfall, but now that darkness was imminent, I was petrified.

To calm myself I cradled my things to me: my water bottle, the edge of my sleeping bag, my thoughts of home. I fished through my fanny pack for peanuts and dried fruit and ate mechanically. The food brought no joy or satisfaction, but the sugar gave me an energy boost.

I realized that the last few minutes of daylight would be my last chance to move. A bathroom break seemed prudent, so I straightened out my legs and groaned myself to a standing position. To shake the pins and needles from my feet, I paced back and forth a few times, turning carefully, never getting too close to the edge and keeping an eye on Rap all the while. At the far end of the precipice, I squatted, fearful that the sound of the trickle would awaken Rap, but he was not in this world.

My last daylight act was to position Sarah's head lamp on the ground with its light trained on Rap. With that, I would not only hear and smell him, but I'd see his every move—if he ever moved again.

Returning to my now familiar niche, I wrapped my sleeping bag around me. The goose down bag had been my first backpacking investment, and I loved the smell and feel of it. The air had not yet chilled, but I needed the bag for psychological warmth. I inventoried my supplies again and settled in.

The sun's last rays spiked up from behind a far-off mesa crowning the rock formation like a halo. At any other time I would have reflected upon a glorious finish to a glorious day, but I dreaded the finale. I mentally hung on to the last wisp of dusky light while the color drained from the canyon, replaced by shades of gray. Within minutes they, too, were gone.

Darkness fell, quick and foreboding. In the thick and humbling blackness, my eyes grew as large as a lemur's and I wanted to cry. Instead I hugged my knees to my chest and buried my face into the sleeping bag with only my eyes on alert, watching the dead man breathe.

I wondered if Rap had a wife. Had he thrown her away to live this crazy life of his? Surely, he had a mother. No doubt, she mourned for the child that he had been, but was no more. Does a mother's love evaporate when a child goes bad or could she feel his pain over the many miles now separating them?

I tried to stretch my senses to feel my own children. James was probably in his office sitting at his computer or bent over drawings, working late. That was typical of him. Maybe Meagan and Ed were home having dinner or out in the brisk autumn air for an evening stroll, holding hands, watching the stars come out.

Scientists say humans use a tiny portion of their brains and have untapped powers of communication, so I tried sending telepathic messages of love to my son and daughter. A lonely echo bounced back at me. I probably asked too much by expecting those powers to activate themselves on such short notice. Maybe later tonight, when their worlds weren't so busy and the reception was better, I'd try the messages again.

Grand Canyon stars were more brilliant than Illinois stars and there were a billion more of them. The moon had not yet shown itself, so the stars sparkled against the backdrop of deep space. My one seminar of astronomy came back to me in tidbits. Orion's Belt, Taurus the Bull, The Pleiades. *Where are they?* Even the Big Dipper was obscured within an overwhelming number of stars. There was nothing familiar to keep me company.

I took comfort from the warmth radiating from the cliff face. Even so, night's chill reached into my sleeping bag. I gathered the bag tighter and tucked myself in along the base of the rock wall, praying that night-crawling scorpions forgave my intrusion.

I tried to keep my eyes on the small shaft of light pinpointing Rap, but the black night swaddled me, muffling my fear. Exhaustion dragged me into dreamless sleep.

22

ON THE EDGE OF MADNESS

Drugged by sleep, I could not identify the sound. I swam to the surface of my consciousness, and the sound became a groan. Once my mind put the puzzle pieces together, my heart missed a beat and my eyes flew open. Lest the other cliff inhabitant hear, I dare not move, dare not let the rustling of nylon alert Rap to my existence. My eyeballs stretched to see the man in the headlamp's hazy light. He groaned again and raised his hand to his head. He let his arm fall and was still.

His resurrection wiped out all thoughts and need of sleep for me.

Fear kept vigil with me for long minutes, maybe hours. My hips and knees demanded I shift position, but I could not comply. A sliver of moon rose and inched its way overhead before Rap made another sound. His groan seethed, but only his arms moved. He fumbled with something from his pocket before his hands went to his face and then dropped again to his side. I prayed that the effort drove him back into oblivion, but within minutes his garbled curses filled my ears.

Some angry evil gave Rap the strength to roll onto his side and push himself into a sitting position. With his head hung loosely from his skinny shoulders, he became precariously erect. He snorted and swayed, moving out of the patch of light and into my blind-spot. I beat my terror back far enough to listen. He slapped his hands against the rock wall. "Let out," he said in thick, garbled syllables. The sound of crunching stones and slapping moved away from me, punctuated by screams of frustration. "Bitches!"

I stopped breathing when his curses and shuffling feet sounded closer and louder. Like a fawn in tall grass, I restrained my muscles and waited for my moment to flee.

Finally, a hint of light given by the slivered moon exposed him. He appeared on the edge of the drop-off ten feet away, making his way back to the boulder that had abruptly ended his cartwheel from above. Trapped and defeated, Rap shook his fists at the night. He wailed and bayed like a hellhound, unleashing his demons into the blackness.

I covered my ears, but could not look away. The canyon had purged itself of the evil of hundreds of previous deaths, murders and suicides and funneled all that pain and anguish into one human receptacle. With his silhouette illuminated by Sarah's head lamp, his body jerked and his arms thrashed. I cringed beneath the weight of the infected spectacle; pinning my spine into the stone wall, seeking invisibility. Hot barbs of fear snagged the blood in my veins, paralyzing me. I prayed that Rap's twisted brain remained devoid of logic and unable to detect me; unable to plunge me into his malevolent world.

Suddenly injected with an ounce of sanity, he stopped his maniacal dance and became more aware of earthly reality. He dropped to his hands and knees, searching, turning over rocks. He crawled across the ledge, sweeping his hands in wide arcs over the gritty stones.

Compressing my body further into my corner of darkness, I pulled my knees tighter and hid my white face within the folds of the black sleeping bag. I feared he'd see my eye movement witnessing his insanity.

More terrifying than his howling, he began to gabble and mutter an incessant string of incoherent words. Only a few were in English.

"Pack whack. Back whack. Whack. Ack. Ack."

The guttural sounds masked the thumping of my frantic heart.

Rap's hands found the headlamp and turned its beam into his face, blinding his crazed eyes, and exposing his contorted mouth. He winced and blinked. Lucid enough to probe the darkness with the light, he searched—methodical, intent, hunting. The beam played across the ledge, slipping past my feet.

My fingers gripped the hilt of Sarah's knife, and I sunk back, trying to become one with the stone. Panic pinched the nape of my neck and stung my arm pits. I feared the animal could smell me. Instinct told me to dash from my cover, to flee, to run from the predator before he devoured me. I exerted all my will power to still myself within my camouflaged blackness, to merely witness and wait.

Suddenly, Rap's muttering stopped. The silence terrified me. He crawled to the edge of our prison and shined the light below. The beam swung back and forth. He inched along the rim, ever closer to my concealment.

I stopped breathing.

A garbled gasp of triumph escaped his lungs. Rap lay flat not three feet from my quaking body, his arms dangling over the edge, reaching and straining. He must have spied his backpack below, snagged in the scrawny shrub sprouting from the canyon wall. Reaching for the pack was futile, but the maniac envisioned otherwise.

Rap jumped to his feet, and as if diving for pearls in an inky black pool, he launched himself into the abyss. One of us screamed. Like a shooting star the LED light held in Rap's hand arced in the night sky, held at its apogee for a moment, and died away.

The thump of a melon breaking against stone came through the darkness. Several seconds passed before I imagined the source of the sound. I gagged and emptied my stomach onto the rocks. I wiped my eyes and then my mouth with my bandana and stifled my cries.

Fearing that the nightmare may not be over, I composed myself and listened for any sound, any movement, any danger. Silence thickened the air. I began to doubt what I had seen and heard.

What if he sprang back over the edge? Was his jump a trick to draw me out of hiding?

I waited, alert and wary, until my legs cramped, and the odor of the vomit next to me began to sicken me again. My hand moved to the headlamp hung around my neck. I clicked on the light to illuminate the spot from which Rap left the ledge. There was no sign that he had ever existed. Slowly and deliberately I unfolded my legs and crawled on my belly to the edge of the cliff, my light searching for life.

My fingers found the edge first and I pulled myself closer to peek into the canyon. The darkness revealed nothing. I listened to the void. All was quiet, so I trained my headlamp on the rocks below. My small circle of light found Rap far below in a broken heap. His puppeteer had snipped his strings, and he lay like a discarded marionette; his arms and legs at odd angles.

Weary, I rested my forehead in the dust and sobbed.

225

Peace returned to the canyon and eventually to my mind. I rolled onto my back and allowed the enormity of the galaxies to overtake my thoughts. I mourned Rap, the human being, but realized I couldn't have saved him. I refused the guilt.

Images of my family floated among the constellations, so I again sent those messages of love to my children. Contemplating the cosmos revealed me to be a mere speck in a vast universe, but not inconsequential. Nature had assigned the roles of loving wife and nurturing mother to me—and I had done my job. My kids sent that message back to me.

Guilt, which John had layered on me for decades, seeped into the gritty soil. His grip on me was suddenly gone. *I'm free,* I thought with a deep sigh. *Is that a good thing?*

The cosmos sent no answers. A cool breeze reminded me I was still alive, so I crawled back to the safety of the wall and cocooned myself in my down sleeping bag.

23

Day 8 - ON THE LEDGE

I awoke to the sound of the tent-fly flapping and figured that the wind had kicked up. My eyes opened. The vast expanse of sky surprised me until I remembered I had no tent.

To the east, night's blackness pulled back, allowing the pink of dawn to reveal itself. The scene reminded me of a young widow's frilly petticoat peeking from beneath her mourning clothes—at odds with events, enticing, and making promises.

The chill of the horrific night clung to the air. I groaned into the folds of my sleeping bag. Razor sharp images of the night before replayed in my mind. My courage needed to be bolstered before I'd be able to peer over the edge at Rap's broken body in daylight.

Guilt snuck back into my thoughts, chiding me for feeling rested and waking refreshed; forgetting for a while that a defective human had departed our world in bizarre fashion. I closed my eyes again to delay the moment when I'd be obliged to view his remains.

A sudden sound from below the edge jolted me to attention. Flup. Flup. Flup. A black specter flew at me. Terrified, I cringed and raised my arms to fend off an attack.

The powerful wings of a condor beat the air in front of my face. Its massive body lifted from the bush at the ledge's lip and rose into the sky. He had been right there, checking me out while I slept. My heart raced at the thought of that carnivore thinking I was dead and pecking at my face with its hooked beak. His foul odor hung like mist around me.

I shuddered as much from the smell as from the scare. Breathing inside my sleeping bag, I kept a wary eye on the gigantic bird. He soared above the open canyon to join another condor balancing on air currents.

They tipped their wings to adjust to the winds and spiraled down into the ravine below me. From a distance their size and grace gave them a majestic beauty, up close they were stinking scavengers. I wished I had food to settle my stomach.

A picture popped into my head and realization slapped me. "No!" I fought to untangle myself from the sleeping bag, struggling with and cursing the zipper. "No. Stop it!" I kicked the bag away and staggered to my feet, stiff and achy. On my way to the edge, I picked up several stones to defend Rap's dignity in death.

The two condors hopped around the body in ungainly maneuvers, perhaps not quite sure of the safety of the unusual carrion. I launched stones in their direction and shouted to no avail. Bigger rocks were needed. I gathered several and wound up my throwing arm. The first rock clattered to a stop ten feet from one of the birds.

That condor lifted from the ground with an easy sweep of its wings, but settled again on Rap's stockinged foot. The second rock bounced near the claws of the other bird. Feathers flew. Not used to carrion retaliating, the birds retreated in confusion, grunting and wheezing.

I hurled a few more rocks which missed their marks, but the scavengers took to the sky to find an easier meal.

Massaging my sore shoulder, I returned to my bedding for warmth and to start the day over. I was exhausted.

My rest was short, interrupted by nature's call. Reluctantly, I sidled over to the far side of the ledge to relieve myself. From where I squatted, I took in the sights revealed by the rising sun. The bright sky made light of the night's terrible events.

Near a stain of blood drying in the rust-colored stones lay a shabby lone shoe. The sneaker gaped open with its tongue hanging out. Rap's sodden gauze bandages had fallen several feet apart. Along the length of the ledge, drops of blood created a meandering trail which had been stomped on and scattered.

No wonder the condors came to investigate my ledge.

My neat-freak compulsion that had ruled me for decades urged me to clean up the mess. The bloody pads could not be left to defile this pristine place. I skewered each of them with a twig and poked them into a zip-lock baggie intended for toilet paper.

I found and examined two tinfoil packets. One had been torn open with residue of white powder inside. The other was intact. I tucked those in my pocket for future reference. There would be questions about how Rap had died.

My stomach growled and begged for food. *Apparently, nothing makes me lose my appetite.* In response, I dug through my fanny pack and found Sarah's tiny backup stove, sent her a *Thank you,* and became almost giddy at the prospect of a steaming cup of hot chocolate to go with my granola bar. I doused my hands liberally with sanitizer and waved them in the air to dry. I then spread my breakfast fixings on a flat rock, set up the stove, found matches and even opened my water bottle before realizing that I had no pot in which to boil the water. I was stunned.

Anger tore at me, bursting my fragile bubble of self control. I wanted to scream and pound my fists on something, to berate God, and throw rocks down on Rap. Suppressed fear and tension that had built up in me overnight refused to be contained or glossed over with happy thoughts and beautiful scenery.

My safe, vanilla life seemed stupid and insipid and never again possible. I could no longer hide. Real life was dirty, low, and would stalk me forever because I had witnessed its ugliness.

My husband left me, my kids don't need me, my job is gone, and crazy Rap dashed his brains out right in front of me.

I prowled the length of the ledge in stiff movements unmindful of the dangerous cliff. I had no idea what to do with my feelings. I could not ignore them. *Where's last night's peace? Where's the cosmos?* My calming thoughts didn't work in daylight, didn't dilute the adrenaline prickling my skin, didn't slow my racing heart.

Suddenly, a rumbling came from my throat and broke from my mouth. I filled the canyon with a howling wail that, until last night, I could never have imagined. I echoed Rap's pain and anger and let howls careen off cold, uncaring walls of rock. The banshee within me screamed until I could scream no more.

Empty, I sat down; exhausted and amazed at myself. My throat hurt, as if stiff bristles had scrubbed me clean and raw. *Where had that come from?*

Taken aback and afraid of my loss of control, I needed a routine task to regain balance.

I resumed my breakfast preparations. I mixed the powered cocoa into cold water, munched on the granola bar, and analyzed what I had just experienced. The feeling wasn't bad, rather cathartic. *Maybe I should have started screaming years ago instead of pretending unpleasant situations didn't exist, instead of making nice.*

The condors still soared overhead, and Rap still lay below like a butchered puppet, but I had turned a page. I was ready to get on with living my life and was excited by the prospects of trying out the new attitude.

I stood, gathered my belongings, and kept an eye on the trail above, waiting for the guys with the ropes.

24

UNDER THE RIM

Craning my neck upward became awkward, so I bundled the gear together at the widest section of the ledge and sat on the pile, waiting. I had a front row seat to view the canyon's morning matinee. The colors, silence, and majesty of the chasm calmed my nerves and mind, transporting me to a place where nature demanded only a person's basic self, no façades; where it was acceptable to simply be. I had found such a wondrous place.

Contentment almost caused me to miss an unnatural sound borne on the wind.

"Amy!" Sarah's voice had a pitch that carried a long way, no doubt agitating dogs for miles around. "Amy!" To me her screech sounded like a Hallelujah choir, but I couldn't tell if her call came from up or down, east or west. Still, joy bounced my heart against my ribs.

"Sarah." Her name fell from my raspy throat and went nowhere. I grabbed my water bottle to wet the dryness and tried again. Then I heard other voices calling, male voices.

"Sarah," I croaked. *Please don't let them march past me.* I dug through my pockets in a panic to find my emergency whistle. I filled my lungs to bursting and shrillness pierced the quiet.

"Amy!" This time my name sounded like *Eureka!* I blasted the whistle again in two friendly toots. Before long, the sound of trampling feet came from the cliff twenty feet above. A few pebbles rained down, and Sarah's face beamed like the sun at the edge.

"Hi," she said. "You okay?"

"I'm fine." And that was the absolute truth. A few of the other rescuers peered down at me, Ranger Glen among them. He took stock of my situation, and his smile warmed the air.

"Good morning, Amy," he said. "We're going to get you out of there."

"Thank you, Ranger Glen. I'd appreciate your help." I pointed tentatively to where Rap had done his swan dive and motioned downward.

Glen nodded somberly. "I see. We'll take care of him. I'm going to rappel down to you, and the crew will pull you up. Okay?"

Everything was very okay.

I heard him giving directions to the men in a firm, sure voice. I caught the words *belay* and *harness*. Soon the end of a rope landed near the blood stain. Glen rappelled from the rim above, his feet nimbly touching against the wall. His boots landed on solid ground, he stepped from the ropes, and gathered me into his arms.

I let Glen cradle me and fought the urge to cry. With his shirt coarse against my cheek, I breathed in his masculine scent, a soapy smell tinged with sweat. His chest pressed hard against my ear. His heart thundered inside and his deep voice reverberated under his ribs.

"I'm so sorry," he whispered.

I looked up with a question, and he framed my face in his calloused hands brushing my hair from my forehead. "If he had hurt you, I . . ." He closed his eyes, the words trailed off, and he rocked me.

Dad's smell. I remembered he had rocked me when I was little, protected me from a barking dog. I wanted to stay wrapped in Glen's arms forever, too, but let him release me so he could do his job.

The crew above had their job to do and did not witness our reunion, but Sarah lay on the edge above with her chin propped on her hand. Our eyes met, and she grinned.

Glen asked me to step into a harness and leaned over to position the straps at my feet. I lay my hand on his shoulder to steady myself. My attention wandered away from his instructions. I became aware of his body heat, hot to my touch. The sensation warmed me to my toes, so I gripped his shirt tighter. He expertly buckled the harness around my waist and thighs as I stood like a docile child. Finally, he hooked up a carabiner to connect me to the suspended rope.

"Now lean back until the rope is taut," he instructed.

"Okay, I got it." I looked at the young man above with the rope held firmly in his gloved hands. I assumed there were several others behind him to whom I would entrust my life and limb.

"That's right, sit back and let them pull you," Glen said. "Now walk up the wall."

He gave me a lift to get started.

Five feet from the top, I looked down at Ranger Glen to give him thumbs up, but caught sight of the drop beneath me and Rap still piled in a heap. I gasped and stumbled, banging my knees into the wall and grabbing at rocks for a hand hold.

"Hey!" The men above shouted and scrambled to dig in, but a foot or two of rope smoked through their grasp. In an instant, the belay men regained their grip and arrested my fall, but I became tangled and off balance. Panic made me clumsy. I found myself twisted around facing the great abyss and tried to stifle my cry.

Glen's steady voice broke through my terror. "Amy, you're okay. Put your hands on the rope."

I dumbly nodded.

"Now turn over and pull up your knees."

I clung to his voice and focused on each detail.

"Good girl. Put your feet under you."

Breathing was as much of a challenge as getting my limbs under control.

"Okay, lean back and walk."

I struggled to the rim where hands reached out to grab me and hoisted me like cargo onto solid ground.

Ranger Glen whooped from below. "Good job."

Five or six well-muscled young men grinned and patted my shoulder in camaraderie, as if I had accomplished some great feat. From under their helmets, beads of sweat sparkled and streamed into their collars. I recognized one of the faces.

"Geraldo, thank you."

"It is no problem," he said, lowering his eyes and making himself busy with the ropes.

I wanted to hug Geraldo even more than the others—maybe because I had belittled his job back at the ranch, not recognizing the hero in him. I thanked him and the rest of the crew profusely. They turned back to the remainder of the job.

My stress and exhaustion caught up with me. I wobbled, but Sarah made her way to me and held me up with a bear hug.

"Do you need anything? What can I do for you?" She held me at arm's length with a strained look in her eyes. "Oh, Amy. I'm so sorry."

"What?"

"I didn't get to the rim until this morning. In the dark I missed a turn and got lost on little animal paths. My light died, and I couldn't find the main trail." Her words tumbled out a mile a minute.

"Sarah! You spent the night wandering in the dark?"

"No, I didn't. When my battery quit, I sat down and waited until dawn. At least I didn't have a killer next to me. Did he hurt you? Did you shove him over the edge? Did you stab him? What happened?"

"I'm fine, really. If you don't mind, I'll tell you everything later." Like rain through a gutter, my energy drained away. "I think I'm hungry."

"Wait. I brought you something." From her fanny pack she pulled a mashed sweet roll.

My mouth salivated immediately. "Thanks." Her thoughtfulness touched me.

"How about tea or hot chocolate," she asked.

"Hot chocolate. Calories be damned."

"Excellent," she said.

My friend fussed over me, and I let her. Right there on the side of the cliff, she set up my stove, and in two minutes I had a steaming cup of cocoa warming my hands.

Sarah and I sat shoulder to shoulder and watched the men work. Ranger Glen climbed from below with my fanny pack and other belongings slung on his back and set them to the side before speaking to the crew. He rested a hand on a man's shoulder while giving out

234

instructions. I didn't see any insignia of rank, but clearly Glen was the leader. The men respected him, perhaps because he was older; maybe because he exuded confidence. The phrase *alpha male* popped into my head.

One of the men rappelled down while another knotted a rope to a backboard which he lowered over the edge. Glen joined our impromptu picnic and squatted next to me. His intense gaze flustered me.

"How are you?" he asked.

"I'm fine. This cocoa has perked me up."

"Uh-uh." He ran his finger along my cheekbone tracing a tender circle. "Any other cuts or bruises?"

"No, not really." I found the bruise with my own fingers and winced.

"Let me clean up the abrasions on your elbows and knees." Without waiting for my answer, he opened his first aid kit and donned surgical gloves. With hands as gentle as my mother's, he cleansed the scrapes and applied antibacterial cream.

"There's blood on your blouse." Sarah pointed out. "Lift your shirt."

Like an obedient patient, I complied. "I cleaned them last night."

"Those scrapes still look nasty. Inflamed," Glen said. "May I?"

I acquiesced, so Glen swabbed my abdomen and applied the ointment. I closed my eyes to ignore the sting.

"I'm sorry this hurts." He unwrapped a large gauze pad and lay the bandage across my stomach. His touch jump started the healing process. I pictured warm blood rushing to repair my injuries.

He broke into my trance. "Do you still have pain in your knee? We can't get a helicopter in here anywhere close, but if you can't handle the hike out, we'll carry you."

I hadn't even thought about my knee. "Seriously, I'm fine—and I still want to finish this hike on my own two feet." My brave words conflicted with my confidence level, but I counted on Sarah to pull me through.

She had moved away to collect her gear which had become strewn about the cliff in yesterday's melee, and I suspect, to give Glen and me a private moment.

Sarah propped up her backpack, and something caught my eye. I squinted, trying to make sense of what I saw. Glen glanced in the direction of my point.

"What?" Sarah asked in confusion.

"Look at your pack," I said.

A knife was embedded up to its hilt in her backpack. Rap's knife. If she hadn't been wearing the pack, the blade would have skewered Sarah right between the shoulder blades. She blanched and backed away.

Glen rose and put his hand on Sarah's shoulder. "I'll get that for you." Using his bandana, he tugged the knife out, examined the broken tip and deposited the weapon into a zip-lock bag that had been in his first aid kit. "May I look through your pack?"

Sarah nodded.

"Looks like you'll need new rain gear," he said. Her jacket was sliced through as was her food bag. Oatmeal and jelly beans spilled out. "The aluminum frame took the brunt of it." Glen showed us the knife point indentation in the metal strip.

"Oh, Sarah." I went to her with my arms wide, thinking of her bravery and how close I had come to losing her. Shaken, she let me hug her.

"Holy crap," she whispered.

"You girls put up one heck of a fight." Glen appraised Sarah. "When you're ready, you'll have to tell me the whole story—maybe over lunch up on the rim?"

"Sure, okay." I answered for us, but still scowled over Sarah's near-miss.

Glen looked me over slowly, taking inventory. "I've asked Geraldo to escort you and Sarah to the next rest stop. I have to take care of things down here, but I'll catch up."

I was too mentally drained to put up a protest, and Geraldo appeared at Glen's side.

"We will start up whenever you are ready, Miss Amy," Geraldo said.

"Thank you, Geraldo. Give us about five minutes."

Geraldo collected pieces of Sarah's gear and helped her stuff them into her wounded pack. He treated her with respect, like one of the guys.

"She's quite a woman." Glen pulled a three-liter Platypus bladder from the pile of emergency gear. "Need a refill?"

"Yes, she is." I found my empty water bottle in the side pocket of my pack which lay on the ledge since the fight with Rap. I steadied the bottle while Glen poured. "You think of everything. Thank you."

"I try. Is there anything else you need?" He spoke quietly, privately.

"How did you get here?" Until that moment I hadn't considered that Sarah had gone up to Bright Angel for help, but Glen had been down at Indian Gardens.

"I heard through the grapevine that a lady was in distress." He grinned and added a sparkle to his eye.

"Seriously, how did you know?"

"Sarah gave her report this morning and mentioned me. The ranger on duty called Indian Gardens, and here I am."

"I'm glad you came." I finished packing my gear into my backpack and snapped the buckles into place.

"I couldn't not come." He shook his head and opened his mouth to say more, but stopped and changed the subject. "Geraldo can carry . . ."

I raised my hand to forestall his offer.

"I will carry your pack, Miss Amy."

"Never mind, Geraldo," Glen said. "Amy is a real backpacker and will carry her own gear." He winked and tipped his hat to me.

"Si. She is a very good backpacker."

"The best," Sarah added.

I blushed at the compliments and attempted to mask the stiffness and groaning of my body as I stood to hoist the pack to my back. "Ready when you are, Geraldo."

Sarah was her audacious self again and obviously pleased to take to the trail. We said our good-byes to Glen and the rest of the crew, and Ranger Geraldo led the way to the main trail.

The steepness soon slowed me, and I looked forward to a rest at the top of every switchback. The ruts made by the mule trains seemed deeper today. My feet stumbled over rocks and worn out timber steps. I couldn't breathe, but my knees were okay. In spite of the hardships, I loved being in the canyon. I loved being alive.

Sarah dropped back to hike with me. "I can't wait any longer, Amy. Tell me what happened after I left."

Little by little, as my gasping for breath allowed, I told my story. Sarah listened in grave silence, as did Geraldo, though he pretended not to eavesdrop. I told them of Rap's crazy dancing and howling in the dark; my absolute terror of being discovered; the sound of the melon; the scavenging condors; and the blood.

"Your voice calling my name this morning seemed like a miracle," I said.

Sarah lowered her head. "I am so sorry, Amy." She apologized for not flying up to the rim in record time. Her voice was stiff and formal while her arms gesticulated extravagantly.

I lay my hand on her forearm to quiet her. "It's okay, Sarah."

"No, it's not. I made stupid mistakes. Backpacking 101." She shook her head. "When the sun set, I couldn't follow the path, and then my batteries died."

"What did you do?"

"I sat out the night at a switchback. I had matches and a candle, but didn't really use them. The stars were awesome."

"I thought so, too." Funny that the stars kept us both company. "Weren't you worried about snakes?"

Her face blanched. Clearly, she hadn't considered that a snake might snuggle up to her for warmth, but she recovered herself. "No." She cleared her throat. "The howling of the wolves creeped me out though."

I shook my head. "There are no wolves in the canyon. That was Rap."

Aghast, she said, "That was ungodly. You must have been scared out of your wits."

I didn't want to relive that terror and shrugged. "I was. Did you get any sleep?"

238

"I may have dozed a bit. When dawn came, I found the trail and ran as much as I could. The guy at Bright Angel lodge called Ranger Jan, the one who gave us the ride, and she got there in two minutes to take my report."

"I liked Jan."

"Yeah, me, too. I couldn't tell them exactly where you were, so she agreed to let me lead the crew down. Like an idiot I missed the little path, and we had to double back. I'm so sorry."

"But you found me."

"I was so afraid he had killed you," she said. "When I heard your whistle I . . ." She cleared her throat. "Well, I'm glad he didn't."

At that moment, I realized Sarah had become the closest friend I'd had in decades. *Is love possible when you've known someone for only a week? Would she understand how I meant it, if I told her?* She and I searched each other's eyes for a long minute, but then got pulled away when the trail narrowed to a single track.

At the next switchback Geraldo sat a discreet distance away while Sarah shared a rock with me during our water break. "Are you going to be okay?" she asked. "I mean, will you be messed up psychologically or something after watching that guy die?"

The experience was already receding into the past. "I've been thinking about that." I didn't know how much to say without sounding melodramatic, but decided to trust my friend. "I was terrified, but in the instant he died everything changed. I changed. My life had seemed like an inflated balloon into which his evil had seeped. When he dove off the cliff, a shard of his insanity poked the balloon and his evil got sucked out of my life; some of my own evil went with it."

Sarah scowled. "You never had any evil inside you."

"Well, not evil exactly, but negative stuff: anger, worry, doubt. Now I feel at peace with myself and very alive."

She considered me and nodded her head. "You look great, glowing. Nothing like spitting into the face of death to perk a girl up."

I laughed and shook my head in wonder. "I can conquer the world."

"There you go." Sarah grinned widely and gave me a high-five.

Strength snuck back into my body. The pain in my knee was manageable, and I vowed to march up to the South Rim without complaint.

After an hour or more of trudging along the trail and having the canyon to ourselves, we came upon a pavilion swarming with people. My aversion to them surprised me. Too much humanity hanging around. Claustrophobia stopped me from entering the structure.

"What's going on here, Geraldo?" I asked.

He laughed, almost to himself. "This is Mile-and-a-Half Resthouse, Miss Amy. Many people walk down from the resorts, but this is as far as they go."

The wilderness aura had evaporated, replaced by the vibe of a tourist trap without the souvenir shops. Most of the people had casually strolled down, some wore flip flops, some carried children on their shoulders. A pregnant woman waddled by and a fat man sat on a stone bench smoking a cigarette.

"What were they thinking? Don't they realize they have to walk back up?" Their ignorance or disregard for the rigors of the canyon irritated me.

Sarah rolled her eyes and consulted the map. "We have another eleven hundred foot gain in elevation from here to the rim. I'll bet more than one heart attack has happened on the way up."

"People are crazy," I said. "Let's rest for five minutes and then get out of here."

We were at the water spigot filling our bottles when Glen caught up to us. "You girls made good time."

Surprised to see him so soon, my heart swelled in my chest. I couldn't stop myself from grinning.

Sarah spoke for me. "You look like you're in a hurry."

"The recovery crew's behind me with the stretcher. I want to get up top ahead of them to make arrangements." Glen took inventory of me again, and his brow furrowed beneath his stiff-brimmed hat. "Are you okay to climb the rest of the way on your own? I need Geraldo to help the crew."

"We'll be fine." I shivered at the thought of the crew's burden. "But I don't want to see or even think about the stretcher. Let's get on our way before they get here."

We left the mob at the pavilion behind. Glen's long stride quickly put him out in front of us, but he turned before he was out of sight and waved. "See you up top."

I was happy to trek along at my own pace. The trail was steep, but in better condition than the rest of the canyon's trails, no doubt to accommodate the steady stream of visitors venturing down to the Mile-and-a-Half Resthouse. People-watching became an entertaining distraction. Twice I spotted Glen several tiers above us.

After an hour's hike, with our destination near, we kept up a steady pace until we heard a commotion ahead. The trail became crowded below the brink. We weaved amongst couples holding hands, and families with children. Two adolescent boys played tag on the trail, chasing and dodging. The air was alive, more like a carnival than a natural cathedral.

We finally stepped foot onto the open plaza near Bright Angel Lodge. I half expected the mass of tourists to clap and cheer for us, as spectators do for marathon runners coming across the finish line. Adrenaline made me think I could still turn cartwheels.

Sarah's elation glowed on her face. "Woohoo! We did it, Amy. High-five!"

We squealed like girls at a rock concert.

Our mood was infectious. The spectators turned and smiled with us. I threw my arms around Sarah, and she picked me up and swung me around, backpack and all.

I spotted Ranger Glen standing in the crowd watching us. Sarah and I linked arms and trotted over to him.

"Congratulations, you hiked the Grand Canyon." He opened his arms wide.

I hugged him. Sarah hugged him.

"Do we look silly to you?" I laughed, but was afraid I should be embarrassed.

"Nope. You look positively glowing," he said. "I remember my first time and envy what you're feeling. You deserve to celebrate."

"I had such a great time, except for . . ." I motioned vaguely toward the depths of the canyon. "Anyway, I'm kind of proud of myself for finishing." The thrill wouldn't go away, and I relished the sensation.

"You should be proud," Glen said. "You hiked twenty-four miles across the canyon and came through harrowing experiences like troupers."

"I can't believe I hiked rim to rim," I said, in awe of my own accomplishment. The journey of a lifetime was over. The pain, exhaustion and terror already seemed like someone else's reality. A huge sense of achievement remained, and I basked in my private moment of glory.

"Can I buy you girls lunch to celebrate, maybe in a half hour? I have a little work to do."

We both said yes and let him go back to being a ranger. I didn't want to come down from my high by thinking about the work Glen still needed to attend to.

He dashed across the plaza to meet a service crew and helped them unload barricades from a pickup truck. They positioned the barricades at the Bright Angel trailhead blocking the entrance. For a while, no one would be allowed to begin their journey below the rim.

Odd, I thought. Within hours tourists will exclaim over the canyon and never know that Michael Rap ever existed, never hear of his evil deeds. The park service would make the canyon once again pristine.

25

BRIGHT ANGEL TRAILHEAD - Elevation: 6,860 ft.

We weren't yet ready to become indoor people, so Sarah and I settled on a bench in a viewing area of the plaza and released ourselves from our packs. I looked over the vast expanse of canyon and marveled at how far we had hiked. The distance was hard to imagine. Simple joy washed over me. Every now and then Sarah would catch my eye, and we'd giggle or bump knuckles or merely grin.

"Hey, you guys!" Kylie dodged through the crowd and jogged toward us.

"Kylie! I'm so relieved to see you. Eric said you hadn't caught up to him." She smelled clean as she hugged my neck and then Sarah's. "Aren't you supposed to visit your sister in Tucson?"

"I'm waiting for Eric." She clapped her hands.

Sarah recovered first from the surprise. "Well—that's good."

"Sit down, Kylie, I have something to tell you." I patted the bench next to me.

Her grin slid from her face as she lowered herself to the bench as far from me as possible. "What?"

"The man who attacked you on the North Rim won't bother you anymore," I said. "He fell off a cliff last night. He's dead."

"Oh." Kylie shuddered beneath a deep frown. "Good," she said before shedding that worry like an old skin. "I thought you were going to tell me something bad about Eric."

"No," Sarah said, "but we wondered about him. What have you've been up to the last two days?"

"I can't talk now." Kylie jumped to her feet. "I have to like run down to the General Store to see if Eric's back yet. Gotta go." She skipped away, throwing the last words over her shoulder.

Sarah called after her. "We're having lunch here. Come back if you can."

"I'll bring Eric." She waved and weaved through a crowd of Korean tourists traipsing behind a guide carrying a bright blue pennant.

"Can you believe that?" Sarah looked after Kylie.

"No, but at least she's safe. I guess I misjudged Eric." I couldn't dredge up much interest in Kylie's drama; maybe I was too tired.

Our discussion was cut short by the arrival of an ambulance on a delivery road at the far side of the plaza. Park Service employees quickly lined the barricades and asked people to keep their distance from the ambulance and from the entrance to Bright Angel Trail.

"They must be bringing him up." The dark side of the canyon became real again.

"Do you want to go somewhere else?" Sarah asked.

"I'm okay. It just means they're taking care of him and the episode is almost over."

A buzz went around the plaza, and curious people wandered toward the barricades for a better look. Before long, the rescue crew appeared at the trailhead. Two men carried the backboard with Rap zipped neatly into a body bag. Alongside, the rest of the crew formed a human shield to block the view of concerned onlookers.

"Is he okay?"

"What happened?"

"Maybe a heart attack."

"Somebody fell."

The conjecture was hard to listen to, but within seconds Rap was loaded into the ambulance and whisked away.

Some tourists worried, "I hope he's all right." Others shook their heads and wandered away to try to forget the scene.

The rescue crew disbursed, sweaty, tired, and no doubt in need of a shower after cleaning up Rap's mess. Ranger Glen remained in the plaza and scanned the crowd until I stood to wave to him. Sarah and I met him half way. His work had left him somber, but he brightened as he approached. "Ready to eat?"

Sarah didn't hesitate. "Yep, I'm starving."

"They'll want to stick us in a corner," I said. "We may be a little ripe." Polite society's hygiene rules hadn't applied in the canyon, but civilization reminded me that we might offend. Sarah and I had merely splashed ourselves clean for the last five days.

"Don't worry. They're used to hikers." Glen had probably showered yesterday and could say that.

Sarah grinned. "You know, we could bottle the smell and label it *eau de canyon*."

"How about . . . *eau de hike,*" I suggested. *"If you love your solitude, you'll love our scent."*

Glen groaned and sniffed Sarah. "I'll bet the hostess seats us outside and down wind." She punched his arm, and he relented. "Seriously, you smell fine."

I wrinkled my nose, teasing. "You don't."

"Ouch. We'll definitely get a table outside." Glen rubbed his bicep and went to put our names on the waiting list.

Sarah and I sat with the packs, waiting. I luxuriated in sunshine and in the sensation of being satisfied with myself and my new friends.

"I hope you don't let that one get away," Sarah said, indicating Ranger Glen strolling back toward us. "He's a good guy."

"Yes, he is." I stood to shoulder my pack.

"I pulled rank," Glen said, "and got a table with a view for me and my girls." He chuckled and led us to an open air patio with no other patrons. "The hostess agreed we might want to be alone."

We submitted our orders and talked about the highlights of our week in the canyon. Glen didn't ask questions about my night on the cliff, and I was in no hurry to relive the experience. Little by little though, the story came out. Having heard the details earlier, Sarah prodded me. Apparently, she worried about my mental health and thought it best that I talk about the incident. Ranger Glen took notes. I assumed he'd use the details for his report on Rap's death.

Our food arrived and relieved me of the need to converse. My meal tasted extraordinarily delectable, probably because it was *not* oatmeal or rice and had never been dehydrated. We cleaned every crumb of food from our plates and sat back in our chairs. The waitress refilled our water glasses for the third time and brought the check.

"Let me get this." Glen reached for the tab and took out his credit card.

"Why, thank you, Glen," I said.

"So what's your plan?" he asked. "Will you be able to stay another night?"

"Not me," I said. "I have a plane to catch tonight." His disappointment made my heart ache. "But we don't have to leave for several hours," I added and looked at Sarah for confirmation.

"Yeah. That's okay with me."

"If you have time," Glen said, "I'll ask Jan to offer you a shower in her dorm room, if…"

"Yes." I didn't have to be asked twice. "That would be wonderful."

We shoved our chairs back to leave, but caught sight of Kylie scanning the dining room.

"Kylie! Out here." Sarah waved her over.

"I need to get started on the report anyway," Glen said, pushing up from the table. "Come to the Backcountry Office whenever you're ready. Good afternoon, Kylie."

She didn't appear to remember the ranger and plopped herself at the table.

"We've eaten, but go ahead and order something," I said. "We'll wait."

"I'm not hungry."

"What's wrong?" The answer was obvious, but Sarah was kind enough to let Kylie explain.

"Eric wasn't there."

"What made you think he'd be waiting for you at the General Store?" I asked and wondered what magic he used to make the girl forget about visiting her sister in Tucson.

"He left me a note on the bulletin board asking me to wait. He wants to be with me." Kylie cheered up a little, removed a paper from her shirt pocket and waved her proof around.

"Then, where is he?" I didn't like the smell of the story and held out my hand for the note, read the scribbled message, and passed it to Sarah.

She read the note aloud. "*I need a ride to Phoenix. If you're going that way, maybe you can wait. I'll be on Hermit's Trail until Friday and will check in at the store. – Eric.* Not very romantic."

Kylie snatched the paper back and tucked his note into the pocket near her heart.

"You waited here for an extra day?" I asked. "What about your sister?"

"I called her and she, like, understood." Disappointed that we did not share her enthusiasm for Eric's suggestion, Kylie dismissed her family.

I pressed the issue. "I hate to see you get hurt, Kylie. Maybe Eric wants the ride and nothing more."

"I know what he wrote." Her words jumped at me, but she then softened. "He's not the romantic type. Maybe if I spend more time with him, he'll love me back."

My heart ached for her.

Sarah was more blunt. "Eric is a user, and he'll leave you hurt."

"I don't think so," Kylie insisted. "Look. He gave me a gift." She unzipped her fanny pack and placed an item on the table. "See? This is a little stove he made from a soda can." Kylie grinned with pride.

Sarah frowned and examined the stove. "Did he give you fuel for this, too?"

"Yep, almost a whole bottle."

I thought the soda-can stove looked familiar. "It's yours, isn't it?"

Sarah nodded.

"What do you mean?" Kylie demanded.

"I'm sorry, Kylie." Sarah did not sugarcoat bad news. "This is the stove I made. These are my initials." She pointed to the bottom. "This went missing from my backpack when we camped at Cottonwood."

"Are you saying that Eric is the thief?" Kylie choked back tears, her face reddening.

Sarah's tone was even and gentle. "No, I'm saying that this is the stove I made."

"He didn't steal it." Kylie stood up, knocking her chair to the floor, and ran through the dining room. A few customers watched her storm out and shook their heads in disapproval.

I put her chair back on its legs and sat down in frustration. "Maybe we shouldn't have told her."

"We had to," Sarah said. "She needs to figure him out."

A few minutes later Kylie marched back onto the patio and slammed Sarah's bottle of fuel on the table. "There. Are you happy?" She sank into a chair and cried into her hands.

Sarah put her arm around the girl's shoulder, and we waited.

Kylie finally raised her head and sniveled. "He has other stuff," she said. "That knife fell from his pack. He grabbed it from me like I couldn't see the tag hanging from it."

"The Buck knife from the souvenir store?" Sarah asked.

Kylie nodded. "He had lights and titanium pots. I thought he just had extra gear. He threw some stuff away. I'm an idiot."

"Not at all," I said. "He spins a good story. Anyone could be fooled."

While we consoled Kylie, I caught a glimpse of three dusty young men trudging through the plaza with strong, straight backs and several days' worth of whiskers. "I'll be right back."

Out in the sunshine I waved to them. "Jeff!"

The Marines turned, wondered who I was, and waved politely.

"Remember helping me and Sarah? You carried her pack for a while."

"Yes, ma'am, hello," Jeff said with a toothy grin. Conor and Jim nodded and let Jeff do the talking. "Did Sarah recover from the snakebite?"

"She's fine, and I want to thank you for your help by buying you lunch. The hamburgers and onion rings here are fabulous. What do you say?"

Before Jeff could answer, Conor spoke up. "Yes, ma'am!"

Like a mallard leading her ducklings, I threaded my way through the restaurant. Sarah rose to meet the young men and gripped their hands in firm handshakes.

Kylie sat, twirling her hair around her fingers, until I introduced the trio. She smiled, and I swear I heard something click between her and Jeff. Conor and Jim pulled chairs to the table leaving the one next to Kylie for Jeff.

The young people placed their orders, and I paid the bill in advance while the Marines gave an account of their adventures on the Tonto Trail over the last three days. Kylie's rapt attention encouraged Jeff to flesh out the details and perhaps embellish a bit.

Before their meals arrived, Jeff smacked Conor's shoulder. "Let's wash up."

The moment the men were out of earshot, Kylie leaned forward with wide eyes. "What do you think? Isn't he gorgeous?"

"Who do you mean?" I asked.

"Jeff, of course. Do you think he likes me?" She knew the answer and grinned.

Sarah laughed. "No doubt about that. You hooked him good."

"Listen, Kylie. Sarah and I need to get on the road. Say good-bye to the boys for us and tell Jeff I need his phone number and address. I must send him a thank you card." I wrote my address on a napkin for her. "You can e-mail them to me."

"Can you take it from here, Kylie?" Sarah asked.

Kylie jumped up. "Yes, thanks, guys." She hugged us, and we wished her well.

Cutting through the Bright Angel's rustic lobby, I caught sight of the gift shop and had to stop. "Sarah, what size do you wear?"

"Extra large, why?"

"I'm buying matching tee shirts," I said.

Leaving our packs in the hall, we went into the small store and dug through piles of touristy shirts. I found two emblazoned with *I Survived the Grand Canyon* and paid for both over Sarah's protests.

"Thank you, Amy." She hugged the shirt to her chest.

We strolled to the Backcountry Permit Office a few blocks away where our damaged rental car was parked as we left it, but covered with a layer of red dust. I dug the keys out of a secure pocket in my pack, unlocked the doors on the passenger side, and threw the two packs in the backseat.

"The first thing I want to do is check my voice mail." Sarah grabbed her phone. "Maybe there's a signal here at the ranger station. Yes, three bars."

Suddenly wanting to reconnect with the real world, I popped the trunk and rummaged through my green nylon bag. I found my phone beneath a plastic grocery bag I'd never seen before. Eager to connect to the outside world, I tossed the tightly wrapped bundle to Sarah's side of the trunk.

Voice mail listed three missed messages. Two from my daughter and one from my son. Surprised, I listened to the messages and immediately dialed Meagan's number. My heart swelled at the sound of her voice, but got her recording. I tried James' number with the same result. I left messages saying I'd just finished my journey and would be home on schedule. "I love you," I added to both messages.

Sarah was on her third call and stopped dialing to ask, "Everything okay?"

"They were expecting a call yesterday when I got out of the canyon. Meagan says she's proud of me."

Sarah grinned. "That's great."

She pressed send. "Hi, Mom."

26

TRAIL REPORT

"Amy." Ranger Jan came from behind the counter in the Backcountry Office and gave me a motherly hug. "Ranger Hawk is finishing up his report. Come on and sit down. Would you like water?"

I filled a paper cup from the water cooler and let Jan usher me to a chair next to her desk. "You've had quite an adventure," she said. "I hope your visit to the canyon wasn't all terrible."

"Mostly I had a great time."

"Ranger Hawk filled me in," Jan said. "Don't let this ruin your perception of the canyon."

We chatted for a while before Sarah joined us. She pulled up a chair and bent toward me. "Mom says Hi. I told her all about you."

A pang hit me. I missed my own mother. "Say hello back the next time you call her," I said. "Jan reminded me that we're on our third incident report."

"See, I told you—trouble follows Amy wherever she goes." Sarah probably winked at Jan over my head.

Jan chuckled and indulged our banter, but then asked if we'd like an update on the man we spotted at the bottom of the ravine near Yaki Point.

I guiltily realized that I hadn't thought about the poor man in days. "Sure. We heard rumors of a murder. Was he the victim?"

"Same guy," said Jan.

"How did it happen?" I asked. "Did they find the murderer?"

"The sheriff's department has cause of death," Jan said, pulling a folder out of the file cabinet, "but no suspects yet."

"Wait. I want to hear this." Glen came from a back office with a sheaf of papers in his hand. He shook the file in disgust. "I love this job, but the amount of paperwork is ludicrous." He straddled a chair and nodded to Jan to begin.

Jan put on her reading glasses and summarized. "The victim's driver's license indicates his name was Jeremy Taylor. The Sheriff believes that he was the driver of the blue Chevy that sideswiped you and was abandoned about a quarter mile east of where you found him. The car was reported stolen in Phoenix and had traces of drugs in the front seat. The County brought in dogs to sniff around."

"So he wasn't an innocent tourist." I regretted wasting sympathy on him.

Jan shook her head. "Nope. His spiderweb tattoo indicates gang membership." She stirred cream into her coffee. "His rap sheet includes auto theft, tried as a juvenile, marijuana . . ."

"Spiderweb? May I see his driver's license?" I asked.

Jan handed me the dark copy of Jeremy Taylor's photo identification. "There were two sets of large footprints around the abandoned car along with yours," she said, glancing down at Sarah's size nines. "That second person could be a witness to Taylor's accident, or could have helped him fall. Either one of them could have tried to pry open your car."

"Sarah, isn't this the kid who tried to steal my gear bag?" I asked.

She studied the picture. "Could be—if you pencil in a goatee and add body piercings."

"I think it's him," I said.

Sarah screwed up her face and shrugged.

"So there were two people," I rocked myself in my seat, letting images swirl in my mind. "Jeremy Taylor, who may or may not have tried to grab my gear, and another man who tried to break into my car."

I wondered about the man at the airport who shoved the tattooed kid, but I couldn't recall his features. "Were there signs of a fight outside their car or maybe at the rim?"

"Hard to tell," Jan answered. "We didn't connect the body in the ravine with the sideswiping incident until after the recovery operation. The shoe prints you found at the rim were helpful, but other evidence may have been trampled during the recovery. The area wasn't a crime scene at that point."

"So why did they call it a murder?" I asked. "Was he stabbed or shot?"

"The newspaper jumped the gun on that story. The Coconino County coroner's report isn't official yet," Jan said, looking over the rim of her glasses. "The body was badly damaged from ricocheting off rocks on the way down, but the coroner found ligature marks on the victim's neck."

The jumble of information fell into alignment. "So," I said, "the abandoned car that sideswiped us was stolen. The dogs sniffed traces of drugs. Jeremy Taylor ends up in the canyon with strangulation marks on his neck."

"Jan just said all that. What are you getting at?" Sarah seemed to expect a Perry Mason moment.

"I think Michael Rap strangled the Taylor guy and threw him over the side."

Sarah and Jan pulled back, studying me.

"Why do you think so, Amy?" Glen stroked his cleft chin and listened.

"Rap never fit with the other hikers in the canyon," I explained. "He didn't have the normal equipment or clothes for a backpacker. He got crazier as the week went on. Sarah suspected he was on something. I think the two men were connected by drugs."

"That's a long stretch," Jan said with a prove-it-to-me look on her face. "The canyon is a big place and there is nothing to put them in the same place at the same time."

I pulled a week's worth of trash from my pockets and deposited a small pile on the desk. Two bits of tinfoil lay among paper, wrappers and tissues. I poked the intact tinfoil packet.

"If I'm not wrong, this is some sort of drugs." I raised my eyebrows at the rangers.

"Drugs are not my expertise." Glen donned bifocals to peer at the packet. "Could be. Where did you get this?"

"Rap," I said. "I found it when I was cleaning up the ledge this morning. I bet there's more in his backpack."

"That's PCP," Sarah blurted. "Dealers wrap tinfoil packets like that." She seemed almost as surprised as me that she had such knowledge and rushed to explain. "PCP started to show up in schools here. I sat in on a teachers' training in Phoenix."

"She's probably right," Jan said, referring to the report. "The Sheriff identified phencyclidine in the abandoned car—street names are angel dust and wack."

"Yeah, and PCP does terrible things to the mind," Sarah said, frowning as she recalled facts. "Even low doses make users crazy. They're impervious to pain and think they can do anything, like fly. High doses kill, but it's cheap."

"So Rap was a drug dealer," I said. *Everything fits.*

"He was certainly a user." Sarah didn't gloat over pegging Rap correctly the day before.

"He did the world a favor by checking out," I said. Any sympathy that I had for Rap evaporated. Launching himself off the cliff to retrieve the stash of drugs suddenly made sense, in a twisted way.

"What about Darren Kreminski?" I asked. "Sarah, can PCP cause a heart attack?"

"Yes, definitely," Sarah said. "Even in young people."

"Who are you talking about?" asked Jan.

"I have the paperwork right here," Glen said rifling through a pile of folders. "Here's a report from the North Rim. Darren Kreminski, twenty-one, cause of death cardiac arrest. That's all, nothing from the coroner."

"I'll bet Darren bought the PCP from Rap behind that souvenir store and had a severe reaction. He went crazy on the bus." I glanced at Sarah to confirm my description. She nodded and rubbed her arms as if they still ached from our CPR efforts.

A frown clouded Glen's face. "I can't remember the last time we had such a crime spree. I'd like to prove Rap and Taylor were the extent of it, and we're done."

"There were also the thefts," I reminded him, "but we have an answer there, too." I recounted Kylie's experiences with Eric and suggested the rangers catch up with him on the Hermit Trail.

Glen heaved a sigh.

I wanted the canyon to be at peace again, too. "I'm sure the violent crimes are connected, and with Rap and Taylor dead, your crime spree should be over." An image buried in my memory came to me. "I think I know the perfect thing to tie it all together."

I paused, enjoying my audience's anticipation.

"Sarah, what do you have in your pocket?"

She looked at me quizzically. "*Mine?*"

"Humor me." I pointed to her thigh pocket.

She tore the Velcro loose and pulled out a plastic baggie and scraps of paper tangled in a shoelace. I pulled the lace loose and held it up.

"This is your murder weapon."

My pronouncement met with skeptical stares until Sarah found her voice. "What are you talking about?"

"Where did you get the shoe lace?" I asked her.

"I don't know. Picked it up somewhere. Litter."

"Exactly. We cleaned up after the tourists that morning near Yaki Point right before we spotted Jeremy Taylor's red jacket in the canyon."

Glen didn't appear convinced, but waited for me to continue. "And I think I know where you'll find the other shoe lace."

"Go on," he said.

"One of Rap's shoes was missing its lace."

"How do you know that?" Glen asked.

I told them about the condor perched on his stockinged foot and the shoe he left on the cliff. Recalling the scene made the taste of vomit rise in my throat, so I poured myself a drink of water. "The shoe on the ledge had no laces. The other shoe stayed tied on his foot."

Glen leaned back in his chair. "We did find a shoe on the ledge and put it in with the body, but I didn't notice the laces. Good job, Amy."

A blush heated my cheeks, and I lowered my lashes. To cover up, I pushed my hypothesis again. "So, if this shoelace matches, that would put Rap at the site of the murder."

"So he's a murdering drug dealer, not just a crazy person." Sarah's face hardened, no doubt replaying in her mind our close encounters with Rap.

"I'll bet you're right," Glen said, "and if that lace was pulled tight around Taylor's throat, there would be embedded skin cells." He held out a baggie into which I dropped the lace.

Sarah shuddered. "I've been carrying that thing around for six days."

"Wow." Another puzzle piece clicked into place. "If Rap was capable of killing Taylor, he might have killed Kylie. I already told her Rap was the attacker, but check the bite marks on his arm."

A scowl creased Glen's forehead, though he encouraged me with a hand motion to dredge up additional memories.

"He screamed at us about stealing his stuff, his 'wack'." A shiver ran across my shoulders, loosening a thought. "Sarah, do you have something wrapped in a grocery bag in the trunk?"

She looked at me like I was crazy.

"I'll be right back."

The three of them were still discussing the events when I returned from the car.

"One thing bothers me," Sarah said. "Why was Rap in the canyon at all?"

"This is why." The package thumped on the desk like a stale Christmas fruitcake. "I'll bet this is PCP. Rap, or the kid with the spiderweb tattoo, slipped it into my bag at Chicago's airport. I must have been distracted by my . . . my personal issues."

Sarah sent sympathy my way.

"They made me a . . . a mule," I said. "Figured I'd be arrested if the package was found." I sank into the chair. "In Phoenix the tattooed kid tried to get the drugs back, but Sarah stopped him from stealing my bag. Rap stalked us across the canyon, but their stuff was in the car all the time."

Glen unwrapped the bundle, glanced inside and held it out for Jan to see. She nodded. The four of us were silent, stunned by the implications.

"Sarah, do you remember Rap saying he cut those guys to get whatever was in his pack?" I asked.

"When was that?" Sarah screwed up her face.

"On the ledge, when he threatened to slit our throats."

Jan and Glen sat back in their chairs, a bit pale, listening.

"The packets he had on him were for his personal use. This bundle must be worth big money. Enough to kill for." I tapped my finger on my forehead, thinking. "They were supposed to sell the PCP in Phoenix, but that Jeremy kid screwed up. Rap killed him to cut him out of the deal."

Certain of my hypothesis, I sat back satisfied and triumphant, as if I had completed a New York Times crossword puzzle. *Okay, that was a goofy comparison.* But I needed to think of the week's drama as a game, a riddle solved with facts and logic. The immediate terror had ended, but I needed to control the images of the horrible events so I could sleep at night.

Another ten minutes passed while we filled out the details of Glen's report on Rap. The incidents seemed otherworldly now; a nightmare that abated once morning dawned, but the details were still sickening.

"You're amazing, Amy. I'll check all this with the coroner and inspect Rap's backpack and shoes." Glen closed the folder and lay his pen aside. "I apologize the paperwork took so long. I know you have a plane to catch." He looked truly sorry.

"Nine tonight," I said. "We should leave soon if I'm going to get through security and check in on time."

"Did I hear someone mention a shower might be available?" Sarah looked at Jan.

"Sure. My place is nearby. Thanks for helping us out here, ladies."

She handed Sarah the keys and gave us the directions to her dorm.

We found the neat little building easily enough.

"I'll go first." Sarah volunteered. "I won't take more than five minutes." She threw her clothes bag on a chair and hurried to the bathroom.

Jan's Spartan room reflected the efficiency of the woman herself. The austerity was relieved with a spark of color from a hand-pieced quilt folded over the foot of her bed, a bear-paw pattern. I sat in a wicker chair and waited a few minutes for Sarah to emerge, still damp, from the shower.

"Your turn," she said. "I'll meet you at the car."

A hot shower and a freshly scrubbed scalp never felt so good, though the jet of water stung and reopened some of my abrasions. I re-bandaged them, but didn't dawdle, and got back to the Backcountry Office in twenty minutes.

Glen stood next to our rental car examining the damage done to the door. Sheepish and not at all like his alpha-male self, he shuffled around and cleared his throat. "Amy, I really enjoyed meeting you and especially the day at the ranch. I'd like to find a way to see you again." His rehearsed words came out stiff. He shifted from foot to foot and looked at a tree, or something, behind me.

Poor guy. I hate to hurt his feelings.

"Glen, you've been wonderful—great. You made the fun parts of this trip fun and the scary parts bearable. You took such good care . . ."

Before I finished my thought, Glen stepped forward and put his finger under my chin, tilting my face up. His clear, open face invited me to search his hazel-brown eyes for trickery. I found only kindness and hope. *What would it be like to . . .* A smile crept to the corner of my mouth.

As if guided by the stars in my eyes, he leaned down to me. His soft lips pressed mine. I would have swooned, if that was still fashionable. All I knew was that my world condensed to that square yard of space and those few moments. The rest of time and space disappeared.

Reality wormed its way into my cozy haze. *This isn't fair to him.* I stepped back. "Glen, I'm sorry. I can't do this."

He winced. "Are you sure?"

I forced my head to nod.

"Okay. I understand."

No, you don't, I thought. *How can you know that I can't trust my feelings; that I don't want to give you false hope; that my love may be only for the canyon?* I hated to see his shoulders slump and the spark go out of his eyes. I wanted to hold him and take away the hurt. Of course, putting my arms around him would have been a mistake. I'd miss my plane. To tamp down the urge, I turned toward the car door.

Sarah tried to lighten the mood. "Hey, let's all do the canyon again next year."

Ranger Glen smiled weakly. "Drive safely, girls."

I fumbled for the car keys. Steeling myself, I turned toward him. "Good bye, Glen. Thank you for always being there."

Sarah hurried to jump in the passenger seat, waving good-bye to Glen from the open window. I started the car and backed up cautiously. I wasn't sure I could concentrate on the road and had to focus.

"Got the map, Sarah?"

"Yep. Right here. Turn left at the corner." She guided us through the busy streets of Canyon Village and onto the highway leading away from the canyon. She held her tongue until the car hummed along on a straightaway.

"Humph."

I glanced over at her. "What?"

"Do you think you did the right thing with Glen?"

"Yes."

"I thought you liked him."

"I think I do, but I don't want to encourage him if I only *think* I like him." A tear rolled down my cheek before I could stop it. Sarah didn't miss anything.

"Do you want to turn around?" she asked.

"No, I'll miss my plane."

"I don't understand you." Sarah's voice rose in exasperation and did nothing to ease my misery. "Why did you blow him off like that?"

"Because I'm afraid." I was surprised I could admit such a thing to her; surprised how far I had come in the past week.

"Of what? Falling in love?"

"No. Yes. No. That I can't trust my emotions. Maybe I need attention so badly, and I'm so vulnerable right now that I would fall for anyone."

"That's ridiculous." She wasn't cutting me any slack.

"What if my attraction to him is vacation-induced? Maybe the canyon gives him a romantic aura. Would he be the same anywhere else? Would I still be attracted to him back in Illinois?"

Sarah stroked her chin as if she had wise, old whiskers. "You are quite the realist, but still, Amy, you can't go through life analyzing everything. Sometimes you have to go for it."

"Maybe it's too soon. I still hurt."

Sarah stopped and sighed. "You're right. There's plenty of time." She reached over and patted my knee, and the issue was left to hang in the air.

To fill the vacuum, I turned on the radio. We listened as John Denver sang his soulful ballad. He claimed that sunshine on his shoulder made him happy, but I heard the sadness in his voice and understood the truth.

We drove away from the trees, away from the great canyon. Hundreds of saguro cacti dotted the desert landscape, sentinels to watch our departure. The Arizona sun beat on them mercilessly; highlighting their stark and lethal spines. One eminently tall saguro stood apart, near the roadside, its arm raised in salute, a bird's nest on its shoulder.

"Amy, are you happy outdoors?"

"Yes, of course. I love it."

"How many men will you meet who will want to share the outdoors with you?"

In response I sighed and stared at the road. I pictured Glen holding my damaged foot so tenderly; rappelling down the cliff; talking about bats with lights in his eyes; his little bald spot and calloused hands.

Sarah waited, and I shrugged in defeat.

"It's too late," I said. "Dating is useless to think about now. I don't know how long it takes to get divorced, and he'll give up on me by then."

"No, he won't." Sarah's firm statement caused me to glance her way. She took a deep breath. "I hope I didn't betray your confidence, but I told Glen that you're about to get divorced."

"You didn't? When did you tell him that?"

"While you showered. Are you mad?"

I wasn't. Suddenly my future brightened up.

Sarah saw the change and knew she was forgiven. "I suggested he wait for you."

"Really?"

"Why didn't *you* tell him John filed for divorce?" Her abrupt question took me off-guard, and I sputtered.

"I don't know. I'm embarrassed. *Divorce* sounds so bad." I stopped myself before I went on a rant and turned my thoughts to more pleasant things. "So that's why Glen thought it was okay to kiss me." My cheeks warmed with the idea.

Sarah raised her eyebrows and smiled. "He probably would have done it sooner, but he thought all along that you were happily married and respected that. Your reactions confused him."

"I guess he has a right to be confused. *I'm* confused."

"When you're ready, contact him." She held up a National Park Service business card between her fingers and waved it in front of me. "You two make a great couple."

My grin grew into a full-blown smile. "Maybe." I snatched the card from her fingers and tucked it into my shirt pocket.

Two hours of driving flew by. We recounted our week together, somehow leaving out the awful parts. The gasoline warning light beeped at me, so we stopped to fill the tank in the suburbs north of Phoenix. I took my turn in the ladies' room while Sarah pumped the gas and paid the cashier. When I slipped back into the driver's seat, Sarah placed a package wrapped in a red bandana on my lap.

"This is for you."

"For me? Why?"

"Because I want you to remember this trip."

The bandana fell away to reveal Sarah's watercolor tablet. "Sarah, I can't take this."

Thrilled with the gift, I gingerly scanned through the paintings to find the three newest illustrations. "Plateau Point, so beautiful. Here's a mule train. These are great. Is this me climbing the rope up the cliff?"

"Of course."

I looked at her skeptically. "I look—brave."

"Amy, you just don't know how courageous you are. You've done amazing things in your life. You've raised two successful children, you ran a million-dollar business, you hiked rim to rim, and you helped rid the world of a drugged out psychopath. Women who do amazing things *are* amazing people. On top of that you're smart, clever and good. Everyone should love you."

I wanted to believe her. I needed to believe her, but the compliments overwhelmed me, and I blushed into my collar. "Thank you" was all I could manage.

* * *

Sarah's MapQuest directions got us directly to the rental car agency. I parked the car and popped the trunk. Sarah rounded the car, took me by the shoulders and stared into my eyes.

"Amy, are you going to fight the divorce?"

"No. I'll give him the divorce. To tell you the truth, once I get past the sense of failure, I'm relieved. One of us finally had the guts to call it quits."

"What if he changes *his* mind?"

"I won't change mine. I like the new me."

"Good," she said. "If you start wavering, call me. My number is on the back of the tablet."

"Don't worry. I'm ready for it now. I don't look forward to all the legal wrangling, but why should it turn into a battle?"

"Good luck with that," she said. "I hope you're right."

"It'll be crazy for a while, I guess, and I'll have to sell the house."

"If you need help with any of that, I'll drive down."

I shaded my eyes from the sun to see her face. "Really?"

"Sure. I'll have time once I'm out of a job. Besides that's what best friends do."

Friends. That pleased me to no end. I stared at her, unable to speak for so long that she tried to retract her offer.

"If you don't want me . . ."

262

"No, no. I'm just clumsy with this. I haven't had a really good friend since high school. Of course, I want you to come."

She stammered. "I thought maybe you didn't want your neighbors and family to think we were . . . maybe a couple."

The thought of making them guess made me laugh. "I don't care anymore what people think. That's the one good thing about being a *certain age*."

"You're right about that," she said. "Hey, if you can't get a new place right away, come stay with me."

"I may do that, so I don't have to make quick decisions."

"I want you to meet my mom."

Suddenly, I wanted very much to meet her mother, to measure up, and meet with her approval. The heaviness of my own mother's death weighed upon me, and I must have frowned. Sarah jostled my shoulder.

"Hey, don't worry. Mom is cool, and she'll love you."

I grinned back at her and shrugged. "What's not to love?"

"Atta girl."

* * *

In the air over the great state of Nebraska, I took Ranger Glen Hawk's business card from my shirt pocket and drew my thumb over the embossed lettering. I flicked the corner of the card several times. It sounded like just the ticket to my next adventure. The Grand Canyon had only been the beginning of a new life.

END

ABOUT THE AUTHOR

In the 1990s Jeanne Meeks was committed to poetry, belonged to Poets and Other Writers, and gave poetry performances as part of that group. Her work appeared in several anthologies. She also self-published a book of poetry, *My Sister's Quilt*. She regularly writes human-interest articles for *Schoolhouse Life* news magazine. She loves attending writers conventions, especially Love Is Murder in Chicago, to learn the craft of writing in the mystery genre.

After twenty-eight years in business, Ms. Meeks and her husband recently sold their security surveillance company. Jeanne Meeks was recognized by the Illinois governor as the Small-Business Person of the Year. She is the Tax Collector for New Lenox Township and has been the President of the New Lenox Chamber of Commerce, on the board of a local bank, and on Silver Cross Hospital's Community Trustee Board.

Ms. Meeks now writes full-time and belongs to Mystery Writers of America, Sisters in Crime, and writers groups in Illinois and Florida. In July of 2013 she won a first place cash prize for a slice-of-life story from Midlife Collage. When not writing, she backpacks, kayaks, volunteers with the local historical society, and plays tennis or golf. She lives with her husband of forty-four years on Florida's gulf coast and in a suburb of Chicago.

Next in the Backcountry Mystery series

Wolf Pack - Murder on Isle Royale

Amy Warren ferries to Isle Royal National Park to reconnect with her daughter, Meagan, by backpacking the island together. When Volunteer Ranger Sarah Rochon, Amy's best friend, is accused by a co-worker of assault and theft, Amy is torn between spending precious time with her daughter and clearing her best friend's name. After rescuing Remington, a prize Havenese show dog, she sniffs out a blackmail scheme, solves a murder, and proves Sarah's innocence.

Wolf Pack - Murder on Isle Royale will be available on Amazon.com and other retail outlets in 2014.

Eternally Yours, Robert

In a long running feud with her husband, Kitty Hanson argues that her ninety-year-old mother should be welcomed into her suburban Chicago home. Rose Turner overhears the threat to put her in a nursing home and takes matters into her own hands.

Looking for the passion she had denied herself years ago, Rose runs away. She knows she'll find Robert at the lovely old Empire Hotel in French Lick, Indiana. Under the scrutiny of the hotel staff, Rose awaits Robert's arrival, lays out a red satin gown, and hopes she'll recognize the man she left behind.

Available as a short story on Amazon.com.

Kind words for *Eternally Yours, Robert*:

"Beautifully written . . . fast-paced"

- Sherry Scarpaci, author of *Lullaby*

"Highly recommended . . . especially for anyone that loves love."

Shelly Lowery, reader from Bettendorf, IA

Home Run

Can deception lead to romance? Jim Szewiski borrows another man's persona to improve his batting average and gets more than he bargained for.

The Southside Chugger's softball team knows Jim as a dependable third baseman. Witzle and Franklin, Inc. knows him as a decent accountant. Jim wants more. He isn't satisfied with first base and decides to swing for the fences—Chicago's night life and rich, single women.

Available as a short story in e-book format on Amazon.com.

Follow Jeanne Meeks:

Website and blog - www.jeannemeeks.com

Facebook - www.facebook.com/JeanneMeeksAuthor

Pinterest - http://pinterest.com/jeannemeeks

e-mail ChartHousePress@aol.com

Grand Canyon trails www.nps.gov/grca/planyourvisit/backcountry.htm

NOTE:

Any error in fact or procedure contained in this story belong to the author and not the professionals to whom she turned for advice and wisdom.